PRAISE FOR THE LORD OF OPIUM

★ "Most young readers who loved *The House of the Scorpion* when it was first released are now adults, and today's teen audience will need to read the first title in order to fully understand Farmer's brilliantly realized world. . . . A stellar sequel worth the wait."
—*Booklist*, starred review

★ "This [is the] highly anticipated sequel to Farmer's National Book Award–winning *The House of the Scorpion*. . . . Once again, Farmer's near-future world offers an electric blend of horrors and beauty. Lyrically written and filled with well-rounded, sometimes thorny characters, this superb novel is well worth the wait."
—*Publishers Weekly*, starred review

The Lord
of Opium

ALSO BY NANCY FARMER

The House of the Scorpion
The Sea of Trolls
The Land of Silver Apples
The Islands of the Blessed
A Girl Named Disaster
The Warm Place
The Ear, the Eye and the Arm
Do You Know Me

NANCY FARMER

The Lord of Opium

A Richard Jackson Book
ATHENEUM BOOKS FOR YOUNG READERS
New York London Toronto Sydney New Delhi

atheneum

ATHENEUM BOOKS FOR YOUNG READERS

An imprint of Simon & Schuster Children's Publishing Division

1230 Avenue of the Americas, New York, New York 10020

ATHENEUM BOOKS FOR YOUNG READERS is a registered trademark of Simon & Schuster, Inc.

Atheneum logo is a trademark of Simon & Schuster, Inc.

For information about special discounts for bulk purchases, please contact Simon & Schuster Special Sales at 1-866-506-1949 or business@simonandschuster.com.

The Simon & Schuster Speakers Bureau can bring authors to your live event. For more information or to book an event, contact the Simon & Schuster Speakers Bureau at 1-866-248-3049 or visit our website at www.simonspeakers.com.

Also available in an Atheneum Books for Young Readers hardcover edition

Interior design by Mike Rosamilia, cover design by Russell Gordon

The text for this book is set in Bembo Std.

Manufactured in the United States of America

This Atheneum Books for Young Readers paperback edition September 2013

10 9 8 7 6 5

The Library of Congress has cataloged the hardcover edition as follows:

Farmer, Nancy, 1941–

The lord of Opium / Nancy Farmer. — 1st ed.

p. cm.

"A Richard Jackson Book."

Sequel to: House of the scorpion.

Summary: In 2137, fourteen-year-old Matt is stunned to learn that, as the clone of El Patrón, he is expected to take over as leader of the corrupt drug empire of Opium, where there is also a hidden cure for the ecological devastation faced by the rest of the world.

ISBN 978-1-4424-8254-8 (hc)

ISBN 978-1-4424-8256-2 (eBook)

[1. Cloning—Fiction. 2. Drug traffic—Fiction. 3. Environmental degradation—Fiction. 4. Science fiction.] I. Title.

PZ7.F23814Lor 2013

[Fic]—dc23   2012030418

ISBN 978-1-4424-8255-5 (pbk)

For Harold, *mi vida*,
and for Richard Jackson,
with deepest gratitude

CONTENTS

CAST OF CHARACTERS

AJO, OPIUM

Matteo Alacrán (Matt): Once a clone of El Patrón, now the new Lord of Opium; age fourteen

El Patrón (deceased): The old Lord of Opium

Celia, cook and **curandera** *(healer):* Matt's foster mother

Tam Lin (deceased): Matt's bodyguard and foster father

Mirasol, also known as Waitress: An eejit; age fifteen

Eligio Cienfuegos: The head of the Farm Patrol

Daft Donald: Bodyguard and best friend of Tam Lin

Mr. Ortega: Matt's music teacher and friend of Eusebio

Eusebio Orozco: The guitar maker; an eejit

Major Beltrán: Pilot working for Esperanza Mendoza

Fiona: Nurse at the Ajo hospital

Dr. Kim: Doctor at the Ajo hospital

Senator Mendoza and Emilia (deceased): Father and sister of María Mendoza

Cast of Characters

SAN LUIS, AZTLÁN

María Mendoza: Daughter of Esperanza; age fourteen

Esperanza Mendoza: UN representative and foe of the drug trade

Sor *Artemesia:* Nun at the Convent of Santa Clara; María's foster mother

THE LOST BOYS, PLANKTON FACTORY, AZTLÁN

Chacho: Recovering from being trapped in the boneyard; age fourteen

Ton-Ton: Leader of the boys; age sixteen

Fidelito: Age eight

PARADISE

Listen: Age seven

The Bug, also known as El Bicho: Age seven

Mbongeni: Age six

Dr. Rivas: In charge of the hospital in Paradise

Dr. Angel and Dr. Marcos: Daughter and son of Dr. Rivas; astronomers

Eduardo: Oldest son of Dr. Rivas; an eejit

THE BIOSPHERE, OPIUM

The Mushroom Master: Leading scientist

AFRICA

Glass Eye Dabengwa: A drug lord; ninety-nine years old

Happy Man Hikwa: Drug dealer working for Glass Eye

Samson and Boris: Glass Eye's Russian bodyguards

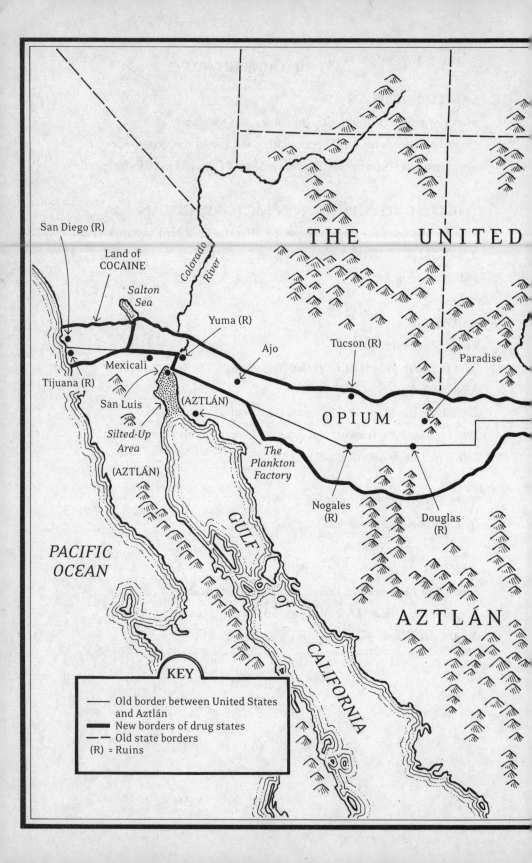

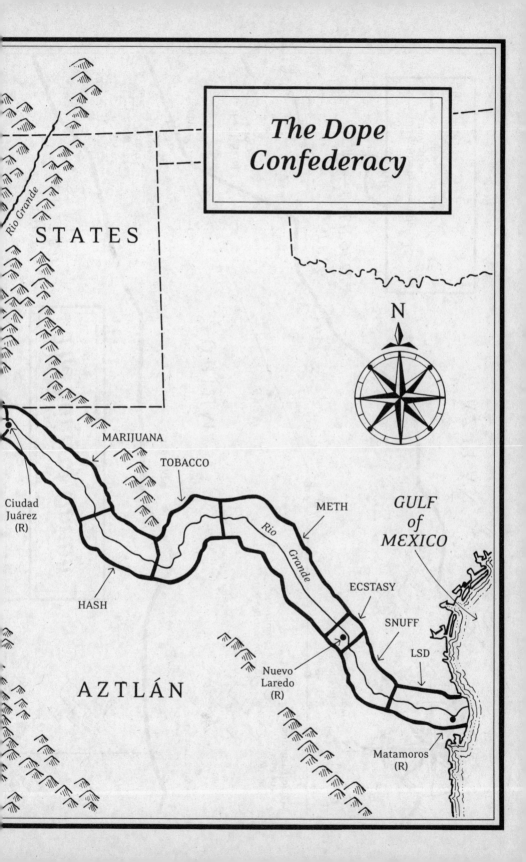

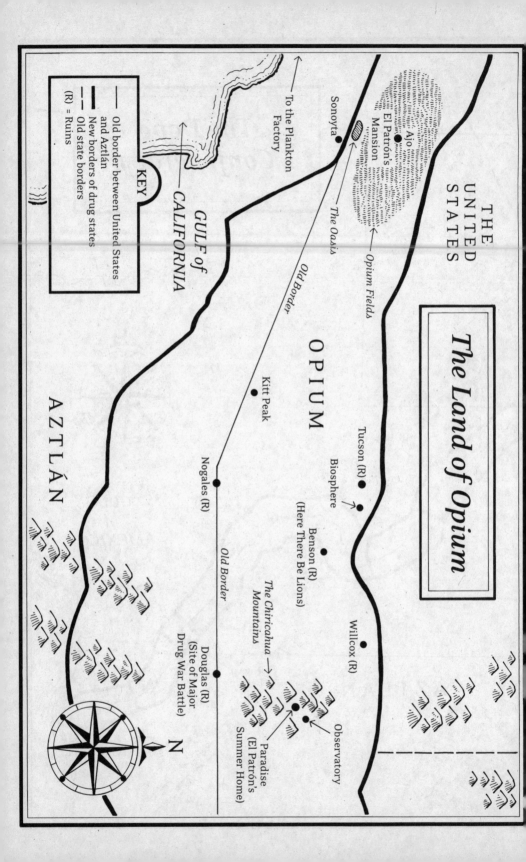

CHRONOLOGY

Birth of El Patrón: 1990
Drug Wars: 2025–2030
Matt harvested: 2122
Death of El Patrón: 2136
Time period for *The Lord of Opium*: 2137–2138

The Lord
of Opium

1

THE OASIS

Matt woke in darkness to the sound of something moving past him. The air stirred slightly with the smell of warm, musky fur. The boy jumped to his feet, but the sleeping bag entangled him and he fell. His hands collided with sharp thorns. He flailed around for a rock, a knife, any sort of weapon.

Something huffed. The musky odor became stronger. Matt's hand felt a metal bar, and for an instant he didn't know what it was. Then he realized it was a flashlight and turned it on.

The beam illuminated a large, doglike face at the other end of the sleeping bag. The boy's heart almost stopped. He remembered, long ago, a note Tam Lin had written him about the hazards of this place: *Ratlesnakes heer. Saw bare under tree.*

This was definitely a *bare*. Matt had only seen them on TV, where they did amusing tricks and begged for treats. The bear's eyes glinted as it contemplated the treat holding the flashlight. Matt tried to remember what to do. Look bigger? Play dead? Run?

The flashlight! It was a special one used by the Farm Patrol. One button was for ordinary use, the other shone with ten times the brightness of the sun. Flashed into the eyes of an Illegal, it would blind the person for at least half an hour. Matt jammed his thumb on the second button, and the bear's face turned perfectly white. The animal screamed. It hurled itself away, falling over bushes, moaning with terror, breaking branches as it fled.

Matt struggled to his feet. Where was he? Why was he alone? After a minute he remembered to switch the beam off to save the battery. Darkness enveloped him, and for a few minutes he was as blind as the bear. He sat down again, shivering. Gradually, the night settled back into a normal pattern, and he realized that he was at the oasis. He cradled the flashlight. Tam Lin had given it to him, to protect him from animals when he was camping. *You don't need a gun, lad,* the bodyguard had said. *You don't want to kill a poor beastie that's only walking through its backyard. You're the one who's trespassing.* Matt could hear Tam Lin's warm Scottish voice in his mind. The man loved animals and knew a lot about them, even though he'd been poorly educated.

Matt found the campfire he'd banked the night before and blew the coals into life. The flaring light made him feel better. In all the years of camping here, he'd never seen a bear, though there had been many raccoons, chipmunks, and coyotes. A skunk had once burrowed into Matt's sleeping bag in the middle of the night to steal a candy bar. Tam Lin had burned the sleeping bag and scolded the boy for foolishness. *Leave food about and you might as well put a sign on yourself saying "Eat me."* Matt had been scrubbed head to toe with tomato juice when they got back to the hacienda.

Matt heaped the fire with dry wood from the supply Tam Lin had always maintained. He could see the familiar outlines of an old cabin and a collapsed grapevine.

Tam Lin wasn't with him. He would never come here again. He was lying in a tomb beneath the mountain with El Patrón and all of El Patrón's family and friends, if you could say the old drug lord had friends. The funeral, three months before, had been attended by fifty bodyguards dressed in black suits, with guns hidden under their arms and strapped to their legs. The floor of the tomb had been covered with drifts of gold coins. The bodyguards had filled their pockets with gold, probably thinking their fortunes were made, but that was before they drank the poisoned wine. Now they would lie at their master's feet for all eternity, to guard him at whatever fiestas were conducted by the dead. Matt drew the sleeping bag around himself, trembling with grief and nerves.

He would not sleep again. To distract himself, he looked for the constellations Tam Lin had shown him. It was early spring, and Orion the Hunter was still in the sky. *Heed the stars of his belt,* said Tam Lin. *Where they set is true west. Remember that, lad. You never know when you'll need it.* They had been roasting hot dogs over a fire and drinking cider from a bottle Tam Lin had cooled by submerging it in the lake.

What a grand existence it must be, mused the bodyguard, turning his battered face to the sky, *to roam the heavens like Orion with his faithful dogs at heel.* The dogs, Sirius and Procyon, were two of the brightest stars in the summer sky. Pinning Orion's tunic to his shoulder was ruby-red Betelgeuse. *As fine a jewel as you'll find anywhere,* Tam Lin had declared.

Matt hoped Tam Lin was roaming now in whatever afterlife he inhabited. The dead in Aztlán came home once a year to celebrate the Day of the Dead with their relatives. They must be somewhere the rest of the time, Matt reasoned. Why shouldn't they do what made them happiest on earth, and why shouldn't Tam Lin?

Matt found Polaris, around which the other stars circled, and the Scorpion Star (but that was so easy even an eejit could do it). The Scorpion Star was always in the south and, like Polaris, never moved. Its real name was Alacrán. Matt was proud of this, for it was his name too. The Alacráns were so important, they could lay claim to an actual star.

Matt didn't think he could fall asleep again, and so he was surprised when he woke up in the sleeping bag just before dawn. A breeze was stirring, and a pale rosy border outlined the eastern mountains. Gray-green juniper trees darkened valleys high up in the rocks, and the oasis was dull silver under a gray sky. A crow called, making Matt jump at the sudden noise.

After breakfast and a short, sharp swim in the lake, Matt hiked along the trail to the boulder that blocked the entrance to the valley. In this rock, if you looked at just the right angle, was a shadow that turned out to be a smooth, round opening like the hole in a donut. Beyond was a steep path covered with dry pebbles that slid beneath your feet. The air changed from the fresh breeze of the mountain to something slightly sweet, with a hint of corruption. The scent of opium poppies.

2

THE NEW LORD OF OPIUM

Matt had left the Safe Horse under a cliff the night before. It was still waiting, as it had been commanded, but its head was down and its legs trembled. "Oh no! How could I have been so stupid?" cried Matt, rushing to the trough. It was half full of water, but the horse had not been given permission to drink, and now Matt remembered that he hadn't watered it the night before. It would stand there, mere inches away from relief, until it died. "Drink!" Matt ordered.

The horse stepped forward and began sucking up great drafts of liquid. Matt hauled on the pump handle, and soon fresh water was pouring over the horse's head and into the trough. It drank and drank and drank until Matt remembered that Safe Horses couldn't stop, either, without a command. "Stop!" he said.

The animal stepped back with its mane dripping. Had it had enough? Too much? Matt didn't know. The natural instincts of the horse were suppressed by a microchip in its brain. Matt waited a few minutes and then ordered it to drink again for a short while.

He climbed onto a rock to reach the saddle. Matt had never ridden anything but a Safe Horse and wasn't skilled enough to vault into a saddle. He'd been considered too valuable to risk on a Real Horse. "Home," ordered the boy, and the animal obediently plodded along the trail.

As soon as the sun rose, the air heated up, and Matt took off the jacket he'd been wearing. They moved slowly, but he was in no hurry to return. There was too much to think about and too much to decide. A few months ago Matt had been a clone. *Make that filthy clone,* he amended, because the word wasn't used without some insult. Clones were lower than beasts. They existed to provide body parts, much as a cow existed to provide steaks, but cows were natural. They were respected, even loved.

Clones were more like cockroaches you might find in an unguarded bowl of soup. Roaches made you feel like throwing up. Yet even they were part of God's plan. They didn't cause the deep, unreasoning hatred that a human copy did. A few months ago Matt had been such a being and then—and then—

El Patrón died.

The original Matteo Alacrán was lying in a tomb under the mountain with all his descendants. Esperanza Mendoza, the representative of the United Nations, had explained it to Matt. In international law you couldn't have two versions of the same person at the same time. One of them had to be declared an *unperson,* but when the original died, the clone no longer existed.

I don't understand, Matt had said to Esperanza.

It means that you are reclassified as human. You are El Patrón. You have his body and his identity, his DNA. You own everything he owned and rule everything he ruled. It means that you are the new Lord of Opium.

"I'm human," Matt told the Safe Horse as it plodded along, neither hearing nor caring. Now they came to the beginning of the opium fields. The crops were planted year round, and all stages of growth, from the first misting of green to brilliant white flowers to swollen seedpods, were visible. Lines of eejit workers, dressed in tan uniforms with floppy hats, tended the older plants. They moved in unison, bending to slash the ripe pods with razors to release sap or, if they were part of a harvesting crew, to scrape the dried resin into metal pots.

Here and there a member of the Farm Patrol watched from the back of a Real Horse. He would tell them when to rest, when to drink water, and when to start work again. For the eejits were just as mindless as Safe Horses. They, too, had microchips in their brains that made them content to do such grueling work. At evening the Farm Patrol would herd them to long buildings with small, dark windows. The ceilings were so low a person couldn't stand upright, but this scarcely mattered. The eejits had no social life.

They were given food pellets from a large bin, and when they had finished eating, the Farm Patrolmen ordered them into the buildings to sleep. Matt didn't know whether they slept on straw or merely stretched out in the dirt. He had never been inside an eejit pen.

In the fields of half-grown opium Matt saw lines of children removing weeds and bugs. Their small hands were much better at tending the delicate plants than adult hands were. These workers ranged in age from six to about ten, although some were so malnourished they might have been older.

Matt was horrified. Before he had seen anything of the outside world, child eejits raised no more pity in him than adults. But now that he'd met normal youngsters, it was unendurable to see them so brutalized. He pictured Fidelito—bright, cheerful, mischievous Fidelito—in a tan uniform with a little floppy hat on his head.

"Stop," Matt told the Safe Horse. He watched the small workers, trying to figure out how to help them. He could take them to the hacienda, feed them well, and give them proper beds. But what then? Could you say "play" and expect them to obey? Could you order them to laugh? The problem was in their brains, and Matt had no idea how to fix that.

He told the Safe Horse to go on. When they arrived at the stables, a young man came out to take the reins. He had dark brown eyes and black hair like most of the Illegals the Farm Patrol caught. Matt had never seen him before. "Where's Rosa?" he asked.

Rosa had been Matt's keeper when he was small. She had been bitter and cruel, tormenting the boy because he was a clone. When El Patrón discovered what she was doing, he turned her into an eejit and made her work in the stables. Dull-eyed and slow-moving, she brought out Safe Horses whenever Matt asked for them.

At first he was pleased with the punishment, but gradually he became uncomfortable. She had been terrible, but it was far worse to see her reduced to a soulless shadow. He spoke to her often, hoping to awaken something buried inside, but she never answered. "Where's Rosa?" he repeated.

"Do you wish another horse, Master?" the new stable keeper said.

"No. Where is the woman who used to be here?"

"Do you wish another horse, Master?" the man replied. He was only an eejit and unable to say anything else. Matt turned away and headed for the hacienda.

El Patrón's hacienda spread out like a green jewel in the desert. It was surrounded by vast gardens and fountains that sparkled in the sun. Peacocks strayed across its walkways, and wide marble steps led up to a veranda framed by orange trees. A few of the gardeners were Real People, and they bowed respectfully to Matt. Under their supervision a line of silent eejits clipped the lawns with scissors.

Matt was startled. Never before had the gardeners bowed to him. They obeyed him, of course, out of fear of El Patrón, but he knew they secretly despised him. What had changed? He hadn't told anyone about his new status, not even Celia, who loved him and didn't care a bent centavo whether he was human or not.

He walked along echoing halls on floors polished so brilliantly it was like walking on water. But he didn't go to the magnificent apartments reserved for the Alacrán family. He had never belonged there and had only bitter memories of the people. Instead he turned toward the servants' quarters and the huge kitchen where Celia ruled.

She was sitting at a scuffed wooden table along with Mr. Ortega, the music teacher; Daft Donald, the only surviving bodyguard; and the pilot who had flown Matt back to Opium. What was his name? Major Beltrán. They were drinking coffee, and Celia had put out a platter of corn chips and guacamole dip. When she saw Matt, she stood up so abruptly her cup tipped over.

"Oh, my. Oh, my," she said, automatically wiping up the spill with her apron. "Just look at you, *mi vida*. Only I can't call you that anymore. Oh, my." The others had stood up as well.

"You can call me anything you like," said Matt.

"No, I can't. You're too important. But I can't bring myself to call you El Patrón."

"Of course not! What a crazy idea! What's wrong with all of you?" Matt, more than anything, wanted to hug her, but she seemed afraid of him. Daft Donald and Mr. Ortega were standing at attention. Only Major Beltrán looked comfortable.

"You told them, didn't you?" Matt accused the pilot.

"It was not a secret." Major Beltrán seemed amused. "Doña Esperanza said I was to find the highest-ranking Alacrán and make a deal with him. Only, there is no such person. They're all dead."

"What do you mean, *deal*?" said Matt.

The pilot shrugged. He was a handsome man with glossy black hair and a film star's face. His spotless appearance made Matt aware that his own clothes smelled of horse and that his face was covered with acne. "We have to open the border," Major Beltrán said. "This place is in lockdown, as you saw when we flew in. Only El Patrón's successor has the power to cancel it, and until I got here, I didn't know who that person was."

"That person is me. Esperanza said that I was his successor."

The pilot shrugged again. "You're a child, and your claim is open to question. El Patrón's great-grandson should have taken over. Or one of his great-great-grandsons. Now, of course, you're all we have left."

Matt realized—how had he missed it before?—that Major Beltrán didn't like him. The ingratiating smile meant nothing. The mocking eyes said, *Three months ago you were a filthy clone, and in my opinion you still are. Never mind. I'll make do until I can find something better.*

That alone made Matt determined not to cooperate. "*I am the Lord of Opium,*" he said quietly. He heard Celia gasp behind him. "I will deal directly with Esperanza. The servants can find you an apartment, Major Beltrán, if they have not done so already, and when I open the border, you can fly home." Matt was trembling and desperately trying not to show it. He wasn't used to giving orders to adults.

Major Beltrán swallowed, and his eyes became cold and distant. "We'll see," he said, and left the room.

Matt collapsed into a chair. He was afraid to speak in case his voice betrayed how nervous he was, but there was only admiration in the eyes of Celia, Mr. Ortega, and Daft Donald.

"*¡Caramba! ¡Le bajó su copete!* You sure put him in his place," exclaimed Mr. Ortega with the slightly flat tone of the deaf. Daft Donald clasped his hands over his head in victory.

"He's been swanking around ever since he got here," Celia said, "giving us orders like he owns the place. He said that international law made you a human the minute El Patrón died—not that I ever doubted it. He said that in the eyes of the law you were El Patrón, but you were too stupid to know what to do. *¡Chale!* I don't think so!" She enveloped Matt in a bear hug, but very quickly let him go. "I can't do that anymore."

"Yes, you can," said Matt, hugging her back.

She solemnly unwrapped his arms and put them down at his sides. "No, *mi vida*. Whatever you may wish, you're a drug lord now and must learn to behave like one." She called a servant to take him to El Patrón's private wing. "You look exhausted, *mijo*. Take a bath and a nap. I'll send you clean clothes."

3

EL PATRÓN'S PRIVATE WING

A servant girl took Matt along various passages and unlocked the heavy wooden door that led to the private wing. It was an area only the most trusted allies of El Patrón had been allowed to visit. A haze of dust hung in the air, as though the windows had been closed for a long time.

As a child El Patrón had been so skinny that chili beans had to wait in line to get inside his stomach. The wealthy *ranchero* who owned his village had amused himself by casting centavos to the boy. El Patrón had to grovel in the dirt to collect them. He had never recovered from this humiliation. He wanted to become so rich and powerful that he could grind the *ranchero* under his heel. Unfortunately, the man died long before El Patrón could carry out his plan.

The insult was forever green in the old man's mind. He built a magnificent hacienda copying the *ranchero*'s estate. That was why most things in Opium were a hundred years in the past, but El Patrón's private wing was even older. He had brought back entire sections of Iberian castles. He had plundered El Prado, the finest art museum in Spain, for paintings and tapestries. These he studied carefully, for his goal was to become nothing less than a king.

The rooms of his private wing were as dark and cheerless as the old paintings. Tam Lin had once pointed out that the reason the pictures were so gloomy was because they were dirty. El Patrón had been furious. He exiled the bodyguard to eejit duty for an entire month.

The colors in this part of the hacienda were various shades of brown and black. Even the walls were a milky color that Tam Lin called "baby-poo." The furniture was made of heavy mahogany and cast iron and took at least three eejits to move. Yet here and there were pockets of beauty—a golden deer with delicate antlers, a statue of the Madonna, a painting of a woman in a white dress lying on a couch. Unlike the other portraits, whose subjects looked miserable, this woman had a mischievous smile. She reminded Matt of María.

The servant led Matt to a bedroom even darker and stuffier than the hall. She bowed politely and left.

Matt stretched out on the bed and closed his eyes, but for some reason he couldn't relax. For a few minutes he puzzled about what was wrong. He got up, pulled back the covers, and there, in the middle of the mattress, was the distinct impression of a man. Matt caught his breath. Of course! El Patrón had lain here for a hundred years. The hollow in the mattress was shaped like the old man, and the horrible thing was that Matt had fit into it exactly.

He tore the covers off, driven by a panic he didn't understand, and heaped them up in a corner to make a new bed. He fell into a troubled sleep, opening his eyes briefly to see the girl enter with an armful of fresh clothes.

Matt awoke hours later wedged under a chair. Above him were strips of ancient leather stained by years of use. A shred of dirty webbing dangled a dead fly next to his nose. He scooted out, vowing to have everything cleaned and to have the windows unsealed. He would send the tapestries back to El Prado and burn the dreadful mattress. Matt yanked at the heavy curtains hanging over the bed. The rotten fabric tore, revealing a bell cord El Patrón used to call servants.

A man appeared in the doorway, answering Matt's call.

"Help me get rid of this stuff," Matt ordered, gathering up the curtains in his arms.

The man didn't move.

Matt took a closer look at his eyes and realized that he was only an eejit. For months the boy had lived with normal people and had forgotten how creepy such beings were. The servant would understand only a few commands. "Get me lunch," Matt said hopefully. Nothing happened. "Call Celia. Make the bed. Oh, forget it. I'm going to take a shower." At the word *shower* the eejit woke up and went into the next room. Matt heard water being turned on and the man reappeared, pushing a wheelchair. He reached for the boy and started to undo his shirt.

"Whoa! Stop! Go away!" cried Matt. The eejit's hands fell, and he left the room as silently as he had come.

Matt heard water thundering in the shower and sprinted to turn it off. It was criminal to waste such a precious resource. At the plankton factory, where he'd been enslaved, clean water was unknown. Everything they used smelled of brine shrimp and strange chemicals. Even the water they drank was polluted and made the boys' faces break out with terrible acne. *Including mine,* Matt thought unhappily, feeling the bumps on his skin.

He saw that the bathroom had been set up for an old man. Handholds were everywhere. The floor was padded against falls. The shower stall was large enough to contain the wheelchair, and there were no mirrors. El Patrón hadn't wanted to be reminded of his age.

Matt took a quick shower and emerged feeling much happier. He discovered his old clothes in a closet and set out to find Celia. The bath eejit stood in the hallway. Only his blinking eyes indicated that he was something other than a waxwork.

On the way to the kitchen, the servant girl who had taken him to El Patrón's bedroom stepped out of an alcove. "Please follow me to the dining room, *mi patrón,*" she said, bowing.

"I don't want to eat in the dining room," Matt said crossly. "I want to have lunch in the kitchen with Celia. And don't call me *patrón.*"

He tried to go on, but the girl hurried past him and bowed again. "Please follow me to the dining room, *mi patrón.*"

"I told you—" He halted, realizing that she was another eejit. He hadn't noticed earlier, because she'd seemed so much more alert. If he tried to go on, she would only try to stop him again and again. Matt didn't have the energy to argue. Shrugging, he allowed her to lead him to a room large enough to entertain a hundred people.

A long table was covered with a white damask tablecloth. At intervals were vases of fresh flowers, and overhead, chandeliers glittered. Only one place had been set, which made Matt wonder. Did the servants decorate this room with flowers every day? They had certainly polished the chandeliers, because dust settled on everything in only a few hours. It was how things were in the desert. El Patrón hadn't minded, though he insisted on cleanliness when there were important visitors. He said that the dust reminded him of his childhood in the dry, dusty state of Durango.

From there, more times than not, the old man had gone on with the story of his childhood, following the well-worn tracks of his youth. Matt knew it by heart. It was like a real place hanging somewhere in space, just waiting to be visited again. Matt shivered. Sometimes it almost felt like one of his *own* memories.

He sat down, and the girl served him watery scrambled eggs, mushy polenta, and applesauce. It was an old man's lunch.

"Would you like me to feed you?" she said.

"Leave me alone," said Matt. He ate morosely, noting the lack of flavor. El Patrón's blood pressure hadn't allowed him to eat salt, chili peppers, or spices.

Heavy curtains had been pulled back from the room's tall windows to let in fresh air, and someone was using a lawn mower not far away. It was a manual lawn mower, because El Patrón hadn't liked modern machinery.

The girl stood silently next to Matt's chair. "For heaven's sake, sit down!" he cried. To his surprise she did, and he studied her more carefully. She was young, possibly his own age. She had silky blond hair and a pale, sweet face that would have been beautiful if her eyes hadn't been so empty. "Do you have a name?" he asked.

"I am called Waitress."

Matt laughed. "That's a job, not a name. What were you called *before*?" He regretted saying this, because he didn't want to think about what she'd been *before*, when she was a normal girl with a home and family.

"I am called Waitress." She stared at him blankly.

"From now on you're Mirasol," Matt decided. It was a name he'd always liked, and for a moment he thought he saw a flicker of emotion. She paused before answering.

"I am called Waitress," she repeated.

"We'll work on it later." Matt turned to the watery eggs. They had cooled off and were even less appetizing than before. "Can't you get me quesadillas or something that doesn't look like it was barfed up by a coyote?"

Waitress sprang to attention and hurried from the room. Matt was startled. Waitress—Mirasol—was showing surprising individuality. Apparently not all eejits were alike. He remembered there had been a huge difference between Teacher, who had long ago tried to teach him numbers, and the mindless zombies who tended the fields.

I've got to find a way to free them, he thought. He'd only returned to Opium yesterday and was still stunned by the change in his fortunes. It was very well to say he was going to end the drug empire, but where was he to begin? The whole thing rested on a vast distribution network that involved thousands of people. They wouldn't like to see their livelihood taken away.

He wished Tam Lin were there to advise him. Tears formed in Matt's eyes at the memory of the man who'd been as close as a father to him, and he hovered between grief and anger. How stupid of Tam Lin to kill himself. How *selfish*.

Mirasol returned with a tray heaped with steaming quesadillas, and Matt fell upon them ravenously. He hadn't had such food for months. All they ate at the plankton factory was plankton burgers, and in the hospital in San Luis, he'd been given dry toast and Jell-O.

He looked up to see Mirasol watching him and realized that

she, too, might be hungry. "I forgot about you," he said. "Please sit down and eat." She obeyed, stuffing quesadillas into her mouth as though she hadn't eaten for a month. He remembered that eejits didn't know when to stop and took the tray away from her.

"The doctors who did this to you are dead," he told her, although he knew she couldn't really understand. "They drank poisoned wine at El Patrón's funeral. Does that make you feel better? No, of course it doesn't, but there must be other doctors around who can cure you."

Talking to an eejit was almost like talking to himself, Matt thought. He wiped her mouth with a napkin, and she patiently endured it. "I wish I'd known you *before*," he said. "I wonder what forced you to cross the border and what kind of family you left behind." He brushed back the silky hair that had fallen across her face. Then, suddenly embarrassed, he took his hand away. "Thank you for the breakfast, Mirasol. I'm going to find Celia now."

"I am called Waitress," she replied.

He left her to do whatever she was programmed to do.

4

CIENFUEGOS

Celia was sitting at the kitchen table with a man Matt had never seen before. He was thin to the point of emaciation, and his skin was the same color as a coyote. His eyes were pale brown and watchful. He was cleaning a stun gun of the kind used to subdue Illegals, or sometimes to kill them.

"Matt!" cried Celia, springing up, but she stopped herself before she hugged him. "Oh, dear, I can't call you Matt anymore. It isn't dignified."

"You need a title," said the strange man, sighting along the stun gun. "This place is like a time bomb. The sooner we establish you as the master, the better."

"He needs a name suitable for a drug lord," said Celia.

"How about El Tigre Oscuro, the Hidden Tiger? Or El Vengador, the Avenger?"

"I don't want a new name," said Matt.

"You're going to have enough trouble controlling El Patrón's empire," the man explained. "You need a title that inspires fear, and you need to back it up with random acts of violence. I can help you there."

"Who *are* you?" Matt asked, instinctively on his guard.

"Oh! I forgot you'd never met," Celia apologized. "This is Cienfuegos, the *jefe* of the Farm Patrol. He's responsible for law and order. You haven't seen him before because he spends most of his time in the fields or at the other house."

"Other house?" said Matt. The Farm Patrol was responsible for trapping Illegals so they could be turned into eejits. They were vicious and dangerous, and Matt wondered why Celia, who had every reason to hate them, tolerated this one.

"The hacienda in the Chiricahua Mountains," said Cienfuegos. "It's where El Patrón went on vacation. It's a very fine place. I'm surprised you never went there."

"Until recently my job was to wait around until he needed a heart," Matt said coldly. "Heart donors don't get vacations."

Celia caught her breath, but Cienfuegos smiled. It made him look even more like a hungry coyote. "*Muy bravo, chico.* I hope you have what it takes to step into El Patrón's shoes."

Matt remembered one of El Patrón's most important rules: *Always establish your authority before anyone has a chance to question it.* "No one is better qualified to run Opium than I," he told the *jefe.* "I kept my eyes and ears open when El Patrón discussed the business with his heirs. I know the trade routes, the distribution points, who to bribe, and who to threaten. El Patrón himself taught me how to intimidate enemies and how to recruit bodyguards from distant countries because they wouldn't be as likely to betray you."

"*¡Hijole!* You looked just like the old vampire when you said that," exclaimed Cienfuegos. "Maybe we aren't screwed after all. Celia, get us some *pulque*. We need to drink to the new ruler of Opium."

"Matt doesn't drink alcohol," Celia said.

"But I do," said Cienfuegos. He leaned back in his chair and put his boots up on the kitchen table. Matt was shocked. If anyone else had tried that, Celia would have thrown him out the door. But Cienfuegos looked perfectly comfortable, as if he'd been doing it all his life.

Presently, Celia returned with orange juice for herself and Matt, and a bottle of *pulque* for the head of the Farm Patrol. Cienfuegos took a long drink, and the acrid smell of fermented cactus juice wafted across the table. "Now, I don't want to be disrespectful, young master," he said, "but I'm certain El Patrón didn't tell you everything about the trade. He had more secrets than a coyote has fleas. Tell me what you want to do with this country you've inherited."

Matt hesitated. One of the first things he wanted to do was disband the Farm Patrol. He couldn't reveal that. In fact, he didn't want to reveal anything to someone he'd just met and didn't trust. He wanted to uproot the opium—or most of it, anyway. That would automatically throw Cienfuegos out of work. With Esperanza Mendoza's help, Matt hoped to shut down the drug distribution network. He remembered the thousands of dealers who depended on it for their livelihood. They wouldn't like their jobs taken away one bit.

The boy felt overwhelmed by the size of the problem he'd inherited. El Patrón's empire was made up of many interlocking parts, and if he removed one piece, the rest might collapse into chaos. He badly needed advice, and he couldn't get it from Celia. She was wise and trustworthy, but she wasn't an expert in this area.

One thing stood out in Matt's mind as most important. "The implants have to be taken out of the eejits' brains," he said.

"That's impossible," Cienfuegos instantly responded.

"You don't know that for sure. If I can cure the eejits, they could be asked to stay on as paid workers."

The *jefe* laughed. "Have you seen what they do, *mi patrón*? No one could stand that job without an implant."

"People have farmed for thousands of years," argued Matt. "They weren't zombies. I'd like to see other crops planted— corn, wheat, tomatoes. I'd like cattle as well." He thought for a moment, carefully gauging the effect of his next suggestion. "I want to end the lockdown. Esperanza Mendoza, the UN repre- sentative, wants to negotiate opening the border."

Cienfuegos wiped his forehead with a handkerchief. "*¡Esa víbora!* I don't know where to begin with that snake."

"Why don't you take Matt for a ride?" suggested Celia. "Let him be seen as El Patrón's heir. You can explain the situation to him on the way."

"Can you ride a horse?" said Cienfuegos. They were at the stables, and the odor of fresh hay prickled Matt's nose.

"Only Safe Horses," he admitted. He could instantly tell the difference between the animals in the stalls. The Safe Horses stood quietly, tamed by the microchips in their brains. The Real Horses put their noses over the gates and begged for attention. They watched eagerly to see whether they would be taken for a run.

"Pity. You won't make a good impression until you know how to ride. When he was young, El Patrón was a fantastic horseman. He could break a wild mustang without even using a saddle."

"That must have been a long time ago," said Matt. El Patrón had been 146 years old when he died.

"The memory is kept alive in *narcocorridos*," said Cienfuegos.

"Narcocorridos?"

"It's an old-fashioned word for personal ballads. Now they call them *gritos*."

"Ah!" Matt understood. He had endured many hours of tuneless yowling from bands hired to celebrate drug deals or spectacular murders. These were politely listened to by El Patrón when drug lords came to visit. The old man had his own praise singers, but they were top-of-the-line guitarists from South America and Portugal.

"I use the old word because that was the term El Patrón preferred," Cienfuegos explained. "He had a fine ear for music. He hired the best composers in the world, and his *corridos* will never die."

"You sound like you admire him," said Matt.

"I do. I know he was evil, but I'm no cherub myself," said Cienfuegos. "Well, if you can't ride, we'd better go by car. You can sit in the back and look menacing."

Matt followed the *jefe* to the garage. Daft Donald was polishing El Patrón's long, black touring car. It had once been owned by someone called Hitler and had a top that could be folded back. Matt had always admired it but until now had not been allowed inside.

Daft Donald nodded silently in greeting. Long ago he and Tam Lin had been Scottish terrorists together and had set a bomb to blow up the prime minister of England. Unfortunately, a school bus had pulled up at the last minute. The explosion killed twenty children and left Daft Donald with a wound that almost severed his throat and had destroyed his ability to speak.

What a fine collection of followers I've inherited, Matt thought. *Citizens of Opium and not a cherub among them.*

Daft Donald grinned and got into the driver's seat. He looked as eager as the horses to be taken for a run. Matt reminded himself that the man, in spite of his evil past, had always been kind. And he was a friend of Tam Lin, which counted for a lot.

Cienfuegos and Matt sat in the back, with Matt on a pillow to make him look taller. "Remember, don't smile," the *jefe* warned him. "You're here to rule, not make friends."

Spring arrived early in Opium, and sand verbenas were already putting out lavender blooms. Desert lilies poked through the warming soil. In the vast gardens of the hacienda, a haze of bees moved over beds of sweet alyssum, and a white-winged dove called *who-cooks-for-you?* from a paloverde tree.

In spite of Cienfuegos's warning, Matt couldn't help smiling. This was *his* home and *his* country. It wasn't full of clanking machines and noxious air like Aztlán—except for the eejit pens, he quickly reminded himself. They were kept out of sight at the bottom of shallow valleys, and it was all too easy to forget about them.

Water from the Colorado River was purified for drinking. The residue, a toxic mix that smelled like rotten fish, excrement, and vomit, was pumped into sludge ponds next to the eejit pens. On still nights the air from the ponds overflowed and poisoned whatever it came in contact with. Then the Farm Patrol ordered the eejits to sleep out in the fields.

The gardeners waved and shouted, "*¡Viva el patroncito!*" as Hitler's old car went by. Matt raised his hand to wave back.

"Don't encourage them," hissed Cienfuegos. "If they start calling you 'the little boss,' they'll never show respect."

Matt put his hand down.

They left the green lawns of the estate and came to the first poppy field. Lines of eejits bent and slashed in a mindless rhythm, and a Farm Patrolman monitored them from the back of a horse.

"¡Hola! Angus!" shouted Cienfuegos. "Come and see the new patrón!"

Daft Donald stopped the car and Angus rode up, tipping his hat. "It's a fine day when we have a new drug lord," he said. "Good fortune to you, sir." He was a bluff, red-faced Scotsman with the same lilting accent as Tam Lin. The man bent down confidentially and said to Cienfuegos, "You might put a word in his ear about the eejit pellets. We've had to cut rations again."

"I'm getting to it," said the jefe.

Angus shot a quick look at Matt and bent down again. "Begging your pardon, sir, but doesn't he look like—"

"It's hardly surprising. El Patrón was the original model."

"You don't say! I'll be burning an extra candle tonight." Angus tipped his hat again and rode off.

"Eejit pellets?" Matt asked as Daft Donald started the car.

"We get their food from a plankton factory in Aztlán," explained Cienfuegos. "With the border closed, we've had to depend on reserves."

"Can't you open it?" said Matt.

"The controls only recognize certain people. The Alacráns activated the lockdown before they went to El Patrón's funeral, and now they're all dead. The system is programmed to kill anyone who isn't authorized. I'm hoping that doesn't include you."

Me too, thought Matt. The old man had booby traps planted all over to keep enemies from gaining control.

Cienfuegos leaned forward and told Daft Donald to take them to the armory.

5

THE DOPE CONFEDERACY

The poppy fields were beautifully maintained, thought Matt, who had learned much about opium farming. Every third year a field was allowed to rest, and eejits patiently massaged manure into it with their fingers to make the soil soft and fertile. The result looked like fine, Colombian coffee grounds. These resting patches of earth brimmed with life. Birds, bees, and butterflies were everywhere. Lizards sunned themselves on fence posts. A falcon hovered over wild grass, looking for the bow-wave of a mouse underneath. Aztlán to the south had been a wasteland compared to Opium.

After a while Matt saw a large building looming in the distance. It had a red tile roof and grilles over the windows after the fashion of old Mexican forts. Outside were picnic tables under ramadas. A few Farm Patrolmen, seated at these tables, snapped to attention when the car stopped.

"At ease," said Cienfuegos. "This is your new leader, *amigos*.

See that you treat him with respect, or he'll have you *cockroached*. You'd do that, wouldn't you, *mi patrón*?"

"In a heartbeat," said Matt, who didn't know what the word meant. From the alarmed expressions on the men's faces, he guessed that it was a serious threat.

"Hugh, get the map of the Dope Confederacy," the *jefe* told a man with cold, humorless eyes. Matt recognized him. Long ago the boy had passed out from bad air near an eejit pen. The man who rescued him had been Hugh, but it hadn't been an act of charity. Hugh had thrown him into the back of a truck and almost crushed the life out of him with a boot. Now the man looked slightly stunned to see his new lord. He hurried to obey.

Cienfuegos ordered everyone away and spread out the map. Matt had seen it before in the Alacrán library. It was a detailed chart of the border between the United States and Aztlán, and over the top was a title printed in gold leaf: THE DOPE CONFEDERACY.

At the western end was the Land of Cocaine, stretching from the Salton Sea to the Pacific Ocean. This had been ruled by Mr. MacGregor until he drank poisoned wine at El Patrón's funeral. Matt wondered who controlled it now. At the eastern end of the Dope Confederacy, from the ruins of Ciudad Juárez to the Gulf of Mexico, were the lands of Marijuana, Hash, Tobacco, Meth, Snuff, and LSD. A tiny sliver—Matt had to squint to make it out—was labeled Ecstasy. Far and away the most impressive country was the one in the middle: Opium.

Matt's heart swelled with pride.

"You do know that all the drug lords were poisoned at El Patrón's funeral," said the *jefe*.

"*All?*" said Matt. This was news.

"It left a power vacuum that immediately led to civil wars.

Most of the Dope Confederacy was rotten to begin with, and it didn't take much for law and order to break down." A breeze lifted the edge of the map, and Cienfuegos pinned it down with a stiletto he flicked out of his sleeve.

Matt was momentarily distracted by the smooth way the *jefe* produced this weapon. One instant the man's hand was empty. The next he had the slim knife poised for attack—fortunately, this time, on the map. *But it could have been me,* Matt thought.

"Whatever you might think of El Patrón, he was a genius at maintaining order," the *jefe* continued. "If anything threatened Opium, the borders were locked down. Anyone who tried to enter or leave was annihilated by unmanned drones. Even during ordinary times, hovercrafts had to get permission before landing. You may have noticed how quiet the skies are over Opium."

"They've been quiet for as long as I can remember," said Matt.

"El Patrón never allowed jets over his territory. He wanted everything kept as it was a hundred years ago. Once, about fifty years ago, a passenger jet carrying two hundred forty-five people strayed into his airspace."

"He didn't—" said Matt.

"He did. Remember what I said about random acts of violence," said Cienfuegos. "That's how you maintain power. El Patrón only had to make his point once."

"But two hundred forty-five innocent people!"

Cienfuegos signaled to someone Matt couldn't see in the Armory, and presently a Farm Patrolman came out with lemonade. The *jefe* poured two glasses and used the jug to pin down another corner of the map. "Mm!" he said, taking a drink. "Not as good as *pulque*, but I promised Celia not to corrupt you."

No, you're only telling me it's okay to shoot down two hundred forty-five people, thought Matt.

"What do you think would have happened if El Patrón had let that aircraft escape?" said Cienfuegos. "Next year another jet would have made a 'mistake,' and then another and another. Eventually it would have led to war. Many more people would have died."

Matt tried to think of a counterargument and failed. "What about Illegals? Are they still trying to cross the border?"

The *jefe* grimaced. "Unfortunately, the border itself is a lethal force field, now that it is in lockdown. It gets them before we do. It's a pity, because we need new workers. The life expectancy of an eejit isn't long."

Matt looked for signs of compassion in the man and found none. Cienfuegos might have been talking about a shortage of Thanksgiving turkeys.

"Show me the lockdown system, and I'll try to open it," said Matt.

"Not so fast. I haven't finished," the *jefe* cautioned. "The governments of Marijuana, Hash, Tobacco, Meth, Snuff, LSD, and Ecstasy collapsed. They were wide open for invasion, and the most vicious of the drug lords took control. You have to really shine in that area to stand out from the others. He was an African called Glass Eye Dabengwa."

"Glass Eye," murmured Matt. He recognized the name. One of El Patrón's homework assignments had been to memorize drug contacts, and Africa was one of the major markets. Matt had to update his information constantly because accidents tended to happen, but Glass Eye had been durable. He'd weathered dozens of assassination attempts. Matt had seen him at Benito and Fani's wedding, and a couple of times later at El Patrón's parties.

He was almost a hundred years old and maintained his

health, as did all drug lords, by raising clones. The truly frightening feature of the man was his ability to stare at someone
without blinking. His eyes didn't seem to need moisture, or perhaps his tear ducts had dried up long before. The whites had
turned as yellow as an old crocodile's.

The rest of the man was a dusty gray, except for his teeth.
They were as strong and white as those of a man of twenty. And
they really *had* come from a man of twenty, because you didn't
need a clone to transplant teeth. Glass Eye Dabengwa found
himself a new donor every few years.

Matt looked at the map with dismay. The combined territo-
ries of the defeated drug empires were as large as Opium. "What
about the Land of Cocaine? Can we ally ourselves with that?"

"Not anymore," Cienfuegos said grimly. "When it became
clear that Glass Eye planned to invade Cocaine, the United
Nations launched a preemptive strike. They called it Operation
Cold Turkey. They firebombed the coca plantations and in the
process killed the eejits. Thousands of them. The land of Cocaine
is now occupied by UN forces under the direction of Esperanza
Mendoza."

"*Esperanza?*" Matt was shocked to his very core. She was
María's mother. She was the one who had saved him in Aztlán
and who'd promised to help him. *This* was her idea of help? But
he also knew she was a fanatic. She'd abandoned her own children to follow political beliefs and might well consider killing
eejits a small price to pay for stopping the drug trade. *That's no
different from El Patrón shooting down a jet plane to avoid a war,* he
thought.

He heard doves calling in the palo verde trees and smelled
dust raised by horses' hooves in a corral. He heard men laughing
as they played cards under the ramadas. It seemed so peaceful

and normal, though of course it wasn't normal. Opium thrived on the blood of Illegals. But if Esperanza had her way, might she not order everyone killed here, too?

"It isn't easy being good, is it?" said Cienfuegos, cleaning his fingernails with the stiletto.

6

MIRASOL

You need Cienfuegos's help," said Celia. She and Matt were sharing an uneasy lunch in the kitchen. Celia insisted that Matt had to keep up his image. No more lounging around the servants' quarters or deferring to people like Daft Donald or Mr. Ortega. He needed to act like a proper drug lord.

Matt, just as insistently, said that drug lords did whatever they wanted. That was the whole point of having power. And so the two of them were eating hamburgers at the old farmhouse table and trying to look comfortable about it.

"I didn't want to call Cienfuegos in," Celia said now, "but there were so few Real People left and thousands and thousands of eejits to control."

Matt reached for the plate of hamburger patties, and Celia firmly took it away from his hands. He was not to prepare his own food, she said. She began to assemble the hamburger, adding pickles, onions, and *pico de gallo* salsa.

Matt thought that not being allowed to do things for yourself could get old quickly.

"I hate the Farm Patrol. I *despise* them. But what was I to do?" Celia said, depositing the hamburger on Matt's plate. "Tam Lin always said that Cienfuegos was the best of the lot, and we certainly needed help."

"Do you trust him?"

"Not really. At least he's not like the other Farm Patrolmen. He wants to end the opium trade."

"*¡Claro, y los chanchos vuelan!* Sure, and pigs fly, too!" said Matt.

"I think he means it. Cienfuegos wasn't the usual thug El Patrón hired. He studied agriculture at Chapultepec University. He told me that the soil in Aztlán had been devastated by industrial waste and that he set out for the United States to find a cure. The Farm Patrol tracked him for three days in and out of the mountains. Cienfuegos killed five of them before they cornered him, and then El Patrón was so impressed by his courage that he recruited him. But Cienfuegos never wanted to be a hired gun. He has never forgotten his mission to heal Aztlán."

"What does he plan to do with the eejits?" asked Matt.

Celia sighed. "I don't know. He says they're incurable."

El Patrón would work them until they died, thought Matt. No one seemed to think they were worth saving.

Until he had met the boys at the plankton factory, he hadn't thought much about the zombielike workers. He felt sorry for them, of course, but like everyone else, he believed they were incapable of feeling. Did it matter what kind of life you had if you couldn't feel pain?

The boys at the factory had been left behind by parents who had crossed the border. Chacho's father had been a guitar maker. Imagine creating something that good and then being turned into a zombie. Chacho's father was probably bending and slashing opium pods along with Ton-Ton's parents and Fidelito's grandmother.

Or, more likely, they were buried under the poppy fields with thousands of other Illegals.

"Cienfuegos paid a price for his life," Celia said, breaking into Matt's thoughts. "He was implanted with a microchip."

Matt looked up, startled. "He's a . . . he's an *eejit*?"

"Don't even hint that you know about it," warned Celia, lowering her voice. "It enrages him. All the Farm Patrolmen are chipped to make them more docile. You can't have murderers and terrorists running around without some kind of control."

"They don't act like eejits."

"There's more than one type of microchip. This kind doesn't blunt intelligence, but there are certain things a Farm Patrolman can't do. He can't harm the *patrón*, for example, or cross the border. If he tries, he's struck by pain so severe that he'll die of shock. Even thinking about it makes him sick."

Matt let out his breath slowly. El Patrón *had* been a genius at maintaining order, and he did have more secrets than fleas on a coyote. There were the hidden underground treasure chambers and the secret passages throughout the hacienda where the old man could spy on people. There were the emergency escape routes and now the invisible chain that encircled the necks of his trained dogs, the Farm Patrol. It was a beautifully constructed system to bring power into one man's hands. El Patrón's hands. And now Matt's.

"Tam Lin told me this privately," Celia said. "Farm Patrolmen never admit to the operation because it makes them seem less than men. It's why they're so cruel to eejits. To prove they have nothing in common with them."

A sudden thought struck Matt. "The bodyguards. Were they chipped?" She nodded. "And Tam Lin?"

Celia smiled sadly. "Him too."

Matt could hardly bring himself to ask the next question, but he had to know. "What about you, Celia?"

Her eyes turned as cold as those of an idol Matt had seen on TV, the Aztec goddess Coatlicue, who wore a necklace of severed hands. He remembered that it was Celia who had brought about El Patrón's death when the armies of Aztlán and the United States had been unable to touch him. "I wasn't worth worrying about," Celia said. "I was only a woman."

Silence hung heavily in the room. They weren't alone, though they might as well have been. Several eejits worked at their appointed tasks. One washed dishes, going over each plate exactly five times with a sponge. He passed it to another man, who dunked the plate exactly five times in rinse water. A woman kneaded bread dough: push, fold, turn . . . push, fold, turn. A teenage boy, who reminded Matt unpleasantly of the boys at the plankton factory, was slicing onions. It took a lot of servants to prepare a meal, because each of them knew how to do only one thing.

"Could I have some ice cream?" said Matt, to break the tension.

"Oh! Of course!" Celia woke up. The goddess Coatlicue disappeared. "Do you want pistachio, mango, or *dulce de leche*?"

"Dulce de leche."

She opened a giant freezer and hauled out a gallon tub of ice cream. Fog swirled around her as she kicked the door shut with her heel.

Matt tried to think of something to say. "What do you know about Waitress, the girl who serves me meals?"

"Her? Why are you asking?"

"No reason. She just seems more alert than most eejits."

Celia dug out scoops of ice cream and poured marshmallow syrup over them. "As I said, not all implants are the same. Most dull the mind so that a person can perform a simple chore for hours without stopping. A few leave a person's basic skills intact. I have a helper who's very good at making sauces. He used to be a French chef."

Matt ate the disgustingly sweet dessert, which he loved, and thought about Waitress. "I want to change her name. Is that possible?"

"Ask Cienfuegos," Celia said impatiently. "He's in charge of training." She went over to tell the boy, who'd run out of onions, to stop chopping.

That afternoon Matt had the old mattress on El Patrón's bed burned. He gave orders for quesadillas, coffee, and fruit to be served for breakfast. He sent the bath eejit away to be retrained.

In the evening he and Cienfuegos sat down to dinner in El Patrón's grand dining room. Now that Matt took the time to study it, he saw how unusual it was. The walls were covered with priceless Spanish paintings of kings and queens. Royal children, dressed in stiff clothing, stared dolefully out of dark nurseries. They didn't look as though they knew how to play, and their only entertainment seemed to be dwarfs. Spanish kings collected dwarfs, to go by the number of them, the way other people collect stamps. A brooding misery hung over all the scenes. There was even, in one shadowy corner, a painting of heretics being burned at the stake.

"Those are all originals," said Cienfuegos. *"Muy, muy valioso."*

"I don't care how valuable they are. I think they're creepy," said Matt.

"They're marks of prestige. A man who can afford such things is like a king."

"Who am I going to impress?" asked Matt. With the border closed, no visitors came to the hacienda. Its rooms and halls were deserted except for the occasional shadowy figure of a servant dusting a statue.

They sat across from each other. The crystal chandelier shed flecks of light over the tablecloth, and they also had a heavy gold candelabra, for the room was large and dark. Waitress served them dinner. She poured *pulque* for Cienfuegos and water for Matt.

"This was where El Patrón entertained his most important guests," said the *jefe*. "Presidents, dictators, and drug lords. Ah, those were the days!"

"Were you invited?" Matt shook his head at Waitress when she tried to cut up his meat.

"I was one of the bodyguards. We stood around the walls and watched the guests."

Unlike now, Matt thought, realizing he might have made a mistake by inviting Cienfuegos to eat with him. It seemed important to show underlings that he was too important to be friendly. Celia had told him he should hire more bodyguards, too, because Daft Donald wasn't enough. A drug lord with only one bodyguard, she said, was like a general with only one soldier. The other drug lords would make fun of him.

"Tam Lin was always present," remembered the *jefe*. "I came when El Patrón wanted to know whether someone was lying. I'm very good at reading faces. For example, I know right now that you're thinking about Waitress."

Matt almost choked on his food. "I am not!" he objected.

"You've been casting shy little glances at her all evening," said Cienfuegos. "She's a pretty thing, isn't she? I'm glad I didn't train her for farm labor. She's much more ornamental here."

A surge of anger almost suffocated Matt. Cienfuegos had captured Waitress and turned her into an eejit. He could have saved her!

"Rage," the *jefe* said calmly, pointing his fork at Matt. "Or perhaps jealousy. You like the girl and think that I'm a rival."

"I'm not interested in her that way," Matt said, trying to keep the anger from showing on his face.

"I'm afraid it's a lost cause, *mi patrón*. Eejits can't feel emotions." Cienfuegos went on eating as though he were merely discussing the weather. "Now let's forget pretty girls for a while and decide what to do about the border."

Matt took careful breaths to calm down. He couldn't afford to quarrel with Cienfuegos. He had too few allies. "Is there a way to communicate with the outside world?"

"The holoport has been locked down along with everything else. You could access it."

"I see," began Matt slowly, wondering what a holoport was. It worried him that Cienfuegos knew so much more than he did. It gave the man power. El Patrón would have surrounded Cienfuegos with spies who would report to him of any disloyalty. And he would have arranged a convenient accident if the reports were bad. Although, if what Celia said was correct, the man would be struck with lethal pain if he tried to rebel.

"I should negotiate with Esperanza first," Matt said aloud. "I'd like to lower the security barrier briefly to allow her daughter María to visit." From the look the *jefe* gave him, Matt realized that he knew about their friendship. "I'll tell Esperanza I must find a way to remove the microchips from the eejits' brains before we discuss anything. It's a humanitarian problem and should appeal to her. Until they're free, the business of shipping opium and bringing in supplies must go on."

Cienfuegos raised his eyebrows. "That's exactly the sort of plan El Patrón would come up with. Esperanza is always bleating about the poor eejits, and we can deflect her until we secure our power base."

"She didn't do anything for them during Operation Cold Turkey," Matt remarked.

"Oh, she wrung her hands and said no one told her what was going on. Esperanza likes to look like a saint."

It hadn't escaped Matt that Cienfuegos had said "we" would secure "our" power base. Somehow, he had to make the man understand that they were not sharing power. "I really do intend to cure the eejits," he said.

The *jefe* held out his hands in mock submission. "One may intend anything, *mi patrón*. The reality, alas, is different. In the old days the drug lords used one microchip the size of a grain of rice. It wore out after a few months and had to be replaced. Now they inject thousands that are no larger than bacteria. These spread out over the brain and form a network, and if one fails, the others take over its function. The effect is permanent."

Matt felt shaken. "If a surgeon tried to remove them . . ."

"It would be like finding the right grains of sand on a beach."

They ate in silence. Waitress brought them crème caramel custards and withdrew to stand by a painting of a Spanish infanta being amused by a dwarf. She looked hypnotized, and the dwarf's face was twisted in an expression that might have been pain.

The windows of the dining room were open, and a cool breeze carried the smell of distant creosote bushes. Matt thought it must be raining somewhere out on the desert. "Please close the windows, Waitress," he said.

Cienfuegos laughed. "You say 'please' to an eejit. You might as well say 'thank you' to a duck."

"It does no harm," Matt said, disliking the man's attitude.

"It doesn't bother me, but you can't do it in front of important people. I'm telling you this for your own good."

Waitress had closed the windows, but she still stood in front of the glass, gazing into the darkness. *What is she thinking?* Matt thought. *Does she know what she's doing? Can she smell the creosote?*

"Please meet me in Celia's kitchen tomorrow morning," he said, turning back to Cienfuegos. "Eight o'clock. You can show me the holoport."

"You almost had it right," said the *jefe*, grinning. "You don't say 'please' to me, either."

"It seems that being a *patrón* means being rude to everyone," said Matt.

"Pretty much," Cienfuegos admitted.

"One thing more. I want to change Waitress's name to Mirasol. Is that possible?"

"Of course. I'll give her a retraining session tomorrow." The *jefe* bowed and took his leave. Matt was left to watch Mirasol at the window.

"Come here," he commanded. He filled a plate with lamb and mint sauce, asparagus, and half a baked potato, as much as he thought healthy for her. "Now eat," he said.

And Mirasol ate ravenously. She acted as though she were starving. The pellets that made up the eejits' diet were running out, so perhaps she *was* starving.

After she had finished, Matt got her one of the custards from the serving table at the side of the room. It was creamy on the inside and brown with caramelized sugar outside. To his amazement, she stopped eating after the first bite. She sat as though stunned, with the spoon in her mouth, and he was afraid he'd made her sick. But then she began to eat again, slowly, keeping the custard on her tongue for a long time. *She had to be tasting it! She had to be!*

"I'll make it up to you," Matt said softly, watching her. "There has to be a way to find all those grains of sand on the beach."

7

MAJOR BELTRÁN

Matt woke up feeling elated. He wasn't confused as he'd been in the morning. He knew he was in El Patrón's bedroom, but the mattress was new and the windows were open, letting out the odors of old age. Today he would have the servants take up the musty carpets and change the curtains. The tapestries would be stored and the walls scrubbed.

I can do anything I want, thought Matt, stretching out on the clean, fresh sheets. It seemed incredible that he'd been here only two nights. The first he'd slept on the ground at the oasis; the second had been spent here in the lair of the old man. *But I can make it my own,* the boy thought happily. He sprang up, eager to explore his new empire.

In the old days he hid in shadows, avoiding the cruel remarks from people who thought him lower than a beast. He'd learned to move like a shadow, eavesdropping and trying to make sense of the world around him. Now he had come into the light.

Today he would contact María. She would come to him, and he would show her how everyone obeyed him and how they need never hide their love again. They would be together always and perhaps become *prometido*, engaged to be married.

Matt halted. What, exactly, was marriage for? María said it was important, but he hadn't paid attention to her reasons. Why would he? At the time he'd been a clone, and they didn't get married. He knew that Felicia had been handed over to Mr. Alacrán as part of a drug deal. Fani had refused to marry Mr. Alacrán's son until her father drugged her. María had been promised to Felicia's son Tom. It didn't matter that Tom's idea of a good time was to nail frogs' feet to the ground.

Nothing about the Alacráns made marriage even slightly attractive.

Before the wedding there was something called dating, for which you needed a girlfriend. Matt had a vague idea of the practice from watching TV, but nothing of the sort existed in Opium. For most of his life he'd had only one friend, who happened to be a girl. Did that qualify? As for having more than one, it hadn't occurred to him until he met the boys at the plankton factory.

Chacho and Ton-Ton bragged about all the pretty *chicas* they knew. There weren't any *chicas* at the plankton factory, but the boys assured Matt that they'd been *muy popular* back in their old homes. Girls, according to them, were the most fun you could have. Especially when they were competing with one another to make you happy. Ton-Ton swore he had at least five following him around.

Matt wondered how Ton-Ton managed this, because he had

a face that looked like it had been slammed into a wall. He didn't dare ask. Nor could he ask Chacho why girls were lining up to take him to parties. He didn't want them to know how ignorant he was. When it came time for him to describe his own adventures, he stole stories from TV shows. He had to be careful, because the only shows El Patrón had allowed were a hundred years old.

One thing had stuck in Matt's mind, though: Ton-Ton said that good girls were always chaperoned. Matt wasn't sure what a *bad* girl was, but María was definitely good. If he invited her, Esperanza would insist on coming along.

Esperanza. Some of the contentment leaked out of the day.

An antique clock struck the hour, and the sun on its face moved forward as the starry night retreated. It was six a.m. Matt had discovered a whole shelf of clocks that did amusing things: An old woman hit an old man over the head with a broom when the hour struck, a rooster spread his wings and crowed, a ballerina turned to the music of *Swan Lake*. There were music boxes, too. On one, an old-fashioned gentleman and lady danced around a sombrero to the tune of the Mexican Hat Dance. Their tiny metal feet darted in and out, and the lady swirled her long skirts. It pleased Matt to know that the old man had such innocent pleasures.

After breakfast he went in search of Celia but found her together with Major Beltrán. The two had their backs to him, and Matt approached with the stealth that had become second nature to him. Celia was holding a coffeepot while the major sampled the brew. "Disgusting! You should never make coffee with tap water," the man said. He was dressed in a uniform that was surely meant for a parade ground. His shoulders were broadened with gold epaulets, and a black military hat made him look tall and powerful.

"Throw this swill out and use distilled water," the major ordered. "Grind the beans just before you brew them. This morning's offering tasted like floor sweepings."

"I'm sorry, *comandante*," Celia said humbly.

"There was an insect in my bedroom this morning," Major Beltrán went on. "A dirty, disease-carrying insect such as you would never find in a decent home. I opened the window and it flew in."

"It must have been one of the bees from the flower beds."

"I don't care what it was. I want the apartment sprayed with insecticide and the flower beds, too."

"Oh, but El Patrón never allowed that—" Celia began.

"El Patrón is dead," the major said bluntly. "Another thing: I won't eat food made by those creatures." He waved his hand at an eejit stirring soup. "They haven't the faintest idea of hygiene."

"I tell them to wash their hands," Celia said.

"Look at this!" Major Beltrán grabbed the soup stirrer's hand and held it out for her to inspect. The eejit did a little dance like a jittery windup toy trapped behind a piece of furniture. It was an activity Matt had seen before when one of the servants couldn't fulfill a task. "There's *dirt* caked under his fingernails," cried the major. "From now on you will prepare all my meals."

"I thought I told you to stay in your apartment," Matt said. The two spun around.

"He didn't like the food I sent," explained Celia. "What was I to do? He's a representative of the UN. *Muy importante.*"

"He isn't important here," said Matt. "Last I heard, Opium wasn't a member of the UN."

"Ah! It's the little drug lord," said the major, with a smile that didn't reach his eyes. "Tell me, don't you feel lonely rattling around in this big mansion? Wouldn't you like some other children to play with?"

"Please return to your apartment," said Matt. He clenched his fists and then unclenched them. He didn't want the man to know that the insult had struck home.

"Be careful, little drug lord. Your country is surrounded by enemies. It isn't wise to offend an ally." Major Beltrán let go of the eejit, and the servant grabbed the ladle and started stirring again.

"Get out," Matt said.

"Make me," jeered the major.

Too late Matt realized that he and Celia were the only Real People in the kitchen. He wasn't strong enough to tackle the man by himself, and Celia was too old. But it was dangerous to let Major Beltrán get away with defiance. A weak drug lord was very soon a dead one.

"You're only a *boy*," the major said scornfully. "Or at least that's the official position. I would call you something else. You can't possibly inherit this country."

Celia watched the man with large, worried eyes.

"You have no authority over me," Major Beltrán said. "I will go and come as I please. All those who would have protected you are dead, and your only guardians are a fat, old cook, a deaf music teacher, and a half-wit bodyguard who can't even speak."

Casually, without any attempt to hurry, Matt walked over to the soup eejit and watched what he was doing. His mind was racing as he hunted for some way out of this situation.

"Quit stalling, little drug lord," the major said. "Doña Esperanza sent you here to open the border, and she doesn't like to be kept waiting."

Matt had gone to the stove with no purpose, or at least none that he was aware of. But once there a voice, deeply buried in his mind, whispered, *He wants to kill you.* It was so real that the boy glanced up to see whether someone else was in the room.

"I'll open the border when I think it's the right time," Matt said, watching the soup eejit.

"If you do it now, Doña Esperanza will be merciful. She doesn't have to be, you know. She has an entire army at her disposal."

Matt felt the back of his neck prickle. He wanted to spin around, to discover what the major was doing, but he instinctively felt that this was bad strategy. He must look as though he were in control. *Do it,* the voice in his mind said. "Do what?" Matt said aloud.

Don't waste time with stupid questions! thundered the voice. *Do it!* As though someone else had taken control of his body, Matt's hands grabbed the pot, and he whirled around. The major was much closer than he thought, and Matt threw the boiling soup at him.

The major jumped back, but not quickly enough. The soup splashed over his coat, and he frantically pulled it off. A knife clattered to the floor. Celia screamed. In the same instant Matt was aware that Cienfuegos was in the doorway.

The *jefe* launched himself across the room, slammed the man into a wall, and punched him three times like a professional boxer. The major collapsed. Cienfuegos casually took a pitcher of ice water from the table and poured it over him.

"It was good strategy using the soup, *mi patrón,*" he said, "but next time throw it at his face." He went to the hall and called for eejits to carry the major to his apartment.

★　　★　　★

Matt's hands were shaking as he clutched the mug of coffee Celia had given him. He didn't know which had upset him more—the major's attack or Cienfuegos's lightning response. "Would he really have killed me?" he asked. "If he had, no one could have opened the border."

"He would have taken you hostage and forced you to do it. I've had my eye on him ever since he learned you were the sole heir," said the *jefe*.

"You need more bodyguards," said Celia, supervising the eejit who was cleaning up the spill.

"I don't know why I threw that soup," Matt said. "Something just came over me."

"That's how the old man was," Cienfuegos remembered fondly. "He was like a samurai warrior, always in the present. No one had time to outguess him." The *jefe* was lounging with his feet up on the table, holding a similar mug, except that his had *pulque* in it.

"I don't really like to hurt people," Matt admitted.

Cienfuegos gazed at him over his drink. The *jefe's* light-brown eyes were intent, like a coyote watching a rabbit. "You get used to it," he said at last.

Celia bustled around, preparing another pot of soup. "I've been thinking about possible names for our new drug lord," she said. "How about El Relámpago, the Lightning Bolt, or El Vampiro?"

"I lean toward vampires," said Cienfuegos. "They come out after dark and drink blood. Very scary."

"For the hundredth time, I don't want another name," Matt said.

8

THE HOLOPORT

When they had finished, Cienfuegos led the way to the holoport, and Matt was surprised to recognize the place. He'd discovered it while exploring the secret passages El Patrón used to spy on people. It was a warehouse filled with computers and surveillance cameras, and normally it would have been full of bodyguards.

"I should have thought of this room," the boy said. "It's one of the few places El Patrón allowed modern machinery."

"You've been here before?" Cienfuegos sounded surprised.

"El Patrón and I used to watch the surveillance cameras together." Matt was lying. He'd never been here with the old man, but it pleased him to keep the *jefe* off balance.

"That's odd. He never let his other—" Cienfuegos halted.

He never let his other clones in on the secret, Matt silently finished. *You can't use the word "clone" around the new Lord of Opium, any more than I can use the word "eejit" around you.*

The *jefe* threw open the doors of a cabinet to reveal a giant screen. It brightened to show an office overlooking a large city. An address at the bottom read HAPPY MAN HIKWA. BULAWAYO, ZIMBABWE. Matt remembered that Happy Man was one of El Patrón's most voracious customers. He distributed drugs under the leadership of Glass Eye and was now probably an enemy.

Matt was pleased to recall the man's identity. When El Patrón was alive, the boy had memorized long lists of drug contacts, trade routes, and the correct *mordidas*, or bribes, to pay.

After a few minutes a new picture appeared of a shed half-filled with boxes: WAREHOUSE #7. ABUJA, NIGERIA. A red light flashed in a corner of the screen.

"They're trying to contact us," explained Cienfuegos. "Everyone wants to know where his shipment of opium is, and I can't answer because I'm locked out. Everyone is. Have you ever used a holoport?"

"I never had reason to," Matt said.

"It's easy if you have access," said Cienfuegos.

And that's why you're willing to serve me, thought Matt. Only El Patrón's handprint—or that of his clone—could unlock the security system and disarm the weapons on the border. For the first time Matt realized what the old man had really intended. It wasn't enough to fill his tomb with slaves for the afterlife. El Patrón had meant to kill everyone in Opium.

With the border closed and no one alive to open it, supplies would run out. Oh, the few Real People might scratch out an existence eating squirrels, but the vast eejit army would perish. And how long could the Real People survive without medicine, seeds, livestock, or food? Opium was a one-crop country, and everything else was imported. When all were dead, El Patrón would rule a kingdom of shadows, with ghostly eejits tending the fields and Celia eternally preparing meals and Daft Donald forever polishing Hitler's car.

But he didn't count on me, Matt thought.

"How do I dial up Esperanza?" he said aloud.

"I don't know, *mi patrón,*" said Cienfuegos. "If you wait long enough, all the addresses will appear."

Matt watched as pictures flashed onto the screen. Places in the United States and Aztlán appeared, although officials in those countries were not supposed to be involved with the drug trade. Warehouses in Russia, India, Japan, and Australia were shown, lingered a few minutes, and faded.

The air in the room was cold, and a hum vibrated almost out of the range of hearing. Matt shivered. He'd gone from near solitude to someone who would have to stand up to presidents and generals. The thought of going toe-to-toe with Glass Eye Dabengwa filled him with dread. He'd seen Glass Eye. The sight of those motionless yellow eyes had turned Matt's spine to water, and the man wasn't even looking at him. No matter how many pillows Cienfuegos put on Matt's chair to make him look tall, Glass Eye would know he was just a kid.

The Convent of Santa Clara appeared with the words ESPERANZA MENDOZA. SAN LUIS, AZTLÁN.

"Put your hand on the screen," said Cienfuegos in a tense voice. When Matt obeyed, a thousand tiny ants swarmed over his skin and his heart raced madly. He'd felt this reaction before. It was what happened when El Patrón's defense mechanism was deciding whether you were friend or foe. He saw the *jefe* step away.

The sensation passed. The screen dissolved into a long, dark tunnel swirling with milky vapors. It looked for all the world like a passageway you could climb into, and Matt found himself attracted to it. He smelled the sharp odor of rain falling on dust.

"Stay back!" shouted Cienfuegos from somewhere nearby. Matt realized he'd been about to fall into the tunnel.

The holoport found its destination, and the scene cleared. A nun, sitting at a table, was embroidering a portrait of the Virgin of Guadalupe. She was as real as someone seen through an open window, so close that Matt felt he could reach out and touch her.

The nun dropped her embroidery. "Oh! Oh! It's a transmission! What do I do? What do I do?"

"Don't be frightened. I only want to talk to you," Matt said, surprised at her panic.

"I shouldn't be here at all," the woman protested. "I'll get into such trouble. I never thought the holoport would activate—"

"If you aren't allowed to talk, please call Doña Esperanza," said Matt. But at that moment Esperanza herself came in.

"*Sor* Artemesia, you booby!" scolded the woman. "You're going to get your head handed to you for poking into places where you don't belong."

"I meant no harm! This was such a nice room to sew in while María was at the hospital—"

"Weren't you supposed to be teaching her math?"

"Well, I meant to. Really I did. But she didn't want to study. She says that visiting the sick is a greater duty and that Saint Francis—"

"Go find her!" thundered Esperanza. *Sor* Artemesia fled.

Esperanza was a small, extremely fierce-looking woman with black braids pinned across her head like a crown. She was dressed in black and wore silver rings on every finger and a large silver brooch with the portrait of an Aztec god. The jewelry did nothing to lighten her appearance. She reminded Matt of a crow on a piece of roadkill. "You survived," she said without a trace of a smile.

"I survived," Matt said, staring back.

"Is that Cienfuegos lurking in the background? Somebody must have left a screen door open."

"I love you, too, Doña Esperanza," said Cienfuegos.

"Well, get me Señor Alacrán or that lump my daughter married, Steven. Whoever's in charge. We've got to unseal the border and allow a peacekeeping mission to enter."

She doesn't know, Matt thought. But how could she know that everyone who had attended El Patrón's funeral was dead, including Esperanza's husband and her older daughter Emilia? "They—uh, they can't come," said Matt, searching for the right words.

"Don't stall for time," the little woman spat at him. "You may enjoy swanking it up in your old home, but I have world affairs to consider. Don't worry, *chiquito.* You'll be well cared for."

"I thought you were going to have me declared the heir," said Matt, stung at being called a little kid.

"Yes, probably. In due time." Esperanza waved her hand impatiently. "If you can't find anyone else, you can rustle up that good-for-nothing husband of mine."

"You have to tell her," said Cienfuegos.

"Tell me what?" the woman snapped. "That they don't want to open the border? Give me a break! Either they let the international peacekeepers in or the whole country will starve to death."

Everything that Cienfuegos had said about the destruction of Cocaine came back to Matt's mind. What would happen if he allowed the so-called peacekeepers in? Esperanza didn't care whether the innocent suffered. She was a fanatic. Somewhere deep inside Matt an old, old voice whispered, *I'm like a cat with nine lives. As long as there are mice to catch, I intend to keep hunting.*

El Patrón, thought Matt, shocked. It was like the voice he'd heard in the kitchen—an actual person whispering in his ear! It frightened him because it was so real, but also comforted him because in a strange way he had found an ally.

"You don't need to have me declared the heir," he said in words he barely recognized as his own. "I *am* the Lord of Opium, the only Alacrán left."

Esperanza's eyes opened wide.

He told her. He described how the eejit children sang the "Humming Chorus" from *Madama Butterfly* at the funeral. The mourners—though you could hardly call them mournful—had waded through drifts of gold coins as they entered the tomb. El Patrón's coffin was laid out like the sarcophagus of an Egyptian pharaoh. His likeness as a young man had been painted on the lid. Then Tam Lin brought out a case of wine that had been laid down the year the old man was born, and Steven, Emilia's husband, had opened the first bottle. *It smells like someone opened a window in heaven,* he said.

How little he knew! Everyone who drank it went straight to the afterlife, though probably not to heaven. All the drug lords died and their wives, too, including Emilia. The others— the priest, Senator Mendoza, Tam Lin—fell with them.

Matt looked for signs of emotion in Esperanza's face, but all she did was sigh. "That certainly makes things awkward," she said.

Awkward? What kind of woman was this who didn't cry when she heard about the death of her husband and daughter?

"I had hoped to negotiate with one of the older family members," she continued. "No offense, Matt, but you're only fourteen years old."

"I'm more than a hundred," Matt said. *And I am,* he thought. *I was grown from a strip of El Patrón's skin.*

"Yes, well . . ." For the first time Esperanza looked uncertain. "We don't really know what happens when clones grow up. We've never had one your age. I do know that you're inexperienced and ill-educated."

Matt smiled. "El Patrón only had a fourth-grade education, and he founded an empire."

"*¡Por Dios!* You sound exactly like him. It's unnatural!" Esperanza cried. She wiped her forehead with a heavily ringed hand. "The situation is more complicated than you think. Most of the Dope Confederacy was on its way out. The land had been farmed until it was exhausted and then polluted with chemicals. The drug lords rode around in hovercrafts and shot all the wildlife. Glass Eye won't find it easy to make money out of his new territory, which is why he's looking toward Opium."

"He is?" Matt asked sharply.

"El Patrón was a monster, but he had a quality the others lacked. I can't believe I'm saying something good about him."

Matt waited as she struggled to control her anger. Through the holoport he could hear doves in a far-off courtyard. When he was recovering in the hospital of Santa Clara, María had pushed his wheelchair into the convent garden. Together they had watched the birds bobbing and cooing in their half-witted way as María threw bread crumbs at them.

"*Saint Francis once rescued a basket of doves from a market,*" she had said.

"*I don't blame him. They taste good with oregano,*" Matt had replied, goading her.

"*Be quiet, Brother Wolf. I'm trying to civilize you. He gathered them in his arms and said, 'My innocent sisters, why did you let yourselves be caught? I will make you nests so that you may raise your*

young in safety.' The doves obeyed him and never flew away unless
they were given permission."

Matt had looked at María's black hair hanging in a bell about her
beautiful face and knew that he loved her utterly and forever.

"Opium is a lifesaver, if used properly," said Esperanza,
breaking into Matt's thoughts. "We don't want to eradicate it,
just to keep it under control. But there's something else about
your country. Do you remember what Aztlán looked like?"

Matt did. His first vision was of a seething mass of factories and skyscrapers. The sky was smudgy as though someone
had been burning rubber tires. Worse than that was the boom-
ing, clanking, thundering din that filled the air. His first day in
Aztlán had been horrible, but he soon got used to it.

"I wondered how anyone could live in such a place," he
said.

"The border area is the worst, but the rest of the country is
a mess too," said Esperanza. "The United States isn't any better.
Wild animals there can only survive in zoos. The flowers that
once covered the countryside have vanished. People huddle in
houses, afraid to go anywhere because of crime, and children
have forgotten what it's like to play outside."

Matt was surprised. So the United States wasn't a paradise
full of Hollywood mansions after all.

"In fact, the whole world is an ecological disaster," said the
woman. "The rich can escape to their little enclaves with gardens and high walls, but even they can't escape the air. It has
become what religious people call God's Ashtray."

"God's Ashtray," repeated Matt, liking the term. It reminded
him of a giant bowl in which rested a single, giant cigarette
butt.

"Opium is the only place in the world with an undamaged

ecosystem," said Esperanza. "The UN has declared it a natural refuge. We hope to use its plants and animals to heal other lands."

"Wait! You're telling me that El Patrón is going to save the planet? He's the patron saint of endangered species?" Matt's whoop of laughter made Esperanza wince.

"This project is too big for you, Matt. You need advisers. You need UN peacekeepers to maintain order."

"Oh, no! We're going to do things my way. I want the border free to bring in food, and I don't want any of your peacekeepers maintaining order like they did in Cocaine. Later on we can discuss exporting the ecosystem. Right now my first concern is to reverse the eejit operation."

"No one can do that," said Esperanza.

"I intend to try," Matt said. "I want you to find me some expert brain surgeons."

"That's going to take time," she protested.

"Do what you can. And I want María and the boys I knew in the plankton factory to visit me."

"Not possible," said Esperanza. "Think! You have Glass Eye Dabengwa leaning on your eastern border. He's not stupid. He's going over and over your lockdown system, trying to find a way to break it open. Do you really want your friends in his path if he invades?"

Matt was deeply disappointed, but he knew she was right. "We'll talk about it later," he conceded. "Right now I want you to find me doctors. I'm going to open the border for brief periods, but be warned—"

Esperanza rubbed her forehead vigorously, and her lips were compressed into a thin line.

"—if your peacekeepers try to get in, I swear that I will fry every gopher, bighorn sheep, and bunny rabbit from here to the Salton Sea. Do you understand?"

From Esperanza's furious expression, he knew she did.

"Fine. I'll call you in a few days to see what progress has been made. How do I turn this thing off, Cienfuegos?" But the *jefe* didn't need to do anything. Esperanza had already broken the connection.

9

THE GUITAR FACTORY

Y ou should have seen him, Celia!" exclaimed Cienfuegos over lunch. They were in the kitchen, feasting on her excellent chiles rellenos. "It was like having the old man back again."

"I don't like the idea of having the old man back again," said Celia, casting a troubled look at Matt.

The boy ate silently, trying to ignore the conversation. He wasn't sure what had happened, and he was certain he didn't like it. Two times a voice had whispered in his ear and made him do things. It was good, of course, to stand up to Esperanza. But where had that courage come from?

"I think we should call him El Relámpago, the Lightning Bolt," Cienfuegos said. "He let Esperanza have it right between the eyes—*Pum!*—'Do what I say or I'll fry the whole country.' Brilliant!"

"That's a terrible thing to threaten," said Celia.

The *jefe* shrugged. "Fear is the beginning of wisdom, *mi cara-melito*."

"Fear of *God* is the beginning of wisdom," corrected Celia. "And I'm not your sweetie pie."

Cienfuegos reached for a tortilla and expertly loaded it with lettuce, beans, and salsa. "What do you say, El Relámpago? Shall we open the border today?"

"Stop giving me nicknames," Matt said. "How fast can we get supplies in? I don't want us vulnerable for more than a few minutes."

"*No problemo*. The train has been sitting in San Luis for weeks," said Cienfuegos.

After lunch they returned to the control room, and Matt found he could pause the lockdown in as large or small an area as he liked, while keeping the rest of the border secure. Cienfuegos focused a screen to show him the border post. Following the *jefe's* instructions, Matt pressed a button. He heard an alarm ring in the distance and saw a mob of work-men running from a warehouse.

"See? They've been waiting for your signal," said the *jefe*. "It won't take them long to unload the train."

Matt saw a train consisting of at least two hundred cars wait-ing in Aztlán. As he watched, it slowly gathered speed and rolled across the border into Opium. The workmen were lined up about a hundred yards away from the tracks.

The crossing took less than fifteen minutes, for which Matt was grateful. He could see a mass of soldiers in green uniforms watching the procedure from Aztlán. Among them were UN peacekeepers in black. They were all heavily armed, and behind the men were ominous vehicles and hovercrafts.

"A whole *maldito* army!" swore Cienfuegos. "Crot Esperanza!"

Matt flinched at the filthy word. "Close the border now, *mi patrón*. I don't trust them to keep their distance."

Matt did so. He had learned from the *jefe* that anyone could activate the lockdown in case of an emergency, but only El Patrón's hand could remove it. It was another example of the extreme control the old man kept over everything. Opening and closing a small portion of the border should have been a simple task, but when Matt was finished, he was utterly exhausted.

"Takes it out of you, doesn't it?" said Cienfuegos. "I've watched the old man fine-tune the border, and he always had to lie down afterward. It has something to do with the scanner."

"It felt like ants were swarming over my skin," said Matt.

"You're lucky that's all that happened. I was worried the first time you used the holoscope. If the machine doesn't recognize you—well, it isn't good."

"How did you find out?" said Matt, remembering how nervous the *jefe* had been when he contacted Esperanza.

"I tried to use an eejit to access the controls," said Cienfuegos. "Don't worry. He was close to his expiry date, so no great loss."

"You sacrificed a *human being*?"

"An eejit, *mi patrón*. No one knew you were coming back, and our goose was rapidly being cooked."

It made sense, Matt realized. One of the Five Principles of Good Citizenship they had to parrot at the plankton factory was that an individual had no value apart from the group. It was the duty of a citizen to sacrifice himself for the good of all. And yet . . .

"What happened to him?" asked Matt.

"The scanner makes you fall apart," the *jefe* said reluctantly.

"I don't quite understand how it works, but it removes the glue that holds your cells together. You melt."

Matt felt sick, imagining what it looked like.

"If it's any help, I don't think the eejit minded," said Cienfuegos. "He looked a little surprised, and then he was only a puddle on the floor. It was a mess to clean up."

"I think I want to be alone for a while," said Matt.

"There's one more thing you should see," said the *jefe*. He refocused the screen on the train, which was now halted on the tracks. Another alarm sounded, and the workmen moved even farther away. Presently, a sheet of light passed over the cars. Even in the fierce desert sunlight it burned bright enough to hurt your eyes. When it was done, it vanished and the alarm rang again. The men swarmed aboard and began unloading crates.

"You see, you can't allow just anything to cross the border," Cienfuegos explained. "You might have weevils or grain beetles on board. The beam kills them."

"What about people?" said Matt, who saw where this was going.

"It eliminates them, too," said Cienfuegos. "I wouldn't put it past Esperanza to hide an army of peacekeepers. We're in luck, though." He pointed at the screen, where one of the workmen was waving a green flag. "No one was on the train. There's nothing there but good cheese, milk, and vegetables."

"And eejit pellets," said Matt.

"Of course eejit pellets, in the last fifty cars," said Cienfuegos.

Matt rested in his room for a while. He drew the curtains and lay down, enjoying the semidarkness and solitude. He listened to the gardeners clipping a hedge outside. El Patrón had wanted to keep his world the way it had been when he was young, and that meant almost no contact with the outside world. The old man had unbent enough to accept a few amenities—refrigerators, for example—but for the most part Opium remained in the past.

What an incredible joke! El Patrón had enslaved thousands of people and grown his crops with polluted water. He no doubt passed this pollution on to drug addicts around the world. Foul pits of chemicals spread death near the eejit pens, but most of the country was untouched. Deer and javelinas still roamed the forests. Wildflowers covered the desert after rain. Every cranny of the wilderness was full of life.

El Patrón craved land because he liked owning things, but he had chosen to neglect vast areas of it. For purely selfish reasons, the old man had preserved what the rest of the world had destroyed.

Matt felt too restless to stay in bed. He went in search of Waitress, but she was nowhere to be found. With nothing better to do, he went to the garage and found Daft Donald playing chess with Mr. Ortega. "I want to get out. I don't care where," he said.

The two men had an odd relationship based on their disabilities. Daft Donald couldn't talk and Mr. Ortega couldn't hear, so they worked as a team, with Daft Donald scribbling notes on a yellow pad of paper he always carried with him. Mr. Ortega translated it into speech. The music teacher was also very good at reading lips, and you could carry on an almost normal conversation with him. Now he suggested visiting the guitar factory.

Matt had often been to the workshops, though not with Mr. Ortega. One building was reserved for making pottery. Long ago El Patrón's mother had gathered clay from riverbeds to make pots in what was then Mexico. She had also woven rebozos on a homemade loom, and so there was a cloth-weaving shed too. Matt sometimes wondered about this shadowy person. In a way she was Matt's mother too, and he tried to imagine the woman behind the smell of wet clay and the sound of shuttles.

These craft eejits, Matt realized now, were implanted with a milder form of microchip that preserved their skills. They were well fed and housed, for they were not expendable like the workers in the fields. Some of them, Mr. Ortega said, had been there for many years. Daft Donald waited in the car with a comic book when they went inside.

The guitar factory was a beautiful building copied from something El Patrón had seen in an old English movie. It was meant to be one of those charming country homes where gentlemen drank tea while their ladies played the harpsichord. It was completely out of place here. The English garden suffered in the dry desert air and was overrun with flower-eating lizards and bugs.

Inside were racks of harps, oboes, zithers, sitars, drums, and every other kind of instrument that had taken the old man's fancy. In one room was a piano. A group of eejit boys were singing German folk songs under the direction of an elderly choirmaster. They were no older than Fidelito, and their voices had the high, pure sweetness of children.

Matt's favorite room, and El Patrón's as well, was full of guitars. At a large table the master craftsman worked alone, for the task was too demanding for lesser hands. At the moment he was sanding a piece of African mahogany, making it as soft and smooth as skin. The man himself was not unlike a tree stump you might find in a forest. His body was thick, with a barrel chest and sturdy legs. The expression on his face, as he bent over the table, was as concentrated as a tree knot, and his large, sloping nose was pure Aztec.

At first glance the man's fingers seemed too clumsy to produce such works of art, but the results of his labor stood against the walls. There was row upon row of the most beautiful guitars in the world. Musicians everywhere coveted them, and El Patrón sometimes gave them to his favorites.

"*Vaya con Dios*, Eusebio," said Mr. Ortega. "May you go with God." The guitar maker kept on sanding.

"You know him?" asked Matt. He had watched the guitar maker for years, but no one had ever given him a name. Like most eejits, he was referred to by his occupation.

"He was my *compadre*. We crossed the border together. Like an idiot, I wanted to be a big star in Hollywood and he . . ." Mr. Ortega paused. "Eusebio has always been happy doing exactly what he is doing now. He came with me for friendship, and look where it got him."

Wsssss went Eusebio's sandpaper as he polished the wood.

"The Farm Patrol shot me with a stun gun. Here." Mr. Ortega pointed to his ear. "In that instant the world vanished, the world for a musician, I mean. It made me stone deaf."

"What happened next?" said Matt. He had never had such a long and personal conversation with his music teacher. In fact, the man hadn't seemed to like him much.

"Eusebio, may God reward him, defended us with a guitar. He played as though we were in a concert hall, not surrounded by enemies. I couldn't hear it, but I could see his fingers moving over the strings. No man was ever a better musician. It was such a unique defense that the Farm Patrol brought us to El Patrón. Later I learned that my friend described me as a famous pianist and himself as the world's greatest guitar maker. Which he is, of course. Unfortunately, it didn't save him from being microchipped. If you hadn't needed a music teacher, I would have ended up here."

Matt didn't know what to say. He had assumed that Mr.

Ortega had been hired as the bodyguards were. When El Patrón wanted something, his dealers in the outside world found it for him, whether it was a doctor, a dentist, a repairman, or a gardener. It seemed odd at the time that the only piano teacher the old man could find was deaf, but Matt had been very young and frightened. He didn't dare ask questions.

"I want to show you something," Mr. Ortega said. He took up one of the guitars leaning against a wall and tuned the strings. He laid his cheek against the wood, and Matt realized that he was listening to the music with his bones. It was the same thing he did when teaching piano. Satisfied, Mr. Ortega proceeded to play the most beautiful flamenco music Matt had ever heard. The notes flowed through the air like water into a desert pool, and it made anyone else's guitar playing seem cheap and tinny.

Eusebio turned toward the sound. His mouth opened as though he were drinking in the music, and his eyes cleared. The sandpaper fell to the floor. On and on Mr. Ortega played until a Farm Patrolman, whose job it was to maintain the craft eejits, came in and ordered him to stop.

The music halted. Matt woke up. He, too, had his mouth open, and it was as though he'd been shaken out of a wonderful dream. "How dare you!" he shouted at the Patrolman in the best El Patrón manner. "Get out and don't bother us again!" The Farm Patrolman did a double take and began apologizing. "Get out!" screamed Matt. The man fled.

But the dream had been shattered. There was nothing—nothing!—Matt hated more than having music interrupted. He wanted revenge! He wanted the Patrolman flogged or, better still, *cockroached*—

"Are you all right?" asked Mr. Ortega.

Matt blinked. No, he wasn't all right. For a moment he had simply vanished into rage. He had no memory of what he'd said to the Patrolman.

"I'll get you a glass of water," said Mr. Ortega. Eusebio went back to polishing. "Celia told me that you were having problems. Cienfuegos thinks it's great when you sound like the old man, but she says it's dangerous. She's a *curandera*, you know, a traditional healer. She thinks you might be suffering from spirit possession."

Matt choked on the water. "That's ridiculous!"

"Probably," said Mr. Ortega. "No doubt there's a psychological explanation, but I always find it useful to listen to Celia. Or read her lips," he amended with a sad smile. "That music you just heard was written by Eusebio. I discovered that he wakes up a little when I play it. I thought you might be interested, since you like talking to Waitress."

Matt was overcome with embarrassment. Was it possible to do anything in this place without being found out? Cienfuegos must have spread the story. "I was curious about her, that's all," he said. "I'd like to go now."

"Would you mind if I stayed?" The music teacher picked up the guitar.

"Not at all."

"You should visit the drug factory," said Mr. Ortega, "keep up with the family business. It's bursting at the seams now because they can't export the opium. The dust alone in that place would knock you on your *nachas*."

"That can't be good for the workers," said Matt.

"They're eejits," the music teacher said. "They don't know when they're stoned."

10

NURSE FIONA

Matt didn't go to the opium factory. Eusebio's reaction to the music bothered him too much, and he told Daft Donald to drive to the hospital. He had no good memories of the place and didn't want to go there now, but he had to learn more about the microchipping process.

The hospital was set apart from other buildings. It was a gray, windowless place surrounded by a wasteland of sand and thorny vines. Dust had drifted over its front steps as though no one had gone inside for a long time. But the door wasn't locked. The smell in the waiting room was sickly sweet and medicinal at the same time, and it stirred terrible images from Matt's past. For the first time in weeks he felt his lungs close up. *Bad air!* his mind screamed as he reached for his asthma inhaler. He staggered outside and collapsed on the dusty steps.

Daft Donald, who had been waiting in the car, rushed over.

"Find help," Matt managed to gasp. The bodyguard nodded and ran inside.

It took Daft Donald a few minutes to return, and by that time Matt felt slightly better. A woman in a nurse's uniform knelt beside him. "Dear me, young master. You want to be lying down." She had the same lilting accent as Tam Lin.

"Not in the hospital," said Matt.

"No indeed! It's like a bloody crypt in there," the nurse said. She and Daft Donald carried the boy to the car, although Matt said he felt well enough to walk. "I'll see you back to your own good bed, laddie. It'll be a fair treat getting out of that hospital, I can tell you," the nurse confided. "All the doctors gone, only the odd gardener coming in with a cut, the halls deserted except for those bloody zombies. Scrub, scrub, scrub, that's all they ever do. It's a wonder the floor hasn't eroded."

By the time they arrived back at the hacienda, Matt had learned a lot about the nurse, whose name was Fiona. He knew where she'd gone to school, her first and second husbands' names, her father's occupation (punter, whatever that was), her mother's problems with varicose veins. On and on the one-sided conversation flowed until Matt was quite bewildered.

"You're the first Real Person I've seen in donkey's years," Fiona warbled, tucking Matt into bed. "'Look after the hospital,' they said, going off to that party they threw for the old man's funeral. The doctors, the head nurses, the lab technicians left me behind because I'm at the bottom of the heap. No vacations for Fiona. She's only a dishwasher. 'We'll be right back,' they said. And didn't they drink poisoned wine at that party! It just shows that good luck has a way of turning on you. Foo! There's a fair pong in this room. Would you mind if I opened a window?"

By now Celia had been alerted as to Matt's illness. She

bustled in with home remedies and a tray of food. Between them, the two women set up a bed table and soon had Matt propped against pillows.

"Where's Waitress?" Matt asked.

"Don't you remember? You sent her to be retrained," Celia said.

A whisper of alarm touched Matt's nerves. "She'll be back, won't she?"

"Of course. Eventually." Celia left.

"Here comes the choo-choo train going to the station," Fiona said brightly. She held up a spoonful of mashed potatoes.

"I can feed myself!" said Matt, shoving her hand away.

"El Patrón used to like this game," the nurse said. "I'd say, 'Here comes the choo-choo train,' and he'd say, 'What's it carrying, Nurse Fiona?' And I'd reply, 'All sorts of delicious treats,' and he'd say—"

"Shut up!" said Matt. And then was sorry because he knew why Fiona was talking so feverishly. She'd been alone too long. "Look, I don't want to hurt your feelings. I'm just not interested in games. I'd like to ask you a few questions."

"All right," said Fiona.

So Matt asked about the chipping process, and it turned out that she knew quite a lot, though she wasn't allowed to do it herself. "They put a drip into the patient's arm," she said, "and then they inject the chips with the liquid. The chips are smaller than blood cells and go right through the heart. Sometimes they get filtered out by the liver, but most of them make it. I've seen them under the microscope. They look like tiny diamonds. One side has a protein that attaches to a brain cell. The other is a mosaic of different kinds of metal and is slightly magnetic."

"Magnetic," repeated Matt. That was interesting.

"I've been told that they're tiny batteries. They work together like a second brain, only much simpler than ours. The process takes less than fifteen minutes, and when it's done the patient—though you could hardly call him a patient, more like a victim I'd say, only don't quote me—is catatonic."

"What's 'catatonic'?"

"It's like a coma. All the brain functions are on hold, so to speak. The doctor marks the forehead with the number 666 to show the operation's been done. Then the orderlies take the patient away to be trained."

"Who does that?"

"The Farm Patrol." For once, Fiona didn't look chirpy. "I hear it's brutal and that they enjoy doing it."

Brutal! And Matt had sent Waitress to be retrained! He pushed the bed table away.

"Lie down, young master! You'll undo my good work if you don't rest," protested the nurse.

"I can't stay. I've got to rescue Waitress." Matt stood up and steadied himself as a slight dizziness struck him.

"If she's an eejit, it won't matter," Fiona said. "They don't feel anything. The doctors say they react to stimuli the same way a dead frog jerks if you give it an electric shock. Mind you, I never liked that part of biology, the poor froggies looking like little old men in green pajamas—"

"Shut up!" cried Matt again. He went straight to the kitchen, where, as he had expected, Daft Donald was having lunch. "Get the car," the boy commanded. "Take me to where the eejits get trained."

They sped through the opium fields with a long plume of dust rising behind them. Matt wished Daft Donald could talk, because he suspected the man knew a lot about the training. It was too late now. The man couldn't drive and write notes at the same time.

They arrived at the armory, and a group of men sitting outside jumped to attention. "Where—" Matt began. Daft Donald took his arm and pulled him through the courtyards surrounding the armory and on to another building behind it.

Matt heard a scream. He shook off Daft Donald and raced ahead. "Step aside!" he shouted at a pair of Farm Patrolmen, and such was the authority in his voice that the men practically fell over getting out of his way. Inside the building, Matt saw a windowless room with a drain in the middle of the floor. At the far end was Waitress, bound to a chair with her hands taped around electrodes, and Cienfuegos in front of a machine. Such was his concentration that he didn't hear Matt enter.

"Your name is Mirasol," the *jefe* said.

"No! No! I am Waitress!" sobbed the girl.

Cienfuegos shook his head and turned a dial. The girl's body jerked.

"Take him, Daft Donald," Matt ordered. The bodyguard lunged past and smashed his head into Cienfuegos's lower back. Matt yanked out the wire leading into the machine. But when he turned, he saw that the *jefe* had recovered from the blow and had cut a slash across Daft Donald's face.

"Stop, Cienfuegos!" shouted the boy. "Obey me!"

The *jefe* aimed another swipe at the bodyguard's face, but Daft Donald was no amateur at this kind of fighting. He produced his own knife from a scabbard on his leg. With this he blocked the *jefe's* arm and inflicted a vicious cut.

"Stop! Both of you!" Matt thrust himself between them, and Daft Donald backed away. Cienfuegos, however, was beyond reason. He raised his stiletto, and his eyes were completely blank.

For a frozen instant nothing happened. Then Matt said, *"I am the cat with nine lives. You will not prevail against me."*

Where had those words come from? They weren't like anything Matt would say.

"El Patrón," whispered Cienfuegos. He dropped the stiletto and doubled up, clutching his stomach. If the cries of Waitress had been bad, the screams coming from the *jefe* were even worse. He sounded like he was enveloped in flames. Daft Donald caught him and mouthed words at Matt. "What do you want? What should I do?" the boy said.

Daft Donald mouthed again, *Forgive him.* Could he possibly mean that? Why would the bodyguard care what happened to Cienfuegos? *Forgive him,* Daft Donald said again. The *jefe's* screams were growing weaker.

"I forgive you," Matt said. Cienfuegos shuddered and relaxed into Daft Donald's arms. Blood dripped from his wound. *The microchip,* Matt thought. *He's under the control of the microchip. When he attacked me, it was programmed to kill him. But El Patrón added a fail-safe to stop the process.*

"Get one of the men to drive," Matt told the bodyguard. "You and Cienfuegos must go to the hospital. Waitress, too." He knelt down beside her and began to unwind the tape holding the electrodes to her hands. "I never meant this to happen, Mirasol, and it will never happen again," he said.

"I am called Waitress," she responded.

11

FEEDING A PET WAITRESS

One good result of the battle was that Nurse Fiona returned to the hospital. Matt did accompany her, taking an inhaler along in case he suffered another asthma attack. He saw at once why Fiona hated the place. The halls and rooms were empty except for a few ghostly eejits going about their chores.

"I have to tell them to do everything," said Fiona. "If I don't give them work, they stand there and jitter, but without patients nothing gets dirty. I have to make them wash perfectly clean floors over and over again. It's enough to make you run barking."

Matt was getting used to her odd language. "To run barking" meant to go crazy. "A fair pong" meant something stank.

"I also have to tell them when to eat, sleep, and defecate. What kind of job is that for someone who got an A in her A-levels?" Fiona said. Matt assumed this was an achievement. He didn't ask about it, because he didn't want a long explanation.

He watched as she disinfected the wounds and, in Cienfuegos's case, put in stitches. "A knife fight! You bad boys," she scolded. "Reminds me of my brothers. They were always trying to see who could lean out the window farthest and coming home with dirty great cuts on their heads. It made no difference to their intelligence, for they had none to begin with. However did you come by those scars?" she asked, examining Daft Donald's neck.

"He tried to blow up the English prime minister and the bomb went off too soon," said Matt. "He can't talk."

"Fancy that! You meet all sorts in this place," Fiona chirped. "Take Mr. MacGregor. There was a nasty piece of work, seducing poor Felicity and driving her mad with drugs. I was present at his operation years ago. He was getting a new liver and a set of kidneys—they usually do that at the other hospital, the one in the Chiricahua Mountains, posh place really, not like this dump. Anyhow, he was prepped and ready to go when they wheeled in his clone. Gracious! MacGregor hadn't allowed the doctors to anesthetize it. A transplant goes better without drugs, but I do think they could have given it a happy shot. It was struggling so hard I was certain it would give itself an injury—"

"Are you as stupid as you sound?" said Cienfuegos.

Fiona's mouth flew open. "Well! Is that all the thanks I get for stitching you up?"

"Do you think it's smart to talk about clones?"

"I don't see why not. After all, El Patrón had clones and—and—" Fiona turned pale. "I didn't mean that! You can't think I was talking about you, young master! Why, Tam Lin used to brag about how clever you were, and I never thought of you that way."

"Just shut up," Matt said wearily. He felt sick at the memory of MacGregor's clone and yet, buried in the nurse's ridiculous prattle were the words *I never thought of you that way.* It was enough to make him forgive her, if not like her. "You have one more patient," he said. "Waitress's hands are burned."

"Oh, but I don't work on eejits," faltered Fiona. "There's the vet hospital for that, over by the horse barn. Only, I don't think they fix eejits either. They replace them."

"You will take care of Waitress's hands and do it immediately," said Matt. "She's as human as you are, and despite your stupid prejudice, she can feel pain. Isn't that so, Cienfuegos?"

The *jefe* had the grace to look ashamed. "Eejits can feel pain, *mi patrón*, otherwise I couldn't train them. I don't think they suffer in the same way we do. They scream, but it's an automatic function, like your heart beating or your stomach digesting food. You don't think, 'Today I'm going to digest that omelet I had for breakfast.' The omelet arrives in your stomach and the reaction happens. To suffer implies emotion, and eejits don't have that."

"I don't believe you," said Matt, and left the room.

He was sitting at the kitchen table with Celia and Mr. Ortega when Daft Donald returned. The man wore a bandage slantwise above one eye, and it was clear to Matt that Cienfuegos had intended to blind him.

"Looks like you poked your nose into someone's business," remarked Mr. Ortega.

Daft Donald wrote on his pad of paper. *Matt and I were rescuing a lady.*

"A lady! Sounds romantic. Was it . . . oh, let me think . . . María?"

"It was Waitress," said Matt, annoyed. Everyone seemed to know about him and María. Daft Donald scribbled busily, describing the fight and how Cienfuegos almost died because he tried to attack Matt.

"Why did he do that?" exclaimed Celia, horrified.

He was out of his mind, wrote Daft Donald.

"But the microchip is supposed to stop attacks against the *patrón*!"

"I've heard that samurai warriors go into a state of no-thought," said Mr. Ortega. "If Cienfuegos wasn't aware of what he was doing, the microchip wouldn't recognize the threat."

I agree, wrote Daft Donald.

"Whatever the reason, *mi vida*—I mean *mi patrón*," Celia said, "you must be very careful around him. You should have let him finish Waitress's training."

"I wouldn't let an animal suffer like that," said Matt.

Celia paused before she answered. "Waitress isn't like an animal . . . or a human. She may *look* like she's suffering, but it means no more to her than rain falling on a rock."

"That's how people used to talk about me," said Matt. "When I was a clone, people insulted me all the time, and I felt it. Why wouldn't she?"

No one said anything for a while. A pair of kitchen eejits peeled potatoes by the sink, and a fussy-looking man measured spices into a pot on the stove. Matt thought he might be the French chef Celia had talked about.

"I'm worried about you," said Celia after a few minutes. "It isn't healthy to care for someone who can never love you back."

"That would be true if Mirasol were a Real Person," Matt argued, "but I've decided that she's a pet. People keep all kinds of things, dogs, horses, cats, even fish. How much love can you get from a fish? They're pretty and fun to feed, and that's about it. From now on I've got a pet Waitress, and I'm going to feed her whenever I like."

"What did he say? Waitress is a *fish*?" said Mr. Ortega, who didn't always understand what people said.

She's the best-looking fish I've ever seen, wrote Daft Donald. *I'd have liked one myself when I was that age.*

"We're in trouble," muttered Celia, getting up to move the French chef to another chore.

That evening Matt and Mirasol sat side by side in a pool of light under the great crystal chandelier. He served the food because her hands were bandaged, and he cut the meat up for her too. "Eat slowly," he urged. But Mirasol seemed to have an on-off switch where feeding was concerned. The command *eat* meant *gobble* unless it was baked custard.

He tried various dishes—asparagus, turkey, fried shrimp, polenta—and they all met the same rapid treatment. For dessert he gave her strawberry ice cream, and she wolfed that down too.

Matt put the small gold statue of a deer he'd discovered in El Patrón's apartment in front of Mirasol. "What do you see?" he asked. She remained silent, staring ahead. Perhaps that was too difficult a problem, he thought. He put her fingers on the cool metal. "What do you feel?" She was silent.

"If you don't know, I'll tell you," he said. "That's a deer. Not a real one, of course. It's made out of gold and is *muy valioso*. Those things on its head are antlers. Real deer are warm because they are alive, but this one is metal and so it's cold. Like this spoon." He moved her fingers off the statue, picked up the utensil, and pressed it against her cheek. "Cold is what you feel when you eat ice cream."

It was no use. She sat there like a stuffed bunny, yet there had to be a way to awaken her. With Eusebio it was music. With her, baked custard. If you could find one pathway, couldn't you find others and gradually open up her soul?

Whatever a soul was. María talked about them, but Matt hadn't paid attention because he didn't have one until El Patrón died. According to the priest, clones went out like candles when they died and didn't have to bother about heaven and hell.

Celia—surprisingly, for she had never before ventured into El Patrón's private wing—appeared in the shadows at the far end of the banquet hall. "It's time for Waitress to go to bed," she said. "She'll be exhausted tomorrow if she doesn't rest."

"Where does she sleep?" Matt asked, interested.

"Far from here. Come along, Waitress."

The girl stood up obediently.

"I don't want her to go to the eejit pens," said Matt. He couldn't stomach the idea of her lying in the dirt next to a toxic waste pit.

"Don't worry, *mi patrón*. The house eejits have their own dormitory."

"She could stay here," he suggested.

"That would confuse the poor girl. She's programmed to go to the dormitory, and any change would require retraining."

Matt recoiled from the thought of retraining. Mirasol left silently, and Celia settled into one of the heavy iron chairs that El Patrón had looted from an old Spanish castle. She looked completely out of place. Her apron was stained with tomato sauce, and there were two brown patches where she habitually wiped her hands. Her dress was cheap and ill-fitting. And yet the vast wealth of El Patrón's private wing seemed ugly next to her. Or perhaps it was the difference between the live deer and the metal one. "I don't like it here," Matt blurted out. "I want to come back to you."

"*Mi hijo,*" she said sadly. "I can call you that when no one is listening. You are the Lord of Opium."

"I don't want to be."

"You have no choice," she said.

"We could run away. I know where El Patrón's wealth is. I can open the border and we can escape to Africa or India or I can buy a little island in the Pacific—"

Celia hugged him as he'd been wanting her to do ever since he came back. "Oh, dear! You're too young for all the problems you have inherited. But God arranges these things for a purpose. What was I but one of a hundred thousand women El Patrón enslaved throughout his long life? Yet Fate decreed that I arrive at the moment you needed me. María befriended you when no one else would. Tam Lin gave you the strength to escape when the time came. Without us, you would merely be a heart beating in an old man's chest. You are meant to end the evil of this place, and you can't run away."

"You sound like María," Matt said. "She's always trying to civilize me."

"She used to call you Brother Wolf," remembered Celia. "Speaking of María, when is she going to visit?"

"Esperanza won't let her come."

Celia thought for a moment. "You know how to use the holoport. Open a channel to the Convent of Santa Clara and ask for *Sor* Artemesia. She's somewhat scatterbrained, but her heart is good. If Esperanza is away, she can be talked into fetching María."

"That's a great idea! I can ask for Fidelito, Chacho, and Ton-Ton, too." Matt was so pleased he couldn't stop smiling.

"We'll have a party. They'll have a picnic on that side and I'll have one here. It's almost like having a real visit, and we can do it every day."

Celia wiped her eyes with her apron. "I must have chopped too many onions," she said. "Later, perhaps, you can ask Esperanza to let the boys visit. She doesn't really care what happens to them. And don't have Cienfuegos with you tomorrow. Sometimes it's good to be alone with friends." She kissed Matt good night, but soon returned with the dusty, chipped Virgin of Guadalupe that she had brought from Aztlán. "There's too much gloom in this place," she said. "You need something gentle to rest your eyes on." And she left the light burning in the hall.

12

THE LONG-DISTANCE PICNIC

Celia brought Matt's breakfast and said that Waitress had been kept in bed to allow her hands to heal. Matt didn't mind, because he was going to visit his friends. He'd seen them five days before, but it seemed more like five weeks, so much had happened. He made a selection of things from El Patrón's apartment—a crystal goblet, the golden deer, a walking stick carved in the shape of a striking cobra—and then put them away. The boys might think he was showing off. In the end he took only the music box with the Mexican gentleman and lady.

Alone in the instrument room, Matt suffered a moment of doubt. María was capable of crying for a dead goldfish. How was she reacting to the deaths of her father and sister? He decided to ask *Sor* Artemesia's advice before summoning her.

Matt held on to a table leg with one hand while activating the screen with the other. He didn't want to be lured into the holoport while it was opening. The room at the Convent of Santa Clara was empty, but a bell summoned a UN official.

"Great regrets, *mi patrón*, but Doña Esperanza is away," the official informed him. "She said to tell you that the doctors you requested are being sought. It might take weeks."

"Very well. I would like to speak with *Sor* Artemesia instead," said Matt.

"Sister Artemesia?" the man asked, clearly surprised. "But she's only a teacher."

"I like talking to teachers. Please call her."

The man went away, and soon *Sor* Artemesia hurried into the room, smoothing the wrinkles out of her dress and straightening the veil she wore over her hair. "I hope you aren't angry because I was here yesterday," she began. "It's such a quiet place, and the light is so good for doing embroidery—"

"I'm not angry at all," said Matt. "Please tell me how María is doing. Is she very upset? I don't want to bother her if she's in mourning."

"Mourning for what?" asked *Sor* Artemesia.

Matt was astounded. Hadn't Esperanza told María anything? "There was some trouble concerning her father and sister," he said cautiously.

"They can't come home yet. Of course her mother told her—not that María would worry about that. Emilia is always picking on her, and her father continually tries to push her into marriage. She's too young, of course, but he doesn't want her to be a nun." *Sor* Artemesia, once she discovered she wasn't going to be scolded, settled comfortably in front of the holoport.

"Could you call her?" asked Matt, hardly daring to hope.

"I'm afraid her mother took her on a trip to *Nueva York*. It was a real surprise, because Doña Esperanza never takes her anywhere. But she says that María has become a little backward where social graces are concerned. She's going to buy her pretty clothes and give her dancing lessons."

And keep her away from me. Clever Esperanza, thought Matt. "Do you know where my friends Fidelito, Chacho, and Ton-Ton are?" he asked.

"Everyone knows where they are," said *Sor* Artemesia, laughing. "When they're not raiding the kitchen, they're picking flowers and digging holes in the garden. Chacho is still recovering from his ordeal, but he follows along readily enough. Ton-Ton is the leader. And Fidelito! Why, he stuck his bottom out a window last night and mooned a night watchman. The watchman threw a stone at him and gave him a bruise to remember. Would you like to see your friends?"

"Yes, I would," said Matt. *Sor* Artemesia, away from Esperanza's critical eye, had turned out to be very likable. He could see the nun letting María shirk her lessons to do the good works she preferred. "Could they bring a picnic lunch? I wish I could send them something, but I don't know how."

Sor Artemesia smiled. "Don't worry about it, *mi patrón.* We've practically got an assembly line feeding those boys." She hurried off and Matt waited, wondering how long the holo-port could stay open and how he could get Esperanza to release his friends.

Chacho arrived first. Then Fidelito burst through the door, to be yanked to a halt by Ton-Ton. "D-don't you listen to anything, y-you turkey!" shouted the older boy. "Sister Artemesia says, uh, to stay away from that s-screen!"

"Matteo! Matteo! Matteo!" shrieked Fidelito at the end of Ton-Ton's arm.

"I'll b-beat the stuffing out of you!"

"You're alive! My big brother!" sang Fidelito, not the least worried by Ton-Ton's threat.

Matt had to swallow hard to keep tears from forming. Fidelito had called him brother! No one had ever done that. He was so moved he could barely speak.

"Are you all right?" said Chacho.

"Yes," said Matt, struggling to gain control of his emotions. Chacho had lost weight in the few days since Matt had seen him, and his face looked haunted. "Are *you* okay?"

"*No tengo chiste.* So-so."

"Me too," said Matt.

"Are you living in a castle?" said Fidelito. "*Sor* Artemesia says you're living in a castle and have thousands of zombie slaves."

"If I had one, I'd tell it to eat your b-brain," growled Ton-Ton. "Now sit!" He shoved Fidelito onto a floor cushion.

"Do your zombies eat brains?" the little boy asked excitedly. "Are they horrible and scary?"

"They're only sad," said Matt.

"Use your head, Fidelito. How could he find enough brains to feed thousands of zombies?" said Chacho. "Do you think he can put in an order to a company in Argentina?"

"As a matter of fact, they eat plankton," said Matt.

"The same crap we, uh, had at the factory?" cried Ton-Ton.

"The same. Here they call it eejit pellets."

"'Plankton is the eighth wonder of the world,'" said Chacho, quoting the guards at the factory. "'It's full of protein, vitamins, and roughage.'"

"Especially roughage. It'll take m-months to get rid of my zits," mourned Ton-Ton. *Sor* Artemesia arrived with a large picnic basket, and Matt was grateful for the interruption. He had his own basket from Celia. The nun also brought a bird in a cage to amuse Fidelito.

"This is María's latest patient," she told the little boy. "It's a finch. See? It has only one leg. María took it away from a cat, but by that time the damage was done."

"Will the leg grow back?" Fidelito put his face close to the cage, and the bird fluttered away.

"Don't scare it, *chiquito*. I'm afraid this one is going to be a permanent guest, like the turtle with a cracked shell, the blind rabbit, and the toothless dog. Sometimes," *Sor* Artemesia said, sighing, "I think God means for creatures to be called to heaven and that we shouldn't interfere."

"But this one is *muy bravo* to be hopping around on one leg," said Fidelito.

"I suppose so," said the nun. "Now you must be very, very careful around the holoport. Stay at least six feet away from it. I have to teach a class in math, but I'll come back in half an hour to check up on you. Ton-Ton, you're in charge."

"Yes, Sister," said Ton-Ton.

Once the woman was gone, the boys fell upon the picnic basket, and Ton-Ton divided up the food. They had ham, chicken, and cheese sandwiches, hard-boiled eggs, celery sticks, and cupcakes. Fidelito poked one of the celery sticks into the birdcage, but the finch only cowered. "Give it cake crumbs," said Chacho, so the little boy broke off a chunk and dropped it inside.

Matt had beef tamales, slices of papaya, and chocolate cake. The tamales were still hot, and a delicious odor wafted out when he unwrapped them.

"I can smell that," said Chacho. "Isn't it strange that sounds and odors can pass through the holoport? I wonder what else can?"

Fidelito threw a celery stick at the screen, and Ton-Ton caught it in midair. "You're going to b-break that machine," he said. "We don't know how it w-works."

"Oh! I didn't think of that," said Fidelito.

"I just remembered," Matt said. "*Sor* Artemesia said that God calls animals to heaven. I thought Catholics believed they didn't have souls."

"*Sor* Artemesia isn't like most of the nuns. She's awesome!" said Chacho. "She read to me for hours when I was in the hospital. She's a follower of Saint Francis and thinks that animals are just as good as people."

"So that's where María got her ideas," said Matt.

"She practically raised M-María," said Ton-Ton. "When Esperanza dumped her kids, S-Senator Mendoza sent them to the Convent of Santa Clara. If I had a mother like, uh, Esperanza, I'd pray to get d-dumped. Not that she hasn't been good to us, but I don't think she likes kids."

"You think zombies are scary, Fidelito, you should see Esperanza in a bad mood," said Chacho. "Speaking of kids, how's Emilia doing? María asked *Sor* Artemesia, but she didn't know."

Matt was dumbfounded. For some reason Esperanza wanted to hide the truth, and until he knew why, he couldn't reveal it. "I haven't seen her," he said evasively.

"I guess Opium's a big place. I mean, you have room for thousands of zombies," said Chacho. To change the subject, Matt brought out the music box, and as he'd expected, they were all enchanted with it.

"It's so clever!" exclaimed Ton-Ton. "I wonder if I could m-make something like that."

"You're good with machinery. I'm sure you could," said

Matt. He wound it up again, and they watched the gentleman and lady dance. Out of the corner of his eye, Matt saw Fidelito fiddling with the birdcage, and the next minute the little boy had the finch clinging to his finger by one claw. "Ton-Ton! Watch Fidelito!" he cried.

The older boy turned and shouted, "Put that back!" The little boy jumped. The bird fell off his hand and flew straight at the holoport. Ton-Ton tried to grab it out of the air, but he was too late. The finch hung in midflight as the opening began to swirl with fog. It had seemed to be only a few inches away, but it moved with painful slowness. Its wings were outspread and its beak was open in a silent cry. Then it fell out the other end and shattered on the floor.

Matt touched it. Ice dampened his finger. The bird had broken into three parts but was melting rapidly into pathetic little heaps. Matt looked up to see the portal trying to re-form. He closed it down before anything else could happen. After a while he wrapped the dead bird in a napkin.

13

THE OPIUM FACTORY

Matt returned the music box to El Patrón's apartment and sat staring out the windows of the bedroom. Celia's picnic basket was on the bed, and in a corner of it was the napkin containing the dead finch. He didn't want to move. He didn't want to make decisions.

How simple it had been at the plankton factory, though of course it had been terrible, too. There he hadn't been responsible for anything. The Keepers could be blamed for problems. He hoped that Fidelito wouldn't get into trouble for losing María's bird. No one knew, after all, that it was dead. Matt could say that it was living happily in Opium, but no, he'd have to tell the truth. Otherwise Fidelito might throw something else into the portal.

He thought about contacting the convent again and was strangely reluctant. The boys were on one side of the portal, having a high old time raiding kitchens and destroying flower beds. He was trapped on the other, with a wall of death in between. It was like watching TV when he was very small and had never seen other children. It was worse than being alone.

After a while Matt went outside and buried the finch, still in its napkin, under an orange tree.

He drifted to the music room, where he'd spent so many happy hours, and played Mozart's "Turkish March." He went faster and louder until it sounded more like noise than music. He crashed both fists down on the keys and stopped. Once, he'd been satisfied by the music alone. Now he had learned about friendship, and it was no longer enough to play without an audience.

Finally, out of boredom, Matt asked Daft Donald and Mr. Ortega to take him to the opium factory. He'd been there many times in the days when he thought El Patrón was preparing him to run the country. He had watched how the dried poppy sap was rolled into black balls the size of coconuts and then pressed into a disk stamped with the scorpion emblem. An eejit assembly line wrapped the disks in waxed paper and stored them in metal cookie cans.

Another assembly line measured laudanum, or opium dissolved in alcohol, into bottles. This was marketed in orange, lemon, cinnamon, and clove flavors. A rose-petal variation was manufactured for the Middle East market. More intelligent eejits processed the raw poppy sap into morphine, codeine, and heroin.

All the storerooms and most of the halls were full of cookie cans and bottles, and the overflow was stacked outside under makeshift ramadas. Matt remembered the lights blinking at various addresses on the holoport. The dealers wanted their shipments, and very soon he would have to deal with the situation.

A fume of dust filled the building. The foreman quickly found respirators to protect the visitors from being overcome, but Mr. Ortega waved his aside. "You know me," he told the foreman. "I'm here to smell the roses." He breathed in deeply with an ecstatic look on his face. "Aaahhh," he said with a sigh. "Don't look so surprised, *mi patrón*. I'm a drug addict. Didn't you ever wonder why my hands sometimes shake?"

Matt hadn't really thought about it. He'd assumed the music teacher was ill.

Daft Donald put a finger to his temple, like a man pretending to shoot himself.

"No, I wouldn't rather be dead," said Mr. Ortega, understanding the gesture. "You've got nerve taking a high moral tone with me after all the murders you've committed."

Daft Donald made a circular motion with his finger: *You're completely nuts.*

"On the contrary, I'm extremely clever," argued the music teacher. "Where else would a drug addict want to be except where there are piles and piles of lovely opium?"

Daft Donald shook with silent laughter.

Their conversation continued, with the bodyguard making gestures and the music teacher replying aloud.

Matt wandered off. The foreman was courteous to him, a change from the old days when the man had treated him like a roach. The boy told him that supplies had arrived from Aztlán. The eejits could go back to full rations. "Very good, *mi patrón*," said the foreman. "We lost a couple of them yesterday and production is down, not"—the man gestured at the overflowing hallways—"that we don't have more dope than we know what to do with."

Matt felt depressed. The eejits—thousands of them—were

programmed to plant poppies, slash pods, and make laudanum, and they didn't know how to do anything else. If they were prevented from working, they *jittered*. Cienfuegos said that after a while these eejits simply keeled over and died. The tension was too great for them. Thus, they had to go on working day after day, while the opium had to keep piling up. It was like a well-oiled machine without an off button.

Matt's choices were to supply the dealers and keep the machine going with fresh Illegals, or to stop exporting drugs and let the current eejits work themselves to death. It was his decision.

"You look tired, sir. Would you like to meditate in our chapel?" said the foreman.

Matt looked up, pleased by the word *sir*. "I thought the chapel was in the church."

"This isn't official." The man seemed slightly embarrassed. "It's just a place to rest for the foremen and Farm Patrol. No one else is allowed in, but as you're the new *patrón* . . ."

Matt followed him, intrigued. The foreman unlocked a small room, hardly bigger than a pantry. It was decorated with flowers and holy candles, and sitting in a chair was a life-size statue of a man. Matt flinched. *It was El Patrón*. Or at least what he had looked like at age thirty. The statue was made of plaster and was slightly chipped, as saints' images tended to be. Its eyes were jet-black. It was dressed in a white shirt with black trousers and wore a black bandanna around its neck.

On a small altar were offerings: plastic flowers, silver charms, pictures. A drawing of a little girl with braids caught Matt's attention. It was hardly more than a stick figure, and the artist had written the name *Alicia* with an arrow, to identify the portrait. "What's this for?" Matt asked.

The foreman hesitated. "Some of the men left family behind

when they came here. They don't have photographs, so they draw pictures."

"Why?"

"To ask the saint for help. That one, if you look on the back, wants his wife to have enough money to raise his daughter. A silver charm means that someone wants a cure—an eye for blindness, an arm for a broken bone. The ear was left by Mr. Ortega."

A cone-shaped lump of copal incense filled the little chapel with fumes. Matt felt for his inhaler, just in case. "What's the saint's name?" he asked, and braced for the answer. But it wasn't El Patrón. The old man hadn't made it that far into heaven.

"That is Jesús Malverde, the guardian of drug dealers," said the foreman. "He was a bandit from Culiacán, with the difference that he didn't keep what he stole. He took from the rich and gave to the poor. They say he was betrayed by a friend, who cut off his feet and dragged his body for miles to get a reward. Malverde's body was hung from a mesquite tree by the local governor, but the poor people cut it down and buried him in a secret place. He has done many miracles."

"Have you ever seen a picture of El Patrón as a young man?" asked Matt, looking at the statue.

The foreman laughed. "No, but I know what you're talking about. You see, there was never a photograph of the original Malverde. When the artist wanted a model for the saint, he asked El Patrón to sit for him. The old man was young then and was flattered to be compared with a saint. In later years no one could see the resemblance, but some of the men have noticed the likeness between Malverde and you."

Matt remembered that first day when Cienfuegos had introduced him to a Farm Patrolman called Angus. Angus had bent down and said, *Begging your pardon, sir, but doesn't he look like—*

And Cienfuegos had replied, *It's hardly surprising. El Patrón was the original model.*

Matt was delighted. Wait till he told María! Brother Wolf had not only become human, he'd turned into a saint. "I'd like to sit here alone for a while, if you don't mind," he said.

"You don't need to ask my permission," the foreman said, almost reprovingly. "You're the *patrón*."

After the man had gone, Matt looked through the offerings. There were various body parts crafted out of silver, even a stomach. Perhaps someone had ulcers. The drawings were mostly of children. Some appeared several times, as though the artist wanted to be sure that the saint noticed them. One was of an old woman. As Matt looked, he felt the ghostly presence of family members who would never know the fate of their men. He assumed that the drawings were by men because women, except for Celia, were turned into eejits.

He read the pleas for help. Most wanted money. Some asked for a dream telling them how their relatives were doing. Some wrote messages that they hoped the saint would pass on.

Toward the bottom of the heap, Matt came across a real photograph. It was of a little girl with black hair cut in the same style as María. She had a serious face, and her hands lay loosely in her lap as though she had been waiting for a long time. He turned it over.

Dear holy and miraculous Malverde, the note said. *My daughter begged me to stay, but I did not listen. I left her with her mother. She was so good. She was so young. I can never see her again, and now my heart is frozen. Please! Please! Please! Out of your mercy, take care of her. I will do anything for you, if only you tell me what it is. Eligio Cienfuegos.*

14

MADNESS

Matt was in an irritable mood that evening, and he had a persistent, dull headache. He ordered Celia to serve him dinner in the kitchen. "I'm a drug lord. I do what I like," he snapped when she tried to argue. Everyone eyed him nervously. Cienfuegos arrived late, slinking into a chair in his usual noiseless way.

"I distributed the eejit pellets," he announced. "There's enough for three months with our current population. Of course, we'll need more eejits as the workers die off." He helped himself to potato salad and turkey. Celia poured him a mug of *pulque*, and he settled back with a satisfied sigh. "How was the convent?" he asked Matt.

"Don't ask," the boy said.

"Ah! The visit went badly. Did Esperanza throw sand in your eyes?" asked Cienfuegos.

"She wasn't there. She'd taken María to New York for

dancing lessons. I talked to my friends from the plankton factory."

The *jefe* raised his eyebrows, and Celia shrugged. "He didn't tell me what happened," she said.

"I had a picnic, okay? I ate on one side of the portal and the boys ate on the other."

"So far, so good," said Cienfuegos. "What went wrong?"

"Fidelito let María's bird out of a cage. It flew through the portal and shattered like a piece of glass."

The *jefe* nodded and took another drink of *pulque*. "The holoport is a wormhole connecting one place to another. Inside, I'm told, it's as cold as outer space. I don't understand the science and neither did El Patrón, but he always had brainy people working for him. It's no great loss. There are lots of birds."

"You don't understand!" cried Matt. "The holoport made me feel like I was really in the same room with my friends. I was happy. Then the bird died, and I knew it was all a big lie. I don't want the boys on the other side of a wormhole. I want them here, and I want María, too. I am *owed* those lives!"

Celia and Cienfuegos looked at each other sharply. "What an odd turn of phrase," murmured Celia.

"It's only a coincidence," said Cienfuegos.

"Another thing," Matt said, close to tears and trying to control it. His head was pounding. "I'm tired of people talking in riddles. Say what you mean or shut up! I'm going to my apartment, and I want my food sent there along with Mirasol." He got up, intending to stride out like a tough guy, but instead he knocked the chair over and almost fell himself. No one tried to help him.

Never had El Patrón's private wing seemed more like a refuge. Matt could shut out the world, and no one could criticize him. No one would expect him to make decisions. Even the gloomy old paintings looked different. The little princess who had seemed hypnotized was merely showing off her dress. She was waiting for a compliment she knew would come. The dwarf next to her wasn't in pain, as Matt had first thought. He was listening to a conversation beyond the edge of the picture.

"Do you want me to serve you?"

Matt turned to see Mirasol carrying a tray. The long table was already set with two places, and the chandelier was ablaze. "Put the tray down. I'll serve you," said Matt.

Mirasol devoured the meal with her usual speed. Matt contented himself with watching her feed. *My pet Waitress,* he thought, and was obscurely pleased that Celia didn't like the girl being there. *It's my apartment. I'll invite who I please,* he thought.

He was still trying to puzzle out how anyone could think of El Patrón as a saint. All those prayers and silver charms were wasted. El Patrón wasn't going to fix ulcers or restore Mr. Ortega's hearing. He'd caused the problems in the first place. And what did Cienfuegos mean, *my heart is frozen*? It didn't seem frozen, the way he begged for help.

Matt noticed that Mirasol had cleaned her plate and was piling on more food than was good for her. "Stop," he ordered. Mirasol stopped and waited for further instructions. One of the good things about her was that she never questioned his commands. She didn't criticize him, and she was always there. Unlike María. How could María go off to *Nueva York* when she knew he was longing to see her? It was disloyal. She *belonged* to him.

Matt remembered the many times El Patrón had described his childhood, using exactly the same words as though he were reciting a long prayer. *The Drug Lord's Prayer,* Matt thought with a twisted smile. María would scold him for disrespect, but why should he care what she thought? She was dancing and partying without him.

El Patrón had a rosary with only one bead on it: He wanted the lost years of his seven brothers and sisters added to his own. Eight lifetimes.

Matt hugged himself. His head pounded, and even his skin was sore. *I'm sick,* he realized with amazement. He'd suffered from asthma and from Celia's doses of arsenic, but never in his life had he contracted an infectious disease. The asthma was caused by being kept in a room full of sawdust as a small child. Celia, of course, fed him arsenic to save him from being used for transplants. He was immunized against everything else.

"Mirasol," he said. The girl sat unmoving. "Waitress . . ." She looked up. Matt sucked in his breath. The light from the chandelier was too bright, and he was suddenly covered with sweat. El Patrón had always called himself a cat with nine lives, and he'd achieved only eight of them. Matt remembered his confrontations with Esperanza and Major Beltrán, and the way words suddenly appeared from nowhere. He remembered the old, old voice whispering in his ear. *What if . . . what if . . . I'm the ninth life?* Matt thought.

"No! I won't let it happen!" the boy shouted, sweeping dinner plates off the table. Mirasol observed him placidly. "I'm not him! I won't be like him! He's dead and I'm alive! I'll cut the cord that binds us together!" Matt grabbed a carving knife and stabbed at the damask tablecloth, slashing until he was so exhausted the knife fell from his hand. He knelt on the floor, sobbing. He'd been alone for years, but it was nothing like this. Then, he hadn't known what friendship was.

He missed the boys, and it wasn't enough to see them on a screen. He missed María, who was moving beyond his reach. "Please! Please! Please! Bring them back. I will do anything for you, if only you tell me what it is," cried Matt, not knowing of whom he asked the favor.

He came to his senses with his head on Mirasol's lap and reeled back against a table leg. But she seemed not to have noticed anything strange. "Go to bed," he ordered.

"Yes, *mi patrón*," she replied.

He lay on the carpet after she left and shivered with fever. The pain in his head eclipsed everything. *This isn't a bad way to die,* he thought in the brief moments he could form an idea, *if only it didn't hurt so much.*

Cienfuegos, Celia, and Nurse Fiona were there, although Matt couldn't remember calling them. Fiona said that his temperature was 104 and that the young master must have run barking, what with the tablecloth and dishes, oh my.

"What's wrong with him?" asked Celia, sounding very worried.

"I'm sure I don't know," admitted Fiona. "I'm not a full nurse, more like an aide, really."

"He needs antibiotics," Cienfuegos said.

"Not if it's a virus," said Fiona. "It's no better than drinking tap water to take antibiotics for a virus. The doctors say you should let that kind of illness run its course, and anyhow I don't know which ones to use or how much."

"Can you bring his fever down?" Celia asked.

"Well, there's aspirin, only he threw up gloriously when I gave it to him, so I don't know—"

"*¡Chis!* Do something besides use up oxygen," snarled

Cienfuegos. "Get ice bags. Lots of them." Fiona scurried off.

"You'll be okay, *mi vida*," Celia said, wiping Matt's forehead with a wet cloth.

Matt's throat was so raw he could hardly whisper. "What happened?"

"I was hoping you could tell me that. No, don't strain yourself. I should have guessed you were getting sick at dinner, but I thought you were immunized against everything."

Fiona came back and to her credit had a washtub full of ice bags. "My mum used to do this when we had a fever," she said brightly. "She packed us up as neatly as mackerels going to market. Twenty minutes on and twenty off is the charm. Up with your arms, laddie."

But Matt was so weak he couldn't obey. Cienfuegos helped him, and Fiona and Celia put ice bags under his armpits, between his legs, and on either side of his neck. The cold was a shock, but after a while Matt's pounding headache settled down to a dull ache.

"Twenty minutes off," announced Fiona. Without the ice bags, the headache soon came back.

"The sides of his neck are swollen," said Celia, feeling gently.

"I hope it isn't mumps," said Fiona. "Oh, look! His tongue is a funny shade of red."

"All those years we were up to here in doctors," raged Cienfuegos. "El Patrón couldn't hiccup without someone rushing to take his pulse. Now there's only one, and he's on the other side of the country."

"If Matt could open the border—" began Celia.

"He's too weak. In fact, I'm wondering if the scanner is what lowered his immune system."

The conversation faded into the background. Matt lay in a

daze as his temperature went up and down. Gradually he was able to swallow when Fiona dripped water into his mouth.

"When did you come?" he managed to say.

"Around ten o'clock. It's two in the morning now," said Celia.

"How . . ." Matt swallowed, and his throat burned. "How did you know?"

"It was Waitress. She came to the kitchen, and I told her to go to bed, but she didn't. She hung around like a dog that wants to tell you something, and I even shouted at her. Then I realized that she wanted me to follow her. The minute I got here, she took off."

"Celia sent a message to me," Fiona added. "I can tell you it gave me the collywobbles to see all those broken dishes. I thought Waitress had gone mad—eejits do, sometimes, although mostly they wander off or lose coordination—"

"She didn't do it," whispered Matt, and paid for it with a flare of pain.

"Don't talk," said Celia.

Cienfuegos returned—Matt hadn't been aware he was gone—and said, "I've readied the hovercraft."

"How many passengers can it take?"

"Three. Me, Fiona, and Matt."

"Oh, dear! I wanted to go," said Celia.

"The small hovercraft is the fastest, and time is important," Cienfuegos said. "Don't worry. If things work out, we'll be back before you know it."

"Perhaps I could take the place of Fiona."

Cienfuegos laughed. "The limit isn't numbers but weight, *mi caramelito*. You weigh twice as much as she does."

"No," whispered Matt.

"What's that?" The *jefe* bent down to hear.

"No Fiona," said Matt.

"I'm sorry, *mi patrón*. If I took Celia, we couldn't get off the ground."

"Mirasol."

Cienfuegos straightened up and brushed back his hair. "Oh, brother! He wants the girl."

"Mirasol . . . or I won't go." Matt had used up all his strength. He waited.

"What about me? Am I chopped liver or something?" cried Fiona. "First the doctors dumped on me and then the nurses, nasty things. I'm glad they're all dead! Fine! Go ahead and take your stupid eejit. I'm going back to the hospital, and I hope you crash!"

Matt heard her slam the door, but he was too tired to care. "How fast can you get Waitress here, Celia?" Cienfuegos said. "She can tranquilize the patient, if nothing else."

15

DR. RIVAS

The stars gleamed through the transparent ceiling of the hovercraft. Matt was too dazed to recognize any of them except for the Scorpion Star. It was in the south, as always, and glittered with a red brilliance. He was lying on a stretcher behind the two seats. In the right chair was Mirasol. In the left was Cienfuegos, piloting the craft.

"There's a water bottle in front of you, Waitress," said the *jefe*. "Take it to the *patrón* and drip it into his mouth until he tells you to stop. Move carefully so you don't tip the craft." Matt was surprised to see that Mirasol understood such a complicated order. She knelt beside the stretcher with barely a whisper of disturbance in their flight and carefully gave him the water.

"Enough." He stayed her hand. "Thank you."

Cienfuegos laughed. "I keep telling you courtesy is wasted on her."

"Isn't," said Matt. He wanted to say more, that she'd saved

his life, that she *cared*, otherwise she wouldn't have fetched Celia. But he was too weak. Meanwhile, he found it soothing to have her near.

The hovercraft was moving at three hundred miles an hour, according to Cienfuegos, yet there was no turbulence. A field of energy repelled all but the fiercest winds. The *jefe* said they could go through a thunderstorm, but at this time of year there were none to worry about.

"Where . . . are we going?" Matt asked.

"To Paradise," said Cienfuegos.

Paradise, thought the boy. That sounded nice. Now that he had a soul, the angels wouldn't turn him away. Or Mirasol either. He would argue for her.

"It's the heart of El Patrón's empire," explained the *jefe*. "It has the best hospital in the world, although right now there's only one doctor. The rest died at the old man's funeral."

El Patrón killed them because he wanted the best possible care in the afterlife, Matt thought. *I wonder if you can get sick in heaven.* Mirasol wiped his forehead with a damp cloth, and he realized that no order had been given for her to do this. She was doing it on her own initiative.

The sky began to soften as dawn approached. The stars went out one by one, with the Scorpion Star lasting the longest.

"We're circling to go up a valley," said Cienfuegos. The hovercraft dipped, and Matt saw white domes here and there among the mesquite trees. They passed over a huge dome that dwarfed all the others. It had a slit in the top like the piggy bank Celia had once given him as a child. She'd handed him shiny new centavos to insert, but Matt hadn't seen the point of that.

I'm trying to show you how to save money, Celia had explained. *That's how people get rich.* But money wasn't used in Opium, and

Matt had preferred to roll the coins around until they were lost down cracks in the floor.

"What you see is the Sky Village," said Cienfuegos. "Long ago astronomers lived here, and each of them had his own observatory. When El Patrón took over, he built his own observatory, larger and more powerful than anyone else's. He bought a giant telescope that he said could see all the way around the universe and look at the back of your neck."

"Don't . . . understand," Matt said. It was hard enough to think without puzzles like that.

"El Patrón didn't either," said the *jefe*. "He was repeating what some scientist told him. He must have had a good reason to build the observatory, because it cost him a quarter of his fortune."

"Maybe . . ." Matt swallowed. His fever must be going up again, because when he blinked he saw lights flashing. "Maybe . . . he was looking for heaven."

Cienfuegos chuckled. "If he found heaven, you can bet the angels were out building fences to keep him away. I'll tip slightly so you can see the trees as we go into the mountains."

Scrubby mesquite and cholla gave way to juniper and oak, and then to pine. Cliffs rose on either side, with folded rocks and caves in which anything might hide. A flock of brightly colored parrots went by. The hovercraft was getting lower as they followed a road with a stream at its side. A mule deer looked up from drinking.

"There it is," said the *jefe*. In the middle of the wilderness was a fabulous mansion, with many outbuildings extending under trees on either side. It was so cleverly built of native rock that at first it looked like part of the mountain. Only up close could you see verandas and reflecting pools and gardens. "El

Patrón loved this place. He sometimes said, 'If there is Paradise on Earth, it is here, it is here, it is here.' That's a quote from an ancient Indian emperor. The old man could surprise you with what he knew, but then he had a hundred and forty-six years to learn. Anyhow, that's why this place is called Paradise."

The hovercraft set down as delicately as a feather, and at once men in green scrubs ran out. They unloaded Matt and carried him to one of the outbuildings. In an instant he was moved from a cool, pine-smelling forest to a bed in a place filled with the odors of medicine and antiseptics. He tensed up. He couldn't help it. Hospitals had never been good to him.

An older man in a lab coat appeared and felt Matt's head. "*Por Dios*, Cienfuegos! Why hasn't anyone treated this boy?"

"I'm sorry, Dr. Rivas," said the *jefe*. "We don't have anyone left at the Ajo hospital except a nurse called Fiona."

Dr. Rivas gave a barking laugh. "Fiona! She's no nurse. She was in charge of sterilizing equipment. She must have taken advantage of the situation and put on a uniform."

"You don't say! She stitched up my arm."

"You're lucky not to have gangrene," said the doctor. "Well, let's look at you, *chico*. Where does it hurt?"

"Uh, Dr. Rivas. This is the new *patrón*."

The doctor flinched as though he'd been shot. "This child? How is it possible? Nobody told me."

"He was, uh, he was . . ." Cienfuegos trailed off.

"A clone," Matt finished for him.

A look of wonder crossed the doctor's face. "This is the one I remember. I thought he'd been harvested." He touched Matt's head again very gently. "Let's get you better before I go off on a tangent." He opened Matt's shirt and pressed his fingers on the boy's chest. "Look, Cienfuegos. That's classic. The skin is red as though scalded, and when I take my fingers away, you can see a white imprint for a few seconds. His lymph nodes are swollen. I'll bet your throat's sore, *mi patrón*. God, it feels strange to call a child *patrón*."

Matt smiled weakly. He wasn't upset that the doctor had called him a child.

"What's wrong with him?" asked Cienfuegos.

"Scarlet fever. I haven't seen a case for years and certainly never expected it in"—he paused—"someone so heavily immunized."

"The *patrón* accessed the holoport twice and fine-tuned the border once in little more than a day," said the *jefe*. "I thought that the scanner might have weakened his immune system."

"Interesting," said Dr. Rivas. "You know, clones aren't exactly like the original. The physical differences are small, but they're there. The scanner might have thought he was an outsider for an instant. Well, I'd better stop nattering and do something." He filled a fearsomely large hypodermic needle from a sealed bottle and swabbed Matt's arm with alcohol. "This isn't going to be pleasant, but the old ways are best with infections of this kind."

Dr. Rivas was correct. It was the most painful injection Matt had ever had, and he gritted his teeth to keep from groaning. "Very good," the doctor said. "Now you try to rest. I'll send someone with fruit juice and water. You're to drink as often as you can stand it, and I'll have the nurse pack you in ice bags until the penicillin takes effect."

Matt caught the doctor's arm before he could leave. "Mirasol," he said. Dr. Rivas looked at Cienfuegos.

"It's a long story," said the *jefe*. "He has a pet Mirasol. Don't worry. I know what to do."

"Mirasol," said the doctor as the two men went out the door. "Is that some kind of bird or what?"

Matt recovered slowly and was allowed out of bed for short periods. "We can't let our new *patrón* take chances," Dr. Rivas said. He spent much time with the boy, and Matt enjoyed his company. The doctor didn't treat him as some kind of ogre, and when he played chess he didn't make stupid blunders to let Matt win. Mr. Ortega and Daft Donald always did. He didn't make jokes about Mirasol, either.

"You say she wakes up when you feed her baked custard. That's interesting," the doctor said one afternoon when they were drinking iced tea on a veranda. In the distance Matt could see the main part of the mansion, where an eejit was removing fallen leaves from a pond. Like most eejits, he wore a faded tan jumpsuit and floppy hat. Without the hat, the man might work in the sun until he died of heatstroke.

Matt raised a pair of binoculars Dr. Rivas had given him for amusement and saw that the man was collecting the leaves one by one. He waded to the side with a single leaf at a time and deposited it in a basket. It was going to take a while to clear the pond.

"Taste and smell endure longer than most memories. You can recall a whole scene from one such clue," said the doctor.

Matt nodded. He knew that the smell of wax from the holy candles Celia burned before the Virgin of Guadalupe was enough to bring back the little house he'd grown up in. "Have you ever heard of an eejit waking up completely?"

"Never," said the doctor, dashing his hopes.

Mirasol sat nearby, her hands in her lap. Matt had given her a glass of iced tea, and she'd bolted it down so quickly he was afraid to give her more. "What if I found more of these clues?" the boy said.

"The reaction disappears too quickly. You could keep feeding Mirasol until she weighed five hundred pounds, but that's all you'd accomplish."

"I've asked Esperanza to find brain surgeons."

Dr. Rivas frowned. "It's going to be difficult to convince anyone to come here."

"I could pay them well," said Matt.

"El Patrón paid them well too, before he poisoned them." Dr. Rivas sent Mirasol for more iced tea, and Matt trained his binoculars on the eejit clearing the pool. Beyond them was an arbor covered with vines. Someone had hung up a humming-bird feeder, and the tiny birds swarmed around it like wasps. Below, half-hidden in leaves, was a child—or perhaps it was a statue. It was hard to see into the shadows.

"Occasionally El Patrón spared educated Illegals. I was one."

"You?" said Matt, looking away from the arbor.

"I crossed the border with my father, wife, and three small children, on the way to a glorious career at Stanford University. Or so I hoped. I had a degree in molecular biology with a minor in cloning. Yes, I said cloning. What a fool I was to think a whole family could elude capture! I had to barter my services for their lives."

Mirasol returned with a fresh pitcher and a plate of sand-wiches. Matt wondered whether the sandwiches had been the cook's idea or hers.

"I started out as a lab technician, growing cells from various drug lords into clones. When I had proved my skill, I was given skin samples from El Patrón. The previous technician had been killed because he could no longer produce results, and I was no luckier. El Patrón's samples were a hundred years old and no longer responded to treatment. Those that grew were deformed. One of my sons was turned into an eejit as punishment, and so I tried harder, invented new techniques, and finally, after repeated failures, I produced you."

Matt turned cold with shock. He had guessed where Dr. Rivas was going when he learned the man was an expert in cloning, but to hear it said so bluntly! To know that this man had selected a cell from skin so old and corrupt that it was little more than carrion was beyond disturbing. The priest had once called Matt unnatural, a soulless creature from the grave. Here was the proof!

"You were a beautiful embryo," said Dr. Rivas. "I watched you through a monitor. I talked to you, and almost as though you could hear, you turned and smiled. Embryos can smile, you know. Who knows what thoughts are passing through their heads? When you were harvested—"

"Don't!" Matt raised his hand to fend off the words.

"I forget that we scientists are used to such things. It wasn't so terrible—bad luck for the cow, of course, but she'd had a happy nine months drifting through a dreamworld of flowery meadows."

"She had a microchip in her brain," said Matt. Somehow it made it worse to call the animal *she*. It made her seem more real.

"When I held you in my hands it was as though you were my own child, the boy I had lost." Dr. Rivas shaded his eyes and fell silent for a moment. "Strange. The grief never goes away. My son was called Eduardo after me."

"What happened to him?" Matt forced himself to ask the question.

"He works in the gardens. El Patrón made certain I knew

where he was in case I had any thoughts of rebelling. That's why I know the eejit operation can't be reversed. I have spent years trying to do it with absolutely no success."

Mirasol was gazing pointedly at the sandwiches, and Matt responded by giving her two. That was surely communication, he thought. He'd become better and better at reading her body language. He winced at the messy speed with which she devoured them and leaned forward to wipe her mouth with a napkin.

"She's got you trained," observed Dr. Rivas. "You were the best of the lot, the most intelligent, the most perfect."

"The best of *what* lot?" Matt said, although he knew.

"The others were used for liver transplants and blood transfusions," said the doctor, ignoring the question. "One, an infant, supplied a heart. It was too small, and the operation failed."

Matt tried to see Dr. Rivas as he'd been a few moments before—a kind, friendly man who had saved his life—and failed. "How could you do it?"

"I had a family to protect. The others, except for you, were merely collections of cells." Dr. Rivas shrugged. "You get used to being evil."

16

DANCING THE *HUKA HUKA* IN *NUEVA YORK*

E speranza is trying to send a message," said Cienfuegos, coming onto the veranda. "In fact, there's at least two dozen people trying to contact us via the holoport."

"The *patrón* has to limit his contact with scanners," Dr. Rivas said sternly. "Once every few days until he's fully recovered."

Matt was eager to get out of the hospital wing and enjoy the fresh air and feel of grass beneath his feet. They passed the pool where the eejit was removing leaves and went up a sweeping staircase to a shadowed porch. Inside were halls even grander than those in the Ajo hacienda. The floors were inlaid with tiles—blue-and-white Chinese willows, geometrical designs from Morocco, flowers from Spain. One room even had a Roman mosaic. The floor-to-ceiling windows were draped with heavy silk curtains. Everywhere were the sounds of fountains and birds.

"If there is Paradise, it is here, it is here, it is here," murmured Matt. It was so delightful he wondered why El Patrón ever left it.

But the room with the holoport was cold and businesslike. The portal itself was enormous—ten feet square—and the addresses were slowly cycling. Right now it showed an office in Sydney, Australia, with a red light blinking in the corner.

"You can select an address by pressing this button." Dr. Rivas demonstrated, and the screen immediately changed to show a multitude of icons.

Cienfuegos cried "Hah!" in surprise. "*¡Por Dios, Doctor! ¡Tiene bien puestos los calzones!* You've got guts!"

"El Patrón showed me the method," said Dr. Rivas, smiling. "You can scroll through the icons by turning this wheel and choose one by highlighting it and pressing the button again. What you must not do, as I'm sure you know, is touch the screen."

"You're telling me!" The *jefe* wiped his face with a handkerchief. "Will you look at all those flashing lights!"

All over the screen, tiny red dots pulsed as drug dealers clamored for their supplies. Matt was bewildered. What if he merely ignored them? What if he cut off *everyone's* opium, kept the border closed, and lived happily ever after?

"I've selected the Convent of Santa Clara," said Dr. Rivas. The familiar room appeared. It was empty, but on a back wall was pinned the altar cloth *Sor* Artemesia had been working on. The Virgin was surrounded by a halo like the sun, and her foot rested on the moon. Around the edge were red roses worked in silk.

After a moment's hesitation, Matt put his hand on the screen. Instantly his skin swarmed with crawling ants and his heart pounded. He tasted vomit. *It's me,* he implored. *You know it's me.* The screen dissolved into a tunnel swirling with mist. Matt sat back, sodden with sweat.

"You're all right," said Dr. Rivas. The boy felt the doctor's hands grip his shoulders. He smelled rain and the crisp odor that follows a thunderstorm. The mist cleared, and the doctor took his hands away.

All was as it should be in the peaceful little room at the Convent of Santa Clara. Esperanza came straight in and started talking as though they'd only broken off contact a moment before. "It's about time! You had me running all over New York for doctors while you've been living it up in Paradise." Esperanza shook her finger at him, exactly as though he were a naughty child. "I've succeeded, not that you deserve it. I've got five of the world's top brain surgeons. They demand a million dollars each up front and a thousand for every day they're working. Are you listening?"

"Yes," said Matt, who was still overcoming the effects of the scanner.

"He hasn't been playing," said Dr. Rivas. "He's recovering from a severe case of scarlet fever."

"Eduardo?" asked Esperanza, squinting to make sure. "I thought you were dead with all the other medical staff."

"*Mil gracias* for your concern, Doña Esperanza," the doctor said. "I'd like to help out with the operations. I probably have more experience than anyone."

"Suit yourself. It's a fool's mission, anyway." The woman inserted a roll of paper into a cylinder like a fat thermos bottle. "I've written down the bank numbers and locations to send money." She threw the bottle into the holoport.

Matt jumped. It felt as though she was aiming straight at him, but, in fact, the cylinder moved as slowly as the bird had, and he had plenty of time to get out of the way. It fell out the other end and struck the floor with a metallic chime.

"Don't touch it," warned Dr. Rivas. "Let it come to room temperature."

Matt saw that the cylinder was covered in ice crystals that were rapidly melting. Cienfuegos nudged it with his foot. "I didn't know you could send things through the portal," he said.

"It isn't recommended, but you can do it in an emergency," said the doctor. "The cylinder insulates the paper against cold."

The wormhole meanwhile was swirling with mist. After a while it reestablished itself, and Esperanza was visible again. "The doctors will come through at San Luis after you've deposited the money," she said. "Inside the cylinder is a list of animals and plants I want. We might as well start the ecological recovery while you're diddling around with the eejits. Major Beltrán can do the collecting."

"I trained in agriculture. I'll collect them," said Cienfuegos.

Esperanza waved a heavily ringed hand. "I don't care who does it as long as I get results. If there's nothing else—"

"Wait!" cried Matt before she could cut the connection. "I want to see María."

Esperanza for once looked almost sympathetic. "You kids. She's been nagging my ears off about you." Matt's spirits lifted. María hadn't forgot him. "I suppose there's no harm in it, but get this clear: You are not to tell my daughter what happened at El Patrón's funeral."

"Why not? She has to find out sometime."

Esperanza held up her palms for silence. The heavy rings, the Aztec brooch pinned to her black dress, the large silver earrings framing her grim face made her look as uncompromising as a stone idol. "Listen to the voice of experience, *chiquito*. No one outside of Opium knows what happened at El Patrón's funeral."

"What difference does that make?" asked Matt.

"As far as the rest of the world is concerned, the Alacráns are still alive along with their friends and bodyguards. Glass Eye may have taken over the smaller drug states, but he doesn't know how many enemies he has inside Opium. That makes him nervous."

Matt could see her reasoning. Glass Eye might want the territory, but he didn't know what would happen if he tried to take it.

"And let's not forget the army of *sicarios* El Patrón has scattered throughout the world. They exist to assassinate his enemies, and as long as they think there's a strong government in Opium, they'll carry out orders. My sources say a lot of people aren't sleeping well these days. What do you think would happen if they learned that Opium was ruled by one inexperienced child? You would get no more supplies on credit. Your bank accounts would be looted."

Esperanza gazed unblinking at Matt. Her will was iron, but so (and it came from some deep source he didn't understand) was his. He would not be intimidated by her. But he had to admit her arguments made sense. "You think that María wouldn't keep the secret," he said.

"Her heart is too soft for this world," said her mother. "I blame *Sor* Artemesia for that. María cannot hide her feelings, and she is afflicted with an irritating honesty."

Matt privately thought that María had been lucky to be raised by the nun rather than her mother. "Very well," he agreed. "Please call her for me." Esperanza left the room.

"Whew! Rather you than me dealing with her," said Dr. Rivas. "She's not going to leave you two alone, you know, not even at the opposite ends of a wormhole. At least we can give you some privacy. Come on, Cienfuegos."

"Give us a report later," said the *jefe*, grinning wolfishly.

The minutes passed. Matt opened the cylinder and read the list of animals Esperanza wanted: Squirrels, sparrows, pigeons, crows, and rabbits. These were so common it gave Matt a shock to think that they were extinct elsewhere. The door opened and María ran in.

"Matt! Matt! I've missed you so much!" she cried. Immediately an arm shot out and grabbed her. "All *right*, Mother! I know I mustn't touch the portal."

"María," said Matt, and instantly found himself tongue-tied. It was a problem going back to his early childhood. Sometimes things were so overwhelming that the power of speech left him. Now all he could do was look. When he'd had the fever, he had tried to call up María's image. He could remember her dark hair and eyes, her hands always in motion, but the spirit of her actual presence was missing. Now—infuriatingly!—she was here and he was rendered speechless.

María understood his problem. She always had. "Take your time, *mi vida*. I have enough conversation for both of us. Gosh, I'm glad to see you! I wish you'd been with me in *Nueva York*. You would have loved the concert halls and operas. I *think* you'd have liked the operas. The sets were beautiful, but I kept thinking, 'How can the heroine stand it when the hero keeps bellowing songs at her face?'"

"I want you with me," Matt managed to say.

"That isn't going to happen," said Esperanza from a chair next to the altar cloth.

María laughed delightedly. "Why can't I visit him, Mother? I used to do it all the time."

"You were a child then." Esperanza in her black dress looked like a patch of midnight in the brightly lit convent room.

"It isn't as though I'd be alone," argued María. "Father and Emilia can look after me."

Matt smiled inwardly as he observed Esperanza's discomfort. *Get out of this one if you can,* he thought.

But she didn't even try. "Tell Matt more about your trip to New York."

And María, swept along on a tide of enthusiasm, obeyed. The buildings were so huge they were like entire cities, she said. Walkways went from one to the other, and you needn't ever set foot on the ground. Which was good. The streets were dangerous. Every kind of food was available for the city dwellers, although she worried about the people on the street. They didn't look happy at all, and she wanted to take food to them, but Mother objected.

"That's right up there with her idea of inviting the homeless in for a bath," muttered Esperanza.

"Saint Francis would have done it," María said.

She had learned the latest dances, the *fósforo,* the *paseo de luna,* the *huka huka* (although that was vulgar and not proper for young ladies). The dance instructor got hair oil on her dress while teaching her, and Mother fired him and bought her a new dress. Oh! The clothes in *Nueva York* were so beautiful! Did Matt know that the latest rage was glow-in-the-dark underwear? Of course you had to wear something transparent over it.

Matt didn't take in much of what she said, although the glow-in-the-dark underwear caught his attention. Mostly he basked in her warmth. If she were there with him, he knew he could face the terrifying problems hanging over his head.

"Who's that?" asked María.

Matt snapped to attention and looked around. He half

expected to see Cienfuegos eavesdropping, but it was Mirasol.

She must have been in the room all along. Matt was so used to her presence that he'd stopped noticing it. She followed him everywhere, sitting (as she was now) on the floor to await orders. She was wearing a sky-blue dress instead of her waitress uniform, and he wondered where she'd gotten it. She was as different as it was possible to be from María—fair-haired and blue-eyed, with a frosting of freckles instead of María's magnolia-petal skin. But the main difference, of course, was her behavior. She was utterly passive, with none of María's fire. She simply waited, her eyes fixed on Matt, for whatever he might require.

"I've never seen her before," said María. "Is she a guest of the Alacráns?"

"A guest—no." Matt scrambled for an explanation.

"Hey, there! What's your name?" called María.

Mirasol rose gracefully to her feet. "I am called Waitress," she said.

Esperanza laughed harshly. It was the first time Matt had heard anything like humor from her, and it wasn't cheering. It sounded like someone choking on a piece of gristle. "She's an eejit," Esperanza said. "You can tell by the eyes."

"An eejit!" María's mouth fell open.

"A very pretty one too," her mother said. "The apple doesn't fall far from the tree, does it? El Patrón used to like pretty wait-resses."

"It's nothing like that!" cried Matt.

"Then . . . what is it?" said María. She had backed away from the portal and was standing next to her mother.

"She's a pet." Matt knew immediately that he'd made a mis-take. The argument might work with Mr. Ortega and Daft

Donald—though he suspected they laughed at him behind his back—but not María.

"You don't make pets out of eejits," she said.

"You made one out of me," Matt said, hoping to deflect her anger. "I used to be an animal, remember?"

"You were a *friend*. Eejits are different. Liking them is—is—perverted." María had a mulish streak, and it was in full display now.

"I felt sorry for her, that's all," Matt said lightly. "Like you do with the homeless."

"It's not at all the same."

María's face was pale, and her hands were clasped—a bad sign, Matt remembered. She did it when she was about to lose control of her emotions. He was close to losing his, too. How dare she attack him when he was trying so hard to do the right thing? All he wanted was to save the eejits.

"I understand about drug lords having girlfriends," said María. "They all do it, and the wives have to put up with it. MacGregor kept Felicia for years. But at least she was a real woman, not—*this*."

"Shut up and listen for a moment," said Matt. "Waitress is just someone I'm trying to help. I don't know where you're getting these crazy ideas, but if you don't like her, I'll send her away. Go to the kitchen, Waitress. Now."

Mirasol turned and glided out of the room.

"I don't know if I believe you. I'll have to think about it," said María.

"Fine! Go ahead and think. You've been doing the *huka huka* with greasy men in New York, but that's okay. You're Miss Butter Wouldn't Melt in Her Mouth. You think you're Saint Francis's baby sister."

"Don't you make fun of Saint Francis!" María's nostrils flared like an angry pony's.

"I will if I like. He's only a myth, anyway," said Matt. He knew he'd gone too far, but he couldn't stop the words from pouring out. *That's the stuff,* an old, old voice whispered in his mind. *Make your women toe the line.*

María gasped and fled the room. He couldn't pursue her. He couldn't do a thing.

Esperanza rose. "Well, that was entertaining."

"It's your fault! You put the idea into her head," accused Matt.

"Did I? Oh, fie! Bad girl!" Esperanza playfully slapped herself on the wrist.

"You won't win this battle. I know María. She'll forgive me, even though there's nothing to forgive."

"We'll see," said the woman. "Just to show you my heart's in the right place, I'll let Ton-Ton, Chacho, and Fidelito visit. They're trashing the convent anyway."

Matt was surprised at her gesture of goodwill, but she had achieved her goal, to drive a wedge between him and María. As for Ton-Ton, Chacho, and Fidelito, Esperanza could easily let go of them. They were expendable. She didn't care what happened to them.

17

THE FOUNTAIN OF CHILDREN

Matt avoided Dr. Rivas and Cienfuegos and went into the garden to think. He didn't even want to see Mirasol. The rage that had threatened to overwhelm him faded, but it still frightened him. *Why can't I control myself?* he thought. *Why can't I be good by merely saying, "Be good"?* But it didn't work that way.

Maybe he should make a list of rules on a card to refer to: *Rule 1: Don't lose your temper. Rule 2: Be courageous. Rule 3: Send Mirasol away.*

She would be miserable if he sent her away. It wasn't her fault that she was programmed to serve him. Besides, he really wanted to help her, only not when María was around. *Rule 4: Don't tell lies.* That was a toughie. Drug lords prospered by telling lies. Even Esperanza thought it was okay.

Matt wandered deeper into the garden. A path led beneath a series of arbors, each one different and each one with its own hummingbird feeder. Vines were hung with clusters of purple and green grapes. A giant squash dangled yellow fruit, and a third arbor was dotted with red roses. Then—most wonderful of all—Matt saw a mass of deep-blue morning glories. Nothing at the Ajo hacienda equaled this waterfall of flowers.

There was a sound coming from the far end of the arbor, a bird or a kitten. Matt listened more closely. Could it be the child he'd seen? It couldn't be an eejit. They were unable to cry. He edged forward, not wanting to startle whoever it was. He saw the vines tremble. The person was *inside* the leaves, hiding in a burrow like a rabbit.

Matt quietly approached and pulled back the vines.

It was a little girl, an *African* girl. She was about Fidelito's age, but much thinner. Her arms were like matchsticks clasped around her skinny chest, and just above one elbow was a vicious-looking wound as though she'd been bitten by a dog.

"Don't be afraid," Matt said. The girl looked up and screamed. She bounded out of the leaves and zigzagged through the garden. "Stop! Stop! I won't hurt you!" shouted Matt. He tried to catch up, but she knew the garden and he didn't. He followed what he thought was her trail and ended up in front of a wall.

By now he was exhausted, what with the aftereffects of scarlet fever and opening the holoport. He leaned against the wall, breathing heavily. Few children came across the border and none, as far as he could remember, had been black.

This girl was no eejit. She had to be someone's daughter, and if so, the person should have protected her from animals. A dull rage kindled in Matt's head. How dare someone neglect such a frail child? Matt would find out who it was and punish him.

For now, though, he was lost. He had chased the girl through

gardens and between buildings until he'd lost his sense of direction. It didn't matter. It was pleasant to be left alone in such a
beautiful place. A fountain cast up a spray of water that flashed
in the sun before raining back on the upturned faces of statues
of children. They held out their hands like real children, and the
sculptor had given them expressions of joy so lifelike that Matt
smiled in sympathy. What a wonderful work of art!

And how strange. Opium was no place for children. Matt
wandered on, and presently he came to a sliding door. Inside he
found a room full of large glass enclosures with no clear purpose. It might have been a zoo, except that the animals were
missing. Long tables were covered with gleaming, stainless-steel
pans and microscopes, and along one wall were giant freezers.
Idly, he opened a heavy iron door, and a dense cloud of fog
swirled out. He saw racks of bottles with tiny writing:
MACGREGOR #1 to MACGREGOR #13 in one rack, DABENGWA #1 to
DABENGWA #19 in another. The bottles were dated. In a third
rack he found MATTEO ALACRÁN with one of the bottles—#27—
dated more than fourteen years before.

Matt slammed the door.

He fled to one of the enclosures and pressed his face against
the glass to calm his nerves. Those bottles were tissue samples.
This was where he had been created. That date, fourteen and a
half years earlier, was his birthday, the day he was harvested from
a cow.

After a while Matt's heartbeat slowed to normal, and he
forced himself to look inside. Mechanical arms reached across
the enclosure, the floor of which was a treadmill. Wisps of hay
were trapped between the joints. Once, a cow had stood here
and her legs had been flexed by the mechanical arms while
the treadmill slowly ground forward. Someone had placed hay

in her mouth, which she chewed mindlessly, dreaming of flowery meadows.

"I was going to give you a tour, but I see you've already found the lab," said Dr. Rivas. He was standing in the open doorway, and behind him was the fountain of children. "You really should rest for a while, *mi patrón*. You aren't well yet."

"I want all the tissue samples destroyed," said Matt.

"That would destroy a hundred years of work. To a scientist, that is a mortal sin."

"I don't understand about sin, but I know evil when I see it," the boy said passionately.

"Cloning isn't the only thing that goes on here." The doctor pulled out a chair and sat down. "The scientists made many discoveries about congenital diseases. Do you know about sickle-cell anemia? They learned to grow healthy bone marrow in this lab to replace the diseased marrow of a victim."

"By using clones, I suppose," Matt said.

"At first. But by sacrificing a few, they saved thousands. They regenerated spinal tissue to heal paralysis. You see, this was the premier research lab in the world, because we could experiment on humans. Well, *almost* humans."

Matt struggled with the idea. The longer he was in Opium, the more the line between good and evil blurred. Of course it was good to save people who, through no fault of their own, were suffering. You cut corners, made compromises, and soon you were in the same position as El Patrón, shooting down a passenger plane to avert a war.

"Where are those scientists now?"

Dr. Rivas smiled sadly. "With El Patrón."

"That's what I would call a mortal sin," said Matt. He looked at the freezers lining the wall. They extended from floor to ceiling, with a ladder on wheels to allow access to the top levels. *There must be thousands of bottles in there,* he thought. "What if we only destroyed the drug lord samples?"

"Surely you want El Patrón's," said Dr. Rivas. "What if you should fall ill and need a transplant? You're the first clone who has lived beyond his thirteenth year, and we don't know whether there are hidden weaknesses in you. Forgive me for using that word, *mi patrón.* I'm a scientist, not a diplomat. But please consider: When you were young, we tried to protect you against everything, and yet you still developed asthma and caught scarlet fever."

"I'll take my chances. There will be no more clones."

"Mi patrón—"

"No more clones!" shouted Matt. He almost walked out before realizing that he didn't know where he was. "Which way is my room? I'd like to lie down."

"Of course! You can rest in the nursery. It's much closer."

The doctor led Matt back along the path by the fountain, and the boy paused to let a breeze blow a fine spray over his face. "This is so beautiful," he said. "Why is it here?"

"El Patrón wanted statues of his brothers and sisters who had died, but of course there were no pictures of them. He selected Illegals for models from what he could remember."

"He used real children?" Matt stepped out of the spray.

The seven statues faced the center of the fountain. The girls were so small, they could not look over a windowsill, not even if they stood on tiptoe. The five boys were larger, and two of them, the ones who had been beaten to death by the police, were almost adults. They were filled with joy by the water that pattered over their faces. Their hands were outstretched to hold this miracle that fell all year long, not just for two months in dry, dusty Durango.

And the models? What had happened to them?

18

THE AFRICAN CHILD

The nursery, fortunately, had normal-size beds. Matt didn't think he could stand a row of empty cribs. It was a brightly lit room with pictures of baby animals on the walls. Stuffed dolls, building blocks, and simple puzzles were strewn over the floor. Matt lay down. He really was tired, and depressed for so many reasons that he had trouble sorting them all out: the fight with María, Esperanza's scorn, the child who had fled from him in the garden, the clone lab, and last of all, the fountain full of El Patrón's embalmed memories.

He fell into a deep sleep and only stirred when he heard a strange noise: *Bub-bub-bub-bub-bub.* A sharp voice said, "You take that out of your mouth, Mbongeni." Matt heard a scuffle and an outraged squawk. He was so tired he didn't want to open his eyes, but the thought occurred to him that the room was littered with toys. Recently used toys.

He opened his eyes. Someone had raised bars around one of

the beds, creating a cage. Inside sat a chubby black boy in diapers. He was too old for diapers, being at least six, and he was rocking back and forth. *Bub-bub-bub-bub-bub,* he said, blowing air through his lips. Outside the bars sat the little girl Matt had seen in the garden. The place where the bite had been was covered by a bandage.

"Do you want a bottle, Mbongeni?" asked the girl. "Nice, warm milk? Nummy-nummy-nums?"

Mbongeni smiled, and a line of drool fell from his lips. The girl got up and went to a small fridge. She removed a bottle and put it into a microwave for a few seconds. She was so tiny and businesslike that Matt was charmed. She had clearly not seen him yet.

The microwave chimed, and the girl expertly tested the temperature of the milk on her skinny wrist before handing it to the boy. "Muh! Muh!" he cried, cramming the nipple into his mouth and sucking lustily.

"That's very good," said Dr. Rivas. He was sitting on the far side of the bed, and the little girl watched him intently. "If you were bigger, I'd let you take Mbongeni for a crawl. I'm afraid you wouldn't be able to stop him if he got into trouble."

"I wish he could talk," said the girl.

"He'll always be a baby, but he doesn't seem to mind." The doctor looked up and saw Matt. "There's someone I want you to meet—*no seas timida*. Don't be shy, little one."

"No," moaned the girl, but Dr. Rivas picked her up and carried her to Matt's bed.

"*Mi patrón*, this is Listen, a very bright girl."

"I saw her in the garden," said Matt. "She was crying because something had bitten her." He held out his hand, but the girl flinched away.

The doctor grimaced. "That, I'm afraid, is an ongoing problem."

"Someone should protect her."

At this, Listen looked up and met Matt's eyes for the first time.

"I want to be your friend," the boy said, extending his hand again. She touched it briefly and retreated. "What kind of name is Listen?" he asked Dr. Rivas.

"African. It may sound odd, but all names have meanings in their original languages. Matteo means 'gift of God,' and Mirasol means 'look at the sun.'"

"'Look at the sun.' Yes, that suits her," said Matt, thinking of Waitress's habit of following him around like a small planet. "Do you listen a lot?" he asked the little girl. She hung her head.

"She does. That's why I'm glad we didn't have to blunt her intelligence when she was harvested," the doctor said.

Harvested, thought Matt. Listen had been grown inside a cow just as he had, and that meant she was a clone. Then the rest of Dr. Rivas's statement sank in. "What do you mean, *blunt*?"

"All such infants are injected with a drug that destroys part of the frontal lobes—all, that is, except El Patrón's clones. He wanted them to experience the kind of childhood he never had."

"So that's what's wrong with Mbongeni," said Matt, looking with horror and pity at the little boy who had finished the milk and was banging his head rhythmically with the bottle. He realized that the bite on Listen's arm came from this poor, damaged child.

"Take his bottle, Listen," said the doctor. The girl fled from Matt and leaned over Mbongeni's cage. She yanked the bottle away from the boy and, before he could complain, popped a pacifier into his mouth.

"Isn't it better that he live as a happy infant, unaware of the hatred people have for clones? When you speak of destroying tissue samples, by the way, he's one of them," said Dr. Rivas.

"He's a child," Matt said.

"Not according to the law. He exists for one purpose only, to prolong the life of his original."

"I make the laws here," said Matt, "and I say Mbongeni is a child."

Dr. Rivas sighed and ran his fingers through thinning hair. "Would you like lunch in the garden, *mi patrón*? The eejits can set out a table under the grape arbor."

"I want Listen and Mbongeni to come."

"I'm afraid the boy would be frightened. Clones like that get very attached to routine and start screaming if anything is changed." The doctor pressed a buzzer, and a pair of eejit women came into the nursery. One of them upended Mbongeni and changed his diaper. The boy howled with rage, but when he was laid back down, fresh and sweet-smelling, the other eejit began to play peek-a-boo with him. Mbongeni gurgled with delight, not tiring of the game. Eejits, of course, never tired of anything.

"They'll do that until he falls asleep," said Dr. Rivas.

Listen wasn't eager to go with Matt, but Dr. Rivas explained that it was her duty. Matt was the new *patrón*, and they had to obey him. She seemed to accept this, although she folded her arms to keep from taking his hand. The doctor must have relayed a message, because the eejits had already put up a table under the arbor by the time they arrived. A fine spray of water cooled the air, and birds flew back and forth through the mist. A mockingbird sat at the top of the arbor and sang.

Lunch was a large pizza and a salad. Listen wriggled in anticipation as the doctor served Matt first, then himself, and last of all her. She inhaled the odor of hot cheese and pepperoni, but she didn't eat until Dr. Rivas had given her permission.

"What do you like to do?" Matt asked her.

"Don't know," said Listen. She ate with surprising delicacy, or perhaps Matt was only used to Mirasol's wholehearted gobbling.

"Do you like dolls or coloring books?" Matt tried to remember what he did at her age. "Do you watch TV?"

"Don't know."

"That's very rude, Listen," said Dr. Rivas. "Answer the *patrón*."

"I like all of them," the girl said sullenly.

"Did you ever see *El Látigo Negro*?" Matt said, naming his favorite show.

"I might have," Listen said.

"I liked the battles El Látigo had with the Queen of Skulls. She was always playing dirty tricks on him."

"She turned into a snake once and he picked it up, thinking it was his whip," said Listen.

"I remember that! It bit him and he almost died." Little by little Matt drew her out until she was almost relaxed, but she kept her distance.

For dessert they had watermelon. It was brought to them by Mirasol, who was followed by a chef in a long white apron. "I had to let her come," he said apologetically. "She kept jittering, and I didn't know what to do."

"That's all right," said Dr. Rivas. Mirasol took up her post by Matt's chair. She was in her waitress uniform again. "Listen, you may take slices of watermelon for yourself and Mbongeni, but pick out the seeds before you give him any." The girl slid out of her chair and made a speedy exit.

The doctor turned toward Matt. "Aren't you going to ask me who Mbongeni's original is?"

"It doesn't matter. I'm not going to allow the boy to be operated on," Matt said.

"He's Glass Eye Dabengwa's clone."

A vague feeling of dread came over Matt. He found it difficult to connect the happy child with the sinister adult, but someday—if Mbongeni survived—he would turn into an elephant-gray monster with yellow eyes. "Why is he here?"

"This hospital was the finest of its kind in the world. It was a safe place for the drug lords to raise their clones, and in those days El Patrón was Glass Eye's ally. That was when he was still president of Nigeria. Now he's retired. El Patrón's great-great-grandson Benito married Dabengwa's daughter."

"Her name was Fani," said Matt. "I remember she had to be drugged into doing it."

"Drug lords marry for power, not love," said Dr. Rivas. "Tissue samples for Mbongeni and Listen were sent here eight years ago. The original Listen was Glass Eye's favorite wife, but the original died before our Listen was harvested."

Matt flinched inside. He would never get used to the word *harvested*.

"Normally, such embryos are terminated, but Glass Eye wanted her spared. She was, legally, no longer a clone. She was human and would grow into an intelligent, beautiful woman. He wanted her raised to be his wife."

"That's disgusting!" said Matt, pushing his chair away from the table. "He's horrible. He's a sadist. He's ninety-nine years old, and he never blinks."

"Drug lords live a long time." Dr. Rivas signaled to Mirasol, and she began gathering up plates. "When Glass Eye is a robust hundred and ten, Listen will be eighteen."

"He's not getting anywhere near her!" Matt could feel rage

rising within him and desperately tried to force it down. But Dr. Rivas's next statement took him by surprise.

"I agree, *mi patrón*. She's too good for him. But consider this: As long as we have Listen and Mbongeni—especially Mbongeni—Glass Eye won't dare to attack Opium. He needs the boy for spare parts." The doctor smiled a friendly, all-encompassing smile. You could almost believe that he wouldn't say *boo* to a baby, let alone harvest it. "They're our insurance policy."

And they were, Matt realized. They would give him breathing space to renovate the hospital, cure the eejits, and replace the opium with real crops. Later he could deal with the problem of Dabengwa, but for now he felt an enormous burden roll off his shoulders.

He noticed that Mirasol was dawdling over the leftover watermelon slices. "Eat," he commanded, and she, with her usual speed, obeyed.

19

DR. RIVAS'S SECRET

What a huge difference the removal of Dabengwa made! Matt had taken on so many problems that he had felt paralyzed, and now he could relax. He could take his time with the other tasks. He accessed the holoport that afternoon—over Dr. Rivas's strong objections—and contacted banks in Switzerland, South Africa, and Japan to move money into the accounts of the new doctors. He sent a message to Esperanza to find qualified nurses and lab technicians. The hospital had to be built up before they could start work on the eejits.

Matt had never handled actual money—it wasn't used in Opium—but he understood the concept of buying and selling. He had studied the ebb and flow of currency and knew that so many US dollars equaled so many pesos, rubles, or rands. Banking was merely a set of numbers to Matt. It was good to have high ones, and if they fell below a certain point, you moved a few tons of opium around and magically the numbers went up again.

Drugs were the real money. Drugs and gold. El Patrón had a lot of that, too.

For the first time Matt appreciated the power he had. He could buy anything he wanted—a castle in Spain, a spaceship, an Egyptian pyramid—and have it shipped to him. When the boys visited, he would throw them a party that would outdo El Patrón's birthdays, and it wouldn't include boring speeches or stiff, formal dinners.

What did Ton-Ton like? Soccer. Matt would have the top soccer teams from Argentina and Brazil flown in. Chacho liked music. Matt would invite the best guitarists in the world. Fidelito liked wrestlers. Or rather, Fidelito's grandmother had liked wrestlers and told him stories about them. The little boy's eyes lit up when he talked about El Pretzel, so called because he tied his opponents into knots. Another favorite was El Salero, the Saltshaker, who threw salt into people's eyes when the referee wasn't looking, but El Muñeco was the best. He was so noble he never played dirty tricks and so good-looking that girls fainted when he stepped into the ring.

Planning the party made Matt feel feverish, and, in fact, he did have a fever. Dr. Rivas ordered him to bed, and Matt thought, *I don't have to go to bed. I'm a drug lord. I can do anything I want.* But he was too tired to argue.

He awoke refreshed and full of confidence. It was time to return to Ajo. The doctors would arrive in a few days, and he had to prepare for the party. And he missed Celia, Daft Donald, and Mr. Ortega. With his newly found power he wanted to give them all presents, but he realized that he couldn't give them the things they really wanted. Daft Donald would want his voice back and Mr. Ortega his hearing. As for Celia, what reward was good enough for her complete devotion?

He was feeding Mirasol breakfast in his hospital bedroom when Cienfuegos slunk in. The *jefe* closed the door carefully and ran a kind of wand over the walls, ceiling, and floor.

"Expecting trouble?" Matt said, picking fragments of toast from the front of the girl's uniform.

"Avoiding it," Cienfuegos said. "I declare this room free of listening devices and spy cameras."

"That's good," said Matt absently.

"A drug lord should never be this relaxed," the *jefe* said. "You act as though you haven't a care in the world, brushing crumbs off your pet eejit, while who knows what plots are being hatched behind your back."

"Even El Patrón took holidays," retorted Matt.

"He did when he was old and had a system of bodyguards and *sicarios* in place. When he was young, he slept with his eyes open."

Matt sighed. "Should I send for Dr. Rivas?"

"No!" Cienfuegos barked. "No," he repeated more softly. "Dr. Rivas is the problem."

"How can I believe you? He saved my life."

The *jefe* pulled up a chair and leaned close, as though he expected someone to be eavesdropping. "He's a brilliant scientist, but he has a family to protect, and that compromises him."

Matt took a second look at Cienfuegos as an idea began to surface in the back of his mind. "I know Dr. Rivas came here with his father, wife, and three children."

"The father died of a heart attack, and the wife killed herself when El Patrón turned one of their sons into an eejit. The eejit is still alive, which is amazing for someone so profoundly chipped, but the doctor has devoted his life to protecting him. I believe you saw the young man removing leaves from a pond."

Matt remembered. Dr. Rivas must have chosen the veranda so he could watch his son. "The other two?"

"They work in the large observatory you saw when we flew in. What you must remember is that the doctor would do anything to protect them." Cienfuegos leaned back, watching Matt expectantly. After a moment he said, "Waitress, go to the kitchen." She rose at once but paused to look at Matt.

"It's all right. Please go to the kitchen," the boy said.

"Did you see that?" exclaimed the *jefe* after she left. "She waited to get your permission."

"Maybe she likes me."

"She was trained to obey everyone, not make choices about who to obey," Cienfuegos said. "The cooks say she jitters when she's away from you. That's a danger sign. Eejits break down if they're under too much stress, and they can die."

Matt was appalled. He hadn't meant to put her in danger. "What should I do?"

"Stop trying to awaken her, *mi patrón*. Let the doctors do it. Right now we have a much more important problem on our hands. Dr. Rivas has been lying to you."

More trouble, thought Matt. *You crawl out from under one rock and another rolls into its place.* He was ready to start jittering himself. "What about?"

"It's better if I show you. Follow my lead," said Cienfuegos.

Following his lead meant wandering through the gardens as the *jefe* explained which plants he planned to collect for Esperanza. He'd already trapped several kinds of squirrels. There were so many around all you had to do was hold out a peanut and they jumped into your arms. He was digging up wildflowers and collecting seeds. "You have to collect them as complete communities," he explained. "You can't mix the ones growing in alkaline soil at a thousand feet with those in acid soil at five thousand feet. You also have to collect the bacteria and fungi living with them."

Matt wasn't interested in soil samples, but he guessed that the conversation was a cover for their real purpose. He knew that hidden microphones and cameras were scattered all over Paradise. El Patrón had been addicted to spying. Dr. Rivas could keep track of their movements, but what difference did that make?

The doctor had a family, and now the idea that had begun to surface in Matt's mind became clearer. He knew little about the outside world except what he'd seen on television. On TV people had brothers, sisters, sons, and daughters. Ton-Ton had parents. So did Chacho. Fidelito had a dearly loved grandmother.

No one in Opium had a family except the Alacráns and their visitors. No one else got married. Until Matt had met the boys at the plankton factory, he hadn't realized how abnormal life in Opium was.

They came to an outdoor shrine dedicated to Jesús Malverde, and Matt was embarrassed to see a small plaster statue of the young El Patrón draped with silver charms. Cienfuegos bowed his head and crossed himself. "That's not a real saint," Matt said.

"I am directing my prayer to God," the *jefe* replied. "It doesn't matter who delivers the message."

Directly behind the shrine was a building almost completely hidden in vines, and Matt heard a girl yell, "Don't touch me!" It was Listen! He started to run, but Cienfuegos held him back.

"Let me handle this," he said. Matt saw that standing in the shadows on either side of the door were bodyguards in the distinctive black suits El Patrón had favored. So they had not all died at the funeral. Some had been kept here, and Matt wondered why. Cienfuegos casually walked toward the men and said, "I've come to fix the electrical problem."

"What electrical problem?" growled one of the guards.

"The current is leaking into the wall, and anyone touching it gets a shock," said the *jefe*.

"Nobody told me about it," said the other guard.

"Dr. Rivas just contacted me. He's afraid one of the children will get electrocuted."

That woke the guards up. "Crap! I didn't know wires could leak. Have you got a pass?" the first man asked.

"Right here." Cienfuegos started unfolding a piece of paper, and the two men bent over to read it. Suddenly, with a speed that made Matt's heart leap into his mouth, the *jefe* flicked a stun gun from a shoulder holster and shot both of them. Twice.

"You killed them!" the boy cried.

"Not quite," said Cienfuegos, prodding one of them with his foot. "You need two shots for some of these gorillas." He bent down and relieved the men of their weapons.

"But why? They were no danger to me. I'm the *patrón*."

"Only if they think you are," said the *jefe*.

"They're microchipped. They can't attack me any more than you—" The minute Matt said it, he realized his mistake. The Farm Patrolmen were chipped, and they didn't want to be reminded of it. A look of pure fury crossed Cienfuegos's face. He leaned against the door frame, breathing heavily.

"Celia told you, didn't she?" he said, shivering with repressed emotion.

"Don't blame her. I'm the *patrón*. I'm supposed to know

everything," said Matt. "She said everyone was"—he searched for a word—"*controlled*."

"You could call it that."

"But your intelligence isn't harmed," Matt said, trying to preserve the *jefe*'s honor.

"Too bad they didn't leave my soul alone." Cienfuegos laughed shakily. "Dr. Rivas is probably wetting his pants right now if he's watching the monitors. Come on. You have to know what he's hiding."

20

THE BUG

Matt looked back, expecting to see more bodyguards running through the garden, but the paths were empty. Inside the building was a large room with swings and a jungle gym and beds. Eejit caretakers were stationed around the walls. One table was set up with art supplies. Another had pitchers of lemonade and sandwiches. It was an ordinary playground for children, or what Matt supposed was ordinary. He'd only seen such things on TV.

Mbongeni was sucking on the bars of a large cage, the floor of which was littered with stuffed toys. He seemed happy enough. Listen's legs were poking out from under a bed, and Matt ran over and dragged her out. "Give her back, you stupid ca-ca face!" a boy roared from the shadows.

The little girl's arms were scratched, and her eyes were wide with fear. Her skin had turned an ashen color. "Carry her to a bed, and don't let anyone near her," Matt told Cienfuegos. A hand raked out from under the bed and Matt jumped back before he got his ankle clawed. The boy's fingernails were long and dirty. Matt dumped a couple of pillows out of their cases and used the cloth to protect his arms. He put his foot temptingly close, and when the hand raked out again, he grabbed it.

A small boy, perhaps seven, came out clawing and spitting like a wildcat. He fastened his teeth onto the cloth hard enough to rip it open. "Cienfuegos!" cried Matt in alarm. In an instant the *jefe* was there, expertly twining a blanket around the boy's body and tying him up with a jump rope until the child looked like a caterpillar in a cocoon. Still the boy thrashed and struggled. Cienfuegos found another jump rope and doubled the bonds.

"Crap eater! Poo-poo brain!" raved the little boy. "I'll have you killed! I'll *cockroach* you!" He was practically foaming at the mouth, but eventually he stopped fighting. His face was red with exertion, and his black hair was plastered down with sweat. "How dare you touch me! I'm El Patrón!" he screamed.

Matt took a closer look at the child. It was hard to see his features, for the boy was not only in a rage, he was also extremely dirty. But the resemblance was unmistakable. "He's—he's—" Matt couldn't finish the sentence.

"A clone," said Cienfuegos. "He thinks he's El Patrón's heir. Those bodyguards at the door thought he was too, and they would have defended him to the death. That's why I had to shoot them."

Matt sat on the floor, far enough away to avoid being spat on by the boy. "Why did Dr. Rivas hide this from me?" he asked. He could hardly take in the reality of the child, his brother—no, *not* his brother, any more than El Patrón was his father.

"Well may you ask," said Cienfuegos. He went over to take

care of Listen, who was beginning to stir. The *jefe* found a bottle of rubbing alcohol and set about disinfecting her scratches, an activity that woke her up quickly.

"Ow! Stop it!" she yelled.

"It's good for you," Cienfuegos said, relentlessly swabbing the wounds. All the while a dozen eejits sat around the walls, oblivious to the battle going on. Presently a bell rang, and they rose to perform their chores. Two of them opened Mbongeni's cage and hauled him off to a bathtub. Others swept the floor and tidied up the room. Still others poured lemonade into cups and brought them to Listen and the boy. They didn't notice that the boy was trussed up in a blanket and couldn't drink properly. The eejit simply poured the liquid over his face.

"Go away! I'll kill you! I'll kill all of you," the boy screamed. Matt thought about helping him, remembered the torn pillow-case, and decided against it.

Listen sat up and dangled her legs over the edge of the bed. "Oh, crot! Now there's two of them," she said.

"Don't use language like that," Cienfuegos scolded her.

"You're not my boss," she said, and let fly with a string of curse words Matt had only recently learned from the boys at the plankton factory.

"You'd better learn manners fast," the *jefe* warned her. "That's the new *patrón*. The other is only a clone."

"They're both bugs," the girl said rebelliously. "Everyone calls the little one El Bicho. The other one is El Bicho Grande." She stuck out her tongue.

Matt knew he ought to be angry, but Listen's performance was so outrageous he laughed. She was fluffed up like a bantam rooster. He also understood her initial fear of him. The Bug had clearly terrorized her. "Why does Dr. Rivas allow El

Bicho to hurt her? I thought she was being protected," he asked Cienfuegos.

"Another lie," said the *jefe*. "Glass Eye didn't ask for her to be spared. The doctor wanted her as a playmate for the others. You'll notice that Mbongeni is kept out of harm's way. He's the important one."

"I am so important," Listen insisted. "I'm going to grow up to be a beautiful woman and marry a drug lord."

"You can do better than that," said Matt, feeling sorry for the unwanted girl. What was he to do with these new additions to his "family"? The playroom was no better than a zoo, and the three inhabitants were practically feral. Nothing could be done for Mbongeni, but Listen could be saved. As for the Bug . . .

"I owe you an explanation," said Dr. Rivas. He had arrived with another pair of bodyguards, who were checking their unconscious fellows for vital signs. Listen ran to the doctor and hugged him.

Cienfuegos went into a defense posture. "Tell them to dump their weapons *now*. I mean it," he said.

"I'm sure you do," said the doctor, gently patting Listen's head. He gave the order and two stun guns, four knives, a knuckle duster, and a garrote wire dropped to the floor.

"Kick them toward me," said the *jefe*.

"Please don't think I was being disloyal, *mi patrón*," Dr. Rivas said. He seemed utterly relaxed, as though no one could possibly suspect him of wrongdoing. "I wasn't sure how to tell you about El Bicho."

"You could begin by telling the *patrón* why he's still alive," snarled Cienfuegos.

"So bloodthirsty," murmured the doctor. "Why don't you ask Matt whether he wants the boy destroyed?"

Matt hadn't sorted out his feelings about the Bug, but he definitely didn't want to order a murder. "I think there's been enough death in this place," he said.

"I quite agree," said Dr. Rivas, smiling serenely. He sat down on a bed, and Listen curled up on the floor by his feet. She held on to his pant leg and sucked her thumb like a much younger child. "Round up some eejits and take the injured men to the hospital," the doctor told the bodyguards. "You know, Cienfuegos, it isn't good for El Bicho to be wrapped up so tightly. He gets into terrible sweats."

"Tough toenails. I'm not letting that little viper loose," said Cienfuegos.

By now the eejits had returned Mbongeni, powdered and sweet-smelling, to his cage. The little boy was massacring a peanut butter sandwich and getting most of it on his face. "Can I help him?" pleaded Listen. The doctor nodded, and she ran to the cage. On the way she kicked the Bug's blanket, and the Bug snapped at her.

"Let me explain how it all happened," began Dr. Rivas. "Would you care for some refreshments, *mi patrón*? I can have coffee and snacks sent from the kitchen. No? Very well. To begin with, El Patrón ordered El Bicho as a backup for you. You had that distressing asthma and strange bouts of illness we couldn't understand."

Matt knew he was referring to the arsenic Celia had fed him. "Go on," he said.

"When El Patrón died, the order came for all of us to attend the funeral. You can't imagine what a momentous event that was. The old man had ruled this country for more than a hundred years, and no one could imagine what was coming. I knew the law—the others didn't—that when the original of a clone dies, the clone takes his place. More important, he inherits. We were told you were dead, and I thought, 'El Bicho is now the heir. If I destroy him, I'll be committing murder.'"

Dr. Rivas spread his hands in a gesture of helplessness. He smiled, and Matt was almost convinced of his innocence, but there was the bite on Listen's arm and her use as a rag doll for the two boys that argued against it.

"So you stayed behind with a few bodyguards and a stockpile of weapons," said Matt. Cienfuegos let out a bark of laughter.

"I couldn't neglect the heir." The doctor seemed affronted.

"I'm the heir, not El Bicho," Matt pointed out.

"No you aren't, poo-poo face!" said the Bug, entering the conversation for the first time.

"Be quiet," said Dr. Rivas with an edge to his voice. To Matt's surprise, the Bug obeyed. "The situation is easily remedied," the doctor said. "I bring the bodyguards together, explain that you are the true ruler of Opium, and they'll switch their allegiance to you."

"Will that work, Cienfuegos?" asked Matt.

"Probably, but I'm staying armed," the *jefe* said.

An ammonia stench reached Matt's nose, and he realized that the Bug had fouled his blanket. "We can't keep him tied up forever," he said.

"I sometimes put him on a leash," the doctor admitted. He called for a group of four eejits, and in a moment Matt could see why. As soon as they unwrapped the Bug, he began kicking, screaming, and biting. The eejits held his arms and legs, reminding Matt of ants holding down a grasshopper, and hauled him off for a bath.

"Is something wrong with his brain?" Matt asked.

"All of El Patrón's clones differ from the original in some way," said Dr. Rivas. "You were the most perfect. El Bicho is almost as good. He's very intelligent and his health is good, but he has no impulse control. If he wants something, he goes straight for it, no matter who or what is in the way."

Matt could hear the Bug screaming in one of the other rooms. If he hadn't known better, he would have thought the boy was being tortured. "What should I do with him?" he asked.

"Put him to sleep like a rabid dog," said Cienfuegos.

Matt frowned. "I was half-mad from neglect when I was six years old, but Celia, Tam Lin, and María brought me back to life. Perhaps El Bicho can be saved."

The *jefe* snorted. The doctor gazed into the distance. Only Listen, who was tucking a sandwich into Mbongeni's mouth, offered an opinion. "He's a bug," she said. "What you need is a big old shoe to squash him."

It's like owning a cage full of pit bulls, thought Matt. He had no idea what to do.

21

THE SCORPION STAR

Matt realized he would have to postpone his return to Ajo. Mbongeni was all right. He was a cheerful infant and his needs were simple, but Listen had to be taken away from El Bicho. Matt moved her next to his room and got one of the nurses to keep an eye on her. Listen didn't like that one bit.

Matt found her surprisingly informed about some things and completely ignorant about others. When he tried to read her *Peter Rabbit,* she sneered at him.

"Rabbits don't wear clothes," she said scornfully. "They don't eat currant buns. That's a stupid book. I hate it."

"It isn't supposed to be real," Matt explained. "You have to pretend you're a rabbit and imagine what it's like being hunted by a farmer who wants to put you into a pie."

"Why would I do that?" asked Listen.

"To grow your imagination. To give your brain a workout."

The little girl considered the possibility that brains needed workouts. "It's still a lie," she decided. "Dr. Rivas says that scientists always tell the truth."

Except when it involves you, thought Matt, but he didn't say it aloud.

Listen then told him about Dr. Rivas's rabbits, which he kept for experiments. She didn't seem upset that he killed them afterward, or that he let her watch dissections. She knew the names of organs and how the bones were put together. When you cut open the stomach, she said, all that was inside was lettuce, not currant buns. Matt realized that she had patterned herself after the doctor. It wasn't surprising, since he was the only normal adult she saw, but she didn't realize that she was just another rabbit to him.

No one had ever sung her lullabies or tucked her into bed. No one had ever held her when she had nightmares, and she did have them. Matt heard her screaming in the middle of the night, but she wouldn't tell him about the dream. She'd never played hide-and-seek, although she'd done plenty of hiding from the Bug. She was, in her way, as isolated as Matt had been at that age, except that she didn't have Celia to tell her stories or Tam Lin to take her exploring. And she didn't have María.

Matt vowed to make it up to her.

The Bug was a much more difficult problem. Once he was cleaned up and his fingernails cut, Matt visited him. Eejits stood on either side, restraining him with a pair of leashes, just as large, vicious dogs were sometimes controlled. The boy's legs were hobbled so that he could walk, but not run. The eejits forced him into a chair facing Matt.

Mirasol brought in a cart with cookies, cheese slices, strawberries, and glasses of milk. For a moment Matt was struck by the similarity between this meeting and when he had first met El Patrón.

Matt had been so traumatized then that he couldn't speak, but he had instinctively liked the old man. Everything was *right* about him, the color of his eyes, the shape of his hands, his voice. Matt went up to the drug lord without the slightest hesitation, and El Patrón had asked him gravely if he liked cookies.

"Do you like cookies?" Matt said now to the scowling, simmering boy.

"Crot you!" said the Bug.

"Dr. Rivas says you're intelligent. You don't act like it." Matt edged the plate of snacks closer.

"I'm smarter than you are, roach face. I'm the boss of this place."

"Doesn't look like it," said Matt, pointing at the eejits holding leashes. "Let's start over. If you're as bright as Dr. Rivas says, you'll want to get along with me."

"When you die, I'm going to take your place," boasted the Bug.

"That's a really stupid thing to say. Only an idiot threatens a man holding a gun."

El Bicho sat very still. After a moment an amazing transformation came over him. His body relaxed, and he grinned like a normal kid who only wanted to make friends. "I guess I acted like a real turkey," he apologized. "You're right. Let's start over."

"Okay," Matt said warily. The shift of personality had caught him off guard. "Do you like cookies?"

"You bet," said the Bug. "I like milk, too. And strawberries and cheese. It was nice of you to invite me to lunch."

"Help yourself," said Matt, and was surprised by the boy's elegant table manners. He'd expected Mbongeni's type of chaos, but of course the Bug had normal intelligence. Better than normal. "What do you do all day?" he asked.

"What do I do?" El Bicho's gaze was far away as he tried to remember. "Sometimes Dr. Rivas teaches me things, and sometimes we go for walks. I watch TV a lot."

"Where do you walk?"

"Here and there," the boy said vaguely. "I like going to the observatory. Dr. Rivas's children are astronomers—well, two of them are. The oldest son is a crot—sorry—an eejit. Sometimes they let me look through the telescope."

It sounded like a normal outing except for the leashes and hobbles. Did the boy wear them most of the time? "Do you like Dr. Rivas?"

"Of course. He's like a father. Or what I think a father is. Like you, I don't know much about families."

For some reason Matt felt like there was a pane of glass between himself and the Bug. What the boy said was reasonable, but it was just words, with no connection to the person behind them. The Bug was saying what he thought Matt wanted to hear.

"El Patrón's father lived a hundred fifty years ago," said Matt. "In a way he was our father too. We had a family back then, but they died long before we existed. It's so strange. Sometimes I feel like an old photograph hidden away at the back of a drawer. Did you ever meet El Patrón?"

El Bicho shrugged. "I don't remember."

"I knew him well. He talked a lot about his brothers and sisters, and it bothered him that they'd never had a chance. That fountain outside the lab is supposed to be statues of them."

"Are they our brothers and sisters?" said the Bug.

Matt shied away from the idea. "Not really. The statues were copied from Illegal children. There weren't any pictures of the originals. People like us have to make our families."

"So that means *you're* my brother," said El Bicho.

"I suppose," Matt said unwillingly. He considered for a moment. "I think that people have an instinct for a family. You look until you find a mother, a father, a sister, a brother. They don't have to be blood relatives. They just have to love you. And when you find them, you don't have to look anymore."

They ate in silence for a while. Matt had no appetite and passed much of his food on to Mirasol. He thought about Celia and Tam Lin, and about Fidelito, who had called him *brother*. Was María his sister? No, she was something more. He kept looking at the Bug's hobbles and wondering whether he dared to remove them. "If I took off your leg restraints," Matt said carefully, "do you promise not to throw a fit?"

"Sure," said El Bicho.

"We could go for a walk."

"I can show you the way to the observatory," said the boy, showing genuine interest for the first time. "It's great! There're all kinds of machines and computers. The smaller telescope looks at the sun, and the big one looks at the rest of the sky."

The Bug's enthusiasm transformed his face, and Matt thought, *What kind of childhood has he had, shut up in a nursery with eejits for company? No wonder he isn't normal.* But that could be changed. He ordered the eejits to unlock the hobbles.

"Remember. No tantrums," Matt warned as they went into the gardens, but he needn't have worried. El Bicho danced around from the joy of being outside before settling down to a steady pace. The eejits followed solemnly, holding their leashes.

To Matt's surprise they went to a hovercraft port concealed behind a hedge. There were a dozen or so small craft parked on magnetic strips, and the Bug went up to one and opened the hatch. "It's a long way to the observatory," he explained.

"I'll get Cienfuegos to pilot," said Matt.

The Bug laughed. "Anybody can fly these," he said, climbing inside. The eejits followed him, pressing themselves against the back wall. "You need a pilot to take up a real hovercraft. This is a stirabout for short hops." He patted the seat next to him.

Matt climbed in, hoping that he wasn't making a mistake. The change in El Bicho had been so gratifying, he didn't want to spoil the boy's mood.

"First, you uncouple the magnets," explained the Bug. He pushed a green button. The stirabout lurched up, and Matt caught his breath. "It's okay. We can't go more than ten feet off the ground," said the Bug. "Now you press the go button and steer with this wheel. I'll let you try it on the way back."

The stirabout obediently followed the road, and Matt's heart settled down to a regular rhythm. For one thing, he was astounded that a seven-year-old could fly anything. El Bicho was clearly intelligent—he spoke of telescopes and computers with easy familiarity just as Listen spoke of rabbit anatomy. They had both copied Dr. Rivas. Matt thought uncomfortably of his own upbringing. At age seven he'd been interested in picnics and Celia's cooking. Nothing much to exercise a brain there.

It occurred to him that El Bicho had become much friendlier when he was in charge. *Power* was what the boy craved, even as El Patrón had craved it all his life.

The valley widened out to a broad plain dotted with mesquite, yucca, and cactus. Here and there were the small observatories once owned by astronomers before El Patrón drove them out. Mesquite trees had grown up around the buildings until their walls were almost invisible. Their round roofs were caked with dirt and bird droppings. Looming beyond them was an enormous white dome, the biggest observatory in the world, Matt remembered, with a telescope that could look around the universe until you could see the back of your neck.

By its side, no less impressive, was a building shaped like the number seven tipped over on its side. The shorter section rose at least a hundred feet into the air. At the top was a solar telescope. The longer section sloped at an angle to the earth and, El Bicho said, extended a thousand feet underground. "Dr. Rivas let me look into it once, but it's nasty. Dark and hot. Only eejits work there."

The boy positioned the stirabout over a strip in the parking lot, and Matt felt the magnetism pull them down.

"What you must always do, when you've gone for a hop," said the Bug in the same serious way as Dr. Rivas giving a lecture, "is recharge the antigravity pods. You pull this lever"— Matt heard a *whump* as a tube with a sucker at the end clamped onto the front of the craft—"and you're set. It takes fifteen minutes to recharge for the distance we've gone."

For all the authority El Bicho tried to project as he led the way into the observatory, he still looked like a little kid on a leash. The eejits followed him as though they were walking a dog, and Matt struggled not to smile. He sensed that any hint of humor would send the boy into one of his rages.

The building was dark, except for the lights on computers, and it was very warm. "You have to keep the telescopes at the same temperature as the outside," said the Bug. "Otherwise, they won't stay still. In winter the astronomers have to wear thick coats."

A woman in a white lab coat hurried out of an office. *"¿Dónde está mi padre?"*

"Dr. Rivas was busy, Dr. Angel," the Bug said grandly.

"You're never supposed to come here without him," scolded Dr. Angel. "But who is this? Ah! Father told me at dinner. You must be the new *patrón*!" The woman bowed as though greeting royalty.

"And you must be Dr. Rivas's daughter," said Matt. "I hope we aren't disturbing your work."

"Not at all. It's a pleasure to meet you," said Dr. Angel graciously. "Would you like a tour?"

"*I'll* show him around," the Bug objected.

"*You* will follow me and keep your hands off the computers," said the woman. "It took us weeks to recover from your last visit."

Matt was afraid the boy would lose his temper, but he merely shrugged. Dr. Angel showed them the image from the solar telescope projected onto a screen. It looked like a pot of boiling fire with whirlpools and tendrils of darker flame writhing across the surface. They climbed stairs and walked along a causeway circling the larger telescope. A man in a white lab coat was lying on a recliner and looking up into the eyepiece. He didn't react as they passed. "That's Dr. Marcos, my brother," said Dr. Angel. "We're all called Rivas, so we use our first names to distinguish us from Father."

Lab assistants stood before banks of machinery, adjusting the focus and movement of the telescope. Dr. Angel explained each activity, but Matt had trouble remembering what she said. It was all so new and unfamiliar that he only took in one word in five. She spoke of *azimuths* and *albedos* and other strange things. Mostly, he was impressed with the sheer size of the instruments. After a while Dr. Angel took pity on him and showed him pictures the large telescope had taken.

He saw Jupiter's moons, Saturn's rings, and a comet that

looked like a dirty snowball with water vapor streaming off it. "That's baby stuff," complained the Bug. "I want to see the Scorpion Star."

"We're not looking at it right now," said Dr. Angel.

"I don't care. I want to see it."

"I'll show you the latest picture," she said. She flicked on a large screen to show . . . Matt wasn't sure what he was looking at. He saw a collection of skyscrapers floating in black space. Light reflected off red walls, and the whole assembly was enclosed in a bubble of some clear substance. A hovercraft was frozen between two buildings.

"Is that a planet?" he asked.

"It's our space station," said the Bug. "Enlarge it, Dr. Angel. I want to see the people."

She went to a computer, and the image grew larger. It felt like flying down toward a city. You got closer and closer to the buildings until you no longer noticed the bubble surrounding them. Windows and walkways appeared. Now Matt saw a man walking through a clear tube connected to another building. He saw a woman standing at a window next to a potted plant.

Dr. Angel moved the image from one part of the station to another.

Matt saw more hovercrafts. The Scorpion Star was so enormous that people had to fly from one end to the other. "There's the best part," said the Bug, pointing. The screen had moved into the heart of the buildings, where another, smaller bubble contained trees and gardens. "That's how they get their oxygen," said the boy. "They grow crops and raise chickens and everything. It's like a whole world where everything is perfect. I wish I could go there!" The longing in the boy's voice was so intense that Matt turned away from the screen to look at him.

"Earth is a good place too," he said.

"No, it isn't! Earth is crappy! Everybody hates me. Up there . . ." The Bug reached out to touch the screen, and Dr. Angel jerked his hand back. "Stop it, you poo-poo brain!" he screamed. "Up there are *real* scientists, not fakes like you! They'll want me. I know they will. Someday I'm going up there, and when I do, I'll burn this place down and you with it! Let go of me!"

By now the eejits had been alerted, and they moved in to hold on to the raving boy. They wrapped the leashes around him and carried him down the stairs and out into the parking lot. Matt followed, with Dr. Angel. "I'm sorry," he apologized. "I thought he would be all right."

"It's nothing I haven't seen before," the woman said. "Come back by yourself whenever you like." She left, and the eejits loaded the boy into the back and sat on either side of him. Matt realized that he would have to fly the stirabout, but fortunately, he had paid close attention to the boy's directions.

He pulled the lever, and the recharging hose dropped away. He pushed the green button to uncouple the magnets and the go button to start moving. The stirabout almost collided with a tree on the way up, but soon Matt was effortlessly following the road back to the hospital. All the while El Bicho screamed and spat on him until the back of his shirt was wet.

The Bug had screamed himself hoarse by the time they arrived at the little hovercraft port behind the hedge. "When you've recovered, we can start over again," said Matt, struggling to stay calm. *Not right away, though,* he thought.

"I'll kill you," the little boy rasped as the eejits unloaded him.

"I'll bring you pictures of the space station, and we can talk about what it's like to live there," said Matt. He was shaking with nerves. Never had he seen anyone lose control so completely.

"Kill you . . . ," whispered El Bicho as he was hauled off to the nursery. Matt went to his room and put on a recording of Hovhaness's *And God Created Great Whales*. The swelling music soothed him with its power, although the great whales themselves were gone and only the echo of their voices remained in the music. He wanted more than anything to lose himself, to disappear into an ideal world where all was orderly and beautiful.

Not unlike the Scorpion Star that El Bicho longed for.

22

THE ALTAR CLOTH

I want to go back to Ajo immediately," Matt told Cienfuegos.

"*¿El Bicho se encabronó, verdad?*" said the *jefe*. "The little pest got your goat, didn't he?"

"You find out about everything."

"It's my job." Cienfuegos grinned. "I won't be sorry to leave this place. Dr. Rivas has too many secrets for my liking, and I can't make up my mind whether he's a villain or not. But then Opium is full of villains." They were sitting under the trees next to a warehouse the *jefe* had used to store the plants and animals he'd collected for Esperanza. Matt could see cages of squirrels, rattlesnakes, and roadrunners.

"Why would anyone want rattlesnakes?" asked Matt.

"They're part of the ecosystem, *mi patrón*. No matter how nasty something is, it has some purpose." Cienfuegos gazed fondly at the animals he'd rounded up. "This is the kind of work I was made for, not hunting Illegals." For a moment he looked sad. It was the first time Matt had seen any sign of regret.

"You can spend all the time you like on it," the boy said, "when you don't have duties with the Farm Patrol."

Cienfuegos grimaced. "I always have duties with the Farm Patrol. It's what I'm *programmed* to do."

Matt paused, understanding what the word *programmed* meant. He tried to think of a way to ask about it without offending the *jefe*. "This programming," he began, "there seem to be several levels. You, for example, show no evidence of control. Mr. Ortega doesn't either, but Eusebio, the guitar master, works like a machine. Music can awaken him briefly, and Mirasol responds to food. The field eejits don't respond to anything. How is this possible?" Cienfuegos stiffened, and Matt braced himself for an attack.

"If you weren't the *patrón*, I would have killed you by now," the man said. "That is the one topic I can't bear to think about. I wake up at night remembering what I've lost and that there's nothing I can ever do about it. I can't kill myself. That's part of the programming too. All I can do is get up, inspect my troops, and send them out on their missions. Now, of course, with the border sealed, there's no one to hunt. Long may it stay that way."

For the first time the *jefe* had let his guard slip. He was a relentless hunter and showed no compassion for his prey, but how much was part of the man and how much was induced by the microchips?

A breeze brought the smell of pinewoods from farther up the mountain and blew dust along the road. Sometimes the winds were so fierce they made the walls of the mansion shudder. It was a place both wild and ultracivilized, Matt thought. Some parts were beyond anything else in the world, like the hospital, but hawks nested in the crags above its roof, and black bears prowled the grounds after dark.

"The microchips form a kind of constellation," Cienfuegos said after a while. "Depending on their makeup, they attach to different parts of the brain. Dr. Rivas knows far more about it than I do. The eejits get a dose like the blast of a shotgun. Everything is shorted out. The lab technicians get enough to control their will, but not enough to dampen their intelligence. Almost everyone in this place is controlled to one degree or another. Celia was spared because she was a woman and not considered important enough to be a threat. Dr. Rivas and his son and daughter at the observatory were left untouched as well."

"Why them?" asked Matt.

Cienfuegos gazed up at the trees, white sycamores that were just coming into leaf. The scanty shade sent speckles of sunlight onto the man's face and illuminated his yellow-brown eyes. "Dr. Rivas was El Patrón's guarantee of immortality," he said. "I don't know why the two astronomers were spared, but you can bet it was for a good reason. Well"—the *jefe* stood up—"I'd better see about packing. We'll need a large hovercraft, though most of the plant and animal samples can go by road."

"Major Beltrán could help with the collecting," said Matt. "He's got nothing better to do."

Cienfuegos's sudden bark of laughter took the boy by surprise. "I'm afraid his job is limited to pushing up daisies right now."

"You didn't!" cried Matt.

The *jefe* shrugged. "He was a security risk."

"But I didn't want him killed! What will Esperanza do when she finds out?"

"Nothing," said Cienfuegos. "She has no problem with

sacrificing people for her schemes, and she's probably forgotten Beltrán's existence. Please don't look so shocked, *mi patrón*. Didn't I tell you Opium was full of villains?"

What would Esperanza do? Matt didn't think she'd excuse an out-and-out murder. Would she permanently keep him from María? And would María even want to see him? She'd always forgiven him before, but this time was different. She wasn't a little girl with simple loyalties and opinions like Listen. She was almost a woman. Matt wished he knew what the dividing line between girls and women was. He might ask Ton-Ton, but he could imagine his friend's reaction. ("*¡Me burlas!* You're kidding! You really don't know what a woman is? Hey, Chacho! Guess what Matt just told me?")

No, he couldn't ask Ton-Ton.

Matt went to the holoport room and sat in front of the giant portal. He hadn't told Cienfuegos or Dr. Rivas where he was going, but why should he? He was the *patrón*, the boss of all bosses. He didn't have to ask anyone's permission.

The icon for the Convent of Santa Clara was winking, but before he reached for it, he looked around.

Mirasol was sitting on the floor, hands folded on her lap. "Waitress, go to the kitchen," Matt said, irritated because she wouldn't leave him alone, and then, "Stop. Stay." He couldn't send her to the kitchen, because she made the cooks nervous. Cienfuegos said they were afraid she would go rogue, something that happened to eejits when their brains were under too much pressure.

Perhaps she would be all right if he gave her something to do. "Come with me," Matt ordered, and Mirasol rose to her feet. He went in search of Listen, but the little girl had dodged her caretaker as easily as she'd eluded the Bug. He found her in Mbongeni's crib. El Bicho was nowhere to be seen.

"Listen, I told you to stay away from here," Matt said.

"Yep, you sure told me," she said, playing peek-a-boo with the little boy, "and I sure ignored you. Mbongeni is my best buddy. I'm not leaving him for anything."

"You aren't safe."

Listen climbed out of the crib and stood before him like a small general. "Why not? I got by before."

"The bigger El Bicho gets, the more dangerous he is."

"Why don't you put him in a cage? Feed him worms or something." Listen folded her arms and thrust out her chin.

"He'll never get better if he's treated like an animal," said Matt.

"Guess what? I don't care."

When Matt tried to pull her away, she shouted insults at him. "I won't desert Mbongeni! I won't!"

Matt gave up. The playroom was a cheerful enough place, with pictures of animals tacked to the walls—probably one of Dr. Rivas's biology lessons. One wall had dinosaurs, another reptiles, and a third insects. Each was labeled with both the common and scientific names. There were no bunny rabbits or kittens.

Six eejits sat in chairs by the kitchen, programmed to fetch food, tidy up, or give baths when a bell rang. "Where's the Bug now?" Matt asked.

"Dr. Rivas took him off for a walk when I got here," said Listen.

At least he's keeping them apart, thought Matt. He'd made it very clear to the doctor that Listen was not to be harmed. "I guess I can leave you for a while," he said.

"Great! Let me show you something Mbongeni loves better than anything in the world." Listen ran to the kitchen and took a bottle of molasses from a shelf. Then she ripped open the side of a pillow and pulled out a chicken feather. "Look, Mbongeni, look," she crowed.

"Muh! Muh!" cried the little boy, bouncing up and down. Listen dabbed a drop of molasses on each finger and glued the feather onto one. "Muh!" he squealed as he transferred the feather from one sticky hand to the other.

"He'll do that until the feather falls apart," said Listen with shining eyes. "He learned to do it all by himself."

Matt looked away, dismayed, but it was clear that the little boy enjoyed the game. "Waitress, I want you to watch over Listen. This is very important. Don't let the Bug hurt her in any way." He waited a bit longer, hypnotized by Mbongeni, until Listen applied molasses to Mirasol's fingers. Like all eejits, she was programmed to copy others and soon she, too, was transferring a feather from one hand to the other.

Matt scrolled through the icons in the holoport room and highlighted the Convent of Santa Clara. The familiar room appeared. *Sor* Artemesia's altar cloth was pinned on a back wall with a vase of red roses placed in front of it, and next to the roses was María.

He thrust his hand against the screen before she could leave the room. As always, he felt sick and his heart pounded, but he knew the sensation would pass. For a moment the wormhole swirled with mist and he lost sight of María. *Don't go. Don't go,* he implored, and sure enough, when the image resolved she was standing directly in front of the portal.

"Don't touch the screen," he gasped, trying to recover from the scanner.

She held her hands clasped over her heart and they gazed at each other, too overcome to speak. They were alone. There was no Esperanza to interfere and no Cienfuegos to make jokes. Finally, she said, "I love you."

"I love you, too," said Matt. How could he have thought her angry and unforgiving? María was made for forgiveness. She was the one still point in a world full of lies and shifting loyalties. "I'm sorry I was cruel to you. I didn't mean it. I would never mean it."

"I know," she said simply. "I lost my temper too. I know you wouldn't betray me."

"Never," he swore. "Mirasol . . . ," he began, not knowing how to explain.

"Mirasol doesn't exist," said María firmly.

"She doesn't exist," he repeated. He didn't believe this. Somewhere Mirasol *did* exist where he couldn't find her, but he wasn't going to risk an argument. "I wish we were together."

"Mother won't let me come," said María, "but I will. I don't know how, but I'll find a way."

"I could come there," Matt said.

"It's too dangerous. I hate to say this—I know it's wicked and God tells us to honor our parents—but I don't trust Mother. She's become so powerful. Presidents and generals listen to what she says, and she's so single-minded. I don't think you'd be safe here." María unpinned the altar cloth from the wall. She put it into one of the cylinders Esperanza used to send messages through the holoport. "Remember me," she said, and tossed the cylinder into the portal.

Mist billowed around the missile as it made its slow journey through the wormhole and fell to the floor with a metallic chime. The image of the Convent of Santa Clara filled with snowflakes, and a finger of icy air touched Matt's face. After a moment the image resolved, but by that time María was gone.

Matt wandered through the gardens in a dream. At last he'd seen María, and although they couldn't touch each other, they were as close as if they were in the same room. Esperanza hadn't been able to change her. Matt smiled. María's mother might have the power to order generals and presidents around, but she couldn't control her daughter.

Matt had the altar cloth folded inside his shirt next to his skin. When he drew the fine silk from the cylinder, it was as though María had reached through the portal and touched his hand. He was transfixed, unable to move for several minutes. He would keep the cloth always. He would never be without it.

Birds crowded the garden, feasting at various feeders that were refilled each morning. Goldfinches clung to bags of thistle, jays squabbled over sunflower seeds, woodpeckers complained loudly when he walked by. Hummingbirds hovered in front of his face, daring him to steal their sugar water. The air was full of their colors—yellow, blue, iridescent ruby, and green—and of the whirring of their wings.

María said that when Saint Francis went into the fields, throngs of birds filled the trees. "My little sisters," the saint told them, "God has granted you the freedom to fly anywhere. He has given you pretty clothing and taught you beautiful songs. He has created the rivers and springs to drink from, the rocks and crags for refuge, and the trees for your nests. The Creator loves you very much. Therefore, my little sister birds, you must praise Him." And the birds rose into the air, singing marvelously and circling ever higher.

I shouldn't have made fun of Saint Francis, Matt thought. Even if he didn't quite believe the stories, she did. He would try to be respectful.

He had no idea how much time had passed. The sun had moved toward the mountains, and the shadows had lengthened. He arrived at last at the playroom, vaguely aware that he had to fetch Listen and Mirasol and enter the real world again.

Mbongeni was asleep in his crib, with Listen curled up beside him. She was sucking her thumb and looked at Matt with wide, scared eyes. Matt immediately looked around and saw the line of eejits next to the kitchen. If they had moved in the time he had gone, there was no evidence of it. Mirasol . . .

Mirasol was standing next to a bed, and around her lay a drift of pictures pulled off the walls—dinosaurs, reptiles, and insects. The thumbtacks had been removed, and now Matt saw where they had gone.

El Bicho was standing next to her and very carefully pressing the tacks into her skin. Her whole right arm glittered with metal as though she were in armor. Mirasol herself showed not a trace of emotion. Her eyes stared straight ahead, unseeing.

Matt hurled himself across the room. "You little crot!" he yelled. He struck the Bug, sending the boy flying across the bed. The Bug screamed and scrambled over the other side. Matt flung himself on the bed, but he was stopped by Listen, who had jumped out of the crib.

"Please, Mr. Patrón. Please help Mirasol," she cried, grabbing Matt's ankle. "I tried to stop him, really I did. He wanted to hurt me, but she came between us. Every time he tried to get me, she put herself in the way."

The red mist that had descended on Matt's brain cleared. He'd been about to kill El Bicho. He knew it. He panted as though he'd been running a race. He sat down on the bed, his heart pumping.

"We've got to take Mirasol to the hospital," said Listen. "She didn't even move when he put those tacks in. She didn't cry or anything, but it's got to hurt."

Matt blinked at her. The Bug was still under the bed, screaming.

"Mr. Patrón? Are you awake?"

"Yes," Matt said dully.

"You can order the eejits to carry Mirasol to the hospital. I can't," said the little girl. "I tried."

At last Matt responded. "Did Dr. Rivas come here?" he asked.

"He dropped the Bug off and left."

The Bug is the wrong one to kill, thought Matt. *Dr. Rivas is the one who knew what would happen.* But he couldn't unleash Cienfuegos on the doctor. He needed him to train the new physicians and nurses. It was another compromise in the battle to save the eejits, like shooting down an aircraft to avert a war. As Dr. Rivas said, you could get used to being evil. Matt got up and gave the orders to the eejits.

23

THE RUINS OF TUCSON

The new hovercraft was large enough to carry cages of owls as well as Matt, Mirasol, and Listen. Listen planted herself sulkily next to the owls, who watched her with round yellow eyes. She had thrown an unholy fit when informed she was to go to Ajo, and it had taken two eejits to subdue her. Only Dr. Rivas's command to obey the *patrón* had made any impression on her. And Matt's promise to send her back later.

Matt had said nothing to Dr. Rivas about Mirasol. What was the point? The girl hadn't minded the tacks, and her injuries had been slight. A disinfectant spray, an injection of vitamins, and a few crème caramel custards had put everything right.

Cienfuegos climbed into the pilot's seat. "You didn't see much on your way here, *mi patrón*. Now you can get a better idea of your country."

They flew down the valley and over the huge observatory. Sunlight glinted off the two telescopes, and soon they were traveling north to go around the mountains. "I could fly over them, but there are dangerous downdrafts in the canyons," said the *jefe*.

Matt looked out the window, entranced. The other times he'd been in hovercrafts, he'd been either sick or scared. Now he watched the landscape unroll beneath him. Here and there were the ruins of abandoned houses or the sketchy marks of agriculture gone back to the wild. After a while he saw a large town that had been deserted. "That's Willcox," said Cienfuegos.

"Where did the people go?" Matt wondered.

"When the Dope Confederacy was established, people were moved either to the United States or Aztlán," the *jefe* explained. "It wasn't a peaceful transition. Thousands died in the conflict."

"*¡Por Dios!*" exclaimed Matt. "Why did the governments allow that?"

"The governments had no control. Drug lords battled homeowners; homeowners fought back. The armies of Aztlán and the United States moved inhabitants who cooperated, but the system broke down in many places. It was a bloody time."

"Was it worth it?"

"For the drug lords, very much so," said Cienfuegos. "As for Aztlán and the United States, they experienced a few drug-free years. In the long run, who can say whether it was worth it? Allowing Opium to return to the wild preserved the ecosystem. Throughout history there have been disasters that have had beneficial results. Bubonic plague killed a third of the people in Europe, but it destroyed the old governments and allowed their citizens to gain freedom. The result was a burst of creativity and prosperity never seen before."

"Dr. Rivas has a supply of plague germs frozen in his fridge," Listen revealed, having gotten over her tantrum. "He's got smallpox and cholera, too. He spanked me hard when I opened the door."

"Now I know he's one of the villains. Show me which fridge the next time we go to Paradise and I'll blowtorch it," said Cienfuegos. She stuck her tongue out at him.

They flew over another deserted town called Benson. It was crossed by a meandering stream that sparkled in the light. "That's the San Pedro River," said the *jefe*. "Not long ago it was dry, but with the people gone, the water isn't being sucked away." Cottonwoods filled the river valley, and the ground was covered in tall grass. Suddenly, a large catlike creature emerged from the grass and bent down to drink from the stream. It was followed by four adults and four cubs.

"That's a lion!" cried Matt.

"Well, what do you know? They've spread from Tucson," Cienfuegos said, pleased.

"Lions don't live here!"

Listen got up and peered out the window. "Looks like they do," she observed.

"They broke out of the zoo during the fighting," said the *jefe*, "along with a lot of other animals. The elephants didn't do well, and the hippos died from lack of water, but there's still quite a wildlife population around Tucson. In winter they stay close to the nuclear power plant, where it's warm. Some of the lions have adapted to the cold and moved away."

Matt saw a herd of antelopes grazing along an old road. "We can collect some of these for Esperanza," he said. "She won't believe what we've got here."

"Let's keep it our little secret, in case we need to negotiate with her," advised Cienfuegos.

As they went on, Matt saw more greenery and more animals.

There were large stretches of desert covered with saguaro, paloverde, and ocotillo, but between them were green valleys where water ran. Clusters of deserted adobe buildings appeared, and rusting metal dwellings that Cienfuegos said were called *trailers*. The dead city of Tucson loomed ahead with skyscrapers like the ones Matt had seen in Aztlán, only these stood against a bright-blue desert sky, not the polluted air to the south.

To the north were two gigantic power plants, one nuclear and the other a cold-fusion energy producer. By the nuclear plant was a large lake surrounded by reeds and waterbirds.

"Are the power plants deserted too?" Matt asked.

"Oh, no," said the *jefe*. "El Patrón had them built. This is where Opium gets its power. Most of it goes to protect the border. We'll land here to recharge our antigravity pods." They floated down to a large hovercraft port and clamped onto one of the magnetic strips.

Immediately, men swarmed out of a nearby building. "I've alerted them to our arrival," said Cienfuegos.

He stepped out, and the men snapped to attention. "At ease, *amigos*. I bring you our new *patrón*. Try to look fierce," he said in a lower tone to Matt.

As Matt stepped out, a cheer went up from the men. "*¡Viva! ¡Viva El Patrón!*"

"I'm not El Patrón," Matt whispered.

"Oh, but you are," said the *jefe*. "You're the old man reborn. I've watched you develop these past weeks. You were nervous at first, but the power grows in you. You'll make a fine drug lord."

"I'm not—"

"Walk past them into the building," said Cienfuegos. "Don't wave. They don't expect it. There's a lunch waiting for us inside." Matt, feeling uneasy, did his best to look tall and

fierce as he went past the cheering men. Mirasol walked obediently at his side, and Listen followed with her head held
high, as though she were already a drug queen. Inside was a
table covered with a white tablecloth and bowls of food. Three
places were set.

"What about Mirasol?" asked Matt.

"She will serve you," said the *jefe*. "You can't be seen treating
an eejit as an equal."

"Oh boy! Apple pie!" said Listen as her eyes lit on the dessert.

"Wait until you're served," Cienfuegos ordered. First Matt,
then the *jefe*, and then Listen were given potato salad, fried
chicken, and candied yams by Mirasol. She filled their plates
until told to stop. When she cut pieces of pie, Listen demanded
three slices, but Cienfuegos stopped her at two.

"I want ice cream and lots of it," said Listen.

After the meal, various men came up and offered their
greetings to Matt. They were all Farm Patrolmen in charge of
supervising the technicians operating the plants.

"Mirasol needs to eat," Matt said after the introductions
were over.

"I'll order a packed lunch. She can have it while she waits
for us in the hovercraft," said Cienfuegos. "Now we get the
grand tour." A technician guided them through the plants,
explaining what each section was for. The man seemed very
intelligent, but there was a deadness in his eyes that spoke of
some form of control. Most of the workers were robots, but a
few human technicians moved among them. They must have
been performing jobs that required great skill, yet their faces
were just as expressionless as the robots. They didn't look up as
Matt and his companions passed.

"They're all men," said Listen.

Matt stopped and looked around. She was right. "Why aren't there any women?" he asked Cienfuegos.

"El Patrón didn't think women were smart enough for this kind of work," said the *jefe*.

"I could do it," Listen boasted. "Show me how and I could run the whole damn plant."

"You can't even reach the on button," said Cienfuegos. The technician who was guiding them went back to work, and the *jefe* led them outside to the lake. Here it was hot and humid, and strange trees formed a dense forest not far away. They were covered with vines, and dark shapes moved restlessly behind shaking leaves. Close by, a bird erupted from the reeds and flew toward them, honking angrily. The *jefe* caught it before it managed to attack and tossed it back into the lake.

"That's an Egyptian goose. She must have a nest nearby. Let's go before she recovers."

There were many kinds of birds Matt had never seen before living in the marsh. Some had built nests like baskets attached to the reeds. Cienfuegos said they were weaverbirds and came from Africa. "I come from Africa too," Listen said proudly. In the water itself were catfish with long whiskers, and Matt saw a pair of yellow eyes gazing up at him from green depths.

Cienfuegos hastily pulled him and Listen away from the edge. "I forgot. There are Nile crocodiles in the lake. We lost a technician last year," he said.

Nile crocodiles? thought Matt. This place was getting more amazing by the minute. When they got to the forest, he saw monkeys slipping through the leaves. Large-billed toucans flapped heavily to keep their balance on the branches, and something howled in the trees beyond. Listen cowered behind Cienfuegos.

"It's a gibbon," the *jefe* said. "Harmless, but noisy. Some of the things here aren't harmless, though. There are Malayan tigers, African river otters that can take a chunk out of your leg, and Tasmanian devils that will attack anything. I think we should turn back. I'd hate to have to kill anything."

Matt vowed to return when they didn't have a little girl to protect. He was enchanted with the lush greenness, the teeming life, the odor of flowers hanging from the trees. "It's a real jungle," he exulted. "Did El Patrón know about this?"

"Of course, but he lost interest in it after a while," said Cienfuegos. "He liked to start things and then move on to something else. Neglect is probably what preserved this place."

"Did all these animals come from the zoo?" Matt asked.

"Yes, but even more interesting is where the plants came from. We'll go there next," said the *jefe*. They retraced their steps and cut through the nuclear power plant to reach the hovercraft port. On the way they passed a shrine to Jesús Malverde, and Matt saw Farm Patrolmen arranging flowers in front of the statue.

"That looks like you," said Listen, pointing.

Matt sighed. "It's a portrait of El Patrón as a young man."

"There's a big chapel in the woods near Paradise," the little girl said. "The nurses were always going out there to worship. Dr. Rivas says that only idiots pray to a chunk of plaster."

"Dr. Rivas doesn't know anything about religion," said Cienfuegos.

"Oh, yes he does. He's a scientist, and they know everything. Religion is crap," declared Listen.

"You're the most obnoxious little brat I've ever met."

"Both of you be quiet," said Matt, who wanted to savor the memory of the green jungle.

They returned in silence as Cienfuegos and Listen simmered with resentment. From all the crumbs inside the hovercraft, it was clear that Mirasol had fed lavishly. She looked up and—was it possible?—*smiled* at Matt. The smile was gone as swiftly as it had appeared, and he wasn't quite sure it had existed.

He sat next to her and let Listen sit in the front. For days at a time he forgot about Mirasol. He was so used to her that she seemed more like a familiar piece of furniture than a person. He took her hand, hoping for a reaction. She let it hang limply in his grasp. Remembering how risky it was to awaken her, he let it fall again.

24

THE BIOSPHERE

They floated over a series of low hills. The canyons were full of streams and a wild profusion of plant life. The dry hilltops were covered with cactuses and paloverde trees. Ahead was a shimmering, transparent curtain that distorted the land beyond.

"That's the northern border of Opium," said Cienfuegos.

Matt had seen the southern border. It consisted of a line of poles with nothing in between. Beyond had been a seething mass of factories and skyscrapers. The air had been a smudgy brown, and the noise emanating from the city had been terrifying. Here, there was only rippling air and vague shapes. This was how the border looked during lockdown.

"We'll land at the Alacrán Biosphere," said Cienfuegos. They paralleled the shimmering curtain, and Matt felt the hairs on his arms stir. Listen rubbed her face. "What you feel is the energy field that protects Opium," said the *jefe*.

Matt could detect vague shapes on the other side of the curtain—specks in the air that might have been hovercrafts. Behind them rose a hazy mountain. "What's that?" cried Listen, grabbing Matt's arm.

There were bodies embedded in the energy field. They were frozen in midstride, as though the men had been running and were still alive, but one skeletal hand stretched bony fingers into Opium. "I wish the news would get out that it's lethal to cross the border," the *jefe* said crossly. "What a waste! There were at least a dozen good farmworkers there."

Listen covered her eyes, and Matt turned away. He saw that they were approaching a collection of huge buildings, each one at least a mile long. Surrounding them was a clear bubble. "That looks like the Scorpion Star," said Matt in amazement.

"The space station was copied from this. I've always wanted to go inside, but I couldn't get permission from Dr. Rivas," said the *jefe*. "Now, of course, I have the new *patrón* to back me up."

"I've seen the Scorpion Star dozens of times," boasted Listen. "Dr. Angel lets me come whenever I want, because I'm clever and I don't break things like the Bug."

"The first biosphere was built in the United States," said the *jefe*, ignoring her. "El Patrón captured it during the drug wars, but the US army drove him away. In revenge, he took every plant and animal with him and destroyed the buildings to keep anyone else from using them."

"He wasn't much of an ecologist, was he?" Matt said.

Cienfuegos grinned. "You could call him an accidental ecologist. His real motive was to collect as much loot as possible. He rebuilt the biosphere, improving and refining it until he had a model for the Scorpion Star."

"Let's go inside," said Listen, her eyes bright with excitement.

"No one has done that since the scientists collected plants to make the jungle you saw," said the *jefe*. "That was eighty years ago."

Imagine being locked up all that time, Matt thought, looking at the miles of buildings. Generations had passed, wars had been fought, and governments had toppled. "Didn't El Patrón get curious about what was going on inside?" *If anything is,* he thought with a thrill of horror. *Maybe they're all dead.*

"He was interested for as long as it took to build the Scorpion Star," said Cienfuegos. "Then he had a new toy to play with. There are lots of things knocking around Opium that no one has bothered with for a long time."

Cienfuegos eased the hovercraft onto a magnetic strip. "I hope to hell the recharger still works. I wouldn't want to get stranded here." He opened the hatch, and all climbed out. The *jefe* produced a device like a TV remote and clicked in numbers. A door in the biosphere bubble opened up. It moved reluctantly, as though decades of dust had found its way into the machinery. "Dr. Rivas says we have to go through a screening process to keep germs from entering."

The door closed behind them, and Matt jumped at a sudden grinding, creaking noise. Ancient robots were coming to life, their arthritic limbs jerking into motion. Smaller machines hurried among them, oiling and flexing their joints. "They look like bugs! Big, horrible, ugly bugs!" cried Listen, trying to wrench open the door. "Don't let them touch me!" She screamed as the fully lubricated robots moved forward, their metal hands clicking.

"Easy, *chiquita*. They're programmed to disinfect us. I'll go first," said the *jefe*. But even he looked nervous as the ancient robots sprayed his clothes and the little machines crawled over him like mice to poke disinfectant into his ears and nose. When they were finished, they moved on to Matt, and he did his best not to panic. Listen tried to climb up the smooth wall of the bubble, but the robots pulled her down.

"Show some class. No drug lord would ever marry such a crybaby," Cienfuegos scolded.

"I don't care! They're big, horrible, ugly bugs!" yelled Listen. She batted away the little machines, but they kept on coming, and finally she rolled herself into a ball and endured the process. Then the robots cleansed Mirasol, who of course showed no reaction at all.

They were allowed through to a second chamber, where they were dried and told to breathe deeply by a large machine that belched scented air. "I believe this is to clear the germs that live inside us," said Cienfuegos. After an hour they were released to yet a third area, where new clothes were presented to them. These were white tunics, and each of them received the correct size. By now Listen had calmed down, and she fingered the cloth with interest.

When they had passed through the final door, they found themselves in a grove of trees whose branches stretched toward a distant glass ceiling. It was like a place in a dream where the colors were unusually clear and bright. The air had the smell of green, growing things. They heard a brook and saw the pond into which it emptied behind a screen of reeds. "It's raining," whispered Listen, her voice muted with awe.

"Yes, it is," said Matt. The room was so huge that clouds had formed between them and the ceiling, and cool drops pattered around them. In the distance, between stands of oak, laurel, and pine, was a field of golden wheat. People in white tunics bent to harvest it. "It's so peaceful," Matt said, and was swept by a longing to live in such a place forever.

Rain pocked the surface of the pond, and a frog suddenly bellowed, *Kre-ek! Kre-ek!* Another frog answered, and soon a whole chorus was calling.

Listen ran over to the pond and thrust her hands into the water. A loud splash followed. "Crap! I almost had him!"

"No, no, no, no, no," came a voice from behind the reeds. A second later a man emerged and shook his finger in front of the little girl's face. "Please do not tease the amphibians," he said. "They must sing if they are to mate."

Listen goggled at the strange man. His tunic and hair were streaming with water. "Are you a scientist?"

"The scientists have been gone for years. I am a frogherd," the man said.

Listen burst into laughter. "A *frogherd*? What do you do? Chase 'em up and down the pool?"

"Frogherd is an honorable profession," the man said stiffly. "You are obviously a brat and should be penned up with the other immatures."

Cienfuegos laughed. "You're right about that, *señor*. But we are visitors and can only stay a few hours."

"Visitors?" The man frowned at the unfamiliar word.

"People from outside."

"I have heard of such beings but thought it was a legend." A frog croaked, and the man's head jerked toward the sound. He seemed to have forgotten the existence of anything else.

"What happened to the scientists?" asked Matt.

The frogherd turned back with a look of impatience. "They have gone to Gaia, but there is no need for them anymore. We know everything about our world and merely care for our companion animals and plants."

"You don't say! Where's Gaia?" Cienfuegos asked.

"Surely you are joking. Gaia is not a place. She is the Mother of All, the Earth Herself. Now I must return to my frogs."

"Wait! I've brought the new *patrón* to see you," said the *jefe*.

"*Patrón?* I seem to have heard that word before," mused the man. "Is it a kind of animal?"

"He's your boss," said Cienfuegos.

"Oh, no, no, no, no, no," the man fussed. "No one owns nature. We are all Earth's creatures." He walked off without saying good-bye.

"What a strange person," said Matt.

"The original inhabitants were top-grade scientists, but at least four generations have passed," Cienfuegos said. "Perhaps their children have gone back to the wild."

They walked on, admiring the birds and trees. "I think this is the ecosystem of northern Europe," the *jefe* said. He pulled out a map and peered at it closely. "Yes. This is northern Europe, or at least the way it was." They sat down on a small hill. In the distance the frogherd swam around the pool, flexing his long, white legs.

"I can see why you wanted to come here," said Matt. "It's the most magical place I've seen."

"I had another reason." Cienfuegos fell silent for a moment, perhaps considering how much to reveal. "Before I came here, I studied agriculture in college."

"I know. Chapultepec University. Celia told me," Matt said.

"If you ever want a story to get all over the place, tell it to Celia," said the *jefe* with some annoyance. "She probably told you that the farmland in Aztlán was poisoned with chemicals." Matt nodded. "It would break your heart to see it. What were once beautiful fields of corn and wheat have turned into desert. The plants grow twisted. Men and women who tend them fall ill with strange diseases. It's like what happened to the Maya in Yucatán long ago. They ruined their environment, and their civilization collapsed. You'd think their descendants would have learned not to kill the earth that feeds them, but humans are endlessly stupid and greedy."

A line of men and women in white tunics walked from the distant grain fields. Each carried a basket of wheat on his or her head, and they walked with such grace that Matt caught his breath. They were like a line of music.

"Originally, I planned to go to the United States," said Cienfuegos. "There's a place in the north where they study how to repair soil, but as you know, I ended up here. Then I heard about the biosphere." A rain cloud passed briefly and pattered rain on their heads. Listen turned up her face and tried to catch the drops in her mouth. Mirasol didn't appear to notice, but somehow in this cool, clean atmosphere, she looked more alive. More beautiful.

"The first biosphere, the one in the United States, had a problem," the *jefe* continued. "No matter how careful the scientists were, they couldn't keep the soil productive. Toxic waste built up."

The harvesters had disappeared among trees at the far end of the building. Matt would have liked to follow them, to see what they did with the grain, but he didn't want to interrupt Cienfuegos.

"El Patrón solved the problem. Oh, not by himself," the *jefe* said. "He hired top scientists to do it. They were the first inhabitants of the Alacrán biosphere, and according to Dr. Rivas, they were imprisoned here. They had to find a way to purify the soil or they would die when the system broke down. A typical El Patrón strategy."

"Why didn't he let them go home after they fixed things?" asked Listen.

Cienfuegos laughed. "Once the old man owned something, he never let it go."

"So they stayed here, had children, and turned into frogherds."

"I think that's what happened," said the *jefe*.

"We're here to find out how they purified the soil," Matt guessed.

"I hope so. This place is huge, and I don't know who to ask. If all the scientists are gone, perhaps no one can explain how it was done." Cienfuegos unfolded the map again and laid it out so the children could look at it. Buildings were labeled NORTHERN EUROPE, THE MEDITERRANEAN, OCEANIA, SUB-SAHARAN AFRICA—

"Let's look at that," cried Listen, poking the map with her finger.

"I didn't know you could read," Matt said.

"Can't read everything. But I know Africa," the little girl declared.

"Let me see. We probably have time to visit four ecosystems on this trip. We can pass through Africa on the way to the Mushroom Forest," Cienfuegos said.

25

THE MUSHROOM MASTER

Matt realized that the biosphere was much larger than he'd imagined. There were dozens of buildings, each a mile or more long. If the Scorpion Star was built on this scale, it was no wonder they needed hovercrafts to get around. Most of the regions were named for parts of the world, but a few were labeled WATER, AIR, KITCHEN and, more mysteriously, GAIA'S DOMAIN, DORMANCY, and BRAT ENCLOSURE. The Mushroom Forest was two buildings away. Beyond it was KITCHEN and a small building labeled EXIT.

Northern Europe was so full of trees they couldn't see the other end of the building for a while, but eventually they came to a long corridor. The air grew warmer and more humid as they walked, and presently they came to the next building, Oceania. Before them lay a wide expanse of water, beside which curved a white sandy beach. The water flowed in and withdrew in a regular rhythm. "Look at that. They've found a way to make tides," said Cienfuegos, pleased.

Listen chased the water as it receded and ran back when it returned. She paddled it with her hands. "It's salty," she cried, licking her fingers. Seagulls floated overhead, and farther out, where it was too hazy to see clearly, a shoal of something dimpled the water. "Oh, boy! I could live here forever!" she yelled, dancing on the sand. Cienfuegos watched her for a while and then urged her to move on because they had to finish the visit before nightfall.

They came to a rocky shore full of tide pools. Sea anemones waved as the water washed over them. Large colonies of purple mussels hung from the rocks, and pale green crabs and orange starfish lurked in shadowy pools. Two men were walking slowly along the beach, one of them busily clicking a calculator. "The mussel population is down," he announced. The other man removed one of the starfish. "Better take a couple of crabs, too," advised the first. "They're upsetting the balance."

The second man dropped the starfish and crabs into a bag tied to his waist. He put his hands together as though praying, and Listen ran up to him. "What are you doing?" she asked. He ignored her, and she tugged at his tunic. "Hey, mister, are you going to eat those animals?"

He looked down, clearly irritated. "You should be in the Brat Enclosure," he said.

"We're visitors," Cienfuegos said quickly. "We're from outside."

The two men looked at him as though he were insane. "Nobody lives Outside," the man with the calculator said.

"There are legends about people who do," the other argued. "Once I saw a UFO fly overhead."

"Only *bobos* believe in UFOs," sneered the man with the

calculator. "You probably believe in the vampire king with his zombie army, too."

"There's no reason to be nasty just because I have an open mind."

Matt trotted ahead, leaving the men to argue, and signaled for the others to follow him. The story of the vampire king was too much like El Patrón for comfort. Listen huffed and puffed after him until they left the rocky shore and came to a mangrove swamp.

Sluggish fish with large fins clustered around the roots. A group of men were hunting them with spears, and a woman warned, "Don't take more than sixteen."

When an animal was collected, the hunter folded his hands and said, "Praise Gaia for this gift of food."

"They *are* praying," said Listen.

"They don't act like scientists," said Cienfuegos. He glanced up at the ceiling. "We don't have much time, so let's keep moving." Listen said she was tired, and he lifted her to his shoulders. "If you pull my ears, you're getting dumped," he warned just as she reached out to do exactly that.

Next was Sub-Saharan Africa. Giant trees, hung with vines, alternated with grasslands dotted with acacia trees. Antelopes lifted their heads and watched as they passed. "Are there lions here?" whispered Listen, as though speaking aloud might attract them.

"I hope not," said Cienfuegos. "I think the main predator here is man. Dr. Rivas said this place wasn't an exact copy of the real world, only an ecosystem that could exist permanently on its own. Its purpose was to create the Scorpion Star, and I don't think they've got lions and grizzly bears up there."

Butterflies as big as Listen's hand flapped by, and praying

mantises the size of mice swayed drunkenly back and forth as they hunted. "So this is Africa." The little girl sighed. Guinea fowl scrabbled in the underbrush, and three-foot-long lizards flicked their tongues at the intruders. Cienfuegos put the little girl down and warned her not to touch anything without asking first. But he needn't have worried. The little girl was cowed by the size and variety of animals around her.

A guinea fowl came right up to Matt's feet and pecked around his toes. "It isn't afraid," he said. He bent down to pet it, and it pecked his hand.

A group of women approached them. One consulted a small calculator and said, "Praise Gaia! There are two excess guinea fowl." Immediately, the others pounced on two birds and wrung their necks.

"Meat!" they exulted, raising their hands to the ceiling. "Meat!" They danced around with the two dead guinea fowls.

"Gaia has given us food," shouted the woman with the calculator. "Gaia is great!"

"Join with us, Sister," cried one of the women, taking Mirasol's hand. The eejit obediently joined the circle and copied what the others were doing.

"Let's get out of here," whispered Listen, but Matt hesitated. Mirasol looked no different from the other women, swaying, clapping, and singing praises to Mother Earth. No one had noticed that she wasn't normal. He wished then that she could stay here forever, but they would soon discover that she could do nothing on her own. He took her hand and led her away.

They hurried through this building because the heat was really unbearable. But the Mushroom Forest was just as warm, and the air was heavy with the smell of fungi. It was also fairly dark. White, brown, orange, and luminous green mushrooms sprouted on every side. A group of teenagers, swathed in gauze masks, were harvesting while others scooped up the soil the plants had grown in.

An old man with white hair rushed up to the visitors. "Hey! You're not wearing masks." He thrust four at them. "If you're not careful, you'll grow a little mushroom forest of your own inside your lungs."

"Mil gracias, señor," said Cienfuegos. "We didn't know there was a danger." He quickly fastened a mask over Listen's nose, and Matt did the same for Mirasol. "This is a most unusual place, sir. I would be most honored if you would tell me about it."

The white-haired man seemed pleased by his interest. "You are obviously a person of intelligence," he replied. "These young ones"—he waved his hand at the teenagers—"are newly awakened from Dormancy and have the brains of rabbits. Not," he hastened to say, "that I have anything against rabbits. All Gaia's creatures are blessed."

He proceeded to list the name of each fungus and what its specialty was. "These," he said, "are Shaggy Manes." Matt looked out over a sea of white humps covered with tattered fringes. "They're experts at killing *E. coli*, which gives you the runs, and *Staph aureus*, which makes you grow pimples. They munch them up like candy. Wonderful plants!" The man's enthusiasm was contagious, and Matt couldn't help smiling at him. "You look as though you could use a little of their help," the man said, smiling back.

Matt self-consciously ran his hand over the remnants of the acne he'd acquired at the plankton factory.

"Never mind. The pimples go away when you get older," the old man said kindly. "Shaggy Manes eat chemicals, too.

Once upon a time farmers put so much fertilizer and pesticides on their crops that the ground became polluted. Nowadays we aren't so foolish, but if we were, the Shaggy Manes would come to our rescue." He smiled proudly at his mushrooms as though they were a herd of prize cattle.

"You mean . . . you mean these little things can pull poison out of the soil?" asked Cienfuegos.

"They not only pull it out, they digest it so that it's harmless. It's like a snack to them. *Mmm! Yummy pesticides!*"

The *jefe* looked stunned. "All those years of failed crops and sickened farmers . . . It could have been avoided so easily."

"Not so easily," cautioned the white-haired man. "You have to learn how it's done—which mushrooms to grow, how to grow them, and what to do with them. The ones that eat mercury, for example, must be burned. You can reuse the metal." The man led them around the fields, pointing out fungi that ate oil or pesticides or bacteria. "This little beauty," he said, gesturing at a dull purple mushroom glistening with slime, "likes radioactivity. Positively wolfs it down. It's called a Gomphidius." He patted it fondly.

"Surely you don't have radioactivity here," said Cienfuegos.

"Never," the old man said, "but if we did, we'd be ready."

"This is what I've been looking for all my life," murmured the *jefe*. "May I ask your name, sir?"

"I'm the Mushroom Master," the man said.

"I would give anything to learn your skill. I could take one day off every week and come here. Please, sir, would you teach me?"

"Of course," said the Mushroom Master, looking somewhat startled by Cienfuegos's fervent plea.

The *jefe* turned to Matt. "You'd order me to come, wouldn't you, *mi patrón*?"

"Of course," said Matt, understanding that Cienfuegos couldn't leave his work unless directly ordered.

"Then it's all right." The *jefe* closed his eyes briefly.

They toured the rest of the building, for only part of it was kept for renewing the soil. The rest grew edible mushrooms. By now Listen was complaining loudly that she was crotting tired, that she'd had it up to here with weird people, and that she was going to eat a Gomphidius, slime and all, if they didn't get going.

"Patience," said Cienfuegos. He picked her up and thanked the Mushroom Master at great length. They headed for the area labeled KITCHEN.

26

THE BRAT ENCLOSURE

In the kitchen, cooks were busily processing food—mostly vegetables—and servers were laying out banana leaves for plates. Groups of men and women drifted in, seated themselves, and were given rice and stew.

"I think we should wait until we get back to the hovercraft to eat," said Cienfuegos, putting Listen onto the ground. "Everything is balanced in this place. I don't know if they have enough food for visitors."

"I wouldn't touch that crap, anyway," said Listen.

The stew consisted of grasshoppers and caterpillars in a thick gluey sauce with chopped-up carrots and onions. The diners ate with gusto, using their fingers. They could have as many helpings as they liked by raising a hand. A server would hurry over and refill the banana leaf.

Matt watched them. "Excuse me," he began, uncertain how to open a conversation. The diners ignored him. "Excuse me," he repeated. "Where are the children?" It bothered him that the only child he'd seen was Listen.

A woman looked up. "You must be newly emerged from Dormancy. Everyone knows they're in the Brat Enclosure." She gestured at a door.

"Those Dormancy graduates," a man said, shaking his head. "Their brains don't wake up for weeks."

"Do children ever leave the Brat Enclosure?" asked Matt.

"Not if I can help it." The woman laughed. The others seemed to enjoy the joke too.

"We take turns watching them," the man explained. "It's tiring to chase after prehumans, and we prefer to keep them corralled."

"I'm a visitor from outside and don't know anything," said Matt. "Please tell me what you mean by Dormancy."

"He's dreaming. Nobody lives Outside," someone remarked.

"Poor *bobo*. He must be from one of the outer ecosystems, perhaps Tundra," said the woman. "I've heard they're not too bright."

"For shame! They're all Gaia's children," scolded another woman.

"All Gaia's children are blessed," murmured the others, as though this were a ritual response. The men and women went back to feeding.

"The job of immatures is to play and to learn to love Gaia," said a man, taking pity on Matt's ignorance. "They don't work. But when they reach the age of fourteen, they are put into a dormant phase for a year or so, and knowledge of the tasks they must perform as adults is fed into their brains. It's very intense, and Dormants take a while to recover from it. You probably went through it recently, and that's why you can't think straight.

Don't worry. You'll get better soon. Everyone does before the first mating season."

"I remember those days," said an older man. He wiped thick, bug-infested gravy off his chin with a finger and licked off the results. "I was allowed to produce three offspring because Gaia took the first one to Herself. I always wondered which ones were mine when I tended the Brat Herd—not that it mattered. All were children of Gaia."

"All Gaia's children are blessed," murmured the group. They started a discussion of past mating seasons. Matt was aware of Cienfuegos watching him with a wicked smile.

"I only wanted to find out about the children," he protested.

"Me too," cried Listen, and before anyone could stop her, she ran over and threw open the door. A din of high-pitched voices, shouts, and laughter poured out. Beyond was a vast space filled with gentle hills and reed-shadowed pools. Flowering bushes surrounded perfect lawns, where children of all sizes, from toddlers to the early teens, engaged in every sort of activity. Babies were being rocked in cradles by adult caretakers. Children of Listen's age were making mud pies. Older ones observed animals and plants under the watchful gaze of teachers. Still others played games or splashed in pools or climbed trees. They shrieked for the pure joy of shrieking.

Adults in white tunics gravely comforted those who had fallen down or who'd been upset. Some of the smaller children were asleep in beds lined up under trees. Matt felt a lump in his throat. So many! All perfect, with no deadness in their eyes. They were loved. They were wanted. They were happy.

"Where did *you* come from?" said a caretaker from the Enclosure, sweeping Listen up in his arms. "You're too little to be running around by yourself."

She screamed, and Cienfuegos reacted instantly, snatching the little girl from the man's grasp. "She's a visitor. She's from Outside. We're leaving now." He slammed the door in the face of the startled caretaker and said, "Come along, you little pre-humans. We have a hovercraft to catch."

Leaving was far easier than coming in. A shuttle cart from Exit took them to the room where their clothes were. After changing, a door opened and they found themselves outside, next to the holoport. *"¡Vete!"* shouted Cienfuegos, scaring off a coyote that was sniffing around the door of the hovercraft. "You'd like some owl tacos, wouldn't you?" He hurled a stone after the fleeing animal.

The *jefe* produced bottles of water and sandwiches for all of them. Listen was so tired, she started crying. Cienfuegos unrolled a foam mattress in front of the owl cages and told her to lie down. "I forgot how short your legs are, *chiquita*. I'm not used to little kids."

"Y-you rescued me." She sniffled. "That man was going to lock me up in the Brat Enclosure, and I'd never see Mbongeni again." She broke into loud sobs exactly like her night terrors that had awakened Matt.

"Don't cry. Please don't cry," he said, his hand trembling over the distraught girl as though she were a flame he dared not touch. "Oh, damn all microchips! Damn everything!" Cienfuegos hurled himself from the hovercraft and disappeared among the mesquite trees. It was so sudden and unexpected that Listen was stopped in mid-howl. She stared at the empty door, still shaking.

Matt scooted over and held her as he'd seen the adults hold unhappy children in the Brat Enclosure. "It's all right," he said,

rocking her back and forth. "People like Cienfuegos are warriors, *muy feroz.* They don't know how to be gentle. He's like the
coyote, always running, and sometimes he bites. But trust me,
he's not angry at you." *He's angry at the microchip in his brain,* Matt
thought. *Something about Listen upset him. I wonder what it was.*

The little girl sucked her thumb and watched the door.
Eventually she stretched out on the mattress and fell asleep.

Cienfuegos didn't return, and Matt worried about what to
do. He couldn't fly such a complicated hovercraft. He checked
the water in the owl cages, and they fluffed their feathers at him.
He pulled the door closed. Who knew what was lurking outside? When Listen woke up, he told her one of Celia's stories
about how Noah put all the animals in a boat and saved them
from a flood.

"How big was this boat?" Listen asked suspiciously.

"Very big," Matt said. "Shut up and pay attention." He continued with the tale, explaining that only two of each kind
could go. All the rest drowned.

"Is that what happened to the dinosaurs?" said the little girl.

"Yes. Noah couldn't fit the dinosaurs in. They swam and
swam, but eventually they got tired and sank," Matt said, impro-
vising. He hadn't heard the story for years and was surprised at
how good it made him feel. He remembered Celia's serious
face in the lamplight next to his bed, where he lay with his
stuffed toys. *Noah sent out a crow to see if there was any dry land
around,* said Celia. *You know how selfish crows are. They don't care
about anyone but themselves, so this one found a cornfield and stayed
there.* She didn't like crows because they raided the garden
behind the house.

"When the crow didn't return, Noah sent out a dove," said
Matt now.

"Was it a white-winged dove?" Listen asked, and after a second added, *"Zenaida asiatica."*

He remembered that she'd been stuffed full of facts by Dr. Rivas. "It didn't have a scientific name," he said. "It was a lady dove called Blanca Luz, and her husband was called El Guapo. They had a nest with six baby chicks."

"I don't believe that," the little girl said.

"How do you know? You weren't there." Matt finished the story, and Listen announced that she was hungry. He searched and found two more sandwiches, which he divided between Listen and Mirasol. They had enough water for several days, but no more food. He told Mirasol to curl up on the foam mattress with Listen, and he kept watch from the pilot's chair. What he would do if a lion got inside he couldn't imagine.

As often happened in the desert, the temperature dropped forty degrees after dark. Matt searched farther and found thermal blankets he used to cover the girls and the owls. The birds began a mournful hooting. Their feet scratched the bottom of the cages, while outside an excited bark told Matt that the coyote was back. He could hear the beast scuffling around the edge of the door.

Tomorrow I'll have to turn the owls loose, he thought. *I'll take Mirasol and Listen back to the biosphere.* Except that he didn't know the combination for opening the door. Could he bang on the walls? Would the inhabitants even notice?

He heard a thump and a yelp from outside. "*¡Maldito sea!* I'll kick you so hard you'll spit out shoelaces," swore Cienfuegos. The man threw open the door. "Why didn't you turn on the outside light? I couldn't see anything in the dark."

Matt was so relieved he didn't take offense. "I didn't know how."

"Tomorrow I'll teach you. You might as well learn to fly, too. ¡Bueno! You looked after the girls and the livestock, and I see you were standing guard like a real man. Move over. I'll do the driving."

Matt happily vacated the seat. *You were standing guard like a real man* played over and over in his head like a piece of music. He'd done the right thing. He was worthy to be *patrón*. He smiled into the darkness as the hovercraft took off and didn't worry that Cienfuegos said not another word until they arrived in Ajo.

27

PLANNING A PARTY

Now came the time Matt had been waiting for. Under his direction, the beam that sterilized trains crossing the border was shut off. Ten doctors and twenty nurses, plus equipment, medicine, and all the other things they would need arrived safely and were loaded into hovercrafts. With them came a dozen hovercraft pilots and a hundred new bodyguards recruited from Scotland and Ireland. This was urged by Daft Donald to shore up security.

The new people went to Paradise for orientation and training. All of the medical staff stayed there, except for one, who came to the hospital in Ajo. With the money Matt was paying them, he wanted them to concentrate on working with Dr. Rivas. Nurse Fiona was reassigned to washing dishes. She complained so bitterly that Matt gave her the job of watching Listen, although this didn't stop the complaints. "What do they think I am? A bloody babysitter?" she yowled to Celia. "That little scrap is the devil's spawn. She's got a mouth on her that would do a sailor proud."

The train returned to Aztlán, bearing Esperanza's samples and several tons of opium.

Matt felt guilty about continuing the trade, but it was only a temporary measure. The cookie cans outside the opium factory by now extended half a mile, and the dealers in Africa, Europe, and Asia were getting hysterical. Happy Man Hikwa, Glass Eye Dabengwa's representative, called again and again. At first Matt ignored him. The last thing he wanted to do was deal with Glass Eye, but Cienfuegos pointed out that this would look like weakness to the sinister drug lord.

"I've seen him at El Patrón's parties," the *jefe* said. "He has an instinct for terrorizing the weakest person in the room. He killed the Old Man of the Mountains, who you may remember was in charge of the Iraqi cartel."

Matt remembered. The Old Man of the Mountains had once been a feared and dreaded drug lord. He was one hundred and twenty years old by the time Matt saw him, broken by illness and stoked up to the eyeballs with hashish. Glass Eye had sat next to him at a banquet. The boy couldn't hear what the African said, but he saw the effect on the Old Man. The Iraqi tried to move away, but Glass Eye detained him with a heavy hand. And then the Old Man slumped facedown into a plate of mashed potatoes.

I should have changed the seating arrangement, El Patrón had said, in a mellow mood after the banquet. *Something about Glass Eye brings on heart problems. Ah, well. There's a silver lining. The Old Man's customers are up for grabs.*

Matt remembered this now as he accessed the holoport and found Happy Man's new address. He was no longer in Africa.

He had a new address in Marijuana, on the eastern border of
Opium, and his light was blinking furiously.

Happy Man Hikwa was sitting in front of the portal. There
was an ashtray full of cigarette butts, a pot of coffee, and a bottle
of aguardente, a villainous Mozambican vodka that smelled like
crushed beetles. Hikwa looked like he'd been living in front of
the portal. His clothes, a plaid suit without a shirt, were dirty,
and Matt could smell stale marijuana smoke. He was a drug
addict.

Matt smiled to himself. Drug addicts were the easiest clients
to handle. They would agree to anything.

"You . . . you . . . ," said Happy Man, having difficulty forming the words. "You *child*! Where is Mr. Alacrán?"

"I am the new Lord of Opium," said Matt. "Mr. Alacrán is
busy. What do you want?"

It took a moment for the African dealer to process this
information. "You're a clone," he finally said. "Clones can't run
businesses."

"I *am* El Patrón," said Matt, smarting from the insult.

Happy Man pushed away from the screen. Behind him was
a room in chaos full of old food containers and weapons, and
beyond was a wide window showing a city. Matt could see skyscrapers chopped in two as though a giant machete had sliced
through them. A line of limousines, not unlike Hitler's old car,
was making its way through rubble. "What's going on?" asked
Matt.

Hikwa looked to where the boy was pointing. "Oh, that.
We're still pacifying the city. A few of the Farm Patrolmen are
holding out." A flash followed by screams showed a building
being blown up. Fires raged in the distance.

"You're destroying your own city," said Matt, appalled.

Happy Man giggled. "We don't need it. We've got more." He reached for the bottle of aguardente and took a swig. "Anyway, this place was a ruin when we got it. It used to be called Ciudad Juarez, and the crotters who ran this place were trying to rebuild. Fat chance. Glass Eye showed them what's what. We"—he hiccuped—"put all their women and children into an empty swimming pool and used them for target practice."

Matt had seen enough. No way was he going to open the border for a shipment to Dabengwa. He reached for the off button.

"Hey! You can't go! We need our opium!" cried Happy Man Hikwa, but by that time the holoport had closed.

Matt sat, shaken by what he'd seen. He knew things were bad in the old Dope Confederacy, but this mindless destruction was worse than anything he'd imagined. He accessed addresses in Nuevo Laredo and Matamoros. In each one a window showed a scene of devastation. What kind of country was Glass Eye building? He and his men acted like a swarm of locusts Matt had seen on an old TV show. *Eat one field, move on to the next.* You needed infinite fields to keep an army like that going.

Matt found a few portals in rural areas where marijuana and tobacco were grown. The crops had withered, and the bodies of eejits filled dry canals.

He was too exhausted to look anymore. Even though the holoport had adjusted to his slightly different handprint, the scanner still made him nauseated. He went to El Patrón's apartment and lay down. The windows opened onto green lawns, and the odors of flowers and cut grass drifted in. The sound of eejits using scissors to trim the lawns soothed him. El Patrón's empire was evil, all right, but it was still alive.

Soon, Matt promised himself, he would rip out the opium

and plant different crops. Cattle would be turned onto healthy fields of grass. When the eejits were free, he would offer them jobs as normal farmers, or they'd go back to whatever lives they'd had before. It would be their choice. Far fewer were dying now that Matt had added meat and vegetables to their diet.

His days were packed with work—learning to ride Real Horses, flying a hovercraft, and even driving Hitler's old car with Daft Donald at his side. The seat was pushed forward so he could reach the pedals, and he enjoyed the cheers from the gardeners and Farm Patrol. *"¡Viva El Patrón!"* they shouted, as though the old man had been reborn. Sometimes Matt had the creepy feeling that El Patrón was actually sitting in the backseat, admiring his kingdom from the dark halls of the dead. *This is the most excitement I've had in years,* the old man said, grinning with delight. Matt shivered. He knew the backseat was empty, but he didn't turn around to look.

Best of all was planning the party. It would be the greatest celebration ever seen in Opium. Ton-Ton, Chacho, and Fidelito were coming on the next train, and their eyes would drop out when they saw what Matt had arranged. They would have a circus, a professional soccer game, a rodeo, guitarists from Portugal, and food undreamed of by boys who had lived in a plankton factory. Ton-Ton had eaten ice cream only a few times in his life, and Fidelito had only seen pictures of it. So many wonderful experiences lay in store for Matt's *compadres.* He had only to stretch out his hand, and whatever he wanted was his.

Cienfuegos had been correct about Esperanza. She seemed to have forgotten about Major Beltrán's existence and had little interest in anything besides the plant and animal samples. Matt managed one unsatisfactory meeting with María, with her mother present, and called the girl his *novia* openly. Esperanza only gave him a tight smile that reminded him of a sprung mousetrap.

As for Cienfuegos, he was short-tempered for reasons Matt couldn't discover. The man was never rude, and yet the boy sensed a gathering tension. It worried him, and finally he approached Celia about it.

"He's being foolish," Celia said. "He knew what Dr. Rivas would do when the new staff arrived."

"Dr. Rivas was going to train them," said Matt. "Is there something else I should know about?"

"Oh, dear," said Celia, putting down the soup ladle she was holding and wiping her hands on her apron. "New staff can't just be turned loose in Opium."

"What are you talking about?" Matt had the queasy feeling that things had moved out of his control.

"Remember what I said about the bodyguards and Farm Patrolmen being microchipped?"

"What do you mean? I didn't tell Dr. Rivas to alter their brains!" cried Matt in horror.

"They're violent men," Celia said. "El Patrón said that chipping them was no different from a rancher turning bulls into steers. Left alone, bulls fight, and it's dangerous for anyone around them. That's why Major Beltrán had to die. He intended to kill you when he discovered you were the only Alacrán left. Cienfuegos understood."

"You knew about the murder! You were in favor of it!" Matt was astounded. This was the woman who had sung him lullabies when he was a small child, but who had also coldly watched El Patrón die.

"I may be only a cook, but I've been close to the center of

power for fifteen years," said Celia. "You don't rule a country by being weak. Thousands have died in Opium and will keep on dying if we don't do something. The drug trade is too powerful to stop without shedding blood. God will forgive us our sins if we manage to stamp it out."

Matt sat down, feeling that the room had suddenly filled with shadows. El Patrón had shot down a passenger plane to avert a war. Esperanza felt righteous about killing the eejits in Cocaine. Dr. Rivas held poor Mbongeni hostage to fend off Glass Eye. Where did it all end? How much wickedness could you do in the service of good before it turned into pure evil?

"Cienfuegos blames me for microchipping the new bodyguards," said Matt.

"He's too personally involved," Celia said.

"What, exactly, is the effect of the process on him?" Matt asked.

The woman frowned. "You know the chips keep him from harming you or leaving the country. They also forbid him to feel pity or love."

Matt thought about the *jefe*'s reaction to Listen's tears. The man had clearly wanted to comfort the little girl, but he dared not do it. If he had touched her, what would have happened? Would he have doubled up in agony as he had when he attacked Matt?

"Cienfuegos is a very unusual man," concluded Celia after a moment's thought. "He fought like a tiger when the Farm Patrol first caught him. Very strong-minded people have more resistance to the microchips."

Without being asked, she dished up a bowl of soup for Matt and set out bread still warm from the oven. The boy wished she would sit with him, but Celia no longer thought it was proper. He ate without much appetite. Cienfuegos did care about people, Matt thought. He liked Listen, pest though she was, and he was upset about the new bodyguards. It was there under the surface, and it was driving him mad.

Matt finished his meal with *dulce de leche* ice cream covered in marshmallow sauce. How Fidelito would like that when he arrived! The thought cheered Matt up, and he made plans to find more things to delight the little boy.

"By the way, you don't have to keep paying the doctors and nurses those outrageous salaries," said Celia, removing his dishes to the sink. "They've been microchipped too. You can't have people who hold the power of life and death out of control either."

Matt eagerly watched the train cross the border on the holoport screen. Workers unloaded suitcases and carried them to waiting hovercrafts. Wonderful, magical passengers disembarked and stretched their legs in the shimmering desert heat. First a group of musicians, five men and one woman, got out, carrying their instruments. They removed their coats and looked around to see what must have been a land of fables to them, a zombie kingdom ruled by an ancient vampire. They wouldn't realize that the workers around them were zombies.

Next came a group of cowboys for the rodeo—short, raw-boned men who seemed made of gristle and steel. Their leather jackets were scuffed from being thrown from horses. After the rodeo, Matt planned to stage a *pachanga*, a kind of bullfight where no animal got killed.

The soccer players from Brazil and Argentina were taller than the cowboys and moved with easy grace like thorough-bred horses. Matt had never seen a soccer match, because El

Patrón didn't like sports. He said that only games with real risks were suitable for men.

The sport he approved of was called *pok-a-tok* and had been played by the ancient Maya. It was somewhat similar to soccer. The players used a hard rubber ball, which they weren't allowed to touch with their hands, and scored points by knocking it through a stone ring. It was more like a religious ceremony than a game, El Patrón said, a symbolic battle between life and death. The winning team represented life, and the losers, who represented death, got their heads cut off.

A troupe of tightrope walkers and trapeze artists hauled equipment out of the train. Long ago circuses had contained lions and tigers, but now those animals were extinct. *Except here,* Matt thought happily. Wrestlers followed, walking with a rolling gait as though they were already in the arena. They were dressed in Levi's and T-shirts, but inside their suitcases were costumes that would transform them into creatures of fantasy.

Matt watched anxiously as the performers were flown off to Ajo. He wasn't going to let them anywhere near Dr. Rivas, and anyhow they were short-time visitors. Now the door of the last car opened and out tumbled Fidelito, pursued by Ton-Ton and Chacho. Matt could almost hear Ton-Ton shout, *C-come back or I'll beat the stuffing out of you!* But he knew the big boy would never do it, and so did Fidelito. The little boy danced around, kicking up sprays of sand. Then a fourth person stepped out of the train.

Sor Artemesia.

Matt's heart leapt to his throat. María was on the train! She had to be. Esperanza had relented at the last moment and decided that he was good enough for her daughter. Matt watched in a fever as the nun stepped down carefully and grimaced when her feet touched the hot sand. She gave a command, and Fidelito immediately stopped prancing and took her hand. Together they walked to the last remaining hovercraft.

Workers swarmed over the train to remove cartons of supplies. María never appeared.

28

SOR ARTEMESIA

Matt and Listen waited at the Ajo holoport to greet his friends. He saw the black craft grow from a distant speck to a sleek ship with a bulging, transparent top. As it settled down, he saw that the pilot was not one of the new pilots he'd hired, but Cienfuegos. Fidelito was bouncing up and down, trying to touch the ceiling, and the *jefe* pushed him into a seat.

"Are those crots?" asked Listen.

"They're Real Children. Don't use that word," Matt said. "It's extremely insulting."

"If they're crots, they won't be smart enough to care," the little girl said reasonably.

"Just stop swearing. It's a bad habit."

The hovercraft set down, and the antigravity recharger snaked up and fastened onto the nose cone. The door opened. Fidelito attempted to jump out and was yanked back inside.

"You turkey," said Ton-Ton. "L-ladies go first."

Cienfuegos helped *Sor* Artemesia step down, and she looked around until she found Matt. "Please forgive me, *mi patrón*. Doña Esperanza sent me away because she says I'm a bad influence on María. I didn't know where else to go."

"You are most welcome here," said the boy, and he meant it. The more he saw of the nun, the better he liked her. "María must be unhappy, though."

"She is. Doña Esperanza hardly ever pays attention to her."

By now Fidelito had wriggled free, and he ran straight to Matt. "You're really here. You're not a picture. Wow! What a great place! Is it all yours?"

"Of c-course it is," said Ton-Ton, catching up to him. "He's the king."

Chacho came behind, somewhat hesitantly. His face was thinner, and he had dark circles under his eyes. "You really are a king. I bet movie stars don't have as much as this."

"I was just lucky," said Matt, embarrassed. "I'm the same kid you knew at the plankton factory." But he could see that wealth made a difference. Both Ton-Ton and Chacho looked amazed by the huge gardens, the hacienda, the many other buildings, and in the distance, the swimming pool winking in the desert light.

"*Mi abuelita* says that if you have food, water, and a roof over your head, you're rich," Fidelito said, quoting his beloved grandmother. "You don't need a lot of stuff. After all, you can't eat a hundred hamburgers or sleep in a hundred beds."

"That's crap," said Listen. "You can save the hamburgers for another day."

"Who are you?"

"I'm Listen, not that it's any of your business."

Fidelito reached out and she slapped him. Hard. "Don't touch me."

"Okay," said the little boy, rubbing his face. He seemed hypnotized by her.

"*¡Que barbaridad!* He was only trying to be friendly," *Sor* Artemesia said.

"Don't want friends," Listen said.

"Whether you want them or not, there's no excuse for being unkind."

Listen made a rude noise. "You aren't the boss of me. I'm going to grow up to be beautiful and marry a drug lord."

"You're already pretty," said Fidelito. Ton-Ton and Chacho rolled their eyes.

"Crot you!" swore Listen. That was too much for *Sor* Artemesia. She picked up the little girl in an expert hold and strode off.

Cienfuegos laughed. "Sister Artemesia knows her way around here. I'll bet she's on her way to the kitchen to find a bar of soap. I'd better calm things down before they go too far."

He left, and the boys went up the marble steps of the hacienda. The trunks of orange trees on either side were painted white, and the dark-green leaves above were starred with creamy blossoms. An eejit was spraying them with water. More eejits dusted and polished furniture in the great entry hall. Like the field workers, they were dressed in drab brown uniforms, but they needed no hats because they worked indoors. "You sure have a lot of servants," remarked Chacho. Matt realized that he hadn't noticed the deadness in the workers' eyes or the mechanical way they went about their chores.

"El Patrón liked a lot of servants," Matt said uneasily. The boys knew about eejits, of course. TV shows portrayed them as crazed zombies that lurched around and ate brains. Nothing could have been further from the dreary reality.

A peacock, sitting in a window, gave a loud cry as the boys passed. "Ohhh," Fidelito said, sighing. "What a beautiful bird!" And so Matt was saved from discussing eejits. They passed a side garden with a blue tile fountain, and Chacho halted.

He went up to the fountain and put his hands into the spray. "Water," he said reverently. He stood there, letting it fill his palms and pour over the sides. "So much water," he murmured. Several peacocks posed like works of art on a velvety green lawn. At the top of a tree, a mockingbird sang. Chacho listened with his mouth open, as it trilled one song after another until it flew away.

Matt heard, in the silence that followed, the sound of an eejit clipping the lawn with scissors. "Let's go," he said. He hurried them on to El Patrón's private wing, where one of the rooms had been cleared for the boys. Matt made a mental note to have another one prepared for *Sor* Artemesia.

Ton-Ton, Chacho, and Fidelito eased their way past a clutter of ancient Egyptian statues and Roman glassware that had, through the centuries, taken on the rainbow color of soap bubbles. The plunder of a long lifetime crowded the halls. Ton-Ton reached for a rooster made of pure gold and hesitated. "It's okay. You can pick it up," said Matt.

"I m-might leave fingerprints on it. My hands are, uh, dirty."

"You can roll it in the mud for all I care. Relax, *compadre*. There aren't any Keepers here," Matt said, referring to the men who had enslaved them at the plankton factory.

"It's too p-pretty." Ton-Ton looked longingly at the golden rooster. "Where did you get it?"

"It belonged to El Patrón. He collected tons of stuff." Matt saw that he would have to do something to put his friend at ease. "You should see his music boxes. Remember the gentleman and lady doing the Mexican Hat Dance? There are dozens more."

Ton-Ton brightened. Machines were something he understood. They went on, past paintings of men and women in somber black clothes. The effect was chilling, as though they were being watched by a throng of disapproving ghosts. "There's a nice one," cried Fidelito. In one alcove was the portrait of the woman in a white dress that had impressed Matt. "Is that María?"

"It can't be," said Matt, smiling because he, too, thought it looked like María. "These paintings are hundreds of years old." The woman smiled as though she had a secret she was dying to tell someone. He thought she was like a ray of light in the dim hallway.

"There's a label," Chacho said. He brushed away a plume of dust from a brass plate below the picture. "It says 'Goya.' What's a Goya?"

"I think it was the artist's name," said Matt.

They gathered in front of the portrait, admiring the skill with which it was drawn. "What I wouldn't give to be able to paint like that," said Chacho.

"You can study art here," offered Matt. "I can hire teachers." Chacho gave him a sad smile that meant, *Oh, sure. Poor boys like me don't get such chances.* But Matt meant it. Why shouldn't the boys stay here forever? They had no homes to return to. Why shouldn't he, with his limitless wealth, give them everything they wanted? Chacho could paint; Ton-Ton could build machines. It was too soon to know what Fidelito was good at, but something would turn up.

They spent an hour playing with music boxes. Ton-Ton took one apart and showed everyone how the gears moved and how a metal hammer hit notes on a tiny marimba. More gears moved the dancers' feet or caused them to twirl around. It was complicated, but the older boy knew exactly how everything fit together. It was the way Ton-Ton thought.

The most interesting box had three people on it—a cowboy playing a guitar, a woman in an old-fashioned dress, and another man dressed in black. They danced around one another, with the man in black always coming between them. Having three dancers meant the mechanism was far more complex than the other boxes, said Ton-Ton. Even he wasn't sure how it was done.

"You'll never know, dear, /how much I love you," the cowboy sang in a tinny voice, *"please don't take my sunshine away."* But the man in black was dedicated to taking the sunshine away, and the lovers never got together.

Celia appeared at the door and announced that dinner was served. Salad bowls had been placed at every setting, and Cienfuegos, *Sor* Artemesia, and Listen were already seated. Listen treated the nun with something close to respect. Matt wondered what had happened.

Long purple shadows flowed out of the west. The tall windows were open, and the smell of freshly cut grass wafted in. Ton-Ton, Chacho, and Fidelito sat up very straight, not touching their salads. Matt guessed that *Sor* Artemesia had drilled them on table manners since they'd arrived from the plankton factory. In the old days they would have fallen on the food like starving wolves.

"Always use the outermost fork first," the nun instructed them. "That is for salad. As the courses appear, you move to the

next fork and the next. The same applies to knives and spoons."
It was no wonder the boys were cowed. Even Matt wasn't sure
how to navigate through twelve utensils. She must have asked
for the place settings in order to teach them.

Mirasol filled everyone's goblets with fruit juice, except for
Cienfuegos, who had his usual *pulque*.

"I've heard of this banquet hall," said *Sor* Artemesia. "Long
ago, before María's parents broke up, they used to come here to
meet with El Patrón and his fellow criminals. I, of course, was
left with the girls. Which reminds me, Matt, how did the
Alacráns take your being the heir? I imagine Emilia's nose was
put out of joint when she discovered she wasn't going to be the
Lady of Opium."

Matt dropped his fork on the floor, and Mirasol quickly
replaced it with another. The boys were already eating, glancing
at *Sor* Artemesia to be sure she approved. Listen was picking
mushrooms, which she disliked, out of her salad. Matt met
Cienfuegos's eyes. How were they going to get out of this one?

"By the way, where are Emilia and her father?" asked the
nun. "I thought they'd be here, if only to hear about María.
What's the matter? Have I said something wrong?"

Cienfuegos nodded at Matt. "You have to tell her."

"Esperanza should have done it," said the boy.

"But she didn't. She tossed the ball to you."

"I don't want the damn ball!"

By now everyone had stopped eating, and *Sor* Artemesia
looked worried. "Is something wrong?" she said.

"You bet there is," said Listen. "They're both dead."

Sister Artemesia gasped and automatically crossed herself.
"Was there an accident?"

"Nope. El Patrón killed them. Everyone who went to his

funeral drank poisoned wine and fell down dee-diddly-dead."

"Shut up, you fool!" shouted Matt. *Sor* Artemesia put her head down as though she were about to faint. He jumped up to catch her, and Ton-Ton put his hands out.

But the nun raised her head again, and although she was pale, she seemed in control. "I shouldn't have been surprised," she said. "Time and again I warned them. 'Don't build your house at the foot of a volcano.' But they didn't listen. The money was too good." She sipped the fruit juice absently. "When Doña Esperanza left, I went with her, and when Senator Mendoza sent the girls to boarding school, I made sure to be one of the teachers."

"What was Esperanza doing for her daughters?" asked Matt. "María thought her mother had abandoned her."

Sor Artemesia sighed deeply. "Some women are not meant to be mothers. Doña Esperanza loved power, and her daughters were merely an annoyance. Which is worse? Someone who is there and resents your existence, or someone who is gone? I did my best for the girls, but Emilia was difficult. She had the worst traits of both her parents, and now it has brought her to this. If you would excuse me, *mi patrón*, I would like to go to the chapel and pray for their souls."

Matt thought briefly of the shrine to Jesús Malverde. That would never do. The church Celia had gone to was several miles away through the opium fields. Its priest had died at the funeral along with the rest. Matt didn't know whether a church was usable without a priest.

"I'll take you," Cienfuegos said. "We'll have to drive, but I'm sure Daft Donald wouldn't mind taking out the car. I'll wait outside the church, you understand. We wouldn't want God to strike it with lightning."

He gently helped the nun to her feet. They walked together, neither looking at each other nor speaking. In the fading light of sunset, they seemed more like figures from the paintings than living beings. No one said a word until their footsteps had faded away and Mirasol had lit the chandeliers.

29

NIGHT TERRORS

P oor María!" Ton-Ton said at last.

"She visited me in the hospital every day," said Chacho. "She brought me sweets when the nurses weren't looking. You know, they only feed you boiled vegetables and soup. Why do bad things have to happen to good people?"

"You were horrible to *Sor* Artemesia," Matt said to Listen. "Didn't you realize she cared about those people?"

"She asked a question and I answered it," said the little girl pertly. She had a heap of unwanted mushrooms next to her salad bowl and now amused herself by flicking them across the table.

"Stop that! Where did you get such an ugly word like 'dee-diddly-dead'?"

"That's what Dr. Rivas says when he kills the rabbits."

"Well, it's nasty, and I don't want you to use it. How did you find out about the funeral, anyway?" said Matt.

"Dr. Rivas and Cienfuegos talked about it. They don't call me Listen for nothing." The little girl scowled. "You're El Patrón's replacement. For all we know you could be feeding us poison right now, and we wouldn't know until it was too late."

"Don't be such an idiot," Matt said, but he considered how she'd been raised, watching the doctor kill animals and hiding out from the Bug. It was going to take work to rehumanize her.

Mirasol took away the salad bowls and began serving the dishes Matt had planned to delight his friends—porterhouse steak, scalloped potatoes, and asparagus. At first the boys were too disturbed to notice what they were eating, but the unfamiliar richness of the food soon got through to them. Ton-Ton attacked his steak as though it might run away, and Fidelito chomped asparagus like a horse eating carrots.

"We should remember our table manners out of respect for *Sor* Artemesia," protested Chacho. But the food was too good, and besides, she wasn't there.

"More scalped potatoes, please," Fidelito said.

"Th-that's *scalloped* potatoes, you loon," said Ton-Ton.

"Waitress, give Fidelito more potatoes," Matt said.

"Why do you repeat orders to her?" asked Chacho. "And why do you call her Waitress? I thought her name was Mirasol."

Matt watched as the girl mechanically filled Fidelito's plate. "That's enough, Waitress," he said. She went back to the serving station and stared out at the room with unseeing eyes.

"That's weird," Chacho said.

"Sh-she isn't normal," said Ton-Ton, suddenly alert. "Her eyes . . ."

"She isn't normal," confirmed Matt.

Ton-Ton got up and looked directly into her face. Mirasol didn't react. "I d-don't believe it. We've been around these, uh, servants for hours and I didn't see it." He took her hand, and she accepted it passively. "She's just a kid."

"El Patrón didn't care about age," Matt said. "There are eejits who are no older than six. He liked them because of their high voices or, if they had no talent for music, their little hands. Child eejits are very good for weeding young opium plants."

"She's a zombie!" shrilled Fidelito. He leapt from his chair and made for the hallway. At the last minute he came to a halt. "There's more of them out there," he whimpered. "All those people sweeping and dusting. They're all zombies. They'll eat my brain." A child of the plankton factory, he grabbed a table knife to defend himself.

"There are no such things as zombies," Matt said wearily. "Eejits are only sad people who've lost control over themselves. They're slaves. If you tell Mirasol to drink water and don't tell her when to stop, she'll drink until her stomach explodes."

The brutal description got to Fidelito faster than any other explanation. "Truly?" he asked. "Her stomach will explode?"

"Probably. I don't plan to find out." In a way Matt was glad he'd waited until now to reveal the existence of eejits. It was harder to evoke sympathy for the mindless robots who toiled in the fields. Mirasol was a beautiful girl who could have been a friend or a neighbor. "Sit down, Fidelito. She hasn't served dessert yet, and I have a lot to tell you."

Warily, the little boy went back to his chair, hitching it closer to the large, protective presence of Ton-Ton. Matt sent Mirasol to get crème caramel custards. Then he told them of all he had learned about the microchips, how some servants were devastated by the operation and others were almost normal. He told them of the dead man he'd seen in the fields long ago, of the eejit pens, the bad air, and the pellets that gave the slaves the bare minimum food for survival. He told them how people like Cienfuegos were controlled—and that they should never mention it in the *jefe*'s presence. He told them of how he'd tried to change Mirasol's name and of the terrible torture she had endured.

Night fell. Neither Cienfuegos nor *Sor* Artemesia returned. In spite of the chandeliers, the banquet hall filled up with shadows, making the gloomy paintings even gloomier. A cool wind rose out of the desert, bringing the mineral smell of dust and bitter, dry vegetation.

"Now I want to show you something," Matt said. He told Mirasol to sit and placed a crème caramel custard in front of her. "Eat, Waitress." As always, she began ravenously, but when the flavor hit her tongue, she paused. She held the spoon in her mouth. Her eyes almost registered intelligence. "This has been the only way I've been able to reach her," said Matt. "It's connected to some memory so powerful that even the microchips can't erase it. I've dedicated my life to freeing her. And the other eejits too."

The solemnity of that statement impressed the boys. They looked at Matt as though he had suddenly grown taller and nobler than the ordinary run of humanity. "Y-you're the only one who can do it," Ton-Ton said at last.

"I'm afraid so," said Matt. "I was given the power. I wish I knew what to do with it."

That night Listen had one of her nightmares. Her screams penetrated Matt's sleep, and he fell out of bed. He fumbled for his flashlight and switched it on. "I'm coming!" he shouted, although Listen probably couldn't hear him.

The boys had tumbled out of their own beds and were

standing in the hallway. "*¡Por Dios!* What's happened to her?" cried Ton-Ton. He and the others followed Matt, but *Sor* Artemesia had gotten there before them.

"You! Take your hands off her!" shouted the nun. The light was on, and Matt saw Fiona shaking the little girl violently.

"She's possessed by the devil," gasped Fiona. "Nasty, spiteful little beast!"

Sor Artemesia sprinted over and slapped Fiona. She pulled Listen away and held her in her arms. The little girl was a terrifying sight, even worse than the times Matt had found her. Her eyes were open and staring in utter panic. Her arms flailed, and she screamed without ceasing, as though what she saw was too dreadful to bear. "It's all right. It's all right," said Matt, kneeling beside her. He stroked her arm, and *Sor* Artemesia held her firmly so she wouldn't harm herself.

"Please wake up," said Fidelito, crying himself. "We're here. We'll protect you."

"She can't wake up," said the nun, rocking the little girl. "This is no ordinary nightmare."

"She's possessed," snarled Fiona.

"Who knows what damage you did, shaking her," said *Sor* Artemesia. "Get this sorry excuse for a nurse out of here, *mi patrón*, and call the doctor." Matt didn't question her authority, in spite of being the boss of all bosses. He rang for help, and soon two of the new guards came in, bowing nervously at being in the presence of the Lord of Opium, followed by the new doctor.

"Take this dishwasher back to her duties at the hospital," Matt said, pointing at Fiona. She yelled curses at them, but the boy had no time to waste on her. Listen was still screaming and staring into a horror only she could see. The doctor, an athletic-looking man who might have been Korean, measured her heart rate and wiped the sweat off the little girl's face.

"It's a night terror," he said. "You did exactly right to restrain her, *señora*. Children can hurt themselves when they're in the grip of this."

"I've seen it before," said *Sor* Artemesia. "She can neither see nor hear us, but the fit will pass."

"Listen has nightmares, but she won't tell me what they are," said Matt.

"She can't, *chico*—Ah! Excuse me! You're the *patrón*. I meant no disrespect, sir." The doctor looked flustered.

"It's all right," Matt said. "Why can't she tell me?"

"Because this is a night terror, something very different from a dream," said the doctor. "It comes from deep inside. It's caused by fever or exhaustion or sometimes by trauma. Do you know if anything bad has happened to her?"

She was terrorized by the Bug. She watched Dr. Rivas turn rabbits dee-diddly-dead. Her only companion was a brain-damaged boy. "Her life hasn't been perfect," Matt said. "Can you help her?"

"I wish I could, but all medical science can do is wait for her to recover. With any luck, she'll outgrow the condition."

"I know something," said Chacho. They turned to him. Matt had forgotten his presence, so different was he from the days when he'd been a noisy, cheerful companion. His face was marked by suffering. He had breathed far less than was good for him when trapped in the boneyard in Aztlán. But more than that, his spirit had been affected by his terrible ordeal. "One of the little kids in the plankton factory had these fits," he said. "The Keepers used to put his feet into cool water. And they washed his neck and chest."

Sor Artemesia immediately set about doing this with the

boys' help, and soon—whether it was the treatment or the fit had run its course—the little girl's cries ceased, and she fell into an exhausted sleep.

"That's one for the books," the doctor said, praising Chacho. "I'll have to remember that." The boy smiled his grave smile.

Sor Artemesia slept in Listen's room, but the boys were in no mood to go to bed. Matt led them to the kitchen, which was of course deserted in the middle of the night. There they made popcorn and feasted on ice cream until Fidelito got sick. "Th-that's the only way you, uh, learn when you've had enough," Ton-Ton said. "By eating too much. N-next time you'll know."

"No, he won't," said Chacho. "Fidelito always eats until he falls over."

"Ohhhh, leave me alone," the little boy moaned, but he soon recovered. Matt led them on an exploration of the gardens, now eerily silent without the bustle of gardeners and eejits. The peacocks were roosting in trees. There was no moon, and the Milky Way provided a strange, silvery light over walkways and the ghostly trunks of orange trees. The air was heavy with the scent of flowers.

"I n-never saw stars like this," said Ton-Ton, as they sat on the top of the marble steps leading out of the hacienda. "They must have always been there."

"The sky was muddy in Aztlán," said Chacho.

"Not on the seashore," remembered Fidelito. "*Mi abuelita* used to find pictures in the night sky—Orion the Hunter, the Seven Sisters, the Big and Little Bears. She told me stories about them, but there was one big, red star she said was new. See? There it is."

"That's a space station," Matt said.

"¿*Verdád?* You can live on it?" asked the little boy.

"It's like a big city inside a clear bubble. It has buildings and even hovercrafts to fly around in. In the middle is a big garden with trees and animals."

"What a great place to live," said Chacho. "You could see the whole Earth. But it would always be night, wouldn't it?"

Matt considered. On TV shows outer space was black, so the skies of the Scorpion Star were probably black too. "There are lights inside the buildings," he said. "I saw close-up pictures of them from a telescope."

"If only I could go there," said Chacho, with the same longing Matt had noticed in the Bug. And then Matt thought, *I own that space station. I can go there whenever I want.*

The thought gave him a chill. When he was young, Celia had told him that the Indians in her village carried charms to keep from being carried off by the wind. And Matt had experienced a strange terror while lying exposed under a dark sky, as though he might lose his hold on the Earth and find himself lost among all those bright, inhuman lights. "Earth is a good place," he said.

"Not anymore," said Chacho, and Matt could find no answer for that. A small sliver of moon rose before the dawn. A rooster crowed somewhere in the shadowy buildings surrounding the hacienda, to be answered by another and another.

Ton-Ton yawned. "I'm too sleepy to, uh, think now, Matt, but tell me more about the m-microchips later. They seem to work together like the inside of a music box."

"What a brilliant idea," said Matt. "They must work together. If you can figure out how to break a music box, maybe you can do the same to microchips."

"Give a box to Fidelito," Chacho said. "He'll break it for free."

30

A VISIT TO THE AJO HILLS

In the morning, as the doctor had predicted, Listen had no memory of her night terror. She shuffled into the banquet room, and Matt noticed how frail she looked. *Sor* Artemesia lifted her into a chair and fetched a bowl of oatmeal. Mirasol waited patiently by the food cart.

"I don't like oatmeal," said Listen.

"Tough," said *Sor* Artemesia.

Only Matt was up, and so they had the huge banquet hall to themselves. It was going to be a hot day. The desert had at last decided spring was over, and a heat haze shimmered over the garden. Birds flew back and forth through a lawn sprinkler.

"María told me about Mirasol," said the nun, buttering a slice of toast.

"She has nothing to worry about. I talked to her alone and told her," said Matt.

"I know you did. As for whether there's something to worry about, I'm not sure."

"You can't think Mirasol is a—is a *girlfriend*," stammered Matt.

"You pity her, which is a good thing, but it must not go any further." *Sor* Artemesia bit into her toast and licked the butter off her fingers.

Matt was almost speechless with outrage. "You've been talking to Cienfuegos. Why does everyone think I'm such a monster?"

"Because you're El Patrón reborn."

"I'm not the same!" Matt felt his face tighten and a current of heat run under his skin.

"Not yet," said the nun. "You've been given great power, and stronger people than you have fallen under its spell. Think of me as the slave that used to stand in Caesar's chariot and whisper into his ear, 'Remember. You, too, are mortal.'"

"How dare you say things like that to me!"

"I dare because I serve God, not the rulers of this world. I thought about El Patrón while I was praying in the chapel. How did a reasonably decent village boy wind up killing so many people? And I thought about whether you were strong enough to avoid his fate. Cienfuegos told me about your party. You've realized that you can have anything and do anything you want. You even have a clone."

"That wasn't my doing!" cried Matt.

"No, it wasn't. But don't you see the tremendous temptation set out before you? To live forever, to have everything you desire. That's what hollowed out El Patrón's soul."

Sor Artemesia was trembling, and Matt realized that she was afraid. He remembered her nervousness when he'd first contacted the Convent of Santa Clara, and her obvious fear of Esperanza. Yet here she was, risking her life for what she believed was right. All Matt had to do was pass the word along to Cienfuegos, and the nun would join Major Beltrán under the poppy fields. He had that much power. Cienfuegos wouldn't want to do it, of course, but he was powerless to disobey a direct order. El Patrón had given such orders many times.

"I'm not angry," he said, although he was, a little. "I think you could stand up to Glass Eye Dabengwa."

The nun laughed shakily. "I'm not that crazy. You're still young. You can change. And now that I've said my piece, *mi patrón*, let's stay friends."

She held out her hand. After a moment's hesitation, Matt took it. "Friends," he said. He saw that Listen was paying close attention to the conversation.

"What party?" the little girl asked.

"Something you won't be invited to if you breathe one word about it," said Matt, for now Ton-Ton, Chacho, and Fidelito had finally rolled out of bed and were sniffing with great interest the food Mirasol had on her cart.

The preparations for the party were in full swing. During the day Matt kept the boys away from the hacienda to keep from spoiling the surprise. He showed them a Safe Horse at the stables and said they could ride it if they liked. They were fascinated, walking around the animal and patting its sleek hide. "You couldn't stand behind a Real Horse like that, Fidelito," said Matt. "He'd knock the stuffing out of you."

"Isn't this a Real Horse?" asked Ton-Ton, and Matt was sorry he'd brought up the subject.

"It's a Safe Horse. They're—controlled."

"That means, uh, they have microchips in their brains."

"Poor creature," said Chacho, stroking the animal's nose. "I remember you telling the Keepers about putting chips into a horse's brain. You said it was a good thing, because horses weren't smart."

"I didn't understand what it meant then," Matt said. He showed them the Real Horses used by the Farm Patrol, and the boys were immediately eager to ride. Matt promised that Cienfuegos would teach them.

They went for a long drive in Hitler's car. Matt drove at first, and after a while Daft Donald showed Ton-Ton how to do it. Ton-Ton was a natural. He took to the machine as though he were part of it. Soon he was cruising around corners at a speed Matt had never dared to try, and Daft Donald grinned and flapped his hands as though they were flying. Suddenly they came around a bend and almost collided with a group of men dressed in tan jumpsuits and floppy hats. Ton-Ton slammed on the brakes.

A Farm Patrolman cantered up and tipped his hat. "Taking the lads out for a spin, are you, *mi patrón*? 'Tis good to see you about." He turned and barked, "Walk faster!" at the eejits. They trotted double time and soon cleared the road. "Well, I'd best be after them before they trample the crop." He tipped his hat again, and Matt nodded stiffly.

The workers disappeared in a cloud of dust kicked up by their feet. Ton-Ton, Chacho, and Fidelito looked stunned. "They're like robots," said Chacho. "They didn't even flinch when the car almost hit them."

"They couldn't," said Matt.

"Was that . . . *a Farm Patrolman*?" Fidelito asked, his eyes wide.

Matt said it was.

"So those are the bastards who took my father," said Chacho. "They took Ton-Ton's parents and Fidelito's grandma."

"They did not take *mi abuelita*!" the little boy cried. "She's in California, living in an orange grove. She has a little house, and she grows corn and sells it in the marketplace."

"All right! All right! Your grandma's in California," said Chacho. "Don't get mad."

"I'm not mad," Fidelito said. "I'm upset because you're telling lies."

"Okay, I'm a big fat liar," Chacho said. "Here. Do you want to punch me? Make you feel better?"

"N-no," said the little boy.

Ton-Ton drove on. They went past more workers bending and slashing opium pods. Every third field lay fallow, and every tenth was covered with young plants that were being weeded by children. Ton-Ton stopped to observe them. "I thought the p-plankton factory was bad," he said. "Do they, uh, work in the other fields when they grow up?"

Matt looked down at his hands. "Most of them don't live that long. I've improved their food, but something about the massive dose of microchips slows down their ability to grow."

"Let's go somewhere else," Fidelito shrilled. Daft Donald took over and drove them toward the Ajo hills. They left the opium plantation and went up a road that hadn't been repaired for a long time. Summer rains had washed out holes, and rocks had rolled down the hillsides. After a while they came to a turn-around and stopped.

Daft Donald wrote on his yellow pad: *Car won't go farther. We walk. Good picnic spot ahead.*

Matt thought they weren't far from the oasis. He hadn't told the boys about the place, and he guessed that Daft Donald didn't know about it either. He was reluctant to reveal its presence, because it was a secret shared by him and Tam Lin, and the man's spirit was still there in some way. The only person who wouldn't disturb this fragile connection was María.

"*¡Ay, que padre!* This is great!" said Ton-Ton. They had come out into a little valley. A stream flowed through the center, rippling around boulders and pooling up here and there into pockets of water stained brown by leaves. Water striders skated over the surface, making diamond patterns of light on the sand below. Rock daisies and desert stars bloomed along the bank, along with pepper grass that Fidelito picked off and chewed.

A scruffy brown animal with a long tail stood up abruptly and twitched its long nose at them. Ton-Ton reached for a rock, but Matt held his arm. "It's a coati. They're not dangerous."

"Looks like a big rat," said Ton-Ton, fingering the rock. The beast decided it didn't like the visitors and loped off with a rolling gait. Its fur was untidy, and its tail had been chewed on. It paused to scratch its butt lavishly before moving on.

"*¡Hombre!* He looks like he's been up all night drinking," said Chacho.

Next to the stream was a smooth, flat rock, and here Daft Donald unpacked the basket he'd been carrying. He put out sandwiches, cupcakes, oranges, and bottles of strawberry soda. "I remember this!" said Fidelito, grabbing one of the bottles. "We drank it when we escaped from the plankton factory."

Chacho turned away. Matt knew he was remembering the boneyard, and it wasn't something he wanted to recall. The boy quenched his thirst from the stream instead.

A small stand of cottonwoods provided shade, and the wind blew through the leaves with a dry, rattling sound. "Do you hear those leaves? Tam Lin used to say—" Matt stopped. He wasn't sure he wanted to talk about Tam Lin.

"He was l-like your father," Ton-Ton remembered. "Where is he now?"

Daft Donald scribbled on the yellow notepad before Matt could answer. *He was at El Patrón's funeral.*

"Oh! I'm sorry!" the big boy said.

Daft Donald wrote again. *He was my friend. He saved my life.*

"How did he do that?" asked Chacho, who had gotten used to the bodyguard's way of communicating and was as comfortable with it as Mr. Ortega.

I was at the funeral too. Tam Lin told me not to drink the wine.

"Why did he drink it?" Chacho asked.

Daft Donald paused for a moment before answering. *I think El Patrón had given him a direct order when they discussed the funeral. Tam Lin couldn't disobey.*

"Microchips," concluded Ton-Ton. The bodyguard nodded.

Matt was overcome by such a feeling of desolation that he trembled. Tam Lin had not committed suicide as Celia had thought. He'd been murdered as surely as if El Patrón had held a gun to his head and fired. It was the same mindless compulsion that made Cienfuegos unable to disobey a direct order or to flee the country or to comfort a little girl. Matt imagined Tam Lin holding the fatal glass of wine and knowing exactly what it would do.

He bent his head and started sobbing. He couldn't stop. It was like Listen's night terrors, except that he knew what was going on around him. Chacho and Ton-Ton put their arms around him, and Fidelito looked up into his face with something approaching panic. "Please don't cry," he said. "Your *padre* was a great hero. Heroes, well, they don't live so long. But they're *muy suave*, and we all admire them."

The little boy's inventive attempt to console him got through to Matt. He shivered and wiped his face on his sleeve. "It's okay, Fidelito. Tam Lin was a hero. I should remember that."

"Hey, we all lose it sometimes. Remember when Jorge was rolling bread crumbs at dinner?" said Chacho, recalling the sadistic Keeper at the plankton factory.

"Heck, yes," responded Ton-Ton. "He was g-giving us the big lecture about not having diseased opinions. He was rolling up crumbs and when he got a big glob, he popped it into his, uh, mouth."

"Only, a roach crawled onto the table and he mashed it up with the rest," Chacho crowed. "*Huck! Huck! Huck! Blort!* All over the table. Wonderful!"

"Yeah, he lost it big-time!" said Ton-Ton. "L-later, when we escaped, Luna, Flaco, and I locked the Keepers into their compound and covered all the exits with bags of salt. Th-they were in there a week, and the only water they had to drink was from the toilet."

"*Huck! Huck! Huck! Blort!*" shrieked Fidelito, beside himself with glee.

Matt knew what they were doing. They were covering for him by coming up with more and more outrageous stories. By the time they'd finished, Matt's breakdown was lost in a welter of crude jokes. Daft Donald wrote on his yellow pad, *You have good friends*, and Matt silently agreed.

When things had settled down and they were back to devouring cupcakes and oranges, Fidelito leaned against Matt and said, "What did Tam Lin used to say?"

"We were sitting under some cottonwoods, same as now, and the leaves were making that rattling sound," said Matt. "I said it was almost as though the trees were talking. Tam Lin said that the Hopi Indians believed the cottonwoods *were* talking, only that the voices were those of the Hopi gods. If you listened and were wise enough, he said, you could understand what they wanted you to do."

"Wow," said Fidelito. He fell silent. The wind gusted through the little valley, ruffling the surface of the pools and sending the leaves into a flurry of sound. After a while it died down, and the little boy said, "I wish I knew what they were telling me."

"So do I," said Matt. "So do I."

31

THE PARTY

A wide swath of desert had been converted into a soccer field and an arena that could be used for a circus, a rodeo, a wrestling ring, and a stage for the musicians. Bleachers had been set up for the boys, Listen, and *Sor* Artemesia. Matt wanted Celia, Mr. Ortega, Daft Donald, and Cienfuegos to be with them, but Celia said that this was a party for children and besides, it wasn't fitting for servants to sit with the Lord of Opium and his guests. She and the others had folding chairs some distance away and supplied themselves with food from a separate table.

It wasn't like El Patrón's parties. Those had been formal affairs with many speeches and hundreds of guests, as well as at least a hundred bodyguards. Dictators, generals, UN members, famous film stars, and even the remnants of old royal houses attended. The most important guests, of course, were the other drug lords, or at least those who weren't at war with Opium.

Glass Eye Dabengwa had been an ally then, but he rarely visited because he had so many enemies at home. No one was sorry about that. Sitting next to Glass Eye was like sitting next to a sleeping crocodile that might wake up at any moment and take a chunk out of you.

In those days there had been many tables covered with spotless white cloths and dishes trimmed in gold. Maids circulated with trays of drinks, and waiters provided cigars or hookahs for whoever wanted them. There was always a fountain of red wine with orange slices bobbing in it, and ice sculptures that melted into puddles before the festivities were over. There weren't going to be any wine fountains or hookahs at this party, and the guests were limited to six, not counting the servants. But in its way this celebration was grander than anything El Patrón had hosted.

The soccer match began after breakfast. It was preceded by Farm Patrolmen on horses, carrying the flags of both Argentina and Brazil. The horsemen galloped around the field in intricate patterns that were almost like a dance. Then the teams marched in. The game itself was a feast for Matt's eyes. He'd never seen a soccer match and didn't know the rules, but he thought that the players' movements were every bit as elegant as the horses' had been. Ton-Ton, who understood the game very well, yelled himself hoarse. The Argentineans won and were rewarded with gold coins.

Matt thought briefly of the Mayan game *pok-a-tok*. If these were the old days, the losing Brazilians would be minus their heads by now. They would have been sacrificed to the god of death who, pleased with the gift, might look the other way when it came time for the ruler of the country to die. Perhaps that was the attraction of the game for El Patrón.

After a midmorning break, trapeze artists swooped back and

forth on swings, moving with breathtaking speed. Five of them balanced on a man pedaling a bicycle across a tightrope. Others juggled flaming torches or chain saws with the motors going. It was almost too much to take in, and Matt realized that he should have spaced the events over several days. By the time the act was over, Listen was cranky. *Sor* Artemesia took her off for a nap, and so they missed the rodeo.

They came back in time for lunch and the *pachanga*, which everyone agreed was the best show yet. Rodeo riders played the parts of bullfighters, except that they carried no swords and there weren't any bulls. A *pachanga*, Matt explained, was far more dangerous than a bullfight because it involved cows. Cows were a lot brighter than bulls and wouldn't be fooled by a cape. They quickly learned that the real target was the man and acted accordingly.

The trick was to lure the cow into an enclosure, but most of the time the men had to run for their lives, with the animals thundering after them. El Patrón had loved this sport and laughed himself silly when someone got trampled. Matt made sure this didn't happen by having Farm Patrolmen on horseback ready to rescue someone who tripped.

Now came the part Fidelito was waiting for. The wrestlers climbed into the ring and swaggered around to let everyone see their costumes. El Pretzel had a black mask with purple and gold rays on it, and purple spandex pants. El Salero was in yellow and had a saltcellar tucked into his tights. La Lámpara, the Grease Spot, was so called because he oiled himself up before a match. He was wearing a slippery-looking green body stocking. El Muñeco, who was supposed to play the Good Guy, had refused to come to Opium. No amount of money would tempt him. As a replacement, Matt had hired El Angel, who didn't look a bit angelic in spite of his white attire and a halo, which he removed before the match.

Fidelito was beside himself with joy. He pointed out the dirty tricks committed by everyone except El Angel. The referee never seemed to see them, and when the boys screamed what was going on, he never seemed to hear them. Finally, after El Pretzel had tied up El Salero in spite of having salt thrown in his eyes, and after the Grease Spot had slithered out of everyone's grasp, El Angel came back from several losses to defeat everyone and be declared the winner.

"That was the best show *ever*." Fidelito sighed, rubbing his stomach as though he'd eaten a big meal.

"They're all cheaters," said Listen. "Even that Angel guy. I saw him trip the Grease Spot and whomp him on the back of the neck."

"I think it's an act," Matt said. "I don't think anyone gets hurt, or not much."

"It's real. My grandma said so, and she never told lies," Fidelito said.

The sun was low in the west when servants brought out the dinner. They had tamales and barbecued ribs, chiles rellenos, and moro crabs flown in from Yucatán. These had been El Patrón's favorite foods, and Matt liked them too. For dessert they had crème caramel custards. Mirasol had been serving meals all day, and Matt made sure she sat down now and ate something. But the food was rich, and both Fidelito and Listen were sick by the time dinner was over. *Sor* Artemesia offered to put them to bed.

The last activity of the day was classical guitar music. Both Matt and Chacho were anxious to hear it, and Ton-Ton stayed to be sociable, although his taste ran more to mariachi bands.

Celia, Daft Donald, and Cienfuegos went off to perform chores, and Mr. Ortega left to select the guitars that would be given to the musicians as awards. Thus, there were only three spectators to watch the concert.

The sky was dark by now. The stage was brightly lit and, unlike the other settings of the day, undecorated. There were no garish masks or prancing horses, no brightly colored streamers or circus folk banging drums to increase the excitement. The stage was bare except for six chairs. The backdrop was a simple white curtain. A light breeze blew through the water sprayers that had been installed overhead to cool the air.

Five men in black suits with stark white shirts filed out along with a woman in a long scarlet dress. The men carried guitars, but she carried panpipes, which she placed on one of the chairs. They began to play, starting with the traditional Portuguese fado, a word that meant "fate." The woman sang of lost love, of poverty, of being abandoned. Ton-Ton leaned over and said, "It's p-pretty depressing," and Chacho told him to shut up.

The next offering was flamenco music from southern Spain. One of the men sang and the woman danced, swirling her long skirt. Then they both danced with a rhythm that set Matt's pulse racing. They were like the gentleman and lady on El Patrón's music box, only much, much better. The man clapped to the beat while the lady danced around him, and Chacho and Matt joined in. Ton-Ton shrank down in his seat.

This was followed by classical guitar pieces by Villa-Lobos and a version of Rodrigo's *Andalusian Concerto* and *Fantasy for a Gentleman*. These had been El Patrón's favorites. He'd had them played over and over because he thought he was a gentleman, and maybe even a king.

Last of all the woman took up the panpipes and, accompanied by one guitarist, played the wild music of the Andes, which sounds so much like wind blowing through icy canyons.

When it was over, Chacho and Matt clapped wildly and stood up to show their appreciation. "Come with me," Matt told the musicians. "I have a workshop filled with the finest guitars in the world. I would be pleased if you would accept one for each of yourselves."

They thanked him enthusiastically, for who had not heard of the fabulous guitars of Opium? They packed up their instruments and followed, with Matt in the lead. It was a long walk, but by now the air had cooled. The black sky and brilliant stars worked their magic on the musicians. Matt heard them whispering among themselves. They had never seen anything like it. The skies over Portugal were murky, as were those of all of Europe. Even in the high Andes, the air was not so clean.

Mr. Ortega had thoughtfully lined the walk with candles housed in yellow sleeves to keep the wind from blowing them out. This, too, impressed the musicians. "They're like Chinese lanterns. So artistic," said the woman.

The guitar factory was ablaze with light. The performers were astounded by the wild variety of instruments hanging on racks, but when they reached the guitar room itself, their amazement knew no bounds. There were hundreds of the instruments. They tiptoed inside, almost afraid to approach such a treasure, and so at first they were not aware of Eusebio and Mr. Ortega sitting in the shadows at the far end of the room.

Mr. Ortega had laid out the six chosen instruments on Eusebio's work table.

First the woman turned and whispered, "Isn't that—"

And a man said, "I thought he was dead. He walked out one day and never came back."

"But it *is* him." Then all the musicians approached the two men and reverently bowed.

"Señor Orozco. Of course no one else could have made such magnificent instruments," said the woman. "We are so honored to meet you."

Eusebio stared straight ahead, not reacting.

"Are you all right, sir? Oh God! You haven't gone deaf?"

"He isn't deaf. I am," said Mr. Ortega, who could read lips. "He is as the others are in this godforsaken place. He is an eejit."

The woman gasped and fell to her knees. She took Eusebio's large, work-roughened hands in her own and gazed intently at his face. The other musicians also knelt, as though they were at a shrine.

"The greatest musician of our age has come to this," murmured one of the men.

But his voice was drowned out by Chacho's cry. The boy pushed past the performers and pulled Eusebio's hands away from the woman. "¡Por Dios! Look at me!" he said. "Don't you recognize me? I'm your son."

"If only I hadn't brought the musicians here," Matt said to Cienfuegos, who had been summoned as soon as the emergency happened.

"Sooner or later Chacho would have found out," said the *jefe*. The musicians had fled, taking their trophy guitars with them. Their faces showed clearly the contempt they had for Matt, though they had the good sense to remain silent. In their eyes he had taken the greatest musician of the age and turned him into a zombie.

"What am I going to do with Chacho?"

The boy crouched next to his father and refused to be moved. Ton-Ton sat with him. Neither of them looked at Matt.

"I can have a bed made up next to Eusebio. It won't be fancy, but I don't think Chacho is used to better."

"No, I mean how can I help Chacho?" asked Matt. "He was already trying to recover from his ordeal in Aztlán. Now he seems completely lost."

Cienfuegos looked at the two boys sitting at the guitar master's feet. They'd been there for an hour, unmoving. "You can't do anything," he said. "All he wants is for his father to be normal, and we know that's impossible."

"No, it isn't!" said Matt.

The *jefe* shrugged.

Mr. Ortega stirred in his chair. He, too, had been silent for an hour. "I remember you, Chacho," he said. "You were such a lively little boy, and so bright! Your mother had died and you'd been taken to your grandfather's house. Eusebio and I went there before we left for the United States. We thought we could send for you once we'd made our fortune, but . . ." His voice trailed off.

"How could Chacho have recognized his father's face after all this time?" asked Matt. "I remember things from when I was eight, but not clearly."

"He had a picture," Ton-Ton said, speaking for the first time. "When he came to, uh, the plankton factory, Jorge took it away from him and tore it up. 'Boys have to be broken and mended before they can become good citizens,' he said. 'No personal loyalties are allowed.'"

"I didn't know that," said Matt.

"Chacho, let me show you something." Mr. Ortega took up

one of the guitars. As before, he laid his cheek against the wood to feel the music with his bones. Then he played the flamenco music Eusebio had written, and it was even better than anything performed that night. The guitar maker turned toward the sound. His eyes cleared. He put his hand on Chacho's shoulder. The boy trembled.

"*Chacho,*" said Eusebio, and convulsed violently. Mr. Ortega stopped playing at once.

"Go on," pleaded the boy, but Mr. Ortega shook his head.

"It's too dangerous. Eejits—men in your father's condition— can't be put under too much stress. They break down and die." By now Eusebio's eyes had resumed their dull expression. "Believe me, this is better. If Matt is successful in his search for a cure, your father will be healed."

"I don't want to leave him," the boy said tearfully.

"Nor shall you," the music teacher said. "I'll move in and keep you company. It wouldn't be good for you to be alone with your father in his condition."

"I'll stay too," Ton-Ton blurted out.

"You don't have to," said Matt. "We could come back during the day."

"He n-needs me," the big boy said. "I don't want a fancy mansion with circuses and, uh, soccer matches. I don't want all that swanky stuff. Besides, maybe my parents are here somewhere, harvesting the d-damn poppies. Maybe Fidelito's grandma is here. Oh, go away and leave us alone!"

So Matt left, deeply shocked by the turn of events. All he had wanted was to make his friends happy, and it had gone horribly wrong. He went back along the path lit with candles. Above, the stars twinkled with a remote light and the Scorpion Star, as always, hovered over the southern hills.

32

DR. KIM'S EXPERIMENT

Matt told *Sor* Artemesia, Listen, and Fidelito what had happened at breakfast. "The poor child," said the nun. "I'll take the little ones over to visit him. Why don't you come with us?"

But Matt was still smarting from the rejection he'd received. "I have work to do."

"Don't leave it too long," advised *Sor* Artemesia. "It's harder to repair a friendship later."

Matt watched as soccer players, circus folk, rodeo riders, wrestlers, and musicians were loaded into hovercrafts to be transported to the departing train. "You don't look sorry to see them go," observed Cienfuegos.

"I'm not. The longer they stayed around, the more they would have found out," Matt said.

"I told them it was strictly a children's party and that the older Alacráns preferred to stay away."

"I wonder if they believed that," said the boy. The last hover-craft, loaded with musicians, took off. They had averted their faces from Matt.

The *jefe* flicked out his stiletto with that lightning speed that disturbed Matt and used it to clean his fingernails. "Sooner or later people are going to wonder why no one has seen Senator Mendoza. They will assume, of course, that Glass Eye killed the drug lords when he took over their countries."

"What about Fani? Isn't Glass Eye worried about her?"

Cienfuegos laughed. "He has more than a hundred daughters. He doesn't keep track."

"What do we do about the doctors and nurses? They surely know by now what happened."

"They aren't going anywhere." Cienfuegos slid the stiletto into its sheath inside his sleeve.

Matt remembered with a sick feeling that they had been microchipped during the orientation process. He wondered how Dr. Rivas had done it. Did he knock them out with sleeping medicine first? Or did he pretend that they needed an immunization shot? Thinking of the doctors, Matt decided he should start asking the one in Ajo how he planned to cure the eejits.

He walked to the hospital with an asthma inhaler in his pocket in case he was affected by the air. But this time he found it clean and fresh-smelling. Obviously, Fiona hadn't kept up the place when she was in charge. Even the bullhead vines had been uprooted and gravel laid down. It wasn't attractive, but at least you didn't wind up with thorns embedded in your shoes.

A nurse immediately ushered Matt to an office and brought him iced tea. "Dr. Kim will be with you as soon as he's out of the operating room," she told him. Matt was surprised, but pleased. It seemed that the doctor was already working on a cure.

He looked through books on a shelf while he waited and discovered they were in an alphabet he didn't even recognize. On the desk was a silver vase with a spray of purple orchids. That reminded him of the greenhouses between the hacienda and the deserted church. He hadn't visited them for a long time. Herbs and vegetables for the kitchen were grown there, but the main attraction for him, as a small child, had been the flowers.

Perhaps Chacho would like to see the flowers. Someday. Matt shrank from a meeting so soon after last night's disaster.

"What a pleasure to see you again, *mi patrón*," said Dr. Kim, coming into the office. He was the man who had treated Listen when she had her night terrors. He moved with the grace of an athlete, and when he shook Matt's hand, the boy felt a restrained power in his grip.

"The pleasure is mine as well," Matt said formally. "The nurse said you were in the operating room. Have you found a way to remove microchips?"

"Only some," the doctor said. "It's early days, I'm afraid."

"But you've had success," Matt insisted.

"Not much," Dr. Kim said. "I used a magnetic probe to take out perhaps two hundred chips from a subject, and yet the remaining number was so great it made no difference. The behavior of the subject before he was sacrificed was unchanged."

"Sacrificed?" asked Matt, thinking, *What are we talking about here? A pok-a-tok game?*

"It's a term scientists use when they terminate lab animals. After the operation, I removed the eejit's brain and homogenized it to estimate the number of microchips." The doctor might have been sharing a recipe for clam chowder.

"You're talking about a human being."

"We could use that term," said Dr. Kim. "But let's face it, he had the intellect of a lab rat." The doctor rang a bell, and an eejit appeared with a tea tray and rice crackers. "I see you have a drink, *mi patrón*, but you might like to try my green tea. It's imported from Korea and has an exquisite background flavor of ripe cherries."

"No, thank you," Matt said. "Why didn't you send the eejit back to work when he'd recovered? Why did you have to kill him?"

Dr. Kim smiled in the same smooth way that Dr. Rivas did when he explained science to a layman. "We have to collect data, *mi patrón*. Other scientists would find our studies useless without verification of the results. In an ordinary experiment, no less than forty lab animals are necessary before a paper can be published."

"I won't let you kill forty eejits!" exploded Matt. "The whole point of the experiment is to save them. *¡Por Dios!* How many have you slaughtered already?"

"Only five," the doctor said, and then he seemed to realize he was arguing with the Lord of Opium, not just a teenage boy. "I thought you had given your approval. Dr. Rivas said—"

"Dr. Rivas is in serious danger of becoming a lab rat himself!" shouted Matt. "Where did you get the eejits? How were they selected?"

Dr. Kim wiped his face. "Believe me, they were close to their expiry dates. Nurse Fiona checked."

"She's not a damned nurse! She's a fraud!" Matt promised to get Cienfuegos after her and lock her up, if there was such a thing as a jail in Opium. "I want this clearly understood, Dr. Kim. You are to sacrifice no more eejits. You will study them and you will cure them. I want results as soon as possible."

Matt's voice had changed. There was a power in it and an

inflexible will that made Dr. Kim turn pale. It was El Patrón's
voice, full of the potential for extreme violence. "I'll do anything you say," bleated the doctor. "I'll tell the other medical
staff."

The boy strode out of the office. *You certainly showed him,*
said the old voice in Matt's mind. *Put a burr up his tail, didn't you?*
I haven't had so much fun in years.

"Go back to where you belong," said Matt. "You've got a
tomb full of servants and treasure to play with."

They're boring, complained El Patrón. *There's nothing like the*
living for entertainment.

"I refuse to listen to you." The boy went to the hacienda and
played the piano until a shimmering curtain of music stood
between him and the voice. Then he went in search of
Cienfuegos.

The *jefe* sent bodyguards to drag Fiona from the hospital. There
were no jails in Opium, none being needed in a society where
everyone was controlled. Doors had locks, but since theft did
not occur, most of the keys had gone missing. "I could unperson her," suggested Cienfuegos, jerking his hands as though
snapping a twig.

"No!" said Matt.

"How about giving her another job, something so isolated
that she can't muck things up?"

"What sort of job?" Matt asked suspiciously.

"Nothing drastic. Something she can easily do." Cienfuegos
held out his hands as if to show he had no weapon concealed in
them.

"I don't want her tortured or killed, just neutralized."

The *jefe* gave his promise, and although Matt was fairly certain a secret was being kept from him, he agreed. "Another thing, Dr. Kim said he was only using eejits close to their expiry dates," said the boy. "You used that term once too. What does it mean?"

"It's an estimate," Cienfuegos said. "Now that you're feeding the eejits better and letting them rest longer, the life expectancy has increased. In the old days, when we could count on a steady supply, we didn't worry about maintenance. An eejit with the maximum dose of microchips lasted about six months."

"That little," murmured Matt.

"Otherwise they tended to pile up," the *jefe* explained. "No use feeding more than we could use, and neither the United States or Aztlán wanted the overflow. The original treaty between them and the drug lords stated that only a certain number could be allowed to cross the Dope Confederacy."

"So some people *were* successful."

"That was part of the plan." Cienfuegos and Matt were sitting in the kitchen, and in the background the French ex-chef fussed over a hollandaise sauce. An eejit boy was taking the strings off green beans. A dull-eyed woman scrubbed the floor. Her skirt was soaked with soapy water as she dragged a bucket behind her. A man followed with a giant sponge that he rinsed in a second bucket.

"If no one had succeeded, the flood of Illegals would have dried up," said Cienfuegos. "We needed a few success stories to whet the appetites of the others. Both of the governments of Aztlán and the United States agreed to this."

"It's so . . ."

"Corrupt," finished the *jefe*. "Now you know how big governments work. Not so different from El Patrón after all."

Celia entered with a basket of vegetables she had personally selected from the greenhouses. She laid out lettuces, tomatoes, celery, and spring onions on the table. "Would you like a salad for dinner, *mi patrón*?" she asked. "Or roasted eggplant with tomatoes?"

"You choose. Everything you cook is wonderful," responded Matt, wishing she wouldn't be so formal. Turning to Cienfuegos, he said, "How do you look up an expiry date?"

"It's tattooed on the bottom of the foot," said the *jefe*.

Matt caught his breath. He had writing on the bottom of his foot: PROPERTY OF THE ALACRÁN ESTATE. He'd meant to have it removed, but with one thing and another he'd forgotten.

"I see," he said.

"A worker with fewer microchips lasts longer and some, like Eusebio, can count on a normal life span. Personally, *mi caramelito*," Cienfuegos said to Celia, "I'd like a big beefsteak for dinner and to hell with the vegetables."

"You'll get what I cook," said Celia.

The *jefe* and Matt went out for a riding lesson. Matt had taken to this with enthusiasm and unmistakable talent, which was to be expected, since El Patrón had been a legendary horseman. They rode to the armory, where Cienfuegos discovered he had work to do. "You can return to the hacienda on your own, *mi patrón*," he said. "You don't need a babysitter anymore. Of course you can stay and watch. We're disposing of a couple of expired eejits in one of the fields."

Matt hastily left. He wondered how many bodies were buried out there. If it took one thousand eejits to run an opium farm, and each one lived for six months, and the ranch had existed for a hundred years . . . It was like one of the problems he'd been given when he studied math. The answer was two hundred thousand bodies. That was if only one thousand eejits were needed. The real number was much higher.

He ought to return to the hacienda to work on the books and answer frantic calls from dealers who hadn't received their shipments. But the weather was too good. He had a bottle of water attached to his saddle—Cienfuegos insisted that he go nowhere without it—and he had a packed lunch. Matt turned the horse toward the Ajo hills.

He skirted the eejit pens, knowing from experience how foul they were. That would be his next project, to construct better, cleaner housing. He could see ponds of fetid waste and a miasma of stinking haze near the water purification plant. An underground canal flowed from where the Colorado River emptied into the Gulf of California, and the water needed extensive cleaning. The river had become so polluted that nothing could live in it except mutated horrors. If you ate one of its fish, your lips blistered.

Long ago the gulf had extended farther north, and the water had been full of life. The great whales had used it as a nursery, but now the whales were gone and their bones filled a great pit near the plankton factory.

It was strange that Opium contained a running sore like the eejit pens. It was completely unnecessary, yet El Patrón had seen nothing wrong with housing his slaves there and feeding them plankton pellets. As Cienfuegos said, he was an accidental ecologist. If he'd paid more attention to the rest of the country, it would have deteriorated like the rest of the world.

The rest of the world had turned into God's Ashtray. Forests had been cut down, animals hunted to extinction, land poisoned, and water polluted. God had finally grown tired of his unruly children and was in the process of stubbing them out.

Matt rode on until he reached the dry streambed that led into the hills. He dismounted, led the horse into the shade of a cliff, and tethered it to a wooden trough. He filled the trough with water from an old, rusty pump, and the animal eagerly began drinking. "I'll be back in a couple of hours," the boy told it, scratching it under the chin at a sweet spot he'd discovered horses liked.

What a difference it made to have a creature that could respond to his voice! Unlike a Safe Horse, it could twitch its hide when flies landed on it and snort when it smelled something interesting. Matt had ordered that no more animals should be microchipped and that the ones already harmed should be cared for until the doctors discovered a cure. If Ton-Ton or Chacho got thrown off while learning to ride a Real Horse, that was their problem.

Thinking of his friends, he sighed and walked up the dry stream. When he got to the boulder blocking the trail, he looked back. Behind him was desert. Ahead—after he climbed through the donut hole—was another world. Matt hadn't been there since the first night he returned to Opium.

Creosote bushes and paloverde trees framed a small, narrow valley, and in the center was the oasis. A ripple of little fish moved away as he approached. "I'm back," Matt announced to no one in particular. He didn't expect an answer and didn't get one, yet he had the feeling that the place wasn't deserted. He sat in the shade of the old grape arbor, after sweeping the ground for scorpions, and ate his lunch.

A small flock of sandhill cranes floated on the far side of the pool. More circled in the air, uttering high, sweet cries. Tam Lin said that in the old days they flew all the way from Siberia to spend the winter here. When spring came they flew back, but El Patrón had fixed them so that they no longer migrated. *That first summer must have been hell for them,* the bodyguard had said. But the birds had adjusted, as the lions had, to the new environment.

"I'm the new Lord of Opium," Matt told Tam Lin. "I don't think you ever expected that. I sure didn't. Everyone treats me differently now. Celia calls me *patrón* and won't eat with me anymore." It felt good to talk, even if his friend couldn't answer.

Matt told him about Dr. Rivas, the Bug, and Listen. "I like Listen even though she's usually a pest. Cienfuegos likes her too. I guess you knew him." Matt talked about losing Chacho's friendship. He described how El Patrón sometimes seemed to be inside his head, telling him what to do.

Not here, said a voice. Matt jumped. He wasn't sure whether it had been an actual voice or an illusion. "What isn't here?" he said cautiously.

Heed the high cliffs, lad. They keep things out. Matt didn't understand the meaning of this. He wondered whether he was remembering something Tam Lin had actually said on one of their visits. He sat quietly for a while. The voice didn't come again.

33

MIRASOL DANCES

He had dinner alone with Mirasol, because everyone else was at the guitar factory. "It's not my fault," he told her. "I didn't turn Eusebio into an eejit, but they blame me just the same. Why can't they understand that I was just as much a prisoner as he was for many years?"

Mirasol watched his face, although her eyes showed no emotion. "I wish you were María," Matt said. "No, I shouldn't say that. You can't help being what you are." He gave her as much food as he thought healthy and then, on a whim, ordered her to take off her shoes. He knew this was a bad idea, but the impulse was irresistible.

The writing on the sole of her left foot was extremely small. He fetched a magnifying glass. It was a three-part number for month, day, and year, and the date had expired three months before.

Matt sat back, shocked. Mirasol looked healthy, and he'd been feeding her well. He tried to limit the amount of work she did, but she was programmed to work. If she didn't, she jittered. She might live for years or she might die tomorrow. The microchips had an unknown physical effect, and the more there were, the more they interfered with life.

"Oh, Mirasol," he said, taking her hands. What if she never awakened? What if she simply went out like a candle? A machine did that. It worked until one day you turned it on and nothing happened. Cienfuegos had warned him that awakening Mirasol could kill her, but what did it matter when she was doomed already?

"What do you like?" said Matt. Suddenly it seemed important to make the rest of her existence happy, if only he could figure out how. So far the only thing that penetrated the dull surface of her mind was a crème caramel custard. And then he thought of Eusebio.

Microchips blunted conscious thought, but certain things escaped them. He remembered Mirasol standing by the window of the dining room and smelling—he was certain of it—a creosote-laden breeze from the desert. She'd responded to his illness by fetching help. She'd wiped his forehead with a damp cloth when he had a fever, and no one had told her to do that. Smell, taste, the sight of pain—all these had gotten through to her.

Mr. Ortega had reached Eusebio with music. The man had been a composer, and music existed on such a deep level with him that nothing could erase it. Matt knew he was the same. "Come with me," he told Mirasol. They went to his music room, and he played the piano and guitar. He put on recordings, and when he played a recent dance piece, she reached for his hand.

She'd never done that before.

"Do you like that? Can you hear it?" Matt asked. The piece

was called "Trick-Track." He'd recorded it when he learned how much María liked dancing. It involved stamping, clapping, and twirling. Every now and then someone would shout, "Trick-Track!" and you had to change partners. Matt had seen it on TV.

Mirasol trembled as he pulled her to her feet. "I don't know how to do this, but we'll play it by ear," he said. It turned out that Mirasol knew all the steps and didn't need him. She was dancing with someone only she could see, and when the recording shouted "Trick-Track!" she moved to another unseen partner.

Matt watched. She was very good, but then she'd always been graceful. When the music ended, her head and arms drooped like a puppet whose strings had been cut. And then she fell.

He caught her. He laid her on the carpet and lifted his hand to ring for help before remembering that he would get Dr. Kim. Anxiously, he felt her pulse. It was normal. Her breathing was untroubled. There was none of the jitteriness that went with an eejit about to go rogue. In fact, she seemed to be deeply asleep, and he watched her for a long time.

Finally, he bent down and kissed her. "Wake up, Waitress," he said. She sat up at once and watched him with incurious eyes, waiting for his next command.

This was a secret Matt intended to keep from everyone. He could imagine what Celia and *Sor* Artemesia would say. Cienfuegos would tell him Mirasol didn't understand what she was doing, and Daft Donald and Mr. Ortega would make sly jokes. As for Ton-Ton, his probable reaction made Matt's blood run cold. *You're d-dancing with an eejit? Way to go,* muchacho. *You're s-so hard up for girls you have to take advantage of someone without a brain.*

The next day he gave orders that no one was to disturb him

when he was at work. He had computers and a desk moved into what had been Felicia's apartment. He aired out the sickly smell of alcohol and drugs and ordered her supply of laudanum to be taken to the opium factory.

He did have work, lots of it. He received reports from all over the country about supplies needed, worker shortages, and the energy flow from the two nuclear plants in Tucson. The doctors in Paradise wanted more equipment. Dr. Rivas said that the Bug had smeared excrement on the walls of the observatory, and they needed to be repainted. Mbongeni kept calling for Listen, which was interesting, the doctor said, because it was the first real word the little boy had learned. Other reports came from places Matt hadn't visited, Farm Patrol outposts close to the border of Marijuana to the east and Cocaine to the west. Fortunately, El Patrón had set up such a well-organized empire that things ran smoothly without much interference.

After a couple of days, everyone except Chacho and Mr. Ortega returned to the hacienda. "He's, uh, pretty torn up," said Ton-Ton. "M-maybe you should visit him."

"He knows where I live," Matt said.

"You know where *he* lives," Listen said pertly. She and Fidelito had formed an alliance and swaggered around arm in arm, getting into all sorts of mischief. "You're the Big Bug. *You* visit him."

"Don't talk about things you don't understand," said Matt, irritated. Still, he was pleased to have some of his friends back, and if they deserted him to visit Chacho he had his new office. And Mirasol.

Matt unbent enough to take them to the greenhouses. As he expected, they were delighted, and he let them select flowers and fruit to take back to Chacho. "It would mean more if you took them," said *Sor* Artemesia. Matt ignored her. His plan was to find a cure for the eejits first and then present Chacho with the happy news.

Weeks passed. Cienfuegos sent plants and animals to Esperanza and ordered supplies. He disappeared once a week to visit the Mushroom Master. Matt would have liked to go too, but there simply wasn't enough time. Opium products moved out steadily. María was allowed access to the holoport a few times with her mother present. The doctors did not find a way to remove the microchips.

Suddenly it was fall. Summer had passed unnoticed in a daily routine of horseback riding, hovercraft flying (Ton-Ton shone there, too), bookkeeping, construction of new eejit pens, and, after the work was done, dancing with Mirasol.

Matt didn't do it too often. He was afraid to, although Mirasol seemed unharmed by the exercise. He'd been unable to find any other piece of music that affected her. By now he was thoroughly sick of the cheesy rhythms of "Trick-Track," but it was worth it to see her briefly awakened. It was like glimpsing a statue at the bottom of a lake. For a few moments the water cleared, sunlight poured into the depths, and the features of the statue became distinct. When the music stopped, the darkness closed in again, and Mirasol fell asleep.

He had kissed her only twice more. It seemed he would be setting out on a dangerous path he might not want to follow. When she lapsed into unconsciousness, he held her. He was holding her now and wondering how long this situation could go on. Outside, the clouds had built up, and thunder rolled around the horizon. It was the monsoon season. The storm made him restless, and he wanted to be out on a horse.

The expiry date on Mirasol's foot was now six months old.

He had protected her in every way possible, but time was running out. He hugged her more closely.

"Wow! So this is what you do in here," said a sharp little voice.

Matt looked up to see Listen standing in the closet doorway. "You! How did you get in here?"

"There's this neat tunnel behind the music room with doors opening into other rooms. Fidelito found it."

"Is he here?" Matt felt sick. Now the story would get out everywhere.

"He saw a big spider and took off," said the little girl, smirking. "It was only a daddy longlegs. They can't bite. Dr. Rivas says they'd like to, but their jaws aren't strong enough."

Matt lowered Mirasol to the carpet.

"What's wrong with her?" Listen asked.

"I've been trying to wake up her mind," said Matt. "She responds to certain things, but the effect doesn't last."

"You mean, like the crème caramel custards?"

"How did you know about that?"

"They don't call me Listen for nothing," said the little girl. "Big people don't pay attention to little kids, and I learn lots of stuff. Dr. Rivas told Cienfuegos that the only way to keep Mirasol awake was to feed her crème caramel custards until she was fat as a pig."

Thunder shook the building, and the lights dimmed briefly. The air outside must be fresh and cool, but inside it was stale. Matt had closed all the windows to keep from being observed. "She also responds to music—well, one piece of music," he said.

"Like Mr. Orozco," said Listen.

Matt remembered that this was Eusebio's other name. "Yes. She dances to it and when it's over, she falls asleep. I leave her alone for a while because I think she needs to rest."

"Wow! It's like *Sleeping Beauty*."

"I thought you didn't like fairy tales," said Matt.

Listen stuck out her tongue. "*Sor* Artemesia says it's 'cultural history.' She says it's no different from anthropology, which is a respectable science."

Clever Artemesia, thought Matt. She'd found a way past Listen's prejudice. "You like Mirasol, don't you?" he said.

"Sure! She saved me from the Bug. She can't help being a crot." (Matt winced inwardly at the word.) "Mirasol's like Mbongeni. He can't help being brainless, 'cause Dr. Rivas made him that way."

For a minute the enormity of what Listen had just said didn't sink in on Matt. "You knew that?" he said in amazement. "And you still like Dr. Rivas?"

Listen squatted next to Mirasol and stroked her hair as you might a dozing cat. "She's really pretty when she's asleep."

Matt nodded. That thought had occurred to him, too. Awake, you noticed the eejit eyes and the utter passiveness. You couldn't get past it. Asleep, you could see that she was outstandingly beautiful.

"Dr. Rivas told me about Mbongeni ages ago," said Listen. "It was when the other Mbongeni was operated on." She stopped stroking Mirasol's hair and turned away. "People hate clones. They're mean to them and say all kinds of nasty things about them. I was lucky because my original died before I was born, but Mbongeni wasn't. Dr. Rivas said that it was right to keep him a happy baby, 'cause then he'd never know when people were insulting him. And he *is* happy. I play with him all the time, and I wish you'd let me go back there."

"What other Mbongeni?" asked Matt.

Listen put her arms around her knees and squeezed her eyes shut. "Not telling."

"There was another clone, wasn't there? An older one." Matt bent down and spoke directly into her face. Listen scooted around until her back was to him. "It's no good keeping your eyes closed. I know what happened and so do you. Glass Eye Dabengwa came to the hospital and the other Mbongeni was operated on."

"Didn't see any Glass Eye Dabengwa. The other Mbongeni was sick. Dr. Rivas said so. He had a bad heart, and they had to take it out."

The little girl was shaking, and so Matt held her. He rocked her back and forth, saying, "That's all right. We won't talk about it anymore." He cursed the doctor for exposing her to things no child should know. He had a good idea where Listen's night terrors came from. "I'm sorry I asked you the question. Let's wake up Mirasol, and I'll take you horseback riding."

"Now? It was raining buckets when Fidelito and I went into the tunnel." Listen gave a sigh and settled into Matt's arms.

"It'll be fun," he assured her. "We'll get wet and the horse will get wet. It's like swimming in the air."

This interested the little girl, who had learned to swim in the huge Alacrán pool. *Sor* Artemesia taught her and watched while she and Fidelito, who'd been taught by his grandmother, splashed around.

"Watch this," said Matt. He clapped three times and said, "Waitress, wake up!" Mirasol shot to attention, ready for orders.

Listen crowed with delight. "It's magic! I mean, 'cultural history.' Can I watch her dance?"

"Not today," Matt said. "I don't know how good it is for her to do it too often. And Listen"—she turned toward him—"let's keep Mirasol's dancing our secret."

"Okeydokey," she agreed. "Only, I get to see her next time."

"Okeydokey," said Matt.

34

THE GREENHOUSES

They left Mirasol in the kitchen with Celia and walked to the stable. The rain swept down, with periods of calm between the storm cells. Matt taught the little girl how to measure how far away a lightning bolt was. "When you see a flash, count one-thousand-and-one, one-thousand-and-two, and so on until you hear the thunder. Every five counts means it's a mile away," he said. As an afterthought he added, "If it's closer than half a mile, we'll go back to the stable." He didn't plan to take her far.

Listen squealed when the rain hit her, but once she got used to it she jumped around in a frenzy of glee. She splashed through puddles and squelched through mud. It was the happiest Matt had ever seen her.

An eejit brought them a Real Horse at the stable. "It's awfully big," Listen said.

"I felt like that the first time I got on a horse," Matt said. "It is big, but you can hold on to me. I won't go fast." They climbed onto a mounting block to make it easier for her, and Matt swung her onto the saddle behind him. As before, he noticed how light she was.

They went out into the rain, and the horse snorted with annoyance. Matt kept the animal at a walk. They circled the stable and then, since the storm had temporarily ceased, went farther to where he could see the cluster of workshops. All the workers were inside.

"Let's go on," Listen urged. "I *like* swimming in the air."

Matt could hear the rattle of looms from the cloth-making factory. A kiln puffed smoke from an enclosure near the pottery shed. The English garden around the guitar factory was a wreck. The roses had been stripped by the storm, and a foot-long chuckwalla was munching petunias, oblivious to the rain.

Matt hadn't intended this visit. It followed naturally from taking Listen for a ride. Matt had noticed that when he was cruel to someone, he often followed it with more cruel things. You got into that mood. But if you were kind, you felt like doing more kind things. He'd started with Mirasol, gone on with Listen, and now it seemed reasonable to finish up with Chacho.

He tethered the horse under a ramada, and he and Listen slopped through the mud to the guitar factory. Child eejits were singing in one of the rooms, not German folk songs this time, but a Christmas carol. El Patrón had liked carols, although, to be honest, the old man hadn't cared about the holiday except as a chance to get more presents.

Children, go where I send thee
How shall I send thee?
I will send thee one by one

One for the little bitty baby
Born, born, born in Bethlehem.

"That's nice," said Listen. "What baby are they talking about?"

"Jesus," said Matt, racking his brain for information about Jesus. He hadn't paid much attention to religion because, until recently, he hadn't had a soul.

"Oh. You mean Jesús Malverde."

"No, not him. Someone much earlier. He was born on Christmas Day. Didn't you celebrate Christmas in Paradise?"

"Dr. Rivas says that religious holidays are crap," declared the little girl.

Matt experienced a new dislike for the man. "We'll celebrate it this year, and *Sor* Artemesia can tell you about the Three Kings who bring gifts to good children. Consider it 'cultural history.'" They watched the choir and their elderly music master. The voices were high and sweet like the sandhill cranes over the oasis.

"Their eyes . . . ," Listen said.

"They're eejits," said Matt, and pulled her on before she could think about it. Outside, the rain began again. Lightning flashed, and he saw the little girl silently count, *One-thousand-and-one, one-thousand-and-two*. Chacho and Mr. Ortega were sitting by a window, drinking maté. Eusebio was stringing a guitar, pausing to listen as he tightened the tension. One end of the room was filled with guitars. *It's like the opium factory,* thought Matt. *It's a machine you can't turn off.*

"Matt," said Chacho, putting down his cup. "Or should I say *mi patrón?*"

"He's come halfway, bug brain. You can do the rest," said Listen.

Mr. Ortega laughed. "I told you, if anyone can nag the dickens out of someone, it's Listen. Welcome, *mi patrón* or Matt or whatever you want to be today. We've been enjoying the storm, although I miss hearing thunder. I can feel it through the earth."

Matt sat across from Chacho. They didn't speak. It was awkward after all this time, but Mr. Ortega expanded on his appreciation of the monsoon, and Listen wandered over to watch Eusebio. She was very much at ease in this place.

Matt thought his friend looked thinner and more haunted, and no wonder. It had to be tough watching Eusebio day after day. "Maybe you can come to the hacienda for a visit," said Matt. "I'd like that."

"Excellent idea!" said Mr. Ortega. "I'll get the umbrellas."

"Father . . ." Chacho looked toward Eusebio.

"Will be better for the break," the piano teacher said. "*Por Dios*, he must be sick of looking at your long face all the time, Chacho. I know I am." He hurried the boy into a raincoat and pushed him out the door. Matt collected Listen and went back for the horse. The eejit children were singing:

Children, go where I send thee
How shall I send thee?
I will send thee seven by seven
Seven for the seven that never got to heaven.

They found Ton-Ton taking apart a music box on Celia's kitchen table. "He says he knows how to put it back together. I sure hope so," said Fidelito. The box was one that fascinated him, because it showed a pirate and a sea captain crossing swords to a song called "High Barbary." No one knew where High

Barbary was, but Fidelito liked to dance to the music, slashing a stick around as though he were fighting pirates.

"If you break it, I'll beat the stuffing out of you," he told Ton-Ton.

"Y-you can try," said the big boy. "Don't look so, uh, worried, *chico*. I took apart all the others and th-they're fine."

"You didn't touch 'You Are My Sunshine,'" said Fidelito.

"That's too difficult," Ton-Ton said. The cowboy, the man in black, and the lady sat among a number of boxes at the far end of the table.

"Chacho!" cried the little boy as he and Mr. Ortega came in. "Look at this music box. It's *padrísimo*!" He reached for "Sunshine," but Celia blocked his way.

"I have to cook here. This isn't a playground," she scolded. Mirasol followed, carrying a stack of mixing bowls.

"Please, please let us stay. This is the best place in the house." Fidelito hung on to her apron and smiled winningly.

Celia smiled back in spite of herself, but her rules were inflexible. "How can I prepare food with grubby hands all over the place?" Ton-Ton carefully put the bits he was working on into a bag. Matt and Chacho moved the other music boxes. They went to a nearby room and found a table that had once belonged to a maharaja. It was made of dark wood inlaid with ivory. Ton-Ton covered it with a sheet so as not to damage the surface.

"I haven't seen this room before," said Chacho.

"You haven't seen a lot of the rooms here," Listen said. "The hacienda is huge. Fidelito and I found—" She was stopped by a frown from Matt. "You wouldn't like what we found, Chacho. It was full of big, horrible spiders."

"I saw one," Fidelito said. "It wanted to bite me."

"Ha! That was a baby," scoffed Listen. "The ones I saw could eat a rat for breakfast." The little boy looked alarmed. Matt had to admire her quick mind. She'd not only stopped Fidelito from talking about the secret passage, she had hit upon the one thing to keep him out of it. She was used to keeping secrets.

Chacho had seen the "Sunshine" music box before, but he willingly watched when Fidelito wound it up. "Tell me, Ton-Ton," he said. "Why are you taking these apart?"

"I'm trying to, uh, figure out how the microchips work. In a machine, you wind it up and it starts moving. One part m-moves the next part and so on. The parts have to be touching." The boy laid out the bits to the pirate box in his slow, methodical way. "The m-microchips in the brain don't touch each other and they don't, uh, have to be wound up. But they're still a kind of machine. Something connects them. This is my way of thinking about the p-problem." He waved his hand at the boxes. "Sooner or later I'll figure it out."

No one argued with this. They were used to Ton-Ton's dogged way of working. It wasn't interesting to watch, however, so Matt suggested they take Chacho on an excursion to the greenhouses. The storm clouds had mostly dispersed when they got outside, and fleeting patches of sun lit up sand verbenas and primroses.

"Look!" shouted Fidelito, dragging Chacho past mango trees, papayas, and granadilla vines in the first greenhouse. "It's like the Garden of Eden."

"The Garden of what?" asked Listen.

"The place where our great-great-great-grandfather and great-great-great-grandmother came from. *Mi abuelita* told me about it. God used to walk around in it and eat mangoes."

"Dr. Rivas says God doesn't exist," the little girl said.

"Dr. Rivas is a horse's butt. *Sor* Artemesia says He does," retorted Fidelito. "Let's look at the other greenhouses."

As Matt had expected, Chacho was overwhelmed by the flower gardens. He was struck speechless by the orchids and their strange shapes and unlikely colors. He stood in front of them for a long time, tracing their outlines in the air. *He really is an artist,* Matt thought. "You can come here whenever you like," he said.

"I'd like to bring my father," Chacho replied.

Matt's heart sank. Eusebio was unable to appreciate anything, but Matt didn't want to discourage his friend. "Of course. Ask Mr. Ortega to help you."

When they had gone through the last greenhouse, Matt noticed another building in the distance. Its walls were of some sort of plastic or glass, and he couldn't remember seeing it before. The sun came out and the walls changed from transparent to milky.

All of them shaded their eyes and looked. The building was perhaps half a mile away, and Matt suggested that they go there. But Listen was unwilling to walk farther, and Fidelito backed her up. Chacho wanted to get back to Ton-Ton. So Matt went on by himself through ragtag bullhead vines and grass awakened by the recent rain. The walls of the building changed color several times as clouds passed overhead.

Close up, he saw that even when the walls were dimmed he could see inside. Vague shapes moved among tables, and long pipes snaked under a ceiling. A constant chuffing spoke of some kind of machinery. Matt opened the door to a small entryway, and an eejit handed him a gauze mask.

Now he understood what this was. Cienfuegos had been busy—*very* busy—to go by the size and complexity of the place.

Beyond the second door was a forest of mushrooms, some growing in boxes of soil, others sprouting from logs or beds of wood chips. The walls dripped with condensation, and the air was thick with the odor of rotting wood. The Mushroom Master and Cienfuegos were inspecting a giant log covered with parasols of cream-colored fungi.

The Mushroom Master had been persuaded to exchange his white tunic for trousers and a shirt. He was wearing moccasins, having no doubt discovered the folly of walking barefoot over bullhead thorns.

"Caught in the act," the *jefe* said cheerfully, looking up. "I was going to tell you when we were further along. Isn't this wonderful, *mi patrón*? It only cost us a ton or so of opium."

Matt was almost speechless. *A ton of opium? Millions of dollars? It cost "us" that much money? There is no "us" involved here. Cienfuegos isn't the Lord of Opium.* "How dare you go behind my back," he finally managed to say.

"I didn't go behind your back," Cienfuegos said quickly. "You wanted to clean the soil around the eejit pens, and this is how we're going to do it. The Mushroom Master inspected them last month and told me which fungi to use. He has methods for getting the mycelia to sprout quickly."

"The what?" Matt asked weakly.

"Mycelia," the Mushroom Master said. "It's like roots, only for mushrooms." Both of the men looked immensely pleased with themselves. They reminded Matt of Listen and Fidelito after the children had pulled off some glorious prank.

"You can't take people out of the biosphere." Matt pointed at the white-haired man who was thoughtfully nibbling one of the cream-colored fungi. "¡*Por Dios!* It was kept isolated for eighty years, and now you act like it's your private playground."

The two men looked at each other. "I made the suggestion to leave," said the Mushroom Master. "I'm one of the few scientists left in the biosphere and almost the only person who knows that a world exists outside. It was decided long ago that we had to adjust to being imprisoned in a small world. We created our own civilization."

"The Brat Enclosure, the Dormancy period," said Matt.

"Yes. We give our immatures a happy, loving childhood so that they grow up contented with their lives. Then, when the time comes, they are put into a kind of sleep where their brains are receptive to learning. They become cooks or weavers, beeherds or frogherds, and they emerge as adults. A few of us learn the old-fashioned way, because Dormants aren't creative. We few cope with emergencies and keep the system going."

Matt put his hand down on a table and recoiled when he felt something slimy. "You program children like robots."

"It isn't that heartless," said the Mushroom Master. "How could children be happy, knowing they were prisoners? It was better for them to believe that the world ended at the wall. By the time the armed guards outside went away, generations had passed and our new civilization was established."

Cienfuegos plucked a cream-colored fungus from the log. "This is an oyster mushroom, *mi patrón*. They're very tasty except when they've been feeding on pesticides. I like to fry them in olive oil, but raw ones have that spicy background flavor." He held one out temptingly. Matt took it, but was too distracted to eat it.

"People out here need me," said the Mushroom Master. "Of what use is the biosphere if we allow the rest of the world to die?"

Of course he was right. Matt had to agree with him. But it

made him uneasy that you could program children into being whatever you liked. It wasn't that far from being microchipped.

"Don't people notice when you leave the biosphere?" the boy asked.

"They assume I'm in another building," said the Mushroom Master. "They're not curious."

"They think I'm a traveler from Tundra, one of the outer ecosystems," said the *jefe*. "Everyone knows Tundrans are idiots, and that excuses the stupid questions I ask."

"Now, now. Tundrans are children of Gaia," reproved the Mushroom Master.

"All Gaia's children are blessed," the two men chanted in unison, and burst into laughter.

It wasn't possible to stay angry with them, even though Matt was annoyed at being deceived. El Patrón would have murdered Cienfuegos for less. Yet wasn't the country's problem that no one except the old man had been allowed freedom?

It had been El Patrón's intent to control everyone's will. From the eejits to the doctors, all had been made part of a monstrous machine. It was a sterile machine, a parasite feeding on the surplus bodies of neighboring countries. There were no families or children. Left alone, it would die.

"I'm glad you decided to help us," Matt conceded. "Have you tried your mushrooms out near the eejit pens?"

"Just beginning to," said the Mushroom Master. "We've got plastic sheets around the pits and mycelia spreading like bullhead vines underneath. It's marvelous!"

"Keep the prehumans away, would you, *mi patrón*?" the *jefe* said. "We don't want Fidelito running around covered with spores."

Matt left the men, laughing and congratulating themselves

on their success. He felt deflated by the easy way they had out-witted him, yet he couldn't argue with the results. He ran his hand over the smooth outer wall of the building. It was made of a photosensitive plastic that darkened in sunlight, ideal for rais-ing mushrooms. It was probably worth half a ton of opium.

Deeply thoughtful, he walked back to the hacienda and encountered Listen and Fidelito in the swimming pool, with *Sor* Artemesia watching at the side. "What was that building?" called the little girl. "Was it another greenhouse?"

"It was a sewage treatment plant," Matt said, and went inside.

35

THE EXPIRY DATE

Chacho did not take his father to the greenhouse. Mr. Ortega explained that removing an eejit (or "a man in your father's condition" as he put it) from his job caused jittering. It was a sign of extreme stress and might actually kill him. This threw Chacho into an even deeper depression. He refused to leave the guitar factory and barely spoke to anyone.

Several days later, after prolonged nagging, Matt let Listen watch Mirasol dance. He turned on the music, and the girl twirled and clapped. She bowed to an invisible partner before moving to the next.

"That's spooky," said Listen. "She's really seeing something."

"It's a memory," Matt said sadly. "Somewhere, the real Mirasol exists where we can't find her."

"What if you played the music over and over?" suggested the little girl.

"I'm afraid to. I don't know how strong she is. She's past her expiry date." Too late Matt realized he'd opened the door to something he didn't want to talk about.

"What's an expiry date?" asked Listen.

"It means . . . the day something is finished," Matt said, thinking rapidly. "It means Mirasol has to be repaired, like putting a new battery into a flashlight."

"So why don't you fix her?"

Matt wished, not for the first time, that the little girl weren't so quick to pick up on things. "The doctors are trying to figure out how. It's part of the microchip problem."

Listen nodded and fortunately didn't ask what would happen if Mirasol wasn't fixed. "How do you know when her expiry date is?"

"It's printed on the bottom of her foot."

By now the music had ended. Matt caught Mirasol and eased her to the carpet. Listen got a magnifying glass and inspected the date. She pulled off her shoes and checked her own feet. "Nothing," she said. "What about you?"

"I have writing," said Matt. "It got me into a lot of trouble when I was at the plankton factory in Aztlán." He'd gotten into the habit of talking to the little girl, always being careful not to give her more information than was good for her. Sometimes he forgot she was only seven years old, she was so intelligent, but he knew she wasn't able to handle many things.

"The Keepers and other boys found out I was a clone. They thought I was lower than the lowest beast . . . except for Chacho, Ton-Ton, and Fidelito. They stood by me."

"You were like Mbongeni," said Listen. For a moment she looked sad, and he realized that she missed her playmate. He would have to figure a way to bring them together, minus the Bug. "I saw writing on Mbongeni's foot," the little girl said. "I didn't know what it meant. Can I see yours?"

For a moment Matt was revolted by the idea. It was a shameful memory, but she had no concept of the beastliness of it. She'd grown up with the idea. It meant no more to her than a freckle or a mole. He took off his shoe, and she got a flashlight to see.

"I don't know all the words. I recognize 'of' and 'the,'" she said. "It says 'Property of the Alacrán Estate.'"

"That means you belong here, huh? It's like a cattle brand."

"I suppose so," Matt said unwillingly.

"Wait. There's more." She fetched the magnifying glass.

More? thought Matt.

"It's a little squinched-up line below the words." She applied both the magnifying glass and flashlight. "It's numbers." She repeated them, and Matt turned cold. It was a date, a number related to the only birthday he would ever have, the day he was harvested from a cow.

His thirteenth birthday.

He was more than fifteen now. Who could tell him what it meant? It couldn't possibly be an expiry date, because he wasn't microchipped. *Or was he?* How could he know?

"Are you okay?" asked Listen.

"It's stuffy in here. Let's wake up Mirasol and go horseback riding." Matt clapped his hands and sent the girl to the kitchen to help Celia. He took Listen to the stables and ordered a horse to be saddled. All the while his mind was churning over the number on his foot. He'd seen the mark before. He'd thought it was a scar from when he fell onto broken window glass as a small child.

They rode past the pottery and weaving factories. The crafts-men and -women were outside, producing their goods in the way people had done for thousands of years. The women patted wet clay onto a potter's wheel turned by pedals they worked with their feet. Others spun wool shorn from a sizable herd of merino sheep. The wool was colored with natural dyes obtained from saffron and indigo plants, and from mushrooms.

Mushrooms. Rose, lavender, yellow, and blue. He remembered seeing them in a barn near the stables as a child. He hadn't been interested enough then to ask about them.

They came to the guitar factory. "Can we go in?" Listen asked.

Matt woke up. He'd forgotten her existence, although she was clinging to his back like a burr. "I don't want to. You go. Ask Mr. Ortega to take you home." She looked at him oddly as he swung her to the ground.

"Are you sure you're okay?" she asked.

"I'm as good as I ever was," he said, and rode off.

The world had changed for him. He barely heard the gardeners shouting, "*¡Viva El Patrón!*" as he passed. He registered that a team of eejits was being moved from one field to the next, and that the Farm Patrolman tipped his hat. Was he one of them on some level? Did something in his brain control him? *Was this where El Patrón's voice came from?*

A trapped feeling like that he'd experienced as a young child in a room full of sawdust came over him. He had trouble breathing and felt for his asthma inhaler.

There was no noxious air or suffocating dust to account for it this time. The reaction was purely in his mind. He was part of the machine El Patrón had created.

He came to the new eejit pens, now built some distance from the evil-smelling pits. They had beds inside and large communal showers. Dining halls with tables and chairs were at the end of each building. The eejits ate a balanced diet of meat, vegetables, and bread, although the Farm Patrolmen were still using eejit pellets for lunch in the fields. Did it matter? Did the workers notice how their lives had improved?

In the distance lay the water purification plant and the polluted pits. Matt headed the horse that way. It was a perverse thing to do. It was guaranteed to bring on a full-scale asthma attack, but he didn't care. Now he understood Cienfuegos's desperation. The head of the Farm Patrol was trapped in an endless round of violence that he wasn't allowed to escape.

Am I allowed? I'll find out, Matt thought savagely.

When he drew near to the pits, the horse began to snort and act up. The stench wasn't too bad, but the animal was clearly alarmed by it. "I don't want to hurt you," Matt said. He rode back to where the air was cleaner and tethered the horse to a fence post. "Someone will find you if I don't come back," he said.

He didn't really want to die. The closer he got to the pits, the more foolish the trip seemed, yet he kept on. He wanted to know how far he could push this death wish. At a certain point he sat on the ground and thought, *I'm not really like Cienfuegos. I left the country, and he can't do that. I can love. I love María.* This made him feel better. He didn't have to kill himself to prove he was free.

One worrisome thing remained, though: the voice in his head. Celia thought he was possessed. Cienfuegos believed that he really was El Patrón come back from the dead. So did *Sor* Artemesia, but she said that he had a chance to be different.

"And I do," Matt said aloud. He stood up and shaded his eyes as he gazed at the polluted pits not far away. The ground was covered in sheets of the same light-sensitive plastic he'd seen at the mushroom greenhouse. A person was tending them, lifting sheets to examine what lay beneath and spraying water from a large hose. The smell wasn't nearly as bad as Matt remembered. He went closer.

It was a woman. She wore a white hazmat suit that must have been hot. Her face was flushed and angry. Her heavy boots came halfway up to her knees. The purposeful way she moved told Matt that she wasn't an eejit. Every now and then she stopped, kicked a stone, and swore a blue streak.

"Fiona?" he said.

She looked up and cursed again. "You did this to me, you pile of eejit droppings! Is this the kind of job for someone who got an A in her A-levels? Who kept the hospital going when all the doctors and nurses buggered off to that party? Served them right to get poisoned. Self-centered duckwits! And didn't I save your life when you got sick? Oh, but nobody cares for Fiona. She's expendable."

"Fiona," said Matt again. "What are you doing?"

"As if you don't know! Cienfuegos said he would *cockroach* me if I didn't work here. He means it too, the bludger. He's got evil, cold eyes like a snake."

Matt barely noticed the smell of the pits, he was so surprised by Fiona's behavior. "I can't help you if I don't know what you're doing," he said.

The woman stopped and scowled at him. "It's perfectly clear, isn't it? I'm tending these ghastly mycelia. They eat filth and they are filth, just strings of rot as far as I can see. The whole place smells like toilet."

Well, it *was* a job, Matt decided. Cienfuegos had kept his word. Fiona was alive and where she couldn't do mischief. "Are you getting fed?" he asked.

"Oh, yes. Prison rations, not that I can stomach it after eight hours of this. I get a bloody cot in one of those new eejit pens. If I want a shower, it's all in together with the zombies, watching them soap themselves in unison."

Matt, in spite of her crimes, felt sorry for her. "I'll see that you get your own cottage," he said, and then, rashly, he said, "Fiona, are you microchipped?"

She appeared to swell up with rage. "You've got a lot of cheek saying I'm an eejit. I don't stumble around like a drunk on Saturday night, thank you very much. You need an eye exam."

"There are other kinds of control, things so subtle you can't see them. Like wanting to do something and discovering you can't."

Fiona turned pale. "I'm sure I don't know what you're talking about."

"Did you have any injections when you arrived?"

"We all had immunizations, didn't we? For the exotic diseases." She seemed to deflate before his eyes.

"Of course. That's all it was," said Matt, unwilling to push the issue. "I'll tell Cienfuegos to find you a cottage." He left her standing by the pits. She didn't move until he was a long way off.

He got the horse and rode on toward the oasis. A few sandhill cranes were huddled in the shady part of the water, panting in the heat. Once there had been thousands of them, but only a few hundred had survived the summers. They moved from pool to pool, seeking coolness.

Matt sat under the collapsing grape arbor and drank some of the water he carried with him. He pulled off his left shoe and looked at the bottom of his foot. The dark line Listen had discovered had always been there, but Matt had never looked at it closely.

Yet he wasn't as worried here as he'd been outside. Something about the place made him feel safe. He looked around at the rocks enclosing the old campsite on three sides. The fourth side was the lake.

Heed the high cliffs, lad. They keep things out. Now Matt remembered that Tam Lin had actually said this once when they camped overnight. The boy had wondered why they could sleep so soundly with mosquitoes whining in their ears and the hard earth under the sleeping bags.

'Tis not bodily comfort we need, the man had said, *but the mind at ease. Something about the rocks holds back the cares of the world. This is the only place in Opium I've felt free.*

That was the time Tam Lin had told him the sad story of the sandhill cranes. The later Alacráns didn't know about the oasis, but the old man did. It was the first place he'd come to in the United States, before he established his empire. He'd built the old miner's cabin and planted the grapevine. Through the years he'd forgotten the oasis and anyhow was too old to climb through the rocks. But in the beginning he'd noticed the sandhill cranes arrive with cold weather and depart in spring.

El Patrón hated to give up anything he thought he owned.

He had his son Felipe net the birds and pull out the lead feathers on one wing. *Birds cannot fly unbalanced,* said Tam Lin. *They tip to one side and fall to earth. The cranes were trapped. Half of them died that first summer, and more the next.*

A few had survived, the ancestors of this flock. Matt watched them now, guiltily enjoying their presence. After a while, his mind at ease, he went back to the horse and rode toward the hacienda.

36

GOING ROGUE

The first sign that something was wrong was Cienfuegos galloping toward him through the poppy fields. "There you are!" shouted the *jefe*, waving his hat. "I've had men hunting all over for you. Fiona said she'd seen you ride this way."

"About Fiona—" began Matt.

"No time for that now, *mi patrón*. We have an emergency. Mirasol has gone rogue." He turned and led the way. When they got to the hacienda, Ton-Ton and Fidelito were waiting outside.

"Don't get mad at her," Fidelito begged. "She thought she was doing the right thing."

"Why would I get mad at Mirasol? She can't help her condition," said Matt, sliding off the horse and leaving Cienfuegos to take charge of it.

"Not Mirasol. Listen," said Fidelito.

"Sh-she was trying to be nice," Ton-Ton said. "They're in your office, the, uh, one we're supposed to stay out of."

Matt ran through the halls, thinking, *Listen has been playing "Trick-Track." She's been trying to wake Mirasol up.* When he got there, he saw that he'd been nearly right. The recording for "Trick-Track" was still in its folder, but music boxes covered the table. Mirasol was lying on the floor, sobbing as though her heart would break. *Sor* Artemesia and Dr. Kim were leaning over her. Listen was huddled in a corner, a ball of total misery.

"I didn't mean it! I didn't want to hurt her!" the little girl cried. "Don't hit me! Don't put me into the freezer!"

What now? thought Matt. "I'm not going to do anything to you, Listen. Mirasol is the one we have to worry about." He knelt next to Mirasol and tried to take her hand, but she threw him off.

"Father! Father!" she screamed.

"It's all right. I'm here. I won't let anyone hurt you," he said. She couldn't hear him. She kept calling for her father and weeping hysterically. "Can you give her a sedative?" Matt asked Dr. Kim.

"It won't save her," the doctor said bluntly. "When eejits go rogue, nothing helps them. The best I can do is give her a lethal injection."

"*¡Jesús, María, y José!* What kind of doctor are you? Give her something to let her rest. I'll take her to the hospital in Paradise. Maybe they're better at their jobs than you are."

Dr. Kim showed a flash of anger, quickly repressed. He took out an infuser, a kind of injector, and pressed it to Mirasol's neck. There was a hiss, and she relaxed. "It won't last long, *mi patrón.* She'll need more and more of these until the sedative itself kills her."

"Give as many as we need to *Sor* Artemesia," Matt ordered. "I'm going to tell Cienfuegos to get our fastest hovercraft." He ran outside to find the *jefe* already waiting in the hallway.

"The hovercraft is ready, *mi patrón*," Cienfuegos said. "I ordered a larger, faster one after your bout of scarlet fever. I hope that was all right."

Matt looked at him, exasperated. Now was not the time to deal with another hidden spending spree. "How many people can it take?"

"Mirasol, a pilot, you, a nurse, perhaps two more."

"You will fly the craft," said Matt.

"*Mi patrón*, that isn't a good idea."

"Do as I say! There's no room for argument." Matt was in full El Patrón mode now. He felt like a general commanding troops. He got Mirasol loaded onto a stretcher and into the hovercraft. *Sor* Artemesia, who'd had first aid training, was installed next to the girl. Cienfuegos was in the pilot's seat. "You come too," Matt ordered Listen, grabbing her by the arm and dragging her into the craft.

"Don't blame her," wailed Fidelito from outside.

The craft took off, first balancing delicately on a cushion of antigravity and then speeding away. It *was* fast. They rose through monsoon clouds and now and then were buffeted by wind or spatters of rain. "If we encounter a thunderstorm, we should go around it. It's safer," said Cienfuegos.

"Do whatever you like," Matt said tersely. Turning to *Sor* Artemesia, he said, "Now tell me what happened."

"I wasn't there at first," the nun said. "Listen was alone with Mirasol."

"I didn't mean to hurt her!" cried Listen.

"Shut up until you're told to speak," Matt snapped. She buried her head in her arms and began to cry.

"I don't think she meant harm," said *Sor* Artemesia, with a quick look at the little girl.

"I'll be the judge of that. What happened?"

"Apparently Listen had the idea that music could awaken Mirasol. She took all of El Patrón's music boxes and put them into your office. She told Mirasol to sit down, and she began to play the boxes one by one. It was all right until she wound up 'You Are My Sunshine.' That particular one seemed to trigger something in Mirasol's mind."

"She started screaming. I was so scared," whimpered Listen.

"Who cares if you were scared?" Matt snarled. "You *knew* you weren't supposed to play music for her."

"I thought she would dance."

"And now you may have killed her!"

"*Mi patrón, mi patrón,*" interrupted *Sor* Artemesia. "Listen is only a little girl. She doesn't have the judgment of an adult. She liked the music boxes and thought Mirasol would too. She came directly to me for help, and I called Dr. Kim."

Mirasol began to stir, and soon she was sobbing again. She sat up and flung her arm at Cienfuegos, who was watching the sky intently. "He killed my father!" she screamed. "He did it! Help me, oh, help me! I can't escape!" She convulsed, and *Sor* Artemesia quickly applied another infuser.

Matt moved into the seat next to the *jefe* and said, "Is that true? Did you kill her father?"

Cienfuegos turned the hovercraft to avoid a pillar of rain descending from an enormous thunderhead. The craft shuddered as a lightning bolt flashed at the edge of the cloud. "The electricity interferes with the navigation of this craft. I have to pay attention. I may have killed her father. I don't remember. There were so many."

There was nothing more to say. Matt watched the *jefe's* yellow-brown eyes as the man maneuvered around the storm.

Cienfuegos's attention was riveted on his task, and no trace of regret was detectable. If Matt distracted him, they might never reach Paradise. "Can you go faster?" Matt said.

"No," the *jefe* said. Now rain began to lash the side of the craft. Another lightning bolt fell, and Listen counted, "One-thousand-and-one." That was as far as she got. Thunder rocked the sky. *Sor* Artemesia silently told the beads of her rosary.

Matt went into the back of the craft and sat by Listen. "I know you're only a child. I was angry, but it was out of fear. I'm not angry anymore." The little girl huddled against him, tears rolling silently down her face. "Did Mirasol say why the music upset her?"

"She said her father used to sing that song. At first she seemed okay. She talked like any other person. She said her father sang to her when she went to sleep, even when they were running away. That's how the Farm Patrol found them. And then she screamed."

Matt put his arm around the little girl. "I might have done the same thing. It was just chance."

Mirasol awoke two more times on the journey, and then they landed outside the hospital in Paradise. Orderlies swarmed out to carry her inside. Matt followed closely. He didn't trust any of the doctors. Their idea of a cure was a lethal injection.

She was taken to an operating room and Dr. Rivas came in, dressed in hospital scrubs, with latex gloves on his hands. "This is going to be brutal. I don't think you should watch," he said.

"What are you going to do?" Matt asked.

"The only thing we can do. Open her skull and pick out the microchips one by one."

"That doesn't work. Dr. Kim tried it."

"So did we. So did I over the years," said Dr. Rivas. "I sacrificed hundreds of eejits trying to find a cure for my son. I tried nullifying the magnetism with electrical currents. I engineered a white blood cell to attack microchips. I induced high fevers, hoping they would destroy the chips before they killed the brain. Nothing worked."

"So this is hopeless," Matt said.

"You can do a procedure a thousand times and sometimes the thousandth time is different. You make a lucky mistake. That's the only hope I can give you."

Matt looked down at Mirasol, her beautiful face composed, for the moment, in sleep. How could he order this mutilation without any hope of success? They said eejits didn't feel pain, but he knew, deep down where no one could detect it, they did. "Leave her as she is," he said.

"Shall I give her a lethal injection?" The doctor removed his gloves.

"No. Give me the infusers. When she starts suffering, I'll give her one."

"She might linger for an hour or two. No more."

Dr. Rivas left, and Matt sat by Mirasol's bed. She awoke, and for a moment her eyes were clear and she seemed to see him. Then the anguish overtook her and she screamed. The last time she looked directly at Matt and he bent over and kissed her. "I love you, Waitress," he said.

She gazed back, really seeing him. "I am called Mirasol," she whispered, and then, as the infusion flooded her veins, she sighed and did not wake again.

37

THE FUNERAL

Matt did not know how much time had passed. He sat unmoving as the small sounds of a hospital went on around him. Air-conditioning clicked on and off. A blood pressure cuff inflated and deflated on Mirasol's wrist. A heart monitor searched for a beat, found none, and searched again. Matt was no stranger to death. It had surrounded him all his life. He had seen El Viejo, El Patrón's grandson, lying in his coffin. He had seen the eejit in the field as a small child. And what he did not see, he was well aware of.

Except for Tam Lin, it had been remote from him. Matt didn't really know most of those people. But Mirasol, dulled and silent though she was, had been a living presence. Her eyes followed him as the sunflower, her namesake, turned its face to the sun. Now something had departed, and he did not know what it was.

Dr. Rivas came into the room. He was no longer dressed for

surgery, but had reverted to a white lab coat. "I'm sorry, *mi patrón*," he said, not sounding sorry at all. "She was a pretty thing and quite bright for an eejit. I imagine you'd like us to take care of the disposal."

"The *what*?" asked Matt, coming out of his trance.

"We have procedures to deal with this situation. Cienfuegos does it all the time. It isn't healthy for you to grieve for someone who wasn't really there."

"Just as you never grieved for your eejit son," Matt said.

Dr. Rivas winced. "I deserved that. But you see, I knew my son *before*. I have memories."

"And I have memories of Mirasol." Matt turned back to the motionless figure on the bed.

The doctor fussed with the equipment, detaching the blood pressure cuff and switching off the heart monitor. "I don't know whether you have any religious preferences," he said. "El Patrón was a Catholic, or at least he liked the ceremonies. I could have *Sor* Artemesia say a prayer over Mirasol."

Matt thought of Listen's quotes from the doctor: *Religious holidays are crap. God doesn't exist. Mbongeni is a happy baby. The rabbits are dee-diddly-dead.* "Please go. And send me *Sor* Artemesia."

The nun was as respectful as anyone could wish. She said a rosary over Mirasol and prayed silently. "I don't think I can give her absolution," she said hesitantly.

"What's absolution?" said Matt.

"When someone is dying, Catholics give them the last rites. The person confesses his sins and is forgiven so that he can enter heaven. Mirasol couldn't have confessed to anything. What sins could she have committed in her state?"

"What happens with dying infants and people in comas?"

"You're right, *mi patrón*. These emergencies do come up, but the rite must be done while the person is alive. Mirasol is dead. It's too late." *Sor* Artemesia tried to pull the sheet over Mirasol's face, but Matt prevented her.

"Not yet," he said. "I say she's still alive."

"But the doctor—"

"Are you going to believe someone whose lifework is turning people into eejits? I am the Lord of Opium, and I say she's alive."

"Oh, dear! Oh, dear! I don't even know whether Mirasol has been baptized," the nun said nervously.

"Then do it now."

Sor Artemesia looked from Mirasol to Matt and back again. "I'm so confused. Perhaps eejits do die in a different way. Perhaps life fades slowly and it would be all right. . . ."

Matt knew she was trying to convince herself. "Saint Francis would forgive you," he said. "He forgave Brother Wolf, after all."

Sor Artemesia left and returned with water, olive oil, and flowers. She poured water over the girl's forehead and made the sign of the cross over her. "I'm doing a conditional baptism," she explained. "If Mirasol has already been taken into the church, this one won't count."

When the nun was finished, she anointed the girl's forehead with oil and spoke in a language Matt had never heard before. He didn't interrupt her, for the ceremony had a quality that moved him deeply. At last she said, *"In nomine Patris, et Filii, et Spiritus Sancti. Amen."* She placed the flowers in Mirasol's hands.

"What language is that?" Matt asked.

"Latin. It was used by priests for many hundreds of years. The church prefers modern languages now, but I've always thought that God pays more attention to Latin."

They stood silently for a few moments, and then Cienfuegos

came to the door. "Dr. Rivas said you needed me to dispose of Mirasol."

"Dr. Rivas can go to hell," said Matt. "We're taking her back to Ajo. She will be buried in the Alacrán mausoleum."

A flicker in the *jefe*'s eyes showed how startled he was, but he didn't argue. "Very well, *mi patrón*. I'll get the hovercraft."

Matt found Listen curled up in Mbongeni's crib. "Come on. We're leaving," he said.

"I won't," she cried, clinging to the little boy. "Mbongeni needs me."

"He'll forget you the minute you're out of the room." Matt roughly pulled her arms away from the boy and dragged her out of the crib. She scratched and kicked him. "Stop that! Mirasol is dead, and we're taking her body to Ajo."

Listen stopped struggling. "Did I kill her?" she wailed. "I didn't mean to."

Mbongeni began wailing too. "Lissen . . . Lissen . . . *muh muh muh muh muh*."

"He's learned to say my name! He won't forget me! Please, please, please let me stay!"

Matt didn't bother to argue. He dragged Listen after him, and the cries of "Lissen . . . Lissen . . . *muh muh muh muh muh*" died away in the distance. Cienfuegos had the hovercraft at the hospital door. Mirasol's body, wrapped in a white sheet, lay on the floor. *Sor* Artemesia had put more flowers on the shroud, and she sat by a window saying her beads.

Listen shrank away from the body. "She's not dead. I don't believe it. She's not a rabbit."

"Don't be afraid of death, child," *Sor* Artemesia said, beckoning to her. "It is when the soul is released to find its true home. Mirasol is not here. She is in heaven and far happier than she ever was on earth. She's with her father now." The nun put aside her rosary and took the child into her arms. "Here. We'll look at trees as we fly."

The hovercraft took off. Cienfuegos went around the Chiricahua Mountains by a southerly route, passing the ruins of a town called Douglas. A great battle must have been fought there, because the ground was scorched black and hardly a trace of buildings was left. Matt saw an ancient road going west, with the remains of cars scattered at the side.

They passed over the ruins of Nogales and crossed a valley filled with deserted farms. "This would be a good place to plant new crops," said Cienfuegos. "The water table has risen and the soil is good."

Matt listened without interest.

"That's Kitt Peak," the *jefe* said, skirting the highest mountain. At the top were two observatories, smaller versions of the ones in the Sky Village. "This is one of the first places El Patrón captured, and it gave him the idea for the Scorpion Star." But nothing could rouse Matt. He was numb. Colors, sounds, and voices withdrew to a gray background in his mind. He couldn't even think of Mirasol.

They landed at Ajo, and eejits carried Mirasol's body, completely shrouded, to the large veranda in front of the hacienda. They laid her on a couch. Matt sat down next to her. A peacock wandered onto the veranda and gave a harsh cry.

Celia, Daft Donald, Mr. Ortega, and the boys came out, and *Sor* Artemesia cautioned them to keep their distance. She herself went up to Matt and said, "*Mi patrón*, please let me help. I think you have never arranged a funeral before."

Matt looked up. "I don't know what to do," he said, dazed. "I

don't want her to be disposed of as though she were an animal."
He looked through the wide portico of the veranda to the distant fields. There were thousands and thousands of bodies out
there. Cienfuegos had told him once that he had flown over the
sand dunes of Yuma on a full moon night. By day you couldn't
see it, but by night the bones of Illegals showed up like a ghostly
army sleeping on the earth.

"We need a coffin," *Sor* Artemesia said. "A beautiful one.
Perhaps one of the eejit carpenters could make it. The children's
choir could sing, and I will say the appropriate words. A priest
would be better, but unfortunately we don't have one."

"El Patrón had a collection of Egyptian mummy cases," said
Matt. "Some of them are very beautiful."

That very evening a procession of eejits dressed in white
robes and adorned with flowers carried the coffin of an Egyptian
queen. It had been buried thousands of years before in the hot
sands of the North African desert. The queen's likeness was
carved on the lid. She wore a crown of gold and lapis lazuli. Her
body was sheathed in white linen, and her arms were covered
with carnelian bracelets. In her hand was a sacred blue lotus.

They came to the Alacrán mausoleum, a building as large as
a house and covered with so many plaster cherubs it looked like
a flock of chickens. Behind them came bodyguards carrying
torches. Celia and the other servants, the boys, and Listen came
next. Last of all walked the eejit children. They hummed the
theme from *Pavane for a Dead Princess*, and the old choirmaster
walked at their side to be sure they did it right.

Matt and *Sor* Artemesia met them at the mausoleum. On
either side of the glass doors were what looked like chests of
drawers. The name of a departed Alacrán was inscribed on each
long drawer, but there were several that hadn't been used yet.

One was pulled out, and here the eejits deposited Mirasol's body in the Egyptian queen's coffin. *Sor* Artemesia performed the funeral ceremony, and two burly bodyguards slid the drawer closed.

They went outside. The sky was clear after rain, and the stars shone brilliantly. One of them fell, a bright streak across the blackness, and Celia turned to Listen and said, "Look, *chiquita*. That's a prayer being answered by God. One of the angels is flying down to carry out His orders."

38

THE MUSHROOM MASTER VS. THE SKY

Matt moved his office to another part of the hacienda. He couldn't bear to be in the place where Mirasol had danced. He closed up the room and ordered the door to be nailed shut. Ton-Ton hid all the music boxes after Matt smashed one of them.

There was plenty of work to occupy Matt's mind. What with sending samples to Esperanza, keeping the opium dealers at bay, and laying out plans for new fields, there was barely time to relax. He moved like a robot from one task to the next. Ton-Ton, Chacho, and Fidelito left him alone, and Listen had been rebuffed so many times that she hid when Matt came into a room.

He didn't care. At one point—it was hard to keep track of the days—Cienfuegos told him that the light for the Convent of Santa Clara was blinking on the holoport. Matt was in the kitchen, dining alone as he preferred now. "I don't want to talk to Esperanza," he said.

"It could be María," suggested the *jefe*.

"She's always with her mother."

"It's better than nothing," said Cienfuegos.

"It *is* nothing." Matt took another bite of a sandwich that tasted like sawdust to him.

"That's no way to treat a friend," said the *jefe*, drawing up a chair. "You liked María before Mirasol came into the picture."

"I loved her," Matt said.

"And still do, *mi patrón*. Please do not speak of her in the past tense. *Es muy antipático*. Disagreeable."

"You don't have to call me *patrón* anymore. I've chosen a new name," said Matt.

Cienfuegos looked surprised and then pleased. "I hope it's frightening. I always thought El Picador—the Meat Grinder— had a certain nasty charm."

"I want to be called Don Sombra, Lord Shadow."

The *jefe* thought for a moment. "It isn't as scary as I'd hoped, but then it depends on what you mean by shadow. A lurking danger, an unseen threat. Yes, it could do."

"It's what I want. You can tell the others. Now leave me alone. I want to think." Cienfuegos withdrew and Matt thought, *Mirasol means "look at the sun." She thought I was the sun, and now that she's gone, there's nothing left but shadow.* He didn't answer the holoport call on that day or on the next five occasions.

The monsoon departed, drifting back now and then to drench the soil and cause flash floods in the hills. The days were hot. Matt wore a hat like the Farm Patrolmen and, when he had time, rode out to inspect the opium fields. Eejits worked to remove stones from new tracts of land where Matt intended to plant with corn.

Field eejits were trained to prepare soil, but they understood only one type of crop. Cienfuegos had tried them out on a small stand of corn, and predictably, they slashed the growing cobs with razors and waited patiently for the resin to ooze out. "I've tried every command I can think of, but they won't change," the *jefe* had said. "It's possible to retrain them, but think of the time wasted, not to mention the high mortality."

"Are they living longer now?" Matt had asked.

"Much longer," Cienfuegos had said. "Of course there are the usual accidents. One of them turned the wrong way and marched out into the desert instead of returning to the pens. No one noticed until the following day. We found him at the bottom of a wash. Two or three go rogue every month."

Matt had turned away. He was preparing fields no one would use unless the Farm Patrol and bodyguards could be persuaded to do it. They wouldn't like it. It was beneath their dignity.

Now Matt walked alone toward the mushroom house. The experiment had worked better than anyone's wildest dreams. Polluted soil now sprouted with grass. Waste from the water treatment plant no longer drained into fetid pits but spread into enclosures, where it was set upon by hordes of ravenous Shaggy Manes. Matt could understand why the Mushroom Master was so proud of his pets.

He saw the Mushroom Master now. The man was carrying a large, brown umbrella that came down past his shoulders and made him look not unlike a mushroom himself. "Hello there!" he called. The man tipped up the umbrella and lowered it again.

"Please forgive me for not stopping, Don Sombra. I was checking a leak in the sprinkler system and must go back inside at once. You are welcome to visit, of course. I have some excellent pu-erh tea." The Mushroom Master scurried through the door as though a rattlesnake was lunging at his heels.

"Is there an emergency?" Matt asked.

"With me, yes." The Mushroom Master furled the umbrella and placed it by the door. "Thank Gaia for this umbrella," he said. "Cienfuegos got it for me. The first time I left the biosphere, I panicked like a newly awakened Dormant at his first mating season. He had to drag me out."

"Is the outside world that frightening?" Matt followed the man through the growing chambers to a small office in the middle of the building. Here the air was pleasantly cool and fresh. A small teapot simmered on a hot plate.

"It's the sky." The Mushroom Master leaned forward as though imparting a secret. "You have no idea how terrifying it is to someone who's always had a roof over his head. It's so big! It goes up and up forever. I feel like I could be sucked into it."

Matt was surprised to find that he understood this feeling. "Once, long ago, I camped out under the open sky at night. I, too, was afraid of falling upward into the stars."

"Stars! I haven't dared to look at them yet." The teapot began to rattle, and the Mushroom Master sprinkled the water with dried leaves. After a few minutes he poured out two cups of fragrant liquid. "This is tea. Have you ever had it, Don Sombra?"

Matt said he had and didn't think much of it. It was brown like old dishwater and tasted much the same.

"Ah! But this is different," said the man. "Tea isn't a plant you can boil like spinach. It must be ripened like a fine cheese. Here. Enjoy the aroma first and then sip carefully."

The boy took the cup with some amusement. The people in the biosphere were peculiar, from the frogherd with his skinny white legs to the people slurping grasshopper stew. But the aroma *was* pleasant. It wasn't like flowers exactly. It reminded him of cedar or sandalwood, of something old but not decayed.

He sipped it. "This really is good."

"You see!" crowed the Mushroom Master. "Even people who have never ventured outside a building can surprise you. Pu-erh is fermented by yeast. Do you know what a yeast is? A fungus! Is there nothing fungi can't do?" The old man warbled on about spores and mycelia, lost in the wonder of Gaia's creations.

Matt liked him and on an impulse said, "Why don't you come to dinner at the hacienda? We can sit outside and stargaze." The Mushroom Master tensed up. "We'll stay close to the door so you can escape if it gets too frightening."

The Mushroom Master considered. "Cienfuegos is always telling me about how beautiful the outside world is, but I'm afraid the farthest he's got me is one trip to the pollution pits. Can I bring my umbrella?"

"Of course," Matt said. "You can sit under it the whole time if it makes you comfortable."

A weight seemed to have lifted from Matt as he made his way back to the hacienda. For weeks he had lived under a cloud, and none of his friends could help him. Everything and everyone reminded him of Mirasol. More than anything, he felt devastated that he hadn't saved her. He should have found other doctors. He should have stopped trying to wake her up.

The Mushroom Master was different, because nothing about him raised unhappy memories. Being with him was like closing a door and looking ahead.

Matt went by the mausoleum, which wasn't far from the hospital. He did this often, though both Celia and *Sor* Artemesia told him it was a bad idea. *I don't even have a picture of Mirasol,* he thought, gazing at the dusty glass doors. How could he have been so careless? He remembered her now, but what about later?

Long ago he'd had a teacher, a woman who was one of the higher-grade eejits. He remembered her as very tall, but then he'd been a little kid. Everyone looked tall. She had brown hair and wore a green dress, and her face . . . was missing. It had vanished from his mind as the woman herself had vanished into the opium fields.

I'll ask Chacho to draw a picture, Matt thought. He went by the guitar factory and invited his friend to dinner.

Eejits moved a picnic table near the veranda and placed lamps at either end. They were powered by solar cells that gathered energy during the day and refunded it as a pearly glow after dark. Matt thought it would appeal to the Mushroom Master. The table was close to a door where the man could dive for shelter.

Servants brought out bowls of salad, salsa, and tortilla chips. A platter of fried chicken sat in the middle of the table. Ton-Ton, Chacho, and Fidelito arrived, followed by Listen and *Sor* Artemesia. Listen went to the end of the table, as far as she could get from Matt.

The Mushroom Master, looking very odd under his dome-like umbrella, was escorted by Cienfuegos. Fidelito hooted with laughter and was threatened by Ton-Ton. "If h-he wants to bring an umbrella, that's his business," said the older boy.

Matt introduced the old man. "He isn't used to the sky and feels safer when he can't see it," the boy explained. He described the work the man and Cienfuegos had been doing.

"So the cat's out of the bag," said the *jefe.* "I'm warning you prehumans"—he shook his finger at Fidelito and Listen—"if you set foot in the mushroom house, I'm going to feed you to the Giant Gomphidius."

"There's no such thing," said Listen.

Cienfuegos smiled wolfishly. "Come and find out."

A servant filled everyone's glass with fruit juice except, as usual, the *jefe's*. "What's that? It smells delightfully moldy," said the Mushroom Master, sniffing from beneath the umbrella. Cienfuegos signaled for another glass of *pulque*.

The sun was setting. One tree was full of redwing blackbirds, singing so loudly it drowned out all the other birds. A peacock settled for the night on a plaster cherub holding a wreath of plaster roses. A line of quails hurried from one bush to another.

"We should eat outdoors more often," Matt said.

"We, uh, did it all the time at the plankton factory," said Ton-Ton. "We didn't have birds, though. The Keepers ate them all."

"Soon the stars will come out," Matt said, steering the conversation away from that unpleasant memory. "You'll be able to see them," he told the Mushroom Master.

"I've seen pictures. I don't need the real thing," the old man said, grasping the umbrella more tightly.

"One of the brightest is the Scorpion Star. You must be interested in that."

"Never heard of it," said the Mushroom Master.

"It's the space station patterned after your biosphere. A place for people to live off the Earth." Matt was amazed that the man had never heard of it.

"Why would anyone want to live away from Gaia?" The Mushroom Master reached for a piece of chicken.

Matt exchanged looks with Cienfuegos. "You know, that's a

good question. El Patrón went to huge expense to create the space station, but we don't know what it's for."

"I know he never went there," said the *jefe*. "Dr. Rivas and his daughter tried to visit once. El Patrón had them arrested in Aztlán and brought back."

"How do people get there?" said Chacho. "On TV they show rocket ships flying to other planets."

"*Pfft!* The other planets are lifeless balls of rock," scoffed the Mushroom Master.

Matt turned to him, or at least to the umbrella. "How do you know?"

"I read books. We have a perfectly good library in the biosphere," said the old man. "It's a hundred years out of date, but that doesn't matter. The planets were dead then and still are. Only Gaia is alive." Salsa and chips were rapidly disappearing under his umbrella.

"People use the Sky Hook to reach the Scorpion Star," said Cienfuegos. "It's a long tether attached at one end to a mountain in Ecuador and at the other to the space station. An elevator goes up and down, carrying people and supplies."

"May I have another piece of chicken?" the Mushroom Master asked.

"You can have as much as you like," said Matt.

The old man sighed with pleasure. He tipped the umbrella slightly to reach the food and quickly righted it again. Matt heard chewing noises from inside.

"You know, it isn't going to rain," said Listen from the far end of the table.

The umbrella tipped up again. "I remember you. I wondered at the time why you weren't in the Brat Enclosure. You'd like it there. Lots of games and playmates."

"I would not like it," Listen said. "Why don't you put that thing away? Nothing's going to fall on your head."

"Are you sure? A star might come loose," the old man said.

"You're making fun of me 'cause I'm a little kid, but I'm smart. A star is a ball of fire millions of miles away. It isn't going to fall on anybody."

"Don't talk back to adults, Listen," said *Sor* Artemesia.

"Listen. What an interesting name," the Mushroom Master said. "You must hear all kinds of things."

"I got ears like a bat," the little girl said.

"It's true that I don't need an umbrella," conceded the old man. "I've lived all my life under a roof, and the sky scares the dickens out of me. But I'm going to put the umbrella away just for you, child." He furled it and placed it on the ground by his feet. Matt noticed that his eyes were closed. "I can do this," he murmured. He opened his eyes and gasped.

A crescent moon hung not far above the horizon. Rose and saffron hues glowed above the western hills, while the sky overhead was deep blue as though saturated with light. The Mushroom Master's eyes filled with tears. "I've seen pictures, but none of them were as glorious as this. Oh, thank you, thank you, Listen, for pulling me out of my shell." The old man gazed, spellbound. Above the moon, gradually becoming clearer, was a brilliant point of light.

"That's the evening star," said Chacho. He, too, was spellbound by the colors.

"That's not a star. It's the planet Venus," said Listen. "You can tell 'cause it doesn't twinkle."

"Sometimes I don't want too much information," Chacho said.

39

MARÍA LEARNS THE TRUTH

Matt hung Chacho's drawing next to the lady in the white dress. It was surprisingly good, considering that his friend had little art training. Chacho said he'd been sketching things for as long as he could remember. His grandfather had encouraged him, buying paper and paints, but when the old man died, all that had ended. Chacho was packed up with dozens of other unwanted children and shipped to the orphanage where Matt had first met him.

"Drawing wasn't allowed there," said the boy. "We worked all day and at night recited the crotting Five Principles of Good Citizenship and the Four Attitudes Leading to Right Mindedness." Matt remembered noticing how clumsy Chacho's hands had seemed, but Eusebio had the same hands. It showed that you couldn't judge people by their outward appearance.

"The picture is really good," Matt said. "Would you mind doing a painting of Mirasol? I'll get you whatever you need."

Chacho looked up and, for the first time in many days, smiled. "I could work at the guitar factory. It would give me something to do."

After he left, Matt continued looking at the drawing of Mirasol and the painting (as he imagined) of María. Mirasol's wasn't as skillfully done, but it showed her bright beauty and her eyes gazing at something in the far distance. They weren't dead as they'd been in life, but still remote. María was altogether more interesting. She smiled as though she had some prank in mind that could get you into trouble, but would be fun anyway. Matt was suddenly overcome by a desire to see her.

He hurried to the holoport room, chose the icon, and activated the screen. The sickness that had come over him when he first used it had gone away. The scanner had evidently adjusted itself to recognize his slightly different handprint, and Matt could now open parts of the border or communicate with people as often as he pleased.

"At last," said a voice behind him. Matt turned to see *Sor* Artemesia standing in the doorway. "Please let me stay, Don Sombra. I've been so worried about María. She must be lonely with me gone and with you . . . neglecting her."

"I haven't been neglecting her," said Matt, stung.

"María doesn't know that. She thinks you've forgotten her."

Matt was annoyed to have company, but he could hardly send *Sor* Artemesia away. She was the closest thing María had to a real mother. By now the portal had cleared, and they saw the peaceful convent room. A small woman in a nun's habit was dozing in a chair.

"*Sor* Inez!" called *Sor* Artemesia. The woman jerked to attention.

"*¡Jesús y María!* Please wait and I'll get Esperanza," she cried.

"Stop!" ordered *Sor* Artemesia. "You are to fetch María alone. Don't bring her mother. Do you understand? Alone."

"Esperanza will skin me alive," said *Sor* Inez.

"She won't if she doesn't know. I have the Lord of Opium here, and you can't imagine the pain *he'll* cause if you don't obey." The little woman scurried off.

"I couldn't possibly hurt anybody from here," said Matt.

"I have found," said *Sor* Artemesia, "that if you give an order forcefully enough, people will obey it without thinking too much." María appeared almost immediately, so she must have been waiting nearby. Matt wondered for how long.

"*Sor* Artemesia!" she cried. "Please come back, or make Mother send me to you. I'm so lonely"—and then she noticed Matt. "*Mi vida*, why didn't you answer my calls? It's been weeks. Have you left me for Mirasol?" Tears began to roll down her cheeks.

Matt felt terrible. He'd been so wrapped up in grief that he hadn't considered the effect of his silence on María. "Mirasol is dead," he said. His throat closed up, and he couldn't speak for a moment.

"How—" began María.

"She was an eejit. They don't live long," said *Sor* Artemesia.

And then María drew the kind of conclusion that was so typical of her and that made Matt love her. "You were trying to save her," she said. "I understand now. You were trying to save her, and she died anyway. How awful it must have been for you!"

The generosity of this conclusion made tears come to Matt's eyes too. He blinked, remembering Mirasol dancing and then falling limp into his arms. It hadn't been as high-minded as María thought. "I want you to come here," he said.

"I'm trying. I keep arguing with Mother, but she's like a brick wall. She's—oh, this is *terrible*—she's trying to arrange a marriage for me."

"You're too young," said *Sor* Artemesia.

"I know. It won't be an actual marriage, more like a betrothal. Honestly!" María stamped her foot and looked, for an instant, like Esperanza in a snit. "You'd think it was the fifteenth century, with girls being given away like favors to slimy old men. It's one of Mother's friends on a human rights board. He's not really old. Thirty-five or so, but he's *hopeless*. He wants me to help him do good works, distribute pamphlets on dental hygiene or getting immunized against AIDS."

Sor Artemesia stifled a snort of laughter. "*Mija*, isn't that what you've always wanted? To emulate Saint Francis?"

María looked daggers at the nun. "Of course, but not with *him*. I haven't got anybody on my side here. Please call Emilia or Dada. Maybe they can back me up."

Both Matt and *Sor* Artemesia flinched. They knew the story of El Patrón's funeral had been kept secret to protect Matt's fragile hold on the Alacrán empire. "What should I do?" the nun mouthed silently.

Matt thought rapidly. Sooner or later the news had to come out. He was a lot more confident of his power than he had been months ago. "I'm going to tell you something that you absolutely have to keep secret," he said, without much hope that María would.

"Aren't Emilia and Dada there?" she said uncertainly.

"Listen to me. It's extremely important. This involves my safety and *Sor* Artemesia's, too. You must promise to say nothing to anyone, including your mother."

"She should have told you long ago," put in *Sor* Artemesia.

"Of course I'll promise. Is Dada in prison?" said María, with a keener sense of her father's activities than Matt thought she possessed.

"He's—he passed away," said Matt. "So did Emilia." How was he going to tell her the circumstances of how it happened?

Sor Artemesia came to his rescue. In a careful, restrained tone she described El Patrón's funeral and the old man's final revenge on anyone who dared to outlive him. "It was quick. They didn't suffer," the nun said.

María looked stunned. "How long has Mother known?"

"Since the first time I saw you through the holoport," Matt said.

"She *lied* to me. She let me write letters to them for months. She gave me their answers. She wrote them herself." María was crying now, but she was also angry. "She wanted to betroth me to that mealy-mouthed creep. She said Dada was in favor of it. *She lied!*"

"We're on your side," said Matt. "I'll tell Esperanza that I won't cooperate with her unless she sends you here."

"She'll find a way around it. She always does." María paced around the room, smacking a fist into her palm. *Sor* Inez came in and signaled wildly. Esperanza was on her way. "Mother's going on a fact-finding mission to Russia next week," María said quickly. "Contact me at the other holoport in Paradise on Tuesday afternoon. I'll have a plan then." She snapped off the connection before Esperanza could come in and discover what she was doing.

Sor Artemesia sat down as mist filled the screen and the Convent of Santa Clara disappeared. She was trembling. "I hate dealing with people like Esperanza," she admitted. "What I wouldn't give for a cottage in a quiet valley where all I had to do was garden."

"Me too," said Matt. "I wouldn't grow opium there either."

Sor Artemesia smiled weakly. "I noticed that the altar cloth I embroidered wasn't fastened to the wall at the convent. I wonder what happened to it."

"María sent it to me." Matt didn't say that it was under his pillow or that he felt for it in the middle of the night when he had trouble sleeping.

The following Monday Matt went to the guitar factory to see how Chacho was getting along with the supplies he'd sent him. Boxes of watercolors, oil paints, and pastel crayons had arrived, along with brushes and various kinds of paper. To his surprise he saw Chacho working on an entire outside wall. It was a mural of people dancing, to go by the sketch done in charcoal on the whitewashed surface. Fidelito, Listen, and Ton-Ton were watching, while Mr. Ortega strummed a guitar.

"H-he's really fast," said Ton-Ton. "Started this morning and now, uh, look." It was indeed impressive. At one end were flamenco dancers, and at the other were more modern figures doing whatever modern dancers did. In the middle was an orchestra led by a man who was unmistakably Eusebio Orozco. In one corner, high up as though she were floating, was Mirasol, doing the Trick-Track with an invisible partner.

Chacho had a stepladder and was working near the top of the wall to draw birds circling over the musicians. "This is the easy part," he called down to Matt. "Doing the actual painting is hard."

Matt sat down next to Mr. Ortega, who continued to play. "Chacho's a natural," the man said. "One of his ancestors was José Clemente Orozco, the best artist Mexico ever turned out. It runs in the family. Eusebio is a good artist too, but he's better at music."

Matt watched in amazement as Chacho dragged the ladder from one end of the mural to the other to add things that had just occurred to him. "What would he be like with training?" he said, turning so Mr. Ortega could read his lips.

"Something wonderful," the man said, his fingers moving over the strings of the guitar. "The original Orozco was mad about painting murals even though he had a weak heart and had lost one hand and an eye at an early age. He had to stop and rest before he could climb a ladder. People like that are driven."

"We absolutely have to find Chacho a teacher," said Matt, thinking that Ton-Ton needed one as well. They had so much talent! And to think that all the Keepers thought they were good for was making ratty sandals out of plastic.

He saw Listen lurking behind Ton-Ton. "I know you're there, so don't pretend you're not," he said.

"I don't see you and you don't see me," she said.

"That doesn't make any sense, *chiquita*." He sat down on the ground next to her.

"Yes, it does. You put me into the freezer and I'm staying here." Listen scooted to the other side of Ton-Ton, who put out a lazy hand and hauled her back.

"L-life is too short for stupid arguments," the big boy said.

"What are you talking about, Listen? I didn't put you into a freezer," Matt said.

She hugged herself and leaned over so she wouldn't have to look at him. "Yes, you did. That's what Dr. Rivas calls 'ignoring people.' You don't talk to them, you don't see them. It's like being a bug on the bottom of a shoe. Dr. Rivas used to put me into the freezer when I was bad. He wouldn't let me play with Mbongeni or anything until I said I was sorry."

Another reason to dislike Dr. Rivas, thought Matt. "This time I'm apologizing. I was so upset by Mirasol's death that I couldn't think of anything else. I think I ignored everyone for a while."

Listen uncurled herself and put out her hand. He took it. "That's okay. I *was* bad and deserved to be punished," she said. "Do you know what I did to make up for it? I told Chacho about Mirasol's dancing, and he put her up there on the wall. It looks like she's flying with the birds."

They sat for a while, watching Chacho speed from one part of the wall to another until he was satisfied with his sketch. "I'll think about the colors next," he said. "I don't know much about mixing oil paints, so it's going to take a while. I have to figure out how to protect the picture from sunlight or rain. Oh, crap! It better not rain." Chacho looked unhappily at a thundercloud rising over the distant mountains.

"I'll have a plastic sheet hung from the roof," Matt assured him. He'd never seen the boy so animated. Chacho, as Listen would have put it, was flying with the birds. "Come and have lunch at the hacienda," Matt said. "You need to rest." Mr. Ortega put down his guitar and led the young artist away.

"I'm going to Paradise tomorrow," Matt told Listen. "Would you like to come?"

"You bet! Can Fidelito come too? I told him he could fly a stirabout and see the Scorpion Star up close."

"You're not running around on your own," Matt said, thinking that not long ago he could have told Mirasol to watch them. Depression settled on him like a fine dust.

In the end he took Cienfuegos, Listen, Fidelito, *Sor* Artemesia, and the Mushroom Master. The last was the *jefe's* idea. "The old fellow has done so much for us. Sooner or later he'll have to return to his cramped life in the biosphere, and I want him to have happy memories."

"Are you sure that going *up* into the sky will give him a happy memory?" Matt asked.

"He can bring his umbrella," said Cienfuegos.

40

THE CLONING LAB

The minute they left the ground, the Mushroom Master gave a wail of despair and jammed the umbrella down over his head so hard that one of the spokes snapped.

The rainy season was over except for a few stray storms. The ride was smooth, and the land below was covered with sheets of golden poppies. Cienfuegos flew low so everyone could admire them. "On the way back we'll fly over the biosphere," he said to the old man. "You'll enjoy seeing it from the air." The only answer was a low moan.

"I told Dr. Rivas that the Mushroom Master is a fungus expert from California," the *jefe* informed them before landing. "I don't think he'd be happy to learn I took someone out of the biosphere."

"I hadn't thought of that," said Matt, whose attention had been focused on seeing María.

"He doesn't like people poking their noses into what he

considers his territory," said Cienfuegos. "All of you keep your mouths shut about the Mushroom Master—pay attention, Listen and Fidelito. There are microphones hidden everywhere. And you, sir," he addressed the old man, "please stay close to me. Bad things happen to people when they're alone with Dr. Rivas."

Matt wondered what the *jefe* was up to. He made it sound like the trip was dangerous, and perhaps it was. Neither he nor Matt had forgiven the doctor for microchipping the new security guards, doctors, and pilots.

When they arrived, the Mushroom Master was escorted inside and allowed to recover from his fright. "Airsickness," Cienfuegos explained to Dr. Rivas, who was waiting to greet them. "Poor old fellow. Barfed his socks up the minute we left the ground." *Sor* Artemesia took Listen and Fidelito away, to visit Mbongeni.

The Mushroom Master was soothed with *pulque*, his new favorite drink. "You must send me the wild yeast responsible for this," he told the *jefe*. He then described the chemical reactions that fungi were capable of, the joy of watching a yeast bud develop, and the different odors produced by the action of mold on old sneakers.

Dr. Rivas's eyes glazed over, and he excused himself quickly to do some work at the hospital.

"I think that went well," said Cienfuegos, and the Mushroom Master smiled.

"I'd like to see the lab where you were grown," said the old man. Matt nodded, although he wasn't happy about showing anyone the unnatural way he'd been created. It still filled him with a sense of shame. They went through the gardens, and the Mushroom Master bravely put aside his battered umbrella to enjoy the trees. "Imagine letting everything grow wild without worrying about whether the ecosystem is in balance. Gaia is an excellent mother."

"We shouldn't talk about Gaia here," warned Cienfuegos, and the old man changed the subject.

They came to the fountain with the children holding their hands out to the water. "Now, that is truly beautiful," declared the Mushroom Master. "One of the chief regrets I have about my, um, home is the lack of art. All is devoted to practical things."

"Those are supposed to be El Patrón's sisters and brothers who died young," said Matt.

"He must have been an extraordinary man, although I'm sure I wouldn't have liked him." The Mushroom Master stepped into the fountain and held his hands up like the children. "Yes, this is a marvelous work of art. I think they are worshipping Gaia."

"We should go on," said Cienfuegos, frowning. They came to the lab, with long tables covered in gleaming, stainless-steel pans and microscopes. A lot of work seemed to have been done recently. They inspected the giant freezers containing bottles labeled MACGREGOR #1 to MACGREGOR #13 and DABENGWA #1 to DABENGWA #19.

One of the glass enclosures was no longer empty. A cow walked slowly on a treadmill as her legs were flexed by mechanical arms. Matt halted in shock. "Who—"

Cienfuegos held a finger to his lips to caution silence. "So that was how you were grown," the Mushroom Master said, peering through the glass. "What an amazing achievement! In some cultures the cow was worshipped as the embodiment of motherhood. I wonder what they would have made of this."

"I know what the people here made of it," Matt said bitterly. "They said I was a filthy clone, worse than an animal, and unnatural."

The old man looked kindly at the boy. "You must not be hurt by other people's ignorance. Where I come from, animals are revered. I would have been honored to have a cow for a mother. The only thing wrong here is that the poor animal has been drugged."

"She has a microchip in her brain. Clones aren't considered human or even animal. They're property." Matt sat down, driven by a desire to show the Mushroom Master just how terrible his childhood had been. He took off his shoe. "There! It's somewhat faded, but that's the mark of a clone."

The old man took out a magnifying glass he used to examine interesting fungi. "'Property of the Alacrán Estate.' That certainly says it all. What does the number mean?"

Matt drew his foot back. "Nothing."

Cienfuegos grabbed Matt's ankle and the boy kicked him, but the *jefe* was very strong.

"I order you to let me go!"

Cienfuegos dropped Matt's foot. "It's a date, and I'm willing to bet that you think it's an expiry date."

"Expiry date?" asked the Mushroom Master.

"They tattoo it onto an eejit's foot to show how long he'll live, but it's very different with a clone. Yours is a 'best by' date, Don Sombra. It tells the doctor when transplants have the best chance of succeeding. You're good for another eighty years." The *jefe* laughed.

Matt grabbed his shoe and sock, furious and relieved at the same time. He wanted to push Cienfuegos's face into the cow patty that had just appeared in the enclosure. He busied himself with the shoe while the Mushroom Master drew the *jefe* away to explore the other freezers.

They opened one door after another until they found racks of trays labeled BUBONIC PLAGUE MONGOLIA, BUBONIC PLAGUE CAIRO, SMALLPOX TEHERAN, and many, many more. The Mushroom Master retreated quickly. They went outside without saying another word.

"Let's take one of the stirabouts," suggested Cienfuegos. "I'm sure you'd like to see the greatest observatory in the world."

"I'd be delighted," said the Mushroom Master, but they went into the flatlands instead, where there was nothing except mesquite trees, cactuses, and a few of the old abandoned observatories.

The *jefe* settled the stirabout down onto a patch of sand. "We should walk some distance away for security reasons. I hope your moccasins are up to it, sir." The Mushroom Master put his umbrella up, for here were no trees. The sun blazed out of an empty blue sky. They walked along a trail until they got to a collection of boulders. Cienfuegos poked around them with a stick to check for snakes before they sat down.

"Is this place really that riddled with listening devices?" asked the Mushroom Master, wiping sweat from his face with a sleeve.

"El Patrón had them everywhere. He had bodyguards whose only job was to listen, and he liked to eavesdrop himself."

"What a dreadful man," said the Mushroom Master. "And now Dr. Rivas is doing it."

"Probably." Cienfuegos took out a bottle of water and passed it around.

"Whose clone is Dr. Rivas growing in that cow?" asked Matt, unable to hold back the question any longer.

"I think it's his son," said Cienfuegos.

"The one who's an eejit?"

"Yes. Eduardo."

Matt remembered the young man who had been picking leaves out of a pool, one by one. "Is—" The boy stopped to gather his thoughts. "Is the doctor going to do a brain transplant?"

"It's been tried, but transplanting a brain is far different from doing a kidney or a liver," said the *jefe*. "I remember that from lectures at Chapultepec University. The brain is shaped by the experiences of the body, and the body is shaped by the brain. When you learn to walk or swim or fly a hovercraft, both are involved. Changing one part results in lethal confusion for the other. I think Eduardo has been dead for a while, and Dr. Rivas is growing a replacement."

"What terrible things have happened since the biosphere was enclosed," said the Mushroom Master.

They sat, each with his own thoughts, gazing out at the low landscape of mesquite trees. The air shimmered over dull green leaves, and in the distance the domes of deserted observatories poked up in the heat haze like Shaggy Mane mushrooms. To the right, completely dwarfing all other structures, was the Alacrán observatory, whose great glass eye was trained on the Scorpion Star. Matt couldn't see it now, but it was there. Always.

"Dr. Rivas has been getting stranger these past few months," said Cienfuegos, "not that he was ever sane. I think the death of his son has pushed him over the edge."

"I'm worried about that collection of germs he has in his freezer," said the Mushroom Master. "Some of those diseases are *legends*. They aren't supposed to exist."

"Listen told me about them," the *jefe* said. "Someday I'm going to take a blowtorch in there."

"Make it soon," said the old man.

"Excuse me, sir, but why did you come to Paradise?" Matt asked the Mushroom Master. "I mean, since you don't like hovercrafts much." He treated the man with the same courtesy as Cienfuegos did. The Mushroom Master might be odd, but there was no mistaking his quality. He was someone even a drug lord could respect.

"I was talking to Ton-Ton about microchips," said the old man. "He's a very clever lad. His methods are slow, but he has one outstanding quality. He overlooks nothing. He has come to the conclusion that the microchips are controlled by an outside energy source. I agree."

All three of them turned to look at the Alacrán observatory. "El Patrón built that with a quarter of the fortune he had at the time," said Cienfuegos. "I don't know what he spent on the Scorpion Star, but possibly twice as much."

"Controlling the eejits would be a compelling reason," the Mushroom Master said.

"Could the Scorpion Star really affect people from so far away?" asked Matt.

"Sunlight reaches Earth from nine million miles away. Without it, life wouldn't exist. Once there was something called a Global Positioning System. It controlled airplanes, ships, and cars from satellites."

Matt's thoughts whirled with this staggering revelation. All they would have to do was shut down the Scorpion Star. He could order that. He had absolute power. And then he thought, *Order who?*

"I wonder why Dr. Rivas hasn't shut down the space station," said Cienfuegos, echoing Matt's thoughts.

"Perhaps he can't," said Matt.

Cienfuegos stood up and startled a lizard that had been sitting on an adjacent boulder. It threw itself off and disappeared into a clump of dry grass. "Let's poke around the observatory and see what we can find out."

41

THE SOLAR TELESCOPE

Matt was greeted warmly by Dr. Angel, but Cienfuegos was clearly not on her list of friends. As for the Mushroom Master—whom the *jefe* introduced as a doctor from California—she quickly decided that he was an eccentric old coot. The Mushroom Master played the role well. He peered nearsightedly at dials, jiggled handles, and poked buttons until Dr. Angel was almost as rude to him as she was to the Bug. Dr. Marcos came out from under the telescope long enough to utter a few surly words of welcome.

The visitors admired pictures of planets and star clusters and endured Dr. Angel's long-winded explanation of focal lengths. But when they got to images of the Scorpion Star, the Mushroom Master was riveted. "Oh, my, that's wonderful! And so *familiar*. If I close my eyes, I can imagine . . ." The old man hadn't seen the biosphere from outside, but he knew the layout. Matt could see him comparing the inner and outer shapes of the buildings. "That could be Africa and that Australia," he murmured. Cienfuegos nudged him and he fell silent.

The Mushroom Master reached out and touched the screen, leaving a visible fingerprint. Matt could see Dr. Angel struggling to control herself. She adjusted the image, and it drew closer to the space station. They saw hovercrafts frozen between buildings and tubelike walkways. People in white lab coats stood at windows. "How many people live there?" asked the Mushroom Master.

"It varies. Around three hundred," said Dr. Angel.

"Ah. So people come and go."

"Scientists are rotated. Six months on and six months off. It's difficult to be isolated for such long periods."

"And how many children are there?"

Dr. Angel looked at him as though he were crazy. "It's a space station. There's no room for children."

"My, my, my, my, my. That's not going to do much for the future of the colony," said the old man.

Dr. Angel looked over his head at Matt, as if to say, *Where did you dig up this idiot?* "Look, I have work to do," she said. "Would you mind wandering around by yourselves? And please don't let *him* touch anything. No buttons, no switches. Nothing."

"We'll keep an eye on him," said Matt. "And thank you for your time."

They went on with occasional stops to watch a technician study graphs or adjust a number on a dial. The Mushroom Master opened every door they passed—carefully, so Dr. Angel wouldn't notice—and discovered a lunchroom with tables. "Excellent! Let's have tea," he said.

Two technicians were sitting at a table, but they left when the visitors arrived. The old man was intrigued by a coffee machine and, by punching a button, managed to scald himself.

"Here, I'll do it," said Cienfuegos, blowing on the old man's hand to cool his skin. "Coffee or hot chocolate? I don't think you'd like the tea."

"Hot chocolate," the Mushroom Master said eagerly. They found a box full of donuts and helped themselves. "This is *extremely* unhealthy," the old man said happily. "The dieticians at home are fanatical about me not eating sugar."

"By the way, sir, you do a fine imitation of a Tundran," said the *jefe*. "Dr. Rivas and Dr. Angel couldn't wait to get rid of you." The Mushroom Master smiled and stuffed another donut into his mouth.

Afterward they explored the solar telescope. A technician carrying a clipboard hurried over and offered to show them around. The man took them to the top of the tower, where the telescope followed the movement of the sun, and then down to the opening of a giant shaft that plunged at an angle into the earth.

"Look at that," cried Matt. A huge tube filled the inner part of the shaft, and elevators enclosed in a chicken-wire wall spiraled slowly down the outer part.

"The elevators are for the maintenance crew. The tube is like a giant thermos bottle, and it needs to be checked constantly for weaknesses," said the technician. "The image of the sun is projected inside the tube from lenses in the tower and filtered to remove most of the heat. Even so, the temperature can be lethal. The final image is relayed to computers in the main observatory to study the weather on the surface."

"The sun has weather?"

"Yes, indeed. The surface is always boiling, and sometimes streams of hot gas are ejected into space. We're concerned with the ones aimed at the Scorpion Star."

Lights illuminated the sides of the shaft, but it was so deep that Matt couldn't make out the bottom. Air conditioners whirred in alcoves at various levels, and a hot breeze rose out of the depths and was sucked through vents.

"Amazing," said the Mushroom Master. "Even with all those safeguards, it's still hot."

"The air-conditioning isn't perfect," admitted the technician. "Every now and then we lose a few eejits."

"What an evil place to work," said Matt, watching the pasty faces of the maintenance crew in their wire cage. They were dressed in the usual tan jumpsuits, and their skin was bleached from lack of sun. They looked like mushrooms. Matt shone Tam Lin's flashlight, and powerful though it was, the beam was lost.

He thanked the technician for his help, and the man went back to his work. Matt continued to look into the hot shaft. More elevators slowly rose and fell along the sides, and some had stopped at alcoves to tend to machinery.

"Triple dare you to go down to the bottom," Cienfuegos said.

"Me? Oh, no! It would be like being buried alive. I hate going underground." Matt remembered finding part of El Patrón's dragon hoard at the oasis. A dark shaft had opened up, and he'd glimpsed strange Egyptian gods and a floor covered with gold coins. It was the first of many chambers the old man had created. The earth around Ajo was riddled with them, all interconnected, with the last one leading to El Patrón's funeral chamber and the bodies of those he had chosen to serve him in the afterlife.

Matt had to hold on to the railing. Looking over the edge made him light-headed.

"And you call yourself a drug lord," the *jefe* said scornfully.

"The Mushroom Master overcame *his* fear and threw away his umbrella."

"Not completely," reminded the Mushroom Master.

"It's a work in progress. A real man doesn't run and hide, Don Sombra. He would be ashamed."

Matt was shocked. Never had Cienfuegos dared to lecture him like this. It was like having Tam Lin back, scolding him for being afraid to get onto a horse. For a second he was angry, but then he realized that what the *jefe* said was true. He could not afford to give in to fear. He was the Lord of Opium. You couldn't be weak and have power at the same time.

"I could have you cockroached for that," he said in an effort to save face, "but this time I'll overlook your insolence. Let's all go down to the bottom."

Cienfuegos grinned. "Very good, *mi patrón*. You're learning."

Of the three of them, only the Mushroom Master was at ease. He was used to dark, enclosed places like the elevator cage. The heat was unbearable. Their clothes quickly became drenched with sweat as the cage crawled into the depths. Matt found himself panting, whether from fear or heat he didn't know. Cienfuegos, for all his bravado, looked nervous in the occasional lights that flashed by. Now and then they passed a platform where there was an alcove gouged into the side of the shaft.

"What does 'cockroached' mean?" said the Mushroom Master. It was a question Matt had wanted to ask. "We have cockroaches in the biosphere, several kinds, in fact. Our founders tried to preserve as many life-forms as possible, although they drew the line at smallpox."

"Cockroached?" Cienfuegos seemed half-asleep. He was panting just like Matt. "It's a punishment El Patrón dreamed up.

He got it from some Indian raja. You tie a person down in a room full of roaches, the bigger the better, and pry his mouth open so he can't close it. The roaches wander around and eventually one of them discovers the open mouth and decides to explore. More follow. There's only so long you can spit them out. It's a way of strangling someone slowly, and for some reason it caught the attention of the Farm Patrolmen. There's nothing they fear more."

Matt felt like throwing up. The more he learned about El Patrón, the more he wished he weren't a copy of him.

"The punishment was never carried out," the *jefe* said.

"Thank Gaia for that!" said the Mushroom Master.

"The old man liked to dream up lurid punishments to scare the crap out of people, but if he wanted to kill someone, he did it quickly and efficiently."

The elevator bumped at the bottom. Here the tube ended in a ring of cement, and Cienfuegos locked the door open before they stepped out. They didn't want to be trapped down here.

They walked around the edge, noting the lights, the air conditioners, and the pipes snaking around the wall. Matt didn't know what they were looking for, but he was glad he hadn't acted like a coward. He walked quickly so they could leave quickly.

On the far side of the tube, a red light illuminated part of the wall. "What's that? Some kind of warning?" said the Mushroom Master. Beneath the light glimmered the red figure of a scorpion.

"Stop!" shouted Cienfuegos as the old man reached out. "I've seen those before. It guards something that only El Patrón was allowed to see. It recognizes his handprint and kills anyone else who touches it. You could open it, Don Sombra."

Both men turned to Matt. He stared at the symbol. There was no telling what it led to, but he was suddenly unwilling to reveal the secret. El Patrón had considered it important enough to hide in this dangerous place. Matt wanted to be alone when he opened up whatever it was.

"I'll come back another time," he said in a tone that allowed no room for argument. "Let's return to the hospital."

42

THE SUICIDE BOMBER

They had lunch under a grape arbor. Fidelito and Listen had quarreled, and *Sor* Artemesia sat between them to keep the peace. "He wouldn't play with Mbongeni," Listen complained.

"Who wants to sit in a baby crib and glue chicken feathers to your fingers?" retorted Fidelito.

"You're jealous 'cause Mbongeni likes me and not you."

"He *bit* me," cried the little boy.

"So? You had molasses on your hand. He likes sweets."

"Both of you keep quiet," said *Sor* Artemesia. She was out of sorts and was distant with Dr. Rivas. He, too, spoke little and appeared agitated. An uneasy atmosphere brooded over the gathering.

Only the Mushroom Master seemed relaxed. He rambled on about how mycelia wrap the roots of young fir trees and draw food to them when the soil is poor. "I think of them as babysitters," he said. "'Time for your three o'clock feeding,' they say, and the little trees sit up and pay attention."

"Shut up!" exclaimed Dr. Rivas. "I can't take much more of your drivel. What in hell are you doing here anyway?"

"He's helping us clean up the pollution near the eejit pens," Cienfuegos said.

"Why bother? The eejits don't care." The doctor glanced toward the lab, where the cow was walking slowly through flower-filled meadows in her mind. "I'm sick of eejits. Nothing fixes them. Nothing works."

"A journey of a thousand miles begins with a single step," the Mushroom Master said brightly. Dr. Rivas threw down his napkin and stalked off.

"I think all of us have been put into his freezer," said Listen.

"He certainly seems nervous," the *jefe* said. "Did you see the Bug when you visited the nursery?"

"Nope. I hope somebody got him with a flyswatter," said the little girl.

They finished lunch, and *Sor* Artemesia took Fidelito and Listen off for a nap. The Mushroom Master said he wanted a nap too.

That left Matt and Cienfuegos. "I'm going to call María, and I want to be alone," Matt said.

"Bad idea," said the *jefe*.

"What? Calling María?"

"Being alone." Cienfuegos looked pointedly at the grape arbor and cupped his ear. Matt understood. Someone was listening. There was an undercurrent of danger in Paradise, and the *jefe* had picked it up. He was practically sniffing the air like a coyote.

Matt felt the strange tension too. Something was building

up, and he wished he could count one-thousand-and-one, one-thousand-and-two to see how close it was. Along with Cienfuegos, he went to the holoport room and opened the wormhole to the Convent of Santa Clara. A UN peacekeeper in full battle dress was standing in front of the portal. He was covered from head to toe with riot gear, and his helmet was darkened so no one could see his expression. The soldier hurled himself into the wormhole.

"Close the portal!" screamed the *jefe*.

Matt was frozen.

"Close it! That's a suicide bomber!"

The figure drew closer with agonizing slowness, and Cienfuegos tried to reach the controls. Matt shoved him away. "We don't know what he is. Stay back! That's a direct order!"

The *jefe* collapsed to his knees. "I can't disobey, but please, please, please close the portal! Esperanza wants to kill you!"

What would El Patrón do? thought Matt as the lethal mists swirled about the figure. The answer came at once. *I'd wait and see,* said the old, old voice in his mind. *I didn't become a drug lord by wetting my pants every time something went wrong.*

Cienfuegos was doubled up with pain, the two directives at war in his mind: to protect the *patrón* and to obey a direct order. It was killing him. Matt laid his hand on the man's head and said, "I forgive you."

The peacekeeper's body shot out of the wormhole and fell with a clatter. The portal closed with a thunderclap that shook the room. Matt kicked away ice, wrapped his hands in a towel, and undid the helmet. The cold still penetrated to his fingers. He blew on a face that was heartbreakingly still and white.

"*¡Por Dios!*" cried Cienfuegos. He raced from the room and returned with a hair dryer. "Quick! Quick! Get the uniform off!" He ran the hair dryer over María's face while Matt undid buckles and snaps. She wasn't breathing, and Matt blew air into her lungs. She shuddered and gasped.

"She's in shock," said Cienfuegos. He called for help. Servants came running and carried her to a hospital room. By that time a doctor and nurse had arrived and began working to keep her warm and to feed oxygen into her lungs. A blood pressure cuff and heart rate monitor recorded life signs. Matt watched in a daze, not knowing what they meant but only that there was still something to measure.

Time passed. She began to breathe regularly. The color had come back into her skin, and the doctor said that she wouldn't lose her fingers or toes. The biggest problem was that she'd gone without air for an unknown time. No one knew how time was measured inside a wormhole.

"I've never seen anything like this," the doctor said. "Astronauts undergo the temperature of outer space, but they have the right protection. This uniform was meant for Earth conditions. I didn't know it could keep out cold."

María had come up with the only way she could escape her mother and used the only kind of uniform she could lay her hands on. "She didn't know either," Matt said.

He briefly went to his room to fetch the altar cloth María had sent to him through the holoport, and this he pinned to the wall in front of her bed. It would be the first thing she saw. All other concerns went out of his head. He sat for hours in her room, refusing food and turning away visitors. Lack of oxygen had harmed Chacho, though he had recovered eventually. He had never lost consciousness like this. Finally, *Sor* Artemesia came and refused to go. "You must rest, Don Sombra. You must eat."

"I'll do it here," said Matt. He had a cot brought in, but when he tried to eat, his stomach revolted and he couldn't keep anything down. This was too much like Mirasol's last hours. He dreaded seeing the doctor come, afraid that the man would tell him the situation was hopeless. Nurses arrived regularly to change the girl's position in bed and to administer intravenous feeding.

And still she did not awake. One of the new doctors measured her brain activity and pronounced himself satisfied with the results. "She seems normal in all respects except one. It isn't like a coma, Don Sombra. It's more like a deep sleep and that gives me hope that she will recover."

Matt said nothing. He remembered Mirasol collapsing after one of her dance sessions, only to be roused by a command. How long would she have slept if he hadn't given that command?

When the doctor had left, Matt said, "María, wake up!" but nothing happened. He talked to her as he'd spoken to Rosa after she'd been turned into an eejit. He told her about the disastrous party he'd thrown for the boys, about Chacho and his father, about the visit to the biosphere. But he left out any reference to the Mushroom Master in case Dr. Rivas was listening.

Day turned into night. He dozed, sitting up each time the nurses came in. They flexed María's arms and legs to stimulate her circulation. On the second day the doctor noted her eyelids fluttering. "She's dreaming, Don Sombra. Her brain is active." Matt wondered whether it was a nightmare or whether she was walking through flower-filled meadows like the cow. At this point he would have welcomed one of Listen's night terrors, if only to prove that María was still there.

Matt fell into a trancelike state. The sight of food revolted him, and he was no longer sure whether he was awake or dreaming. Nurses came and went. The sound of voices echoed distantly from the hall. The window lightened and darkened as the sun moved across the sky.

Matt saw Dr. Rivas bent over María and wondered vaguely why the man hadn't come before. The doctor held up a syringe, tapped it to dislodge air bubbles, and squirted a small amount of liquid from the tip.

"What are you doing?" asked Matt.

"Giving her a stimulant," said Dr. Rivas.

Something was wrong—the doctor's smile didn't reach his eyes, and behind that smile his teeth were clenched. Matt jumped up and smashed the syringe out of the doctor's hand.

Dr. Rivas backed away, hands in the air. "I meant no harm, Don Sombra. I exist to serve."

"Like you served El Patrón by carving up his clones."

"Good heavens! I'm your best hope for María's survival. Look. She's stirring."

Matt turned to see her fingers fluttering on the sheet. "María, it's me. I'm here. You made it. You're safe." The girl tossed her head from side to side. Her dark hair whipped across the pillow. "What's wrong?" the boy cried.

"She's trying to wake up. This will pass," said Dr. Rivas. And indeed, after a moment María calmed down and breathed easily again. Her lips opened slightly as though she wanted to speak. Matt watched, fascinated, willing her to come to life.

"I'm sorry I snapped at you, Dr. Rivas," said Matt, holding her hands and feeling warmth return to them. He turned, but the room was empty.

43

THE CHAPEL OF JESÚS MALVERDE

He rang for a nurse. No one came. He rang again and went out into the hall. The nurse's station was deserted. There were no voices, no whirr of machines, only the sound of eejits going about their tasks. He went back to the room. María seemed to be all right. Her blood pressure and heartbeat, as far as he could tell, hadn't changed.

He was afraid to leave her. He sat there, watching for any change in her condition. He realized that he shouldn't have struck out at Dr. Rivas. The man was understandably upset about his son's death. Matt should have been more patient.

"Don Sombra," came a soft voice from the door. Matt looked up to see *Sor* Artemesia. "You must come, Don Sombra. I think Dr. Rivas has gone mad. He's been fighting with the other doctors and destroying equipment."

Matt felt heavy with lack of sleep and food. His mind wasn't functioning clearly. "I'll deal with it later," he said.

"You must come now," urged *Sor* Artemesia. "There was trouble at one of the labs. Something about a dead cow. Dr. Rivas killed an eejit."

Everyone kills eejits, Matt thought wearily. Dr. Kim, Esperanza, even Cienfuegos on occasion. Nothing abnormal about that. "I need coffee," he said. The nun hurriedly fetched him a cup from the nurse's station. Matt waited for the bitter brew to work its way into his consciousness. "I can't leave María now. Especially if Dr. Rivas is going rogue. Where's Cienfuegos?"

"He flew the Mushroom Master back to the biosphere. When he returned and found the doctor growing more erratic, he radioed to Ajo for Daft Donald and the bodyguards. Oh! María's eyes are open!"

The girl was blinking, as though she didn't know where she was. Matt immediately went to her side. "You're safe, *mi vida.*"

Suddenly she was wide awake. "Matt?"

"I'm here. You should have asked me to come to you. I would have done it no matter how angry Esperanza was."

"But you *have* come," she insisted. "I had such a fight with Mother! You wouldn't believe how inflexible she can be when she wants something. She kept pushing me to get engaged to that creepy friend of hers. Honestly! He reminded me of a plucked turkey."

The excited flow of words told Matt that María had come back in full force. He was so grateful that he promised himself to apologize to Dr. Rivas as soon as possible. But then . . . perhaps recovery hadn't been the doctor's real intention. Matt remembered him tapping the syringe and claiming it was a stimulant. Why wait so long to give her a stimulant? Why wait until María was almost well?

He remembered Nurse Fiona's words: *They put a drip into the patient's arm and then they inject the chips with the liquid. The chips are smaller than blood cells and go right through the heart. The process takes less than fifteen minutes.*

"I'll kill him," he said.

"Don't bother," María said brightly. "I put him in his place. He tried to kiss me, and I gave him a slap he won't soon forget. *Sor* Artemesia, how wonderful to see you! Did Mother let you come back?" She sat up, and the intravenous needle popped out of her arm. "Ow! What's going on here?"

"It's all right, *mija*. You're in the hospital." The nun gently forced her to lie back down. She swabbed the blood from María's arm with a cotton ball.

"Hospital? I'm not sick. It's probably one of Mother's schemes to keep me under lock and key." She had no memory of going through the portal, and when she learned that she was actually in Opium, she was all for getting up to explore. "I've only been to Paradise as a small child. I remember wonderful gardens and deer that would eat out of my hand. The hummingbirds were everywhere."

"You haven't eaten real food for a week. You must take things slowly," said *Sor* Artemesia. She and Matt jumped when they heard the rattle of a machine gun.

Matt ran to the window and signaled for the others to stay back. He saw the shadow of several hovercrafts pass overhead. He heard the clap of stun guns, more machine-gun fire, then silence. They waited. "It came from the direction of the observatory," said Matt.

"Closer than that." *Sor* Artemesia shivered. They waited for a long time, and no more sounds came. Matt ventured into the hallway and found it deserted.

"I took Fidelito to a place of safety," said *Sor* Artemesia. "I tried to bring Listen, but she wouldn't leave Mbongeni. Chacho and Ton-Ton are okay as long as they stay in Ajo."

"You seem to have expected trouble," said Matt.

"Let's just say I know Dr. Rivas. We should take María away. I don't trust him."

They unpinned the altar cloth and eased María out of bed. Her legs gave out when she tried to stand, and they had to support her. "I wish we could get one of those little stirabouts," she said. "I remember floating around the gardens in one."

"We're less noticeable on foot," said Matt, remembering the shadows of large hovercrafts overhead.

Half-filled coffee cups sat on the nurses' desks, and half-eaten sandwiches had been knocked to the floor. The station had been abandoned in a hurry. They collected a full thermos of coffee and unopened packages of cookies.

"Why don't we go to the holoport room and call Mother?" suggested María.

"Later," said Matt. The sooner they got under cover, the better. *Sor* Artemesia led them along a stream in a direction Matt hadn't been before. For a while María had to lean on the others, but she recovered swiftly. She looked around eagerly and chattered about how happy she was to be here. Matt didn't tell her about Dr. Rivas. Sycamores twisted white branches over the path, and cottonwoods whispered among themselves. The shadows of birds followed them as they traveled.

The Paradise hospital and observatory were the most advanced of their kind in the world. Yet a short walk took you into a world that looked as though it hadn't been disturbed since the beginning of time. Pronghorn antelope and white-tailed deer swiveled their ears toward the travelers. A coyote slipped into tall grass, and Matt saw his yellow eyes peering at them through the leaves. He reminded the boy of Cienfuegos.

A fork-tailed hawk crested the trees in search of prey, and a family of quail sat as still as a painting in the dappled shade of a bush. Nothing was unduly alarmed by the people moving through their domain. The animals were cautious, as they would have been with one another, but not frightened. They had not been hunted for a century.

Matt saw a white building with stained-glass windows beyond a woven fence of reeds. "Is that a church?" he asked.

"Not exactly," said *Sor* Artemesia with a crooked smile. "It's the chapel of Jesús Malverde."

There had been a small shrine in Ajo and near the nursery in Paradise, but this was a building as big as a church. A long room had pews on either side and an altar at the end. Store-rooms and a kitchen were separate from the main chapel. This was a serious meeting place, and Matt wondered what sort of rituals were performed for a saint who answered the prayers of drug dealers. Stained-glass windows showed Malverde stand-ing in a marijuana patch, giving money to the poor, casting blindness on a troop of narcotics agents, and warning a drug mule to flee.

The altar was covered with silver charms, candles, and gifts like the one in Ajo. On a dais behind it was the saint himself, sitting in a chair. A cactus wren had made a nest in the timbers over his head, and wisps of grass had fallen onto Jesús Malverde's black hair.

This was a far better statue than the other ones Matt had seen. The saint's hair was carefully combed, and his face was painted with care. He wore a white shirt and bandanna. His trousers were black and his shoes were polished and expensive-looking. In one hand he held a bag of money. In the other was a sheaf of dollar bills. At his feet was a carpet of gold coins.

"María!" squealed Fidelito, popping up from behind a pew. The little boy ran up and hugged her. "I was so worried about you. Are you all waked up? Did you see things when you flew through the wormhole?"

But María couldn't tell him, because she had no memory of it.

"Be gentle with her, *chico*. She's been ill," said *Sor* Artemesia, untangling the little boy's arms.

"Where's Listen? I found dolls at the back of the altar. She'd like them."

Sor Artemesia shuddered. "That's *brujería, mijo*. Witchcraft. Those are voodoo dolls meant to curse someone, and it's better if you don't touch them. I couldn't get Listen to leave Mbongeni." The nun found the dolls and threw them away. She draped the altar cloth in the appropriate place and stood back to admire her work. "There!" she said. "That should take some of the curse off this place."

Sor Artemesia had planned the refuge carefully. She had stashed bottles of drinking water along the walls, and crackers and beef jerky were stored in plastic boxes to keep them from the mice. She told Fidelito to fetch sleeping bags from a cupboard and lay them on the pews for beds.

"Won't the saint be angry that we're living in his house?" said the little boy.

"That saint," said *Sor* Artemesia, "wouldn't care if you turned the place into a nightclub."

They made María lie down and propped her up with pillows. The nun insisted that she eat some jerky and drink a little coffee with lots of sugar. Matt also drank coffee, although he didn't like it. He'd been fasting for days and felt light-headed.

"I don't want to leave you," he said.

"You have to, Don Sombra. You have duties," said *Sor* Artemesia.

"I never asked for them," he said wearily. "I'm tired of cleaning up El Patrón's mess and watching the opium farms churn out drugs. I'm tired of watching eejits die. It's like a giant machine with no off button. Why shouldn't I stay here with people I love and forget the whole miserable thing?"

"You can't, Brother Wolf." María had been silent until now, but the food had brought life back into her eyes.

"The problem is too big, *mi vida*," said Matt. Thousands of people and billions of dollars are involved. We need an army to deal with it, and I can't trust anyone who has one." He threw up his hands. "If I had such a force, who would I attack? What would I invade?"

"You must begin by freeing the eejits," María said gently.

"Oh, sure! Like I haven't been working on that."

"I spoke with Cienfuegos before he went away," *Sor* Artemesia said. "He says the Scorpion Star is the source of the power that controls the eejits. You have to destroy it."

Matt looked at her in amazement. This was not the gentle, compassionate nun he was used to. "There are three hundred people on that space station."

"And at least ten thousand times that number are buried under the fields."

"So what am I supposed to do? Shoot it down? What would Saint Francis recommend?"

The nun was unmoved by Matt's sarcasm. "He'd tell you to get off your butt and do the job God has given you."

The boy had no answer for this. He was bone tired. He wanted to hand the problem to someone else. He wanted to move into the biosphere and herd frogs for the rest of his life. But that wasn't allowed. He took María's hand and felt its warmth. "I'll return when I can," he said.

"I can help you," she said. "I don't want to be left behind. I didn't risk death to be tossed aside like a kitten that's only good for chasing feathers."

Sor Artemesia laughed. It was the first wholehearted laugh Matt had heard from her in days. "I remember the arguments we used to have at school when she wanted to care for lepers. 'We'll have to import them,' I told her. 'Leprosy has been extinct for fifty years.' I remember her turtles with cracked shells, the birds with broken wings, and the three-legged cats. You have a drive to do good, María, but you'd slow Matt down in your present condition."

"*No te preocupas, mi vida.* Don't worry. Your turn will come when I've sorted out the Scorpion Star," said Matt, holding her hands and gazing into her eyes. "There will be thousands of people who will need your help."

"Well, then," she said, gazing back. He kissed her and left before she could think of an objection.

"Don't forget Listen," called Fidelito as Matt left the clearing where the chapel of Jesús Malverde stood.

44

EL BICHO

Matt moved stealthily through the gardens surrounding El Patrón's mansion. Peacocks fluttered and cried as he passed. Giant carp stuck their noses out of ponds. The old man had imported them from Japan, and they were so tame people could feed them rice balls. They were more than two hundred years old. Animals, both wild and tame, inhabited the gardens, as well as eejits toiling in their drab uniforms and floppy hats.

Matt tiptoed over the tile floors of the main house and came at last to the room he was seeking. The holoport was swirling with icons, and he intended to call Esperanza. He wanted to tell her about her daughter and also ask whether she knew a way to jam the signal, if signal there was, from the Scorpion Star.

On the floor, in front of the screen, was the Bug.

"What are you doing here?" cried Matt. He knelt by the child and felt his head. A ripple of energy like a low electric current ran through him.

The Bug moved feebly and held up his right hand. Matt saw to his horror that it had *melted*. All that was left was a sticky-looking knob of flesh. "He wouldn't take me," whimpered the little boy.

"You put your hand on the screen, didn't you," said Matt.

"Dr. Rivas told me to open it. And I did—I did—" El Bicho's voice trailed off.

"Does it hurt?" Matt didn't know what he would do if the boy said yes.

"It feels—funny. Like ants crawling. Will it grow back?"

No, thought Matt. *Not unless you really are a bug.* "I'll ask the doctors."

"He wouldn't take me," said the Bug.

"Take you where?" Matt said, although he knew.

"To the Scorpion Star."

And that was how Dr. Rivas had tricked the boy. He knew how much El Bicho longed to be in that ideal world. But the boy's hand was too small for the scanner to recognize. It must have partially accepted him, or else he'd be a puddle on the floor.

The Bug touched Matt's face with the knob. It was an instinctive gesture, a child reaching out for comfort, but Matt jerked away. It was disgusting, the feel of that boneless mass of flesh. He felt bile come into his mouth.

"Are you strong enough to walk?"

"I tried. I can't stand up."

Matt was confounded. He didn't have time to carry the boy to Malverde's chapel. He had to locate Cienfuegos and find out what those large hovercrafts were doing and why someone was firing machine guns. And then he noticed that the portal had changed. The edge of the screen was supposed to be red. Part of it turned green when Matt opened a section of the border to allow the passage of supplies, but now it was all green.

That was what the doctor had been up to. That was why he'd sacrificed the child. He'd ended the lockdown and left Opium defenseless.

Matt restored the lockdown at once. "How long has this been open?" he demanded.

"Don't be angry," wailed the Bug.

"I'm not angry, but we may have been invaded." Matt realized that the little boy was too shocked to answer questions. "Listen to me," he said urgently. "I have to get help. I have to rally the Farm Patrol. The whole country is in danger. Do you understand?"

"Don't leave me," cried El Bicho. He grabbed Matt's sleeve with his good hand.

Matt pulled away. "None of us is going to survive if I don't get help. I won't forget you. You're my brother, and I won't desert you. Try to stay strong."

"Don't leave me!" screamed the boy.

Matt fled the room. The Bug's screams followed him. He slammed the door and leaned against it, breathing heavily.

Being a drug lord isn't all guitar playing and pachangas, said the old, old voice in Matt's head. *I left my dying mother to build an empire. I sacrificed my son Felipe to the drug wars. I shot down a passenger plane to preserve the peace.*

Be quiet, said Matt.

El Patrón chuckled. *I am the cat with nine lives. I've had eight, and you are the ninth.*

Leave me alone!

Matt realized that he hadn't contacted Esperanza, but he couldn't bring himself to go back into that room. He ran to the armory, hoping to find Cienfuegos or Daft Donald, but it was deserted. *Where is everyone?* Matt thought. The silence was unnatural.

He selected a stun gun. He'd never fired one and now cursed himself for overlooking a basic drug-lord skill. He strapped a knife to his leg and another to his upper arm. He filled his pockets with tranquilizer beads. When you threw them at someone, they exploded, and the gas knocked the person out. That was how the Farm Patrol had captured Cienfuegos when he was trying to reach the United States.

Matt had never used a weapon in his life or even gone hunting. He didn't know whether he could kill someone. *You'd better make your mind up fast,* advised El Patrón. *We're not playing soccer here. This is* pok-a-tok.

Matt crossed the gardens, heading for the nursery, where he thought Listen and Mbongeni were. He felt the hidden knives pressed against his skin and mentally copied the swift movement that Cienfuegos used to produce a stiletto. He knew that he could never equal it. He'd seen Daft Donald pull a switchblade from a pant leg. It wasn't simply a matter of practice, but will. You had to want to kill someone. *You think too much,* complained El Patrón.

He kept to the shadows of trees, and every moving branch or birdcall made him flinch. He simply didn't know where the dangers were. But the children weren't in the nursery. A line of caretakers sat along a wall, and at their feet was a dead eejit. It was probably the one who let the cow die, the animal Dr. Rivas was using to grow a replacement for his son.

Matt ran to the main part of the hospital, and at last he saw normal people. Nurses in white scrubs were standing outside an operating room with doctors in gauze masks and latex gloves. The operating room door opened, and the medical staff went inside.

Matt edged forward, and his foot bumped against something. He glanced down and saw a body. It was a soldier, and the smell of hot metal rose from him. He'd been killed with a stun gun, and very recently. Matt backed away, but an African man in a military uniform came out of the operating room and shouted, "Stop him!" Instantly, soldiers poured out of the operating room. They grabbed Matt and removed the stun gun and knives as easily as peeling the skin off a banana. They shook the tranquilizer beads out of his pockets, but it was Matt who was overcome by gas, not his enemies. He passed out almost instantly.

45

PRISONERS

He woke up on the floor. He was in a hospital room, and on a bed, clenching her teeth like a little wild animal, was Listen. He stood up and almost passed out again. He fell against the bed.

Then he noticed the men sitting by the door. They were squat and broad-chested, your standard-issue thugs. Their booted feet looked twice the size of those of a normal man.

Matt was swept with dizziness again, and his stomach heaved. Listen sat up. "There's a bathroom next door if you want to barf."

Matt staggered inside, lost the coffee he'd drunk earlier, washed his mouth out, and staggered back. He collapsed next to Listen. "Don't bother trying to talk to them. They're Russians," said the little girl. "They've been jabbering at me for hours, but I've been ignoring them."

"How many of them are there?" asked Matt.

"Only two. Dr. Rivas said the border closed before more

could get in. I didn't know we were at war with the Russians."

"We aren't. They're working for Africans," said Matt. He knew now who had taken advantage of the open border. Just as El Patrón preferred Scottish bodyguards, Glass Eye Dabengwa had preferred Russians. Foreigners weren't as likely to betray you as your own kind.

"Africans! I'd sure like to meet them," said the little girl.

"Don't get your hopes up. Thugs come in all types. Where's Mbongeni?" he asked.

"Dr. Rivas says he's very sick and needs an operation."

Matt couldn't speak for a moment. He knew what kind of operation the doctor had in mind, and that meant that Glass Eye needed a transplant. "And where's Dr. Rivas?"

"Don't know." The little girl shrugged. "First he came for the Bug, and then he came back for his son and daughter. They were going on a trip, but the bad guys got here first. Can you make those men let us go?"

It was worth a try. Matt pointed at the door, nodding to show that he wanted it open. One of the men rubbed his chin with a rasping sound like sandpaper. *"Nyet,"* he said.

Matt tried to walk past them and got pushed back. It was a lazy gesture, like shooing a fly, but the strength behind the man's hand propelled Matt across the room and into a wall.

"Maybe they'll fall asleep," said Listen. The men showed no indication of sleepiness. They rumbled to each other in Russian and smoked a hand-rolled cigarette that they passed back and forth.

Matt recognized the smell from El Patrón's parties, where guests were offered hookahs. "If they keep that up, they'll pass out," he said. But the guards showed no sign of passing out, either.

After a while someone knocked on the door and handed through trays of food. It was a kind of beef stew with tomatoes and onions. On each tray was a slab of polenta as heavy as a brick. But the food was surprisingly good and the polenta okay if you ignored the rubbery texture. The guards ate enthusiastically, using their fingers and wiping their hands on their pants. They cleaned up the leftovers from Matt's and Listen's trays.

"I'm thirsty," complained Listen. She opened her mouth and pointed down her throat. One of the men went into the bathroom and returned with two plastic cups. "I sure hope he got that water from the sink," said the little girl.

Time passed slowly. To keep Listen amused, Matt told her one of Celia's Bible stories. "Samson was a very, very strong man," he began. "When he was a baby, he could pick up his crib and throw it across the room."

"The Bug tried that once," said Listen. "He rocked Mbongeni's crib back and forth until it fell over. Dr. Rivas put him into a straitjacket for a whole day."

Matt had forgotten about the Bug. With luck, someone would have heard his screams by now, although Matt didn't think his chances were good with Glass Eye Dabengwa's soldiers. Of course, Dr. Rivas could have helped him, but the Bug was of no further use to him. The boy was just another rabbit.

Matt's head hurt, and the aftereffects of the tranquilizer beads made him queasy.

"Hey, are you okay?" asked Listen, shaking his arm.

Everything's fine, Matt thought. *Sor Artemesia, María, and Fidelito are hiding. Cienfuegos is missing. The Bug has lost a hand. Glass Eye Dabengwa has taken over Opium, and Mbongeni—*

Glass Eye had needed a transplant as soon as he arrived. Matt was suddenly alert. That meant he was seriously ill and was probably close to death. Too bad Dr. Rivas hadn't waited a few more hours before opening the border.

Matt shied away from what must have happened in the operating room, but he had to face it. He remembered the first time Celia fed him arsenic. She had known, as he did not, that El Patrón had suffered a heart attack. She had forced him to eat before going to the hospital, supposedly to visit the old man, but in reality to have his heart cut out.

The arsenic had made Matt so sick that he was unusable for a transplant. And El Patrón had to make do with a piggyback transplant, with a heart too small to do the job properly. Just as Glass Eye was making do with poor Mbongeni.

"I wish we could get fresh air," Listen said. "The smoke is making me sick."

Matt looked up to see the guards passing their hand-rolled cigarette back and forth. He pointed at the smoke and pretended to gag. One of the men opened the door. *"Izvineete,"* he said.

Matt calculated how fast he'd have to be to scoot out the door, but he couldn't leave Listen behind. "Let's see. Where was I? Samson was strong because he never cut his hair. It was a kind of magic."

"Dr. Rivas says there's no such thing as magic," said Listen.

"Dr. Rivas is a jerk. One day Samson was out walking, and a lion attacked him. He killed it with his bare hands. Later he saw that a hive of bees had moved into the lion's skin, and he ate some of the honey."

"Didn't the bees sting him?"

"They sure did, and Samson brushed them off like bread crumbs. Heroes don't worry about things like that." Matt told her about how Samson's girlfriend Delilah betrayed him by cutting his hair off, and how Delilah's friends turned him into a slave.

"His hair must have grown back," said Listen, with her usual logic. "Then he could beat everyone up."

"His hair did grow back, but nobody noticed because he was a slave. Samson waited and waited until he got his enemies all in one place. One night they had a big party, and they brought Samson out so they could make fun of him. Samson got hold of the posts holding up the house and pulled them down. The building fell on top of everyone and squashed them flat."

"And Samson lived happily ever after," finished Listen.

Too late Matt remembered how the story ended. "Not exactly," he said.

"He got out, didn't he?"

"I'm afraid not. He died along with his enemies. But he got revenge, and that's important."

"I don't like that story," Listen yelled. "I want a happy ending! He should have picked up a rock and let 'em have it." She grabbed a pillow and began to pound it with her fists.

"It didn't really happen," said Matt.

"It's a *Bible* story. *Sor* Artemesia says they're all true."

Listen started to cry, and one of the guards came over and thumped himself on the chest. *"Samson,"* he announced. He flexed his muscles.

"Did you understand what we were talking about?" asked Matt.

"Nyet. Samson." Thump, thump.

"That's his name," Listen said delightedly. "What's the other guy called? Delilah?"

"De-lee-lah," said Samson, pointing at his fellow guard and mincing around.

"Boris," corrected the other guard. Now he came over and with gestures invited Listen to a game of scissors, paper, rock. They had seen that the little girl was upset and wanted to cheer her up. For thugs, they weren't too bad.

Night came, or what Matt supposed was night. There was no window in the room. The men made gestures that indicated sleep. They turned off the light but left the bathroom door ajar. Matt still had Tam Lin's flashlight, and they used that to move around in the dark.

Listen curled up on the bed, but it was too small to include Matt, and he had to sleep on the floor. Exhausted though he was, he couldn't get comfortable. He dozed and woke and worried. The Russians snored erratically and occasionally woke each other up with a snort.

Sometime during the night Listen climbed out of bed and sat down next to Matt. "I get scared in the dark," she told him. "Most times I used to climb into the crib with Mbongeni. I tried to teach him scissors, paper, rock, but it was too hard for him. We played paper and rock instead, but you need scissors to make it work. Anyhow, he liked moving his hands around." She began to cry softly, and Matt held her until she fell asleep again.

They lost track of time. Air seeped in through a vent, but it was never fresh, and the fumes from the guards' cigarettes made them sick. The same food was brought three times a day, but the Russians got most of it.

At night Matt went over his last sighting of Glass Eye Dabengwa. It had been at El Patrón's birthday party three years before. Silence radiated from wherever the African drug lord walked. It reminded Matt of a large predator arriving at a waterhole. The birds stopped singing, the monkeys faded through the trees, and the antelopes clustered together, hoping that there was safety in numbers.

But there was no safety in numbers where Glass Eye was concerned. He had wiped out entire villages for trivial slights. Matt hoped that by imagining the man he could get used to his presence. But the memory of those unblinking yellow eyes appeared to him in dreams and lingered long after he'd awoken.

Matt practiced Russian with the guards and managed to communicate a few basic requests, such as soap, towels, and toothbrushes. Boris and Samson seemed unaware that such luxuries were necessary, but they were eager to please. They passed the requests on, and the supplies arrived.

"Ask them for deodorant," suggested Listen.

"For us?" asked Matt, surprised.

"For them."

"Boris would probably eat it," said Matt. He suspected that even if he learned fluent Russian, the guards wouldn't have much to say. They were stoned all the time. They sat in front of the door in a state that was almost hibernation. But they could wake up quickly. Matt tried to sneak Listen past them, and they hurled him across the room without even breaking into a sweat.

Once Listen sat up in the middle of the night and screamed, "I want Dr. Rivas! I want Dr. Rivas!" The guards fell over themselves trying to calm her down. Boris sang her a Russian lullaby so melancholy that Listen went into hysterics.

46

GLASS EYE DABENGWA

And then, one morning, they were awakened by a knock on the door. The light was already on, and the guards were passing their cigarette back and forth. The same man Matt had seen outside the operating room marched in. He was dressed in a general's uniform, with so much gold braid on the shoulders you could hardly see his neck. The guards snapped to attention and ground the cigarette under a heel.

"Idiots! You don't get stoned on duty!" shouted the man. He slapped Boris hard and shoved Samson against the door. Matt watched hopefully—they could have snapped the officer in two—but the guards only cowered before his obvious authority. The man turned to Matt and Listen. "Come on! Hurry up!"

Boris and Samson herded them down the hall, with the general striding in front. "Hey, mister! Are you an African?" yelled Listen, running to keep up.

The general halted and turned around. She almost ran into him. "Why do you ask?"

"'Cause you're dark like me. I'm an African. My name's Listen, and I'm going to grow up to be a drug queen."

The man's eyes widened. "I once knew a woman called Listen, but she died long ago."

"I know," the little girl said excitedly. "I'm her clone—or I woulda been if she'd lived. Tell me about her. What was she like?"

The general knelt down beside her. "She was a most beautiful and kind lady." The hard expression faded from his face, and he smiled.

Matt did a double take. He'd seen this man before, whining for a shipment of opium. At the time he'd been dressed in a plaid suit and high-heeled boots. The uniform made him look almost respectable, but Matt knew he didn't deserve to wear it. He wasn't a real general. He was a drug addict. "You're Happy Man Hikwa," Matt said. "Are we going to a costume party?"

The hard expression came back. "You'll soon learn what kind of party we're going to." The man picked up Listen and continued down the hall.

What a fool I was to walk into the hands of our enemies, Matt thought as they walked on. He should have hidden until he found Cienfuegos. How easily the soldiers had disarmed him. He might as well have handed the weapons over and saved them the trouble.

I wonder what shape Glass Eye is in, said El Patrón in a casual, chatty way. *His replacement parts used to wear out faster than mine.*

Do you know something I don't? thought Matt. He heard a dry cackle and imagined the old man sitting in the back of Hitler's car, enjoying the homage of his slaves.

Just because they took your weapons doesn't mean you aren't armed, said El Patrón. Matt waited for more information, but the voice only came when it felt like it. He had no control over it.

Matt experienced a moment of abject terror when he entered the hospital room. Glass Eye Dabengwa almost over-flowed the chair he was sitting in. His legs were like tree trunks covered in gray bark, and his toes, with their gnarled and dis-colored nails, spread out like the talons of a bird of prey.

He was dressed in a skimpy hospital gown, and his seamed arms, repaired from many battles in his youth, bulged out of the sleeves. His body was massive, nourished, so rumor said, on the blood of children. But much the same rumor had been circu-lated about El Patrón. It could be said of any drug lord who harvested clones.

The only mercy was that Dabengwa's eyes were cloaked by dark glasses. The curtains in the windows were drawn too, and the only light was from a dim lamp covered by a shade. Matt wondered whether something was wrong with the man's vision. He certainly hoped so.

Dr. Rivas was seated in another chair across the room, and Listen immediately flew to him. A pair of nurses cowered against a wall. The rest of the space was taken up by African soldiers.

"Who is this child?" Glass Eye said in a voice that resonated like distant thunder.

"The baby *patrón,*" said Happy Man.

"Baby Patrón. I like it. Come closer, boy," said Dabengwa.

Matt struggled to hang on to his courage. Was it his imagi-nation or did he hear an odd sound in the room? "I am the heir of El Patrón," he stated as firmly as he could. "I am the Lord of Opium."

Dabengwa's large head turned toward him. *Click. Whirr.* There were those strange noises again. "I see only a boy."

"Appearances are deceiving. I'm actually a hundred and forty-seven years old."

Glass Eye wheezed. It took a moment for Matt to realize it was a laugh. "You sound like the old vampire, at any rate."

"We don't know how much of the personality clones inherit," said Dr. Rivas. "None has survived this long."

Glass Eye dismissed the comment. "No matter. He's in my power now."

Dr. Rivas paused before saying, "*Mi patrón*, let me warn you that he still has an army. There are men in Ajo—"

"Silence!" Glass Eye nodded to a nurse, who looked perfectly terrified as she approached with a bottle of some liquid. The man sucked on a straw. *Click. Whirr.*

Matt thought, *So Dr. Rivas is calling him* patrón *now.* He was disgusted, but not surprised.

"Where's Mbongeni?" Listen suddenly asked. Dr. Rivas shushed her, but it didn't work. "Mbongeni's my best buddy, and I want him back."

Glass Eye seemed to notice her for the first time. "Another child," he said.

"I'm Listen," said the little girl, wriggling out of the doctor's grasp. "I want my buddy, and I know he wants me. Do you know where he is?"

Matt grabbed her before she could get too close to the ancient drug lord. She didn't seem to understand the danger she was in. Dabengwa removed his glasses, and there *they* were, the yellow eyes that never blinked, the eyes of a crocodile peering up through leaf-stained water. They whirred as he focused on her.

"*I* am Mbongeni," said Glass Eye.

Matt felt sick. Part of him was, of course—the heart, maybe the liver.

Listen laughed. "You're making fun of me 'cause I'm a little kid. Mbongeni is about so high"—she held out her hand, palm down—"and he's not too bright, but that's not his fault. He's a baby and always will be."

Glass Eye was paying close attention to her. He reached out his hand and turned hers over. "This is how they measure size in Africa. With the palm up." Matt shuddered to see his massive paw enclose hers, but she shook him off.

"I'm an African, but I've never been there," she said.

"Is your name really Listen?"

"She's your wife's clone," said Happy Man Hikwa.

"I'm *not* a clone, you turkey. Once the original dies, the clone becomes a full human." The little girl folded her arms and scowled at Happy Man.

Glass Eye grinned, something Matt didn't think was even possible. The famous teeth of a twenty-year-old gleamed in his weathered face, and something squeaked in his neck. "She's as cheeky as the original," he said with approval.

"Tell me about her, Mr. African. I always wondered what she was like."

"Well . . ." The yellow eyes swiveled, remembering. "She was very clever, *too* clever really. How she could hide when she was naughty! I would look for her all over the presidential palace. I would send guards to seek her out, but she always escaped them. Then, when I was worried enough to forgive her, she reappeared, hanging her head as you do now and promising never to do whatever it was again."

"She was like one of those brightly colored hummingbirds

you have here," said Happy Man. "They hang in the air, and when you try to grab them, they disappear."

"Nobody but a dum-dum would try to catch a humming-bird," Listen said scornfully.

Glass Eye wheezed again. He was pleased with her. "You do remind me of her. So quick. So pretty. I'm glad you didn't terminate her, Dr. Rivas."

Matt could see the little girl trying to figure out the word. Fortunately, it wasn't part of her vocabulary.

"How come you don't blink, Mr. African?" said Listen, gazing into his face. "If I don't blink, my eyes hurt."

"Listen! Don't ask rude questions!" cried Dr. Rivas.

Dabengwa waved his hand at the doctor. "It's all right. Her original would have said the same thing. My eyes are artificial, child. They are machines, like little cameras. Dr. Rivas made them for me many years ago, after I was injured by a car bomb. He replaces them every so often."

Listen was impressed. She went up close and watched as he swiveled them back and forth. "Is that why they make squeaky noises?"

"They should not do that," grumbled the drug lord. "I need them replaced, but one cannot have several operations at once. Parts of my body are artificial. I was not blessed with a fine hospital and many clones as El Patrón was."

The little girl cocked her head to one side. She was clearly pondering the meaning of that last sentence. "Why is it important to have many clones?"

"Let the man rest," interrupted Dr. Rivas. "Please overlook her questions, *mi patrón*. She chatters like a tree full of birds, and half the time she doesn't know what she's saying."

"That's not true!" cried the little girl. "I'm smart. I can recite the names of planets and the twenty biggest stars in the sky. I can dissect a rabbit, or could if Dr. Rivas would let me."

"Now is not the time," said the doctor, pulling her away roughly. Glass Eye slumped in his chair, and the nurse came forward again with a glass of liquid.

"We will conduct more business tomorrow," Happy Man announced. "The drug lord is tired." He went to the door, but Glass Eye wasn't finished.

"Tomorrow," he said heavily. "I will see you tomorrow, Baby Patrón. And then you will open the border for me."

Never, thought Matt as they were led away.

47

HAPPY MAN GOES HUNTING

Why did Dr. Rivas call Mr. African the *patrón*? Aren't you the *patrón*?" asked Listen when they had returned to the room.

"He's not called Mr. African. His name is Glass Eye Dabengwa, and he's trying to take over the country."

Boris and Samson had settled by the door, this time with two cigarettes. The visit to their boss had unnerved them so much that they were trying to get high as soon as possible. They puffed vigorously until a smoke alarm on the wall went off. Samson bashed it with his fist until it stopped.

"I guess Glass Eye got in when the Bug opened the border," said Listen.

Matt sat up. "You knew about that?"

"Dr. Rivas said they were going to do it. He told the Bug they were going to the Scorpion Star, and oh boy, was he happy about it. He said he was going to aim a big missile at the nursery and blow me up."

Matt sighed inwardly. He kept trying to feel sorry for El Bicho, but it was difficult. "I closed the border again. That's why there aren't more bad guys."

"So are you the *patrón* or not?"

"We're still arguing about it."

Matt, in spite of the desperate situation, knew he had a few things in his favor. Glass Eye had few allies in the country, and Cienfuegos, if he was still alive, would make sure that number went down. As for opening the border, no one except Matt could do it. Dabengwa could rage and threaten all he liked, but he couldn't kill his only chance of escape.

But as the day dragged on, some of Matt's optimism seeped away. Nothing said that Glass Eye couldn't *torture* him until he gave in. How much pain could he endure? He thought of various things Glass Eye could do and listed them on a scale of one to ten. *You think too much,* complained El Patrón.

Matt and Listen were sitting on the floor with the evening food trays on their laps. Beef stew and polenta again. Listen had developed a dislike for polenta almost equal to her hatred of mushrooms. She flicked bits of it on the wall to see if it would stick.

"Stop that. If you don't like it, give it to Boris."

"I want to see if he'll eat it off the wall," the little girl said. Matt got up, took the tray away, and dumped the remaining polenta on Boris's tray.

"There! Finish the stew," he said, replacing it on her lap.

"I miss Mbongeni," she said. "And I miss Fidelito and *Sor* Artemesia and Cienfuegos, too." Her mouth turned down, and she looked dangerously close to crying. "There sure are a lot of people missing."

"They aren't missing. They know exactly where they are," Matt said. He watched her eat and then tucked her into bed. "Try to sleep," he said. He shone the flashlight Tam Lin had given him on the wall and made shadow animals with his hands. Celia had done that for him when he was small. He did a rabbit, a goose, a coyote, and an eagle.

Boris came over and hunkered down. He'd learned a few English words and used one of them now. "Lullaby?" he offered.

"Nyet," said Matt.

Boris continued looking at the little girl. "Glass Eye bad," he announced.

"You can say that again," said Matt. The Russian twisted his hands as though he were snapping something in two. Then he shook his head.

"What does that mean?" said Listen after the Russian had gone back to his post.

"It means he'd like to kill Dabengwa but can't. He's controlled by a microchip."

"It was nice of him to think of it," said the little girl, snuggling into the covers.

"Being here isn't nearly as bad as when I was thrown into the chicken litter," Matt said. "I was alone except for Rosa, my caretaker. She hated me. All I had to play with were cockroaches. But a dove used to come through the window and visit me."

"Was it the same dove Noah sent out to look for land?" Listen said suspiciously.

"Her great-great-ever-so-great-granddaughter," said Matt. "María rescued me, even though she was only six years old. She brought Celia to the window, and Celia went to El Patrón." He told her how Tom—a certified bad guy—had come to the window and shot him with a peashooter until he was covered with bruises. "But then I threw a rotten orange at him, and it fell apart on his face and covered him with wiggly worms."

Listen crowed with delight. "Did they get into his ears and mouth?" she asked.

"Yes! And two of them went up his nose." But Matt saw she was getting too wild, and so he made her lie down again and told her about the oasis instead. "It was a secret world. No one except me and Tam Lin knew about it. We had picnics and campfires. We went swimming in the lake. It's not like being in a swimming pool. The water makes you feel alive, and it's full of little fish."

"I wish I had a secret world," Listen said wistfully.

"I'll take you there when we get out," Matt promised.

Later, when he attempted to snatch a few minutes of sleep, he felt Tam Lin's flashlight under the pillow and wished they were in the oasis now. There sure were a lot of missing people, and tomorrow there might be two more.

Dr. Rivas arrived about noon, accompanied by two African soldiers armed with machine guns. "This place stinks. We'll go to the nursery," he said. He was in a grim mood and shoved Listen away when she tried to hug him.

She didn't stay depressed long. It was too wonderful getting outside, and she danced for joy. She was dressed in a yellow pinafore and bright pink sandals that had been delivered the evening before. Eejits went about their work in the gardens, clipping grass with scissors, refilling hummingbird feeders, and taking litter out of ponds one leaf at a time.

"Look!" cried Listen. Over one part of the hospital was a column of smoke. "That's the lab where all the freezers are!"

Five soldiers were scooping buckets of water out of the

fountain where El Patrón's brothers and sisters stood. If only five had been spared to fight the blaze, Matt thought, Glass Eye couldn't have that many men. Perhaps hundreds of eejits were around, but they hadn't been trained to throw buckets of water on a fire. The whole hospital could burn down around their ears and they wouldn't notice.

"A century of research went up in those flames," said Dr. Rivas. "My life's work. I begged Glass Eye for more help. I told him his health depended on the lab, and he said that his life depended on being guarded. Cienfuegos is at the bottom of this. I hope he's proud of his stupid Neanderthal act of terrorism. He must have used a flamethrower."

He probably is proud, Matt thought. *Among those samples were the deadliest germs known to humankind.*

The same caretakers were sitting along the wall of the nursery, but the dead eejit had been removed. Listen peeked into the kitchen, the bathroom, and the cupboards. "Where's Mbongeni?" she said.

"You know where he is," Dr. Rivas said impatiently.

Listen looked wary. "How would I know?"

"Because I explained it to you when the first Mbongeni was sacrificed. He's been used for spare parts," said Dr. Rivas.

Listen shrieked, "You did it! You said you wouldn't do it, and you did! You did! You did! You did!"

"You're a beast," said Matt, trying to calm the little girl.

"We're all beasts." The doctor sat down on one of the beds, and one of Mbongeni's stuffed toys fell to the floor. "*Sor* Artemesia can talk about souls all she likes, but when we die, we turn into compost like any other piece of rubbish."

"Mbongeni was not rubbish!" Listen shouted.

"For twenty years I have been El Patrón's slave. I created life out of nothing, fed it, cared for it, and in the end killed it to prolong his existence. That's what clones are for, Listen. You knew that, so don't pretend you didn't. It's no different from dissecting rabbits."

"You don't cut up people!" she cried.

"Clones aren't people. They're collections of cells."

Listen threw herself at the doctor, but Matt held her back. He was afraid for her. She'd hidden the truth from herself for years. She knew on one level what had happened to the older Mbongeni, and she knew what the fate of the younger one would be. But it was too much for a seven-year-old child to face consciously. The truth had only surfaced in her night terrors.

The African soldiers kept glancing outside as though expecting trouble. Boris and Samson had, Matt noticed, armed themselves with stun guns. A breeze laden with smoke from burning cholera, smallpox, and plague germs stirred the curtains of the windows. It was another beautiful day in the drug neighborhood.

"You're one of the lucky ones, Listen," said Dr. Rivas. "Glass Eye likes you. He wants you to grow up to become his hundred and fiftieth or two hundredth wife. I forget how many there are."

The little girl refused to look at him. "I'm putting you into my freezer," she hissed.

Matt longed to lunge at the doctor and silence him forever, but the soldiers would stop him. "Glass Eye won't live that long," he said, lifting Listen onto one of the beds.

The doctor laughed bitterly. "Oh, yes he will. He isn't in as good a shape as El Patrón was, but we can do wonderful things with machines. I can build a mechanical heart that will keep him going. Just think, Listen. In ten years you'll be seventeen. You always wanted to be a drug queen, and here's your chance."

To Matt's surprise, Listen didn't look grief-stricken, as he'd expected. The expression on her face was rage. It made her seem a lot older than seven.

"I think it's time for lunch," said Dr. Rivas, getting up and brushing the wrinkles from his lab coat. He sent the eejit caretakers to the nursery kitchen, and they soon returned with cheese sandwiches and chocolate milk. Matt didn't think he could eat, but he'd grown so tired of stew and polenta that the new food was welcome. Listen spat on her sandwich and threw it on the floor. The soldiers and Russian bodyguards stood by the door and watched.

Matt picked up Mbongeni's stuffed toys and put them into a cupboard, where Listen couldn't see them. He rolled the crib into the kitchen, but the eejits, when they tidied up, put everything back. They'd been programmed to keep things in order, and it was useless to argue with them.

"Happy Man has been going on hunting parties," Dr. Rivas said suddenly. "He and a few friends have been flying around in those little stirabouts."

"I suppose they want to turn this place into a wasteland like the rest of the Dope Confederacy," said Matt.

"They've been extremely successful." The doctor smiled, pleased that he'd gotten a reaction. "The animals here have never been hunted, and they didn't know they were in danger. Happy Man bagged a dozen pronghorn antelope, even more white-tailed deer, two bears, a jaguar—they're very rare—and a puma. It won't take him long to clean this place out."

For the first time Matt realized that the doctor was not only evil, he was *insane*.

"The machine guns were so powerful, they blew the animals to bits. One of the antelopes was standing in front of a window at Malverde's chapel. I suppose the beast thought it was under the saint's protection, but it soon learned its mistake. When the buzzards came down to feed, the soldiers blasted them, too."

"Why tell me?" said Matt. He carefully kept his face blank at the mention of the chapel.

"Because I want you to see your country in ruins. I want you to watch your friends die and know that you yourself have fallen into the hands of your worst enemy."

"What do you have against me? I didn't do anything to you."

"You destroyed my son and drove my wife to suicide," said the doctor, as though he hadn't heard Matt. "You burnt up my life's work, but it's all worth it if you suffer."

"El Patrón did those things, not me." Matt despaired of getting through to the man. He was locked into a mental bubble.

More soldiers came to the door. They talked excitedly in some African language. Boris and Samson jumped from one foot to the other, trying to make themselves understood.

"I'm not El Patrón," Matt repeated.

"Oh, but you are," Dr. Rivas said softly. "You have the same gestures, the same body, and the same voice. You're the most perfect copy of him I ever made."

The soldiers beckoned to the doctor, and they conferred in low voices. "Glass Eye had a slight relapse this morning," Dr. Rivas said when he returned. "That's why he didn't call for you. It seems that Happy Man took advantage of the situation to go hunting again. He didn't come back."

"Tough toenails," said Matt. With any luck, the fake general was in the stomach of a jaguar (very rare).

"It means that your time has run out. Dabengwa wants the border opened, and he wants it now."

Matt grabbed a fork from a table and stabbed at his right hand, but he wasn't fast enough. The African soldiers were as well trained as the Farm Patrol, and one of them twisted his arm behind his back while another kicked him in the stomach. Matt collapsed, gasping for breath.

"That was a trick worthy of the old man," Dr. Rivas said. "Too bad it didn't work. Your hand is going to stay in perfect condition until we've had the use of it."

The soldiers pulled Matt to his feet and shoved him out the door. He wondered how long he could endure pain. He'd heard about things Glass Eye had done to his enemies. Unlike El Patrón, the African drug lord didn't dispose of them quickly. Terror was the way he kept power.

"I'll die before I betray Opium," he said.

"Oh, you won't be the one to suffer," Dr. Rivas said, nodding at Listen as they hurried across the garden. "*She* will be."

48

EL PATRÓN'S ADVICE

You're in a fine mess, aren't you? said El Patrón.

Stop gloating and help us, thought Matt.

Why should I? I've already told you what you need to know, the old man said peevishly. Matt imagined him sitting under a grape arbor, watching the statues of his seven brothers and sisters.

Tell me again. If I don't survive, your ninth life is over. Matt knew there was no use appealing to El Patrón's better nature. He didn't have one. But only silence followed this appeal to self-interest. The old man had gone back to whatever entertainments the dead had.

They passed a stirabout and a heap of ruined animal skins. They hurried through the halls of the hospital. Samson carried Listen, who was trying to shred his arms with her fingernails. He bore it stoically.

There was chaos in Glass Eye Dabengwa's room. Bottles had been overturned, a lamp lay shattered, a nurse knelt at the drug lord's feet, holding her arm and sobbing. Soldiers were ranged against the wall in postures of defense. Glass Eye himself was swaying like a heavyweight boxer about to land a crushing blow.

"I'll kill him," he snarled. "I'll kill him." No one dared to answer. Either Happy Man really had run off, or he was pushing up daisies in the forest. "You! Boy! Open the border. I will have more men now!"

Matt flinched. The yellow eyes swiveled toward him, their lids shrunken and dry from lack of use. He swallowed. His throat closed up. "No," he managed to croak.

"YOU DO NOT SAY NO TO ME!" roared the drug lord.

Matt swallowed. He heard the *click, whirr* of Dabengwa's eyes, the creak of his neck, the tiny groans of various parts of the man's anatomy as he moved. Dear God, was any part of him still human?

"You leave my friend alone!" came a sharp little voice directly under Glass Eye's nose. "If you're not careful, I'll put you into my freezer."

Dabengwa looked down as though he could scarcely believe what he was seeing.

"If you don't know what that means, I'll tell you," said Listen. "I won't see you and I won't hear you. You'll be a big old lump of ice to me."

"Listen, please come away," begged Matt.

She looked directly into the drug lord's yellow eyes and tapped her foot impatiently. It was like watching a bantam rooster challenge a rottweiler. Utterly courageous and crazy. The rottweiler always won.

"Let me tell you about your original," rumbled Glass Eye, momentarily distracted. "She was a girl from a small village. I sent for her and she defied me, so I killed her brothers and sisters.

She ran away, and I killed her parents. Then she came, hanging her head and apologizing, but she was never obedient. Always she ran, and I had a tracking device injected under her skin. The last time, I broke her neck."

Listen wavered a little, but she stood her ground. "That was dee-diddly-dumb. You remind me of the Bug. He's always breaking things, and then he doesn't have them anymore."

"The Bug?" said Dabengwa.

"Another clone of El Patrón," Dr. Rivas explained quickly. "She used to play with him."

"Dead, I suppose," said the drug lord.

The doctor nodded, but Listen said, "He's not dead. He's running around, opening doors and all sorts of secret places."

"That's a lie!" the doctor cried.

"Nope. Dr. Rivas had him open the holoport. Then he took him to other places full of jewels and gold and everything. Ask him to show you."

"She's raving, *mi patrón*. She makes up stories."

Glass Eye signaled, and a couple of the soldiers restrained the doctor. "This is very interesting, child. Tell me more."

The little girl took a deep breath. "See, the big people don't pay attention to me. They don't think I can understand, but I'm not called Listen for nothing. I heard Dr. Rivas and his son and daughter talk about a room at the bottom of the solar telescope. It's where El Patrón kept his money. Boy, did they get excited! Dr. Angel and Dr. Marcos loaded a hovercraft and took off for the Scorpion Star, but they didn't get more than a tiny bit of the stuff." She smiled winningly, an adorable child trying to please.

Dr. Rivas struggled with the soldiers, but they only tightened their grip. "You can't believe a seven-year-old! Children that age have no understanding of reality. And you need me,

Glass Eye. You aren't out of the woods yet. You need a heart monitor and another clone—"

Glass Eye swung at the doctor and struck him such a blow that Matt heard the man's neck crack. Dr. Rivas slid to the floor with a look of immense surprise. He lay there, his eyes open, his body trembling for a moment before it became still.

That's why I always got the better of Dabengwa, commented El Patrón. *Poor impulse control.*

Matt was too frozen to respond. It had been so quick! The doctor, who had maintained El Patrón's zombie army for twenty years, who had created his clones, who had created Matt himself, was dead!

Happy Man Hikwa came to the door, supported by a shambling field eejit in a jumpsuit and floppy hat. His black general's uniform was torn and smeared with blood. "Oh no." He moaned. "You shouldn't have done that, Glass Eye. Oh, no, no, no."

Dabengwa looked like a man waking up from a trance. He seemed to have trouble focusing. "Where've you been?" he asked.

"A few of us went to that abandoned church in the forest," said Happy Man. "But the damn stirabout ran out of energy. We stalled. And this—this monster came out of the church—seven feet tall, I swear! His neck was covered in scars."

Daft Donald, thought Matt.

"Where are my men?" thundered the drug lord.

"Please don't blame me, Glass Eye! There were enemies everywhere. We didn't stand a chance. I was the only one who got away. I ran until I fell over a tree root and sprained my ankle. I saw this eejit and ordered him to help me." Happy Man slumped and the eejit slumped too. Like most zombies, he tended to copy his master.

"We've got to go," Happy Man bleated. "Please, Glass Eye. We can't survive here. There aren't enough of us. Make the Baby Patrón open the border."

"Why am I plagued with such stupidity?" shouted Dabengwa. "Who told you to go joyriding when we're in the middle of a war? I should have you skinned and nailed up on a wall as a warning to others."

"I meant no harm," babbled Happy Man. "I've always been your most loyal follower."

"Drop him," said Glass Eye. The eejit obediently opened his arms, and Hikwa fell to the floor with a loud shriek.

"Ai! It hurts! I need a doctor!"

"This is the treatment you get," said Dabengwa, kicking Happy Man's ankle. "Now you will open the holoport, boy, and end the lockdown."

Matt gathered up his courage. "I'll never do that," he said, and braced himself for a blow. But it didn't come. Instead, Glass Eye turned to Listen and grabbed her by the throat. She tried to pull away, but he tightened his grip and she struggled for breath.

"You have seen what I can do. Think carefully." Glass Eye loosened his grip slightly, and Listen gasped.

Matt dropped his hands to show compliance. He knew the man could snap the little girl's neck. And he knew that nothing he tried would make the slightest difference. If he attacked, the soldiers would be on him. If he agreed to open the border, it would only postpone the inevitable. Ultimately, Glass Eye would not let either of them live.

Death then, he decided. It would trap the invaders, and Daft Donald and Cienfuegos could finish them off. Opium would remain sealed. Once, he had believed that the country would die without supplies, but that was before he had learned about the biosphere. When the rest of them were dead, the Mushroom Master would free his people and Opium would become the new biosphere.

Matt looked at Listen and hesitated. His hand brushed against a lump in his pocket, and suddenly he remembered El Patrón's advice: *Just because they took your weapons doesn't mean you aren't armed.* He grabbed Tam Lin's flashlight and turned it to maximum. A beam ten times the brightness of the sun shot out and struck Dabengwa's eyes. The drug lord screamed and dropped Listen. He clawed at his face, making mindless groans. His whole body seemed to convulse, as though the various parts of it were at war with one another.

Matt turned off the flashlight. Even the reflection of it dazzled him, and he couldn't see where to go. But a hand reached through the brilliance and dragged him away. "Good thing I had the sense to close my eyes," a man said.

They ran until they got outside, and Matt's vision began to recover. He saw the eejit with Listen slung over his shoulder. "Put me down. I can't breathe," she cried. She swayed and held on to him. "Crap! What happened back there?"

"Something I'm sure *Sor* Artemesia would call a miracle," said the eejit. "It's a good thing you still had Tam Lin's flashlight, *mi patrón*, because I didn't know how I was going to take on so many."

Matt's heart skipped a beat. "Cienfuegos?"

"At your service," said the *jefe*, bowing.

"How did you—"

Cienfuegos smiled. "Nobody notices eejits. I had a devil of a time locating you, Don Sombra. Couldn't you have dropped a few bread crumbs on the trail?"

"I was out of bread crumbs," said Matt. He felt like collapsing, the relief was so great.

"I tossed tranquilizer beads around as we left, but we'd better make ourselves scarce." They walked through the gardens at a normal pace so as not to draw attention. Cienfuegos went in front, with the hangdog posture of an eejit.

49

THE ABANDONED OBSERVATORY

They passed the soldiers throwing water on the lab.

"I couldn't believe how easy that was," said the *jefe*. "I simply walked inside with a flamethrower, and no one questioned it. People ignore eejits at their peril."

"Where are we going?" asked Matt.

"We can't stay here, and it's too dangerous to cross the hospital grounds and head for the chapel. Our friends are fine, by the way. Daft Donald has set up a command post nearby. No, I think we'll head for the observatory."

Matt fell silent. Sunlight shone through the trees and cast patterns on the ground. Here and there a beam caught the flash of mica on a stone. Birds swooped out of trees and flew close to the ground until they reached the safety of a yucca. Matt felt the wonder of being alive, of *staying* alive. Listen, too, was uncharacteristically quiet.

They went to the hovercraft port, but the energy signal on

all the stirabouts was flat. Happy Man hadn't bothered to recharge them. Matt, Listen, and Cienfuegos would have to walk, and the way was long, treeless, and hot. It quickly became clear that Listen would need frequent rest stops. Cienfuegos himself was uneasy about traveling without cover in daylight. "I wish I'd thought to bring water," he said.

He broke into one of the small, abandoned observatories on the way. A mesquite tree had grown up in front of the door, and his hands got gouged by thorns when he cleared its branches. "Sometimes I forget that everything in this desert is out to get you," he said, sucking blood from his fingers. "The cactuses, the trees, the bullhead vines. If you lift a board, you find a rattle-snake. If you take a nap, the conenose beetles crawl into bed and suck your blood. Dark corners are the happy homes of black widows and brown recluse spiders and *these* suckers—!" He squashed a bark scorpion running for cover.

"Still, it's all part of the ecosystem," he said, patting the single bed inside and releasing clouds of dust. "Just as *I* am part of the ecosystem, along with my venomous brothers and sisters." Once he was satisfied that the bed was safe, he told Listen to lie down.

The air was cool and shadowed. Ancient photographs of star systems covered the walls, and a desk with a bookcase stood against a wall. A small kitchen with dishes and a sink was attached to the building, but of course nothing came out of the faucet except a centipede.

"Let me look outside," said Cienfuegos. They heard him pulling away bushes and cursing. They heard banging and clank-ing, and the *jefe* eventually returned soaking wet. "Water," he announced. He had discovered a hand pump and by pounding it with rocks had worked the rusty handle until he got a stream of reddish-brown liquid. Matt and he filled pans and bowls.

"At least it's wet," conceded Cienfuegos.

"Looks like mud," said Listen.

"Give it a few minutes. The sediment will sink, and you can pour off the top."

They rested, waiting for dusk, when it would be safer to travel. "Whoever owned the place walked out one day and never came back," observed Matt. A leather-bound book lay open on the desk next to a pair of wire-rim glasses. He recognized these from old TV shows. No one wore glasses anymore.

"Be careful with the books," said Cienfuegos. "I'll take them to the Mushroom Master. He'll know how to preserve them."

Listen pointed at a photograph. "That's an African," she said. Matt blew gently to dislodge the dust and saw a man in an astronaut's uniform. The symbol on his sleeve was of the old American empire, and he stood next to an antique escape pod.

"Who was he?" said Matt. But they found nothing about him in the papers scattered on the desk.

They exchanged news of what each had been doing during their separation. Cienfuegos revealed that he'd been responsible for the dead soldier outside the operating room. "Then I had to run," he said. "There were too many of Glass Eye's troops on the ground. I realized that the border was open and went to the holoport, but you'd already closed it. That's when I found the Bug."

"How was he?" asked Matt.

"Buggy," the *jefe* said. "Half the time he screamed and the other half threatened. I was seriously tempted to leave him, but . . ."

"You felt sorry for him."

"Not really. He was making a racket, and I didn't want Glass Eye's troops to show up. I carried him to Malverde's chapel. *Sor*

Artemesia is looking after him, and good luck on that job. I'd rather take care of a rabid skunk." Cienfuegos got up and poured clear upper water into another basin.

"There's a dead mosquito in it," complained Listen.

"Yum," said Cienfuegos, picking it out and eating it. It was difficult to gross out the *jefe*.

Matt revealed what had happened just before Cienfuegos arrived in Glass Eye's hospital room, and the man was impressed. "*You* killed Dr. Rivas?" he asked Listen.

"I guess I did. I made Glass Eye mad," the little girl said uncomfortably. "But Dr. Rivas killed my best buddy. He promised not to, but he did it. He did." The energy went out of her and she bent over, grieving silently.

"Well, I think you're crotting marvelous. If I'm ever elected head of the UN, I'll issue you a Hero Medal."

"You said a curse word," she said.

"It's okay when I do it. Did you really hear Dr. Rivas and his son and daughter talk about the room at the bottom of the solar telescope?"

"They said it had a big secret inside and they wanted the Bug to open it, but he couldn't. Dr. Rivas thought I wouldn't know what they were talking about. Big people ignore little kids, and they shouldn't."

"I'd never ignore you, *chiquita*. You're too dangerous," said the *jefe*. "So Dr. Angel and Dr. Marcos escaped."

"I think so," the little girl said. "They didn't get any loot, though. I made that part up. I'm hungry."

They found rusty cans of food in the pantry, which Cienfuegos said were too old to be safe. The loaves of bread crumbled into dust when Listen touched them.

"It's like an Egyptian tomb with all the things the owner

needed for the afterlife," said Matt, thinking of El Patrón and also of Mirasol. The flowers that had been heaped around her must have withered by now. Or perhaps they didn't in the world of the dead. Perhaps they still bloomed, and she was dancing with the people she had loved. He had left the music box in her tomb.

"There are clothes in the closet and a toothbrush on the sink, except that the bristles have fallen out," said Matt. "All we need is a sarcophagus with a pharaoh painted on the lid." *And servants,* he thought. Real pharaohs needed servants to get through the afterlife.

"There's a lunchroom at the observatory," Listen said. "You can get hot chocolate and donuts and sometimes turkey burritos. We should go there now."

"Patience," said Cienfuegos, leaning back in a chair and half-closing his eyes. "Your ancestors didn't whine about turkey burritos when they were on a hunt. They waited like lions for the game to get careless."

"So we're lions," the little girl said, interested.

"Oh, yes. We're hunting the biggest game of all."

"The Scorpion Star," said Matt.

The *jefe* smiled gently at the dark ceiling draped with ancient cobwebs and dust. "The Mushroom Master thinks the eejits' brains are controlled by an energy source on the Scorpion Star. And that the observatory controls the Star. We'll begin our hunt by looking into that room at the bottom of the solar telescope."

Matt didn't like the plan, but he couldn't think of a better one. He helped Listen search through the desk while they waited. Dried-up fountain pens of a sort only seen in museums filled one drawer. In another were colored scraps of paper that Cienfuegos said were used for sending letters, a concept he had to explain. These were in an envelope labeled FOREVER STAMPS.

The little girl unfolded a large diagram on the floor. The folds cracked, and each section separated from the others.

"That looks familiar." Cienfuegos got up and weighted the pages with stones to be sure they didn't get mixed up. "It looks a lot like the biosphere. There's Northern Europe and Africa. And at the far end is Tundra. It's even got the name printed on it."

Matt knelt by it. "It could also be the space station." The longer they studied it, the more likely this seemed. The diagram was covered with strange symbols and mathematical formulas. Between each ecosystem was a series of zigzag lines and notes like *gauss here* and *outgauss there*. In the margin was written *500 teslas. Excessive? No!* At the bottom were two words: *Couple* on the left, and *Uncouple* on the right.

Cienfuegos carefully gathered up the sheets, keeping them in order. "This is gibberish to me. I'll take it to the Mushroom Master later. It's strange. He knows more about science than we do, and he's a hundred years in the past. He says we depend too much on machines. All we know how to do is press buttons, but he knows how the buttons work."

50

THE SECRET ROOM

When the sun slipped behind the Chiricahua Mountains, they left the abandoned observatory. Heat still radiated from the ground, and a wind had whipped up a dust storm. It blew into their eyes and dried their lips, but it also made them less easy to spot on the treeless road.

The white dome of El Patrón's observatory loomed against the shadow of night rising in the east. To the south appeared the Scorpion Star, always the first to be seen at evening and the last to disappear at dawn. They slipped into a side door and tiptoed along the dark, curved wall to the door of the lunchroom. No one noticed them. The technicians were busy with screens and computers.

The room was deserted, and they helped themselves to hot chocolate and donuts. Only the greasy wrappers that had been around the turkey burritos were left. "We're taking a huge chance, but I think Listen is right. We need a pick-me-up before tackling the solar telescope," said Cienfuegos. Matt found a machine that served boxes of apple juice, and he pocketed a few of these before they went to the other building.

He dreaded the giant shaft plunging beneath the solar telescope in a way that wasn't quite rational. After all, they had survived it before. Yet something about the enclosed space, the hot air gusting up, the darkness and awareness of tons of earth over his head made him break out in a sweat before they even got to the elevator.

"I wish we could leave Listen up here," Matt whispered when they had reached the shaft door.

"She's safer with us," said Cienfuegos.

"Don't worry, Listen. We did it before and we can do it again," said Matt, more to reassure himself than her. He held on to the elevator door, wishing he could back out.

"I'm not scared of heights," the little girl said.

"You can't be sure of that. You've never seen a drop like this."

"She'll be fine," said the *jefe*, pulling the door closed. And then they were sinking at a forty-five-degree angle. Round and round they spiraled the huge tube of the telescope. Dim lights gleamed on its dark-green surface. "It's hot down here," said Listen, pulling her blouse loose. She was already drenched in sweat.

Air conditioners whirred at various levels, and a warm breeze rose out of the depths. They passed another elevator slowly rising and saw the sickly faces of the eejits moving up.

The heat was unbearable, even at night. Soon they were all panting, and Matt opened one of the apple juice boxes and handed it to Listen. They passed a platform in an alcove and saw eejits mending a pipe with an oxyacetylene torch. Sparks showered into the elevator cage. More heat.

The elevator bumped at the bottom. They moved quickly, but before they got to the door, they heard the sizzle of more sparks. Cienfuegos signaled for them to stop. Matt saw an eejit trying to cut through the wall to the forbidden room.

Listen grabbed Matt's arm. "I can see Dr. Angel and Dr. Marcos," she whispered.

Suddenly there was a flash of light, and a lightning bolt snaked out of the wall and incinerated the eejit. The odor of burnt flesh drifted through the hall. "Next!" shouted a voice Matt recognized. Another eejit took up the torch. There was a line of them waiting in the space between the telescope and the wall.

"This won't work," said Dr. Angel. "We've tried it before."

"When I want your advice, I'll ask for it," said Happy Man Hikwa. "Each time the wall will degrade a little more. Eventually, we'll break through."

"It isn't just the substance the door's made of, it's the force field running through it. There's a plasma current that reacts to energy," said Dr. Marcos. "The more you pour in, the more powerfully it pushes back. We've tried this before."

Happy Man barked a command, and a soldier struck Dr. Marcos on the head with the butt of a gun. The doctor fell to his knees. The next eejit blasted the wall until another tongue of fire erupted from it. The remaining eejits watched passively.

"Can we do anything?" whispered Matt.

Cienfuegos watched as the next man moved into position. He drew his stun gun and fired at Happy Man twice in rapid succession, a lethal shot. The *jefe* jumped back, pulling Matt and Listen with him. "Run," he said, but when they got to the elevator, it was gone. They had forgotten to prop open the door, and someone had called for it. They could see it slowly spiraling upward. "Climb!" the *jefe* said desperately.

There was a chicken-wire barrier enclosing the elevator shaft, and Matt tried to haul himself up, but the openings were too small. His feet didn't fit, and he could only cling with his fingers. Cienfuegos tried to boost Listen into a position to climb, but the structure of the barrier was against them. She wasn't strong enough to hold on. The *jefe* turned, thrusting Matt and the little girl behind him, and took aim at the soldiers.

He brought two down, but a third one shot him. It was an old-fashioned gun with metal bullets, and the impact threw Cienfuegos against the barrier. He raised his weapon and was struck by several more bullets. He crumpled to the floor. Listen screamed. The soldier took aim at Matt and a voice shouted, "Stop!"

It was Dr. Angel. "Stop! He's the only one who can open the door! That's El Patrón's clone!"

The soldiers halted. They looked back. "We only take orders from our *patrón*," one said.

"You don't have a *patrón* anymore," Dr. Angel said. "If you want to survive, join us. If not"—she looked upward—"the Farm Patrol will take care of you."

Dr. Marcos came up behind her. His head was bleeding, but he seemed to have recovered. "Take the boy," he ordered. "Leave the girl and the eejit."

"Stay with him," Matt whispered, hoping that Listen would, for once, follow orders. She did. She fell over Cienfuegos's body and clung to his shirt, which was beginning to ooze blood. Matt forced himself to look away. He couldn't think about it now. He couldn't fall apart.

"I thought you were on your way to the Scorpion Star," he said as soldiers shoved him down the hallway.

"We had to turn back at the border," said Dr. Angel. "Someone reactivated the lockdown, but no matter. There are worse things than becoming the Lady of Opium."

The door glowed faintly with residual heat, but the mark of the scorpion was still visible. "Let it cool," Matt said. "If you burn my hand, nothing's going to happen." The charred lumps of the two eejits had been kicked aside, and the body of Happy Man was slumped against a wall. The other eejits were waiting for orders. "What happened to Glass Eye?" Matt asked.

"You killed him," Dr. Marcos said. "The bright light sent his brain into shock. Half of it was nuts and bolts anyway." He splashed water from a bottle against the door to cool it faster.

"You tried to cut through this wall before," stated Matt.

"Father did," said Dr. Angel. "He used up more than a hundred eejits, but that was in the good old days when we had more than we needed. Now, with the border closed, we have to treat them like pampered, pedigreed cats. Good food, new houses, rest periods." She shook her head over the foolishness of it all. "I suppose we have you to thank for that, Matt."

"You're not calling me *patrón* anymore, I see."

Dr. Angel laughed. "We're the *patrón*s now. If you're good, we'll let you live, and maybe that foul-mouthed little imp, too. How did you train an eejit to kill? Father was never able to do it."

"The eejit has to have been a soldier or policeman *before*," said Matt, who realized that the doctor hadn't recognized Cienfuegos.

"Interesting," said Dr. Angel. Matt could see who the dominant member was in this family. He wouldn't give much for Dr.

Marcos's chances if he tried to order his sister around. Neither of them seemed to be grieving for their father.

"I think it's cool enough," said one of the soldiers. "What happens if one of us touches that scorpion?"

"Try it and see," said Dr. Angel, but the soldier, who'd seen lightning come out of the wall, was in no mood to experiment.

Matt flexed his hands. He was a little frightened himself of touching that wall. Who knew what changes all that fire power had caused? But the sooner he satisfied the greed of these doctors, the sooner he could get back to Listen. He would not think about Cienfuegos. Not yet. Not if he wanted to stay sane.

He put his hand against the scorpion. Ants crawled over his skin. His heart shuddered with the impact of the scanner. And then the reaction faded. The door in the wall slid back, and he heard a collective gasp behind him. Dr. Angel shone a flashlight inside.

Thousands of gold coins formed a path down a long, dark hallway. They winked and glittered as the flashlight in the doctor's hand trembled. The soldiers had their own lights, and soon a dozen or more beams were illuminating the walls and discovering side chambers.

On either side of the door were the grim statues of Mayan warriors, not genuine ones, of course, for none had survived the Spanish conquest. These statues were copied from wall paintings. They were beautifully done, their heads long and slightly deformed from the way Mayan infants were bound to their mothers' carrying boards. Their noses were large and aristocratically curved. Their ears were heavy with turquoise and gold. They wore loincloths of jaguar, and the teeth of jaguars hung about their necks. They were *pok-a-tok* players.

Dr. Angel rushed down the dark hallway, followed by Dr.

Marcos and the soldiers. In the distance were more treasures—real art works from Babylon and Mohenjo-daro and many other ancient, forgotten places. There was a room made entirely of amber, and a diamond throne that had belonged to the shah of Iran. Matt heard exclamations as each wonder was discovered. He followed them a short way, but his attention was drawn to something else near the door.

It was a diagram etched in metal. It was very close to the one he'd seen in the abandoned observatory, and now he realized that the man who had lived there was one of the designers of the Scorpion Star. What had happened to him? Had he been drawn by the chance to build something so marvelous that the ethics about its use hadn't bothered him?

What had driven him out in such a hurry that a book lay open on his desk and his glasses were left beside it?

The diagram wasn't exactly the same. Some of the buildings were of different sizes, and an area called Savannah was missing. There were no cryptic notes or formulas, but at the bottom was a pair of glowing scorpions and the words COUPLE and UNCOUPLE.

Matt knew more or less what those words meant. "Couple" was to bring together, as happened when people married. They became a couple. And "uncouple"?

Matt reached out and pressed his hand against the scorpion above UNCOUPLE. The familiar energy went through him, so something was happening. He waited a few minutes and stepped back. Outside, the eejits were waiting. He put his hand on the door, and it slid back into place. "Come with me," he told them.

51

UNCOUPLING

Listen was lying where he'd left her on Cienfuegos's body. Matt touched her, and she shook her head violently. "Not moving," she said.

"You have to," Matt said gently. "Cienfuegos is no longer there. I don't understand much about death, but María says the soul lives on. So does *Sor* Artemesia. When I go to the oasis, I feel that Tam Lin is still there, sitting by my fire and listening to me. People can return to those they cared about."

Listen shrugged off his hand. "Cienfuegos is alive."

Matt sighed. He was trying very hard to stay in control. He felt just as devastated as she did, but he knew the *jefe* was dead. He knew how many times the man had been shot. "Come with me, *chiquita*. I'll call down the elevator."

"I'm not leaving," the little girl said. "I left Mbongeni for just ten minutes, and look what happened to him. I'm staying put."

Matt saw the elevator descending and a group of unusually active eejits inside. They were talking excitedly, and one of them called to someone on the ground. He looked at the eejits who had come with him and saw that they, too, were animated.

Had he actually disrupted the signal from the Scorpion Star? For the first time Matt thought clearly about what might happen when the eejits were freed. He'd imagined them waking up like people who have had a very long sleep. But the shock might send them into convulsions, like Eusebio. Or they might all go rogue.

"Hey, you guys!" shouted Listen. "We got a sick man here, and he needs to go to the hospital."

"Don't attract them," said Matt, warily eyeing the eejits as they got out of the elevator.

"You don't understand," Listen said fiercely. "All this talk about Cienfuegos coming back for chats by the fire is crap. He isn't dead."

"You poor child, he has to be."

"What do you think I've been doing here? I've been listening to his heart. It's beating, and you can't say that about a dee-diddly-dead rabbit. Hold that crotting elevator, you guys!"

The eejits were awake, no question about it, but they were bewildered. They seemed to have no memory of how they had arrived in this hot, dark pit, and they willingly followed Listen's orders. They chattered to one another as the elevator slowly began to ascend, asking about relatives and towns they had left behind.

Cienfuegos stirred and gasped. The harshness of his breathing frightened Matt. He might yet die—and to think that he'd almost been abandoned! Thank God for Listen's persistence!

"What can you remember?" Matt asked one of the eejits.

"I crossed the border. I was with my wife. Then the Farm Patrol came and there was pain. Pain." The man's voice trailed off. Matt wondered what his reaction would be if he learned that the man they were trying to save was the head of the Farm Patrol.

The scene outside was chaos. Eejits wandered about, calling the names of friends and family members. The technicians, who were far less affected by the microchips, had some memories, but they also seemed bewildered by what had happened. "I was twenty when I came to work here," one of them said. "It was like yesterday, but now I look fifty."

Matt put the technicians in charge of the eejits. "I'll send people who can explain later," he said. "There's been a national disaster. Get these people food and send them to their shelters to rest."

"Are we at war? Look! There's a rocket!" cried one of the eejits. A fireball streaked across the sky. Then another and another.

"It's a meteor shower," said a technician. "A nice one too."

The stirabouts at the observatory hadn't been drained of their power, and Cienfuegos was loaded into one of them. He groaned and spat blood. Matt flew the craft, and Listen curled up by the *jefe*.

"Dr. Angel," the little girl said suddenly. "I bet she's trying to blast her way through that secret door."

"She doesn't have to. I opened it for her." Matt swooped up as gently as possible to avoid jarring Cienfuegos.

"You did? Were there jewels and gold inside?"

"There was enough gold to satisfy a hundred Dr. Angels. There was a room made out of amber and a diamond throne that once belonged to the shah of Iran."

"Wow! I bet that made her happy."

"Very happy. She and Dr. Marcos and all the soldiers ran inside. The soldiers filled their pockets with gold coins." Matt could see the lights of the hospital ahead and a crowd of eejits milling around. He landed outside the emergency room. He got out and ordered them to carry Cienfuegos inside. Listen ran in front to find a doctor.

Fortunately, like the technicians, the doctors had noticed little difference when their microchips were deactivated. And since they had been recently hired, they weren't disturbed by the passage of time. They hurried the *jefe* to the operating room and began working on him at once. "¡*Por Dios!* Do you see what he's wearing under that jumpsuit?" one of them cried.

"We'll have to cut it off," another said.

"You'd need bolt cutters," said the first doctor, and in the end they had to ease it over Cienfuegos's head. It was a silky vest, now bloodstained, and when it was removed a clatter of bullets fell to the floor. "That's what saved him," the doctor said.

They sent Matt and Listen to another room to wait. Matt knew he should go outside and try to restore order, but he was too worried. They sat in the room where he'd seen the dead soldier and where Dabengwa's men had ambushed him. "Is Glass Eye dead?" Listen asked.

"Yes," said Matt.

"Good. I didn't like him." She thought for a moment. "What about Happy Man?"

"He's dead too."

"So the only ones we have to worry about are Dr. Angel and Dr. Marcos."

"I think they'll be happy with the contents of the secret room," said Matt. By now they would have discovered that the door was closed. The soldiers would fire their weapons at the wall—much good it would do them—and then their flashlights would fail. They would be alone in the dark with the *pok-a-tok* players.

"You can see him briefly, *mi patrón*," said a doctor at the door of the operating room. "He's heavily sedated, but he seems to have an amazing resistance to drugs."

"He would have," said Matt.

He and Listen stood by Cienfuegos's bed and saw, from his eyes, that he recognized them. "He thought you were dead, but I knew you weren't," said Listen.

The *jefe* smiled.

"That's the most amazing bulletproof vest," said a nurse who was sitting by the bed. "I've heard of them, but this is the first one I've seen." She pointed at the garment soaking in a bucket. "It's pure spider silk, stronger than steel. They say it's harvested from giant African spiders and that little girls are trained to reel it out as it's produced." The nurse shuddered. "The jobs some people have!"

They left, to allow Cienfuegos to recover, and the doctor explained his injuries outside. "Mostly broken ribs. The bullets didn't get through, but the force of the blows must have been terrific. There's some damage to the liver, and a broken rib pierced a lung. Fortunately, his heart is unharmed. He'll be laid up for a long time."

The gardens were filled with eejits—or ex-eejits, Matt reminded himself. *Paisanos,* he would call them. Fellow country-men. He supposed he should address them, but he was too exhausted. Instead, he gave orders to the nurses and lab techni-cians to see to their needs. He would tackle the problem in the morning.

"I'm really tired," said Listen, trotting by his side.

"Me too, but there's something we have to do before we can rest," Matt said. For once she didn't complain about the long walk. They were both too anxious to see their friends. Matt lit the path by the stream with Tam Lin's flashlight, and they saw the gleam of rabbits' eyes as the creatures hopped out of their way.

The chapel was visible long before they arrived. Dozens of candles had been lit and fastened to rocks. The inside of the building as well was illuminated by flickering light. All around the outside were newly freed eejits, Farm Patrolmen, and bodyguards, among them Daft Donald. *Sor* Artemesia stood in the doorway with María, Fidelito, and the Bug. The Bug was on a leash.

"You did it!" shrieked Fidelito when he caught sight of Listen. He ran through the crowd and hugged her. "You can slap me all you like for touching you. I'm so glad you're okay."

"It isn't worth it," she said, hugging him back. "You'll only do it again."

Matt and María held each other's hands. They were more restrained, being older, and somewhat embarrassed by the large audience. "Well, then," said Matt.

"Well, then," replied María.

"I guess things have worked out." He wished they could be alone.

"God has answered your prayers," said *Sor* Artemesia in a ringing voice. "He has sent his messenger."

"What in hell are you up to?" asked Matt. He saw the gathered men kneel. Some were weeping openly.

"You know who you resemble," said the nun. "These men are frightened, and they need sympathy. Try to look saintly."

First Cienfuegos tells everyone that I'm El Patrón, and now I'm supposed to be Jesús Malverde, thought Matt. *When will I ever be myself?*

Matt spoke what he hoped were consoling words and sent everyone away to their hostels and bunkhouses. Then he went inside with María, and they embraced behind the statue of Malverde, where the Bug couldn't spy on them.

"I've got so much to tell you," he said.

"Me too," said María. "I was outside when the first meteor fell. It was the brightest I've ever seen, and then I saw another one. Not long after, the men began to show up. They were so lost, *mi vida.* They didn't know what had happened, and they were calling for their families. *Sor* Artemesia said that Malverde was the only shred of religion they'd had and that we must honor it."

"I'm really interested," said Matt, yawning broadly, "but I've been through so much I can't even think straight."

"That's all right," she said in the understanding way he loved. "We have the rest of our lives to talk."

He kissed her sleepily, staggered to the front of the chapel, and passed out on one of the pews. In the middle of the night he awoke when a bright light passed over the forest. It was the last of the meteors, perhaps Tundra.

The Scorpion Star had uncoupled, each building separating from the others, and the carefully maintained orbit had failed. One by one they had fallen. Matt tried not to think of the terrified people inside. He'd been no better than El Patrón shooting down a passenger plane.

52

THE GHOST ARMY

It seemed unfair that Matt could remember everything awful that had happened, but few of the good times. The months after the Scorpion Star fell were some of the good times. They were a golden blur. Many of the *paisanos* left, with money to get established in their new lives. Nothing, of course, could make up for what they had lost. Some remained who had little to return to.

One of the most difficult problems was getting Aztlán and the United States to take back their citizens. These people had no passports, the governments argued. They were unpersons and therefore Opium's responsibility. Matt understood that *paisanos* had little value in lands where machines did most of the work, and for this problem he called on Esperanza.

She looked like a small black thundercloud ready to spit lightning when he accessed the Convent of Santa Clara. "What have you done with my daughter?" she shouted.

"I didn't do anything. María came here of her own accord," protested Matt.

"Then she *is* with you," said Esperanza, and Matt realized he'd been tricked. María's mother hadn't known where she was.

"She's happy," he said.

"She probably is, the little fool. What I can't figure out is how you got your hands on her. The last anyone saw of her, she was in this room. Then the sisters discovered that the door lock had been melted with a laser. By the time they broke it open, she was gone. What did you do? Send a commando unit and then fuse the lock to provide a distraction?" Esperanza was practically incandescent with rage.

"I didn't do anything. She came through the portal," Matt said.

Her eyes widened. "That's impossible! It's a *wormhole*. It's the temperature of outer space." The intensity of her rage reached through the portal, and Matt, in spite of knowing he was safe, took a step backward.

"You're lying. You lured her through, and now she's dead," said Esperanza.

"No!" Matt cried. "She dressed herself in a UN peacekeeper's hazard gear. She almost died from lack of air, but she recovered and has no permanent damage. I'll bring her. You'll see."

He turned to call a *paisano*, but Esperanza impatiently waved the man away. "This is extremely interesting. A person went through a wormhole and survived. Don't you see the military importance of such a discovery?"

It wasn't just a person, Matt thought. *It was your daughter.* As before, he was amazed at how coolly she received bad news. Her husband and older daughter had died at El Patrón's funeral, and Esperanza's only reaction had been, *That certainly makes things awkward.*

"With the right gear and a supply of oxygen, I could transport a soldier anywhere in the world," said Esperanza. "I'll have to find out how long it takes to cross a wormhole."

"If you're thinking of sending peacekeepers here, think again. Armies can go both ways," Matt said, with what he hoped was El Patrón's menace.

"It won't be necessary," said Esperanza, brushing off his threat. "Some very unusual things have been happening. The Scorpion Star, that monstrosity El Patrón planted in the southern sky, fell out of orbit and burned. And the eejits under Glass Eye Dabengwa's control went rogue and wiped out his army. Reports are that he's missing."

"He's dead," Matt said. He filled her in on all that had happened. "Those eejits aren't rogue, they're awake, and so are the ones in Opium. The Scorpion Star was controlling their brains, and I destroyed it." He waited to see whether she would congratulate him. She didn't. "Most of the ex-eejits want to go home, but the countries they came from won't take them back."

"I'll organize a committee to study the situation," said Esperanza.

"Oh, no you won't. A committee would string things out for years. I want you to lean on those governments until they back down. Otherwise, I won't send you any more bunny rabbits and squirrels." The woman frowned, ready to do battle, but Matt added, "You'll never believe what we discovered near Tucson. Lions and tigers from a zoo that went wild during the drug wars."

Esperanza was so startled she forgot to scowl. She clasped her heavily ringed hands until they looked like a ball of silver and turquoise gems. "Lions? They survived in the desert?"

"Tucson isn't quite a desert anymore," said Matt. "It's hot, but lions are used to heat. I also discovered a jungle with monkeys and toucans and crocodiles. And there's a biosphere with eco-systems from every part of the Earth. Think about it, Esperanza. Opium holds the seeds of recovery for the entire planet. The scientists in the biosphere have also found a way to clean up pol-luted soil."

She was stunned. She opened her mouth and no sound came out. As Cienfuegos had suggested, keeping the lions secret had been a good idea.

"I can't believe it," she murmured at last.

"Believe it. I'll send you pictures."

"We built a park near the ruins of Tijuana for the samples you sent," she said. Her expression had changed completely. She was no longer harsh and uncompromising. She looked twenty years younger. "It's a very small place, but we planned to expand it slowly. If there's a way to recover polluted soil . . ."

"There is. Do we have a basis for negotiation?" asked Matt.

"Oh, yes. Yes." Esperanza's face was radiant with joy. It almost made the commander of the UN forces likable. But when they had finished their conversation and Matt had shut down the portal, he remembered.

Esperanza had entirely forgotten about María.

Most of the Farm Patrolmen stayed because they had prices on their heads in other lands. Samson and Boris opted to stay as well. Cienfuegos recovered slowly. Once Matt found him weep-ing, and he turned away quickly to hide it. "I remember too much," he explained. "But don't worry, Don Sombra. People like me have an infinite ability to forgive themselves."

Matt offered to help find his family in Aztlán, but he shook his head. "My daughter was ten when I left her, and now she'd be almost thirty. She'll have married and forgotten about me. As for my wife, she'll definitely have remarried. It would be amusing to walk in on her and her new husband, but I've lost my taste for blood sports."

With Matt's help, Cienfuegos sent samples of the fungi used by the Mushroom Master to his old university. "What I would most like is to grow something here that isn't narcotics," the *jefe* said. "It would be wonderful to produce life instead of taking it." Matt promised that he could do whatever he liked. "Of course, if you need me to kick butt with the Farm Patrol, I'd be willing to help," Cienfuegos said, with a flash of his old spirit.

Matt set about finding jobs for the remaining *paisanos*. Most of the opium was uprooted, and soon alfalfa, corn, tomatoes, wheat, and chilies took the place of the old fields. The population of Opium, minus the men who had gone home, was very small compared to that of other countries. Most of the land would be left untouched.

María, of course, was in her element. She gathered the ex-eejit children into small houses and, with *Sor* Artemesia's help, hired women from Aztlán and the United States to be surrogate mothers for them. None of the children, as far as they could tell, had any family left. Those who were musical were given lessons by Mr. Ortega and the newly freed choirmaster.

Eusebio wasn't interested in giving lessons. Chacho said that his father awoke that memorable night when the Scorpion Star fell, turned on the light, and inspected the rows and rows of guitars propped against the walls. "Who left these here?" he demanded. "They should be in proper cases and not lying around where mice can get at them."

Chacho sat up, utterly amazed. "You made them, Father."

"Me? Pah! I don't remember doing it. And who are you?"

For a moment Chacho was speechless. "I'm your son," he managed to say.

"Nonsense! *Mi hijo* is only so high, not a hulking teenager like you. Where's Mr. Ortega?" By now the light had awakened the piano teacher, who stumbled out of bed and tried to explain the situation. It took a while for Eusebio to realize that his friend was deaf.

"What a pity! What a pity!" the guitar maker exclaimed. "And you such a great pianist. Are you ill, *mi compadre*? You look so old. It must be the dry desert air."

"I advise you not to look into a mirror," retorted Mr. Ortega. Gradually, he and Chacho told Eusebio what had happened. Chacho said he was worried about his father's reaction, but Eusebio was far more interested to learn that he could write music here and not be concerned with finding work. He lived for music, just as it seemed Chacho would live for art.

He was hugely impressed with his son's artistic ability. "Runs in the family," he bragged. "All of us Orozcos are born with either a paintbrush or a guitar pick in our hands."

Ton-Ton was a problem. He admired music and art from a distance, but he had little talent in those areas. Most of what sent Chacho into transports of joy passed over Ton-Ton's head. María drafted him to teach the ex-eejit children. "They can learn so much from you," she enthused. "You can show them gears and screwdrivers and those little round things you use to feed wires into boxes."

"Grommets," said Ton-Ton.

"Yes! Such a cute name!" But when she found him threatening to beat the stuffing out of a five-year-old who had rearranged Ton-Ton's computer parts, she was outraged.

"It's a j-joke," he explained when she pulled the howling boy away. "Fidelito and Listen aren't scared of me. Kids, uh, break stuff if you don't w-watch them all the time."

"You can't threaten them," she cried.

"W-why not, if it works?" he argued. And so the experiment with Ton-Ton as teacher was over.

Matt tried to involve him in farming, but years of toiling under the hot sun at the plankton factory had killed the interest. Medicine and astronomy, two other possibilities, were too "brainy," according to Ton-Ton. Yet Matt knew that nothing was wrong with the older boy's brain. He simply approached problems in a different way.

It was finally Daft Donald who came up with the solution. *He thinks with his hands,* wrote the bodyguard on his yellow pad of paper. And so he introduced Ton-Ton to the inner workings of Hitler's car. The boy was enchanted. From there they went on to Celia's freezer, to Dr. Kim's electron microscope at the hospital, to the irrigation system at the mushroom house, and to many other delights.

"The secret of successful education," the Mushroom Master said wisely as Ton-Ton moled around the fungus gardens with pipes, "is finding out how a particular person learns."

Matt fulfilled his promise to take Listen to the oasis. He worried that she would destroy the quiet nature of the place, but she seemed awestruck by it. "We won't tell the others," she said. "They don't need a secret world, but we do. Those sure are some funny-looking rocks."

Matt looked up at the range he'd climbed to escape Opium.

"That's how I got to Aztlán. There's a ridge of mountains where you can see all the opium farms at once."

"I don't mean those," the little girl said impatiently. "I mean *these*."

And Matt saw the rocks that surrounded the old miner's cabin and collapsed grapevine. They were some distance away, on three sides with the fourth side opening onto the small lake. In the middle, next to the water, was the campsite where he and Tam Lin had toasted hot dogs.

Now he saw what Listen was talking about. The color and texture were strange. He walked to the nearest one and scratched it with his pocketknife. It was very hard, but a few brown flakes came loose. "This looks like some kind of metal ore," he said.

"Dr. Rivas had a box that looked like that," said Listen. "He put an eejit inside. He was trying to block out something, but he wouldn't tell me what."

Matt remembered asking Tam Lin why they could sleep so soundly at the oasis with mosquitoes whining in their ears and the hard earth underneath. *'Tis not bodily comfort we need,* Tam Lin had replied, *but the mind at ease. Something about the rocks holds back the cares of the world. This is the only place in Opium I've felt free.*

Of course. The metal ore blocked the energy from the Scorpion Star. "What happened to the eejit?" he asked.

"He was okay as long as he was inside, but he went rogue the minute he got out. Dr. Rivas tried it about a hundred times." Listen yawned and lay down on the sand next to the water.

That left only the Bug to deal with. If El Bicho had learned anything from being treated kindly—gratitude, for example—

no one saw evidence of it. He was as vicious and demanding as ever. Finally, after consulting everyone, Matt asked permission to install the child in the Brat Enclosure. "My opinion, which you won't listen to, is that we put him to sleep like the rabid coyote he is," said Cienfuegos.

"I thought you didn't have homicidal impulses anymore," said Matt.

"A few may have been overlooked," admitted the *jefe*.

"We've had *bichos* like him before," said the Mushroom Master. "We treat them with love, and if that doesn't work, we give them an extra-long Dormancy to be sure they don't do harm when they wake up."

As for El Bicho, he approached the Brat Enclosure with suspicion. He found the peaceful groups of children threatening, and he immediately destroyed a sand castle they had built. The children only looked at him and began building another. "Do you remember the Scorpion Star?" Matt asked him. "This is its original. When you grow up, you'll join the scientists. You'll be one of them and never be lonely again."

The Bug looked at Matt as though he were a rat dropping. But he went willingly into the enclosure, and the last they saw of him, he was squatting by a pool with other children, feeding giant carp with rice balls. "Do you know," said Matt, "his hand has started to grow back. It's like he's a frog or something."

"Then he'll fit right in here," the Mushroom Master said tranquilly. "We admire frogs."

One moonlit night Matt flew María over the sand dunes west of Yuma. They passed the ruins of the old city, a sketchwork of deserted houses and dry fields. To the south was the glow of San Luis on the border of Aztlán, and when they went close to the ground, María gasped. "Those are bones! There are skeletons down there!"

"Cienfuegos told me about this," said Matt. "They're only visible under the full moon, and sometimes they're hidden by shifting sand. Those are the bones of Illegals who tried to cross over."

"So many," said María.

"They've had a hundred years to accumulate. It's extremely hot and dry here. El Patrón didn't bother to send out the Farm Patrol."

"But why didn't their own governments stop them?"

Matt looked out over the thousands and thousands of skeletons strewn like a ghost army over the earth. "These were surplus people. They had few skills that Aztlán and the United States wanted. The governments were glad to get rid of them."

"This must never happen again," said María, with a firmness that reminded Matt of her mother.

"I've been thinking about that," he said. "I have to fix the border so that other people can open it in an emergency. Power has been in the hands of one man for too long. But there are problems with giving people freedom. Some of them will abuse it. Both Cienfuegos and *Sor* Artemesia say it's inevitable. Cienfuegos says he can organize the Farm Patrol into a decent police force, and *Sor* Artemesia will try to look after people's souls. Our old, predictable lives are going to change." He idled the hovercraft over the dunes, and it bobbed gently on a cushion of antigravity.

"I'm thinking of *not* opening the border until people adjust to the new system. We'll soon be self-sufficient, especially if we can persuade women to join us. I'm thinking of turning Opium into a larger biosphere, or as close to it as we can get."

"The drug dealers won't like it," María pointed out.

"Crot the drug dealers," said Matt. "It will be an adventure, and it may not work, but it's worth trying. And one thing more, *mi vida*."

She turned toward him.

"I want to marry you."

She smiled mischievously, so like the lady in the Goya painting. "I'm only fifteen, you know. It's illegal."

"I'm fifteen too, and I'm the Lord of Opium. I say it's legal."

"Mother will be furious."

"That's one of the side benefits," said Matt. They said nothing for a while.

María gazed out at the field of bones, and the moonlight painted the world with a pale blue light. "You sure picked a weird place to propose," she said.

"I think it's peaceful."

"You'll have to bring in a real priest. I'm not going to be a drug lord's floozy."

"You can have ten priests if you want them."

"You're crazy, but okay. I accept. After all, who's going to say no to the Lord of Opium?"

"Only the Lady of Opium," he said, putting his arms around her.

APPENDIX

JESÚS MALVERDE

Jesús Malverde is a Robin Hood figure known as the "generous bandit" and "angel of the poor" because he stole from the rich and gave to the poor. He was supposedly killed on May 3, 1909, a day that is celebrated at his shrines. He is an unofficial saint who isn't recognized by the Catholic Church. People pray to him for many things—good health, money, family problems, and finding a job—but he is best known as the patron saint of drug dealers, especially those from Sinaloa. There is no evidence that he was involved with drugs during his life.

Although movies have been made about him, there was never a picture of him. At some point someone made a statue of him, but no one is sure who the model was. In my book I have made El Patrón the model, as a young man. If you go to zazzle.com on the Web, you can find a Jesús Malverde T-shirt with the words *El Patrón* written below the saint's image. Also on the web you can find statues, votive candles, incense, and even Malverde cologne for that special someone.

Recently a pair of dim-witted drug dealers not only parked the wrong way on a Chicago street, they parked in front of a police station and had a statue of Jesús Malverde on the backseat. Not surprisingly, the police were curious. They opened the trunk, found more than a million dollars' worth of cocaine, and arrested them.

THE BIOSPHERE

This information comes from Wikipedia.

Biosphere 1 refers to the entire system of life on earth. Biosphere 2 was built north of Tucson, Arizona, around 1990. It was an effort to create a complete, enclosed world where people could live forever without going outside. It was meant as a model for space exploration. It contained a rain forest, a small ocean with a coral reef, a mangrove swamp, a grassland, a desert, a farming section, and a place for humans to live. Eight people were locked inside for two years, and later a crew of seven people were locked inside. They grew bananas, papayas, sweet potatoes, beets, peanuts, beans, rice, and wheat. During the first year the inhabitants complained of constant hunger, but during the second year the crops improved. The inhabitants also had four nanny goats, a billy goat, thirty-five hens, three roosters, two sows, and a boar pig, plus tilapia fish. Beside these were wild animals and insects to keep the ecosystem going.

It was a noble experiment, but the scientists soon discovered that it wasn't easy duplicating what Mother Earth does. They found, for example, that trees need wind in order to grow strong. The soil bacteria produced more carbon dioxide than expected, and most of the vertebrate animals and all the pollinating insects died. The cockroaches did well, though. They always do. The scientists also forgot that when you bottle people up together, fights break out. Secret food caches were discovered. Supplies were smuggled in, and half the participants weren't on speaking terms by the time the experiment was over.

You can visit Biosphere 2 today, in the town of Oracle, north of Tucson. It is run by the University of Arizona, and they conduct tours. It's used as a research facility, but people aren't locked up in it anymore.

THE HEALING POWER OF MUSIC

Oliver Sacks, a great doctor, has written a book called *Musicophilia*. It is about the deep way music affects people and how it can reach those who have had strokes, amnesia, and Alzheimer's disease. If you go on YouTube and enter "Alive Inside" or "Old Man in Nursing Home Reacts to Hearing Music," you will see an amazing demonstration of this. Henry Dryer, age ninety-two, suffers from dementia and is in a near-complete stupor. The nurse puts earphones on his head and plays the music of Cab Calloway, the old man's favorite. Immediately, his eyes light up. He sways to the beat, sings, and remembers who he is. The effect wears off, but for a while after the music has stopped playing, Henry Dryer is awake. It is a deeply moving scene and one that I found almost too heartrending to watch. I used it in the book for Eusebio and Mirasol.

THE MUSHROOM MASTER

There really is a Mushroom Master. His name is Paul Stamets, and he runs a company called Fungi Perfecti in Washington State. His specialties are mycoremediation and mycofiltration, ten-dollar words for "cleaning up the soil using mushrooms." He wrote a book called *Mycelium Running: How Mushrooms Can*

Help Save the World. It's very good, but very demanding, and you need to know a lot of science to understand it. But you can go to YouTube and look up "Paul Stamets" and "6 Ways Mushrooms Can Save the World" for an eighteen-minute description with pictures.

You can also Google "Paul Stamets," "Going Underground," and "the Sun" for an interview that gives a simple, but fascinating description of his work. If you're really interested, you can go on his company's website, fungi.com, order a chunk of wood full of spores, and grow your own mushrooms.

JOSÉ CLEMENTE OROZCO

In my opinion, José Clemente Orozco was the greatest artist Mexico ever produced. He grew up during the Mexican civil war of the early part of the twentieth century. What he saw gave him a lifelong aversion to politics. As a young man he contracted rheumatic fever, which gave him a permanent heart condition. On one of his early jobs he mixed chemicals to make fireworks to sell on Mexican Independence Day. The chemicals exploded. He lost one hand, part of his hearing, and the sight in one eye. Now picture this: We have a young man missing a hand, an eye, part of his hearing, and with a heart so weak he has to rest every few minutes. He wants to paint huge murals on the sides of walls. And he does! And they're good! Whenever I feel like whining about my problems, I think about Orozco. I have made him one of Chacho's ancestors.

THE GHOST ARMY

Long ago my mother-in-law told me this story. If you fly over the sand dunes near Swakopmund, Namibia (which is in southern Africa), on a full moon night, you can see a vast field of skeletons. They are only visible on full moon nights. She thought they were horses used by German troops during World War I. The curious thing is that each horse (or mule—they were there too) has a bullet hole in its skull.

The truth is this: The animals belonged to South African troops battling the Germans. There was an outbreak of glanders, a fatal, highly infectious disease, and the ship carrying the vaccine was wrecked before it could reach the army. To keep the other horses from being infected, the soldiers killed 1,695 horses and 944 mules. It must have been a traumatic thing to do, because the men were fond of their animals. But they had to do it to save the rest. This happened in 1915, and today, almost a hundred years later, the skeletons are still there. I found this image haunting and used it at the close of *The Lord of Opium*.

PARADISE

The setting for *The Lord of Opium* exists. It is the two towns of Portal and Paradise in the Chiricahua Mountains of Arizona. Portal contains the Sky Village, consisting of small, private observatories. It also consists of a small town with a library, café, and post office. I live in Portal. Higher in the mountain is Paradise, and between them is the American Museum of Natural History Southwestern Research Station. This is where I put El Patrón's mansion and hospital. Near it is the oasis, although I placed it south of Ajo in *The House of the Scorpion*.

This area is a Sky Island, a unique setting where many different species of plants and animals can survive. Half the animal species of North America live in our Sky Island. We are also on a major drug smuggling route for the Sinaloa Cartel.

A Reading Group Guide to
The Lord of Opium
By Nancy Farmer

About the Book

Matt, the clone of the evil and powerful drug lord El Patrón, was harvested to provide spare parts for the old man. When El Patrón is assassinated, Matt is reclassified as a human and named Lord of Opium, ruler of the largest and most powerful territory in the Dope Confederacy. The problem is that Matt is only fourteen years old, and his life as a clone gave him no experience for leading an empire. To make matters worse, there are forces inside and outside his land that are attempting to dethrone him. Matt wants to rid the empire of the evil ways of El Patrón, but he must first learn to recognize his friends from his enemies. As Matt sets out on his journey for truth, he learns that a ruler and a dictator require different skills and that he must earn the trust of his people to accomplish his mission.

Discussion Questions

1. At the beginning of the novel, Matt is at the Oasis and is dealing with grief and nervousness. What is the reason for his grief? Name at least five things that contribute to his anxiety.

2. Explain the following quote: "The air changed from the fresh breeze of the mountain to something slightly sweet, with a hint of corruption." To what is the quote referring? Document hints of corruption throughout the novel. Who are the central characters responsible for the corruption?

3. Discuss how Matt makes the sudden transition from "filthy clone" to human and to the new Lord of Opium. What are his greatest challenges? How does exposure to "real humans" change Matt's view of eejits? What does he mean when he thinks, "Talking to an eejit was almost like talking to himself"? Explain how this shapes his dream of changing life in Opium.

4. Celia tells Matt, "You're a drug lord now and must learn to behave like one." Make a list of behaviors that Celia might think a drug lord should possess. Explain why Cienfuegos thinks that Matt needs a name that instills fear. Discuss Matt's greatest fears. At what point does he gain the courage to face his fears?

   Discuss whether Matt fears power. How does fear give him the wisdom he needs to carry on his attempt to change life in Opium?

5. The quest to belong is one of the themes of the novel. Trace Matt's struggle to belong from the beginning of the novel to the end. Why is he uncomfortable in the apartments of the Alacrán family? What is the pivotal point when Matt finally gains a sense of belonging? Which characters help him the most with his struggling identity?

6. Good versus evil is the central theme of the novel. Matt understands that the land of Opium is evil, but it takes him a while to distinguish the good and evil characters. What must Matt learn about trust before he recognizes the good and evil players? Which character disappoints him the most? Discuss what Cienfuegos means when he tells Matt that it isn't always easy to be good.

7. How does being Lord of Opium change the way people view Matt? Discuss whether it changes the way he views himself. How is he overwhelmed by his duties? What compromises must Matt make as he rules the empire? What is significant about Matt's desire to be called Don Sombra, Lord Shadow?

8. Symbolism in literature conveys a "deeper meaning" that a writer is trying to convey. What is symbolic about Matt giving Waitress the name Mirasol? Explain the symbolism of El Patrón's touring car.

9. Discuss the view of women in the Land of Opium. How might Matt's relationship with María change that view?

10. Matt hears El Patrón's voice in his head. On the subject of the evil forces taking away Matt's weapons, explain what the voice means when it says, "Just because they took your weapons doesn't mean you aren't armed." What weapons did the evil forces take? How is Matt "armed" to defeat them?

11. Explain Matt's reaction when he learns the purpose of the Scorpion Star.

12. One of the main themes of the book is family. Matt believes that there is an instinct for family members, whether you are born with them or not. You search until you find a parent or sibling. What is the relationship he has with Celia, María, Listen, the Bug, Cienfuegos, and El Patrón?

13. Listen is the only character Matt allows to visit the Oasis. Discuss why she, and not María, is taken there.

14. Listen influences major events in the book, although she is very young. Discuss why she has this effect while others do not.

15. Matt strives for Cienfuegos's approval, but he never trusts him. Is this because Matt is growing up and trying to reject parental authority, or is it because of serious flaws in Cienfuegos's character?

Activities

1. Explain the following simile: "It's like owning a cage full of pitbulls." Who are the pitbulls in the novel? What is the cage? Identify other similes in the novel. Then write a simile that Matt might use to describe one of the following characters: María, Esperanza, Cienfuegos, Celia, Dr. Rivas, Listen, or Glass Eye.

2. El Patrón bought paintings and tapestries from El Prado, the finest art museum in Spain, for his home. Research the most famous painters and paintings that hang in El Prado (museodelprado.es/en/the-collection/online-gallery). Use books in the library or sites on the Internet to research the technique and style of one of the artists.

3. Read about the global drug-trafficking industry and how it affects crime and health issues in the United States. The

following website is helpful: policyalmanac.org/crime/ archive/drug_trafficking.shtml. Which government agency handles this issue? Write a letter to the agency and make one suggestion for a solution for solving the drug trade in our society.

4. Discuss the meaning of the word *humanitarian*. What are Matt's most humanitarian efforts? Write a declaration that the United Nations might present to Matt at the end of the novel for his humanitarian deeds. Cite at least ten points in the declaration.

5. Write a brief opinion essay that addresses the following question: Is it easier to be "good" or "evil" in the Land of Opium? Use specific scenes from the novel to support ideas. Encourage peer editing from your reading group for grammar and clarity of thought.

6. Antique books often have decorations at the beginning of each chapter. Make a decoration for each chapter of *The Lord of Opium* that is symbolic of the chapter content. Include a one-sentence annotation that summarizes the chapter.

7. Discuss the ecological message of the novel with your group. Use books in the library or sites on the Internet to identify the greatest ecological issues facing our nation today and then stage for the group a news talk show, including visuals, that presents the issues and possible solutions.

8. At the end of the novel, the idea is expressed that some people don't know what to do with freedom, and therefore

they abuse it. Divide the group into two opposing sides and ask them to discuss the following: "Should freedom be denied all because some abuse it?" Cite specific ways characters in the novel may abuse freedom. Are there correlations to our current society?

This guide, written to align with the Common Core State Standards (corestandards.org) has been provided by Simon & Schuster for classroom, library, and reading group use. It may be reproduced in its entirety or excerpted for these purposes.

NANCY FARMER

is the author of nine novels, including *The Ear, the Eye and the Arm* and *A Girl Named Disaster*, each a Newbery Honor Book, and *The House of the Scorpion*, winner of the National Book Award, as well as being a Newbery Honor Book and a Michael L. Printz Honor Book. For somewhat younger readers, she has written a trilogy inspired by Norse mythology: *The Sea of Trolls*; *The Land of the Silver Apples*; and *The Islands of the Blessed*.

Nancy Farmer lives with her husband in the small town of Portal, Arizona, which is one of the settings for *The Lord of Opium*. Visit her online at nancyfarmerwebsite.com.

A THRILLING FANTASY TRILOGY OF DANGER AND ADVENTURE FROM THREE-TIME NEWBERY HONOR WINNER NANCY FARMER!

★ "A tale of high adventure and exploration that reads with unexpected sensitivity, warmth, and humor."
—*Bulletin of the Center for Children's Books* on ***The Sea of Trolls***, STARRED REVIEW

★ "[Draws] readers into this complex world and [leaves] them looking forward to more."
—*School Library Journal* on ***The Land of the Silver Apples***, STARRED REVIEW

★ "Farmer's richly imagined saga is filled with danger, action, [and] delightful comedy."
—*Booklist* on ***The Islands of the Blessed***, STARRED REVIEW

PRINT AND EBOOK EDITIONS ALSO AVAILABLE

Atheneum

From Atheneum Books for Young Readers

HEED THIS WARNING, MORTAL:

stay far away from me and my sisters, the three Fates. For if we come to love you, we might bring about the end of the world.

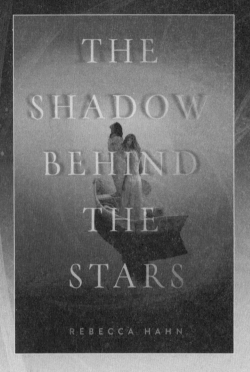

★ "A heartbreaking fantasy that tackles life's big questions. Shattering and transcendent."
—*Kirkus Reviews*, starred review

★ "Hahn captures the dueling beauties of human life and inhuman fate in poetic prose. . . . It builds to a conclusion that is satisfying and true."
—*Publishers Weekly*, starred review

★ "A strange and wondrous course through questions of fate and free will . . . Hahn expertly tackles the power of belief and choice in this thoughtful and introspective work."
—*School Library Journal*, starred review